"I'm going to bunk here so I can keep an eye on things..."

Lizzie was going to sleep in the stable? On the floor?

It felt wrong to leave her there, which was silly because Heath had spent many a night in the lambing barns. But this wasn't him. It was Lizzie. And when she stuck a ridiculously small pillow behind her head, he wanted to snatch it, send her to bed and say he'd watch the horse.

She gazed up at him, looking so much like the girl she'd been twelve years before. But different, too.

"It's my job, Heath." She kept her voice quiet. Matter-of-fact. And quite professional. "People don't inherit a quarter share of a ranch worth millions without putting in some time. I'll see you tomorrow."

She was right. He knew that.

But walking away from her—moving through the door into the cold spring night—was one of the toughest things he'd done in a long time.

He did it because it was the right thing to do. But he hated every minute of it.

USA TODAY bestselling author **Ruth Logan Herne** loves God, her country, her family, dogs, chocolate and coffee! Married to a very patient man, she lives in an old farmhouse in upstate New York and thinks possums should leave the cat food alone and snakes should always live outside. There are no exceptions to either rule! Visit Ruth at ruthloganherne.com.

Award-winning author **Myra Johnson** writes emotionally gripping stories about love, life and faith. She is a two-time finalist for the ACFW Carol Award and winner of the 2005 RWA Golden Heart® Award. Married since 1972, Myra and her husband have two married daughters and seven grandchildren. Although Myra is a native Texan, she and her husband now reside in North Carolina, sharing their home with two pampered rescue dogs.

Her Cowboy Reunion

USA TODAY Bestselling Author

Ruth Logan Herne

&

Hill Country Reunion

Myra Johnson

LOVE INSPIRED
INSPIRATIONAL ROMANCE

LOVE INSPIRED®

INSPIRATIONAL ROMANCE

ISBN-13: 978-1-335-45617-5

Recycling programs for this product may not exist in your area.

Her Cowboy Reunion & Hill Country Reunion

Copyright © 2020 by Harlequin Books S.A.

Her Cowboy Reunion
First published in 2018. This edition published in 2020.
Copyright © 2018 by Ruth M. Blodgett

Hill Country Reunion
First published in 2018. This edition published in 2020.
Copyright © 2018 by Myra Johnson

This edition published by arrangement with Harlequin Books S.A.

For questions and comments about the quality of this book, please contact us at CustomerService@Harlequin.com.

Love Inspired
22 Adelaide St. West, 40th Floor
Toronto, Ontario M5H 4E3, Canada
www.Harlequin.com

Printed in U.S.A.

CONTENTS

HER COWBOY REUNION

Ruth Logan Herne

This book is dedicated to Casey…

I was blessed to help raise you and I'm absolutely delighted with the wonderful young woman you've become. You are a part of us…and always will be. You can't get rid of me easily! Love you, kid.

And above all these things put on charity,
which is the bond of perfectness.
And let the peace of God rule in your hearts,
to the which also ye are called in one body;
and be ye thankful.

—*Colossians* 3:14–15

Chapter One

This is the chance you've been waiting for. Hoping for. Praying for. Don't blow it.

Lizzie Fitzgerald climbed out of an SUV more suited to her rich past than her impoverished present.

Her late uncle's Western Idaho ranch splayed around her like an old-fashioned wagon wheel, spreading wide from the farmhouse hub. Straight south lay sheep barns forming a huge letter *T*. The sound of sheep and dogs rose up from beyond the barns where woolly creatures dotted rolling fields like white sprinkles on a Kelly-green cake.

On her left the long, curving graveled drive wound past a copse of newly leafed trees to the two-lane country road above. Behind her was a classic Western home. Two stories, wrapped in honey-brown cedar and a porch that extended across the front and down both sides. Two swings and a variety of rockers decked the porch.

"No doubt I will spend my share of time on that porch as the weather warms," said Corrie as she stepped from the other side of the car. "What a pretty place this is, Lizzie-Beth! But I can see your attention is drawn to what brought us here." She dipped her chin toward Lizzie's right. "Your uncle's passing and his love for horses. A family trait. Or downfall," she added softly.

"It won't be this time." Lizzie strode toward the freshly built stables. "Not with someone willing to put in the effort. It wasn't horses that brought down Claremorris," she reminded Corrie, the stout African American woman who had raised Lizzie and her two sisters at the stately Kentucky horse farm. "It was greed and dishonesty. This will be different, Corrie. You'll see."

"I'll pray it different, right beside you," Corrie declared. "Then we'll see, Sugar. You explore your new place. I'm going to see if there's a restroom close by."

Lizzie walked toward the classic U-shaped stable configuration while Corrie disappeared into the house. Two equine wings stretched from opposite ends of the central barn. A row of stable doors faced the groomed square of grass that was surrounded by a hoof-friendly walking area. Six windows lined the face of the central barn, facing the equine courtyard. Curtains in the upper windows suggested living quarters, much like they'd had in their Kentucky stable. The whole concept was modeled after the Celtic horse farms her great-grandparents had known in Ireland. Uncle Sean might not have liked the newspaper publishing business that made the family's fortune, but he clearly appreciated their Irish roots.

A horse nickered from its stall. Another answered softly.

Then quiet stretched as if wondering about her. Testing her.

Footsteps approached across the gravel. She turned.

A cowboy strode her way, looking just as classic as the ranch around him. Tall. Broad-shouldered. Narrow-hipped. And…familiar. As if—

Lizzie pushed that thought aside. She'd loved a cowboy once, with all the sweet intensity of first love, but that was a dozen years and a lot of heartache past. And yet—

The cowboy drew closer.

He raised his head and looked at her, as if throwing down a challenge. And she knew why.

Heath Caufield. Her first love, with his coal-black hair and gray-blue eyes. Eyes that seemed to see right through her and found her wanting.

Her heart went slow, then sped up.

Adrenaline buzzed through her. She stared at him, and he stared right back. Then he said two simple words. "You came."

"You're here."

"I live here."

"You worked for my uncle?" None of this made any sense. Her uncle Sean hadn't had contact with Lizzie's lying, scheming father in decades. He'd purposely gone off on his own after serving in the Marines, as far from the Fitzgerald News Company as he could get. He'd spurned the newspaper empire, took his inheritance from Grandpa Ralph and gone west. And that was all she knew because that was all Corrie had ever told her. So how'd he hire Heath?

"I've been here twelve years. Been manager for three."

She flushed.

He didn't seem to notice her higher color. Or he simply ignored it. "I came here the same time you went off to Yale to get your fancy degree in journalism like your daddy and grandpa. How's that working out for you, by the way?"

He looked mad and sounded madder, as if the demise of her family business, horse farm and estate was somehow her fault. It wasn't, and she didn't owe Heath any explanations. In her book, it was the other way around, but she'd put the past behind her years ago. She had to. He'd be wise to do the same. "Journalism with an MBA on the side. From Wharton. And enough expertise with horses and business to handle this, I expect."

Her words and Ivy League degrees didn't seem to impress him, but she wasn't here to impress anyone. She was here to do a job, a job assigned to her by her dying uncle. If she and her sisters put in a year working the equine side of Pine Ridge Ranch and brought it out of the red and into the black, his estate would be split four ways, according to the lawyer's formal letter. Her, her two sisters, and the current farm manager, who appeared to be Heath Caufield.

His look went from her to the stunning barn behind her, then back. "Twenty-eight horses, with eight of them bred to championship lines. And you show up on your own. Where are Charlotte and Melonie?"

His attitude caused a hint of anger to fire up inside her. Should she snap back?

No. There was nothing to be achieved in that. She kept her face and her voice even. "They'll be along. They had things to finish up. And while they'll be living here, don't expect them to take on major horse work.

Char just finished her veterinary degree and Melonie doesn't do well in a barn."

"She'll adjust."

The lick of anger burned a little brighter. "I believe Uncle Sean's will said that Charlotte, Melonie and I had to live here for at least a year to earn our bequests. And that we needed to focus on getting the horse breeding business up and running or sell it off. Correct?"

He held her gaze with hard eyes and nodded. Slowly.

"Trust us to disburse the jobs as we see fit. They'll do their share, but make no mistake about it, Heath." She folded her arms and braced her legs because if there was one thing she was sure about, it was her ability to run horse from every aspect of the business. "I'll be the one putting in the time in this stable. With whatever help you have available."

"Help's tight at the moment. We've got one last herd of sheep going into the hills since the government reneged on our grazing rights, and that leaves us short down here. For the next six weeks at least."

"Then we'll have to figure things out," she told him. "Because the girls won't be here for a few weeks, either." She didn't tell him why she was available at a moment's notice, how the illustrious corporation her great-grandfather began had fired her as soon as the Feds indicted her father on multiple charges of embezzlement and money laundering. No publisher in today's struggling print economy wanted their name connected to Tim Fitzgerald's misdeeds. She was guilty by association. End of story.

Not out here. Not on this ranch. Or so she'd thought

until she came face-to-face with Heath again. Who'd have thought her road less traveled would lead to this?

Not her. But that was okay because she'd grown up since then, and this ranch, those beautiful horses...

This job was made for her. She knew it. She was pretty sure Heath knew it, too. And if they both stayed calm, cool and collected, maybe they could make it work. As long as they both stayed on their own side of the ranch.

She'd come.

Heath hadn't wanted her to. He'd have been fine leaving the past in the past, but now it rose up to meet him, and all because his friend and mentor's life had been cut short...with a herd of pricey horses to comb, curry, exercise and tend. And not one lick of time to do it.

Sean's cancer did this. He'd invested a crazy amount of money to begin a horse breeding enterprise, the kind of horses that required substantial bankroll, then took their own sweet time about paying it back.

Beautiful horse flesh, the kind that ranchers and rodeo riders alike loved. With Sean's death, they had no one to oversee the million-dollar industry. No one except Lizzie and her sisters, straight off a pretentious Southern horse farm that had been seized by the government. Sean had called it God's timing.

Heath considered it more like cruel fate. Either way, she was here, and if he was honest with himself, she was even more beautiful than she'd been a dozen years before. Long chestnut-toned hair, pulled back. Cinnamon eyes that almost matched the hair, and skin as fair and freckled as he remembered.

"Heath Caufield."

He turned swiftly toward an old, friendly voice. "Corrie?"

She hugged him, laughed, then hugged him again as Lizzie began to retrieve bags from their vehicle.

"You came all the way up here? I can't believe this."

"Did you think I'd send any one of my babies on alone?" She stared at him as if aghast. "Not on your life! My girls will begin this new adventure with me by their sides. Caring for horses does not come easy and it's a night-and-day enterprise. But that's something you already know."

He sure did. He'd spent seven years working their grandfather's horse farm before he'd been banished.

Corrie offered him a frank look, a look that made him wonder how much she knew. And then it was gone. "Do you expect there's room in the kitchen for one more? I don't want to step on any toes."

"There aren't any paid positions open right now, Corrie." He didn't want to say money was tight on a ranch valued in the millions of dollars. But it was.

She shrugged. "I put some money by over the years, and followed some investing advice. Money's not what I'm after. A roof over our heads, and food to eat—that's not a bad day, is it? I'm not handy with horses, but I'd like to learn my way around sheep. Such docile creatures. And the lambs, so small, like a painting from the Good Book." She indicated the size of a newborn lamb with her hands. "And of course, I am good in the garden. Always was, and fresh-grown food is a blessing." She gave him a quiet scan. "You look good, Heath. Older. And wiser."

"Smarter, for sure." He didn't look at Liz. He didn't have to look at Liz to remember the strength and urgency of young love. How could one forget the unforgettable? He couldn't, but a smart man put it all in perspective. "Steadier."

"Steady is good." She put a hand on his arm. "You're married."

She'd dropped her gaze to his left hand where his plain gold band glimmered. "I was." A rogue cloud passed between them and the sun at that moment, chilling the spring air as it dulled the light. "She died from complications after having our little boy. Now it's me and Zeke. My son. We do all right."

Corrie did what she'd always done.

She prayed.

Right then and there, her hand on his arm, head bowed, she whispered a prayer for him and his child.

Then she stared up at him, and he couldn't bear to see the pain in her eyes, in anyone's eyes, because he'd moved on. He had no choice because he might have lost Anna but he still had his son, Ezekiel Sean Caufield. And Zeke came first now. In everything.

Lizzie had drawn close. He wanted to avoid her, especially now, remembering the birth of his son. His wife had risked her life and lost, but she'd been willing to go the distance for their child.

That set the two women a long ways apart. One who was willing to sacrifice for a child, one who couldn't be bothered.

He had no time to dwell. He had work to do and a son waiting for him. A spunky little boy, waiting to play with his dad.

He started to turn. Lizzie turned at the same moment, and there they were, face-to-face.

Anger bubbled up from somewhere so deep it should have stayed buried, but Corrie's words about his wedding ring had opened it like a fresh-dug grave.

Lizzie started to speak, then didn't.

Just as well. They had nothing to say to one another.

He reached out and hoisted two duffel-style bags, then moved toward the porch.

"Where are you going?"

"Inside?" he said, because it was fairly obvious.

She hooked a thumb toward the stable. "Who's living in the barn apartment?"

"No one."

"Well, there is now." She grabbed a rolling bag by the handle. "Leave the right-hand duffel here, please, but go ahead and take Corrie's into the house. First rule of horse is to have someone close by that knows how to rule the horse."

"You're going to live in a barn?" He looked back at Corrie. She remained quiet, just out of the way, watching their back-and-forth.

"At least until I get a feel for the place." She kept walking toward the barn. "Is it furnished?"

It wasn't because Sean had cared for the horses until he got too sick, and he'd lived in the house. "No."

"Wi-Fi?"

Sean had the equine offices built on the first floor purposely, facing the pasture. If he was throwing down a major equine business deal, he didn't want the walk back to the house to interrupt. The vision of pricey mares and geldings in the rich, green grass added enticement to the deal. "Yes. There's a full office set up with all the records. Hard copy and online. I can show you all that."

"Corrie, I'll see you once you're settled." Liz motioned toward the house. "The sooner I get set up, the quicker I can grab some furniture off Craigslist."

Used furniture?

Living in the barn? Was she serious?

One look at her face confirmed that she was. Maybe he'd been wrong. Maybe she understood the stakes. Maybe she had what it would take to help make things right.

He hauled Corrie's things inside and up the main stairs. He set the duffel inside the first room, then repeated the trip with the smaller bags and boxes.

His phone rang as he backed out of Corrie's room. The name of a well-known Pacific Northwest grocery retailer flashed. He took the call, and by the time he'd finished a deal for four hundred fresh market lambs for wedding season, nearly a quarter hour had passed. That meant he'd left Lizzie to do all her own lifting and carrying.

He hurried back outside because no matter how rough their past had been, he wasn't normally a jerk. At least he hoped he wasn't, but with Pine Ridge teetering on the brink, he might be testier than normal. It wasn't fair to lay that at her door, but there wouldn't be time to sugarcoat things, either.

Lizzie wasn't in his line of sight when he stepped outside. He started for the nearest stairs at the same time he heard his five-year-old son sigh out loud as he gazed out through the square, wooden spindles. "You're so beautiful."

Heath turned in the direction his son was facing and swallowed hard, because Zeke was one hundred percent correct. Standing on the graveled yard below, Lizzie Fitzgerald was absolutely, positively drop-dead gorgeous in an all-American girl kind of way. That thick, long hair framed a heart-shaped face. A face he'd loved once, but he'd been young and headstrong then. Somewhere along the way, he'd grown up.

"You're quite handsome yourself." Lizzie smiled up at Zeke, and despite Heath's warnings about strangers, Zeke grinned back, then raced down the broad side steps.

"Are you staying here?" He slid to a quick stop in front of Lizzie. There was no curtailing his excitement. "My dad said we've got people who are coming here to stay, so that must be you. Right?"

"Correct." She didn't look at Heath and wonder about his dark-skinned son, and he gave her reluctant points for that. Zeke's skin was a gift from his African American mother, but his gray-blue eyes were Caufield, through and through.

Lizzie squatted to Zeke's level and held his attention with a pretty smile. "My name's Lizzie. My friend Corrie and I are living on the ranch with you. I hope that's all right."

"Do you snore?"

She paused as if considering the question. "Not to my knowledge. But then, I'm asleep, so how would I know?"

"I do not snore," declared Zeke. He shoved his hands

into two little pockets, total cowboy. "But I have bad dreams sometimes and then Dad lets me come sleep with him."

"I'm glad he does."

"I know. Me, too."

Heath came down the stairs. Zeke smiled his way. "This is the first girl visitor we've ever had, Dad!"

Lizzie raised her gaze to Heath's. He thought she'd tease him, or play off the boy's bold statement. There hadn't ever been a woman visitor to the ranch house, except for the shepherds' wives.

She didn't tease. Sympathy marked her expression, and the kindness in her eyes made his chest hurt.

Maybe she'd grown up, too.

Maybe she could handle life better now. That was all well and good, but he'd lost something a dozen years before. A part of his heart and a chunk of his soul had fallen by the wayside when she chose school over their unborn child.

Guilt hit him, because he was four years older than Lizzie, and it took two to create a child. He'd let them both down back then, and the consequences of their actions haunted him still.

"You've got your daddy's eyes. And the look of him in some ways."

"And his mother."

He didn't mean the words to come out curtly, but they did and there was no snatching them back. Lizzie stayed still, gazing down, then seemed to collect herself. "That's the way of things, of course."

"Do you look like *your* mother?" Zeke asked as Lizzie stood up.

"I don't. I look more like my dad and my Uncle Sean. My two sisters look like my mother."

"Mister Sean was your uncle?" That fact surprised Zeke. "So we're almost like family!"

"Or at least very good friends." She smiled down at him. "I think I'd like to be your friend, Zeke Caufield."

"And I will like being your friend, too, Miss Lizzie!"

"Just Lizzie," she told him. She reached out and palmed his head. No fancy nail polish gilded her nails. And from the looks of them, she still bit them when she got nervous. Was the move to the ranch making her nervous? Or was it him?

"But Dad says I'm asposed to call people stuff like that," Zeke explained in a matter-of-fact voice. "To be polite."

"I think if you say my name politely, then it is polite. Isn't it?"

"Yes!"

She looked at Heath then.

He tried to read her expression, but failed. What was she feeling, seeing his son? Did her mind go back to their past, like his did? Would this old ache ever come to some kind of peace between them? How could it?

"Dad, I'm so starving!"

"Hey, little man, lunch is ready inside." Cookie, the ranch house manager, called to Zeke through the screen door. He saw Heath's questioning look and waved toward the road. "Rosina had a doctor's appointment, remember? So Zeke is hanging with me for a few hours."

He'd forgotten that, even though he'd made a note in his phone. What kind of father was he?

"I'll see to him, boss." Cookie's deep voice offered reassurance, but it wasn't his job to watch Zeke, and keeping a five-year-old safe on a working ranch wasn't a piece of cake. "No big deal."

It wasn't a big deal to the cook because he had a good heart, but it was a huge deal to Heath. His first priority should be caring for his son, and since he'd lost his friend and mentor, Heath was pretty sure he'd fallen down on that. He'd add it to the list of necessary improvements, a list that seemed to be getting longer every day.

"Maybe I can be with you?" Zeke had started for the stairs, but he paused and looked back at Lizzie. "Like while Dad's working and Cookie's busy. I won't get in the way." He shook his head in an earnest attempt to convince her. "I like almost *never* get in the way."

Cookie bit back a laugh.

Heath didn't. He slanted his gaze down. "Miss Lizzie will be busy. You stay here with Cookie. Got it?"

Zeke peeked past him to Lizzie, then sighed. "Yes, sir."

"But for now we can have lunch together," said Lizzie as she followed Zeke up the stairs.

He couldn't stop Zeke from eating with Lizzie, and the reality of having her here was a done deal. But he could set limits when it came to Zeke. He was his father, after all.

But when Zeke aimed a grin up to Lizzie and she smiled right back down, another dose of reality hit him.

He couldn't enforce sanctions on emotions. And from the way his son was smiling up at Lizzie, then reaching for her hand...

He swallowed a sigh and headed for the barn.

Emotions and Lizzie were a whole other rodeo. One he knew too well.

Chapter Two

"Sean did something your father never seemed to understand," Corrie said softly as she and Lizzie approached the stablemaster's quarters after a quick lunch. She indicated the sprawling ranch around her and the pristine buildings, a trait for classic perfection that came straight from Lizzie's grandfather. "He worked hard and made his own success."

In sheep...and now horses. Only he was gone too soon.

Lizzie found the whole thing pretty unbelievable, even though she was a huge fan of great woolens made by pricey designers. Or had been, when she'd had money for such things.

"Liz."

Oh, be still her heart, hearing Heath's voice call her name. She'd hoped for that long ago. Prayed for it. It had never happened, but for one swift moment she longed to turn and run to him, like she'd done long ago.

She didn't.

She tucked the momentary surprise away. She stopped moving to let him catch up, but then another cowboy came their way on horseback. He drew up, dismounted and gestured toward the western hills.

A deep furrow formed between Heath's thick, dark brows.

A long time ago she would have smoothed those furrows away. Not now. She'd learned a hard lesson back then, but one she carried with her still. Strength and independence had become her mainstay and they had gotten her this far.

He turned back toward the long drive, then whistled lightly through his teeth. She used to call that his pressure cooker release valve, when they were young and in love. But that was a long time ago, too.

"If you've got work, Heath, we can find our way around," she told him. "We'll take our own personal tour of the place."

He went all Clint Eastwood on her. He didn't blink. Didn't flinch. Didn't roll his shoulders the way John Wayne would have. But then, she wasn't exactly Maureen O'Hara, either.

Then his expression darkened. "There's a problem up top." He pointed toward a far-off pasture dotted with hundreds of recently sheared sheep. "Some folks hiked in and thought they'd set up camp. Campers mean campfires, and if you're green to these parts, you don't always understand the dangers. And even though it's still spring, we don't encourage people to camp on the ranch. I'm going to head up and explain where the campgrounds are."

"He didn't tell them to move on?" Lizzie motioned toward the cowboy moving toward the barn.

"Jace did. They called him names and didn't believe he had the authority to evict them."

"Called him names?" Lizzie stared after the retreating cowboy before bringing her attention back to Heath. "I don't—"

"Slurs," said Corrie.

The older woman lifted her chin and Lizzie finally understood. The trespassers had spurned Jace because they doubted a black man had the authority to send them packing. "Someone called him out because he's dark-skinned? That's some crazy, foolish nerve right there. Want help moving them off?" She raised her gaze to Heath's and stood firm. "Give me a horse. One of the ranch ponies. I'm ready to ride."

"Whoa, girl." Corrie put a hand on her arm. "I appreciate your willingness to stand up for truth, justice and the American way, but how about we unpack before you get yourself shot again?"

"Again?" Heath looked shocked.

"Grazed. No biggie. Part of the job, at least the one I had back then."

"What kind of a job allows shooting at women?"

"I was overseeing the Mid-Central region, from Ohio to Indiana and all points south. A political story got too hot and I was with the investigative team when someone tried to scare them off. I got grazed by a bullet. It was long before the executive team decided that having a Fitzgerald on staff seemed imprudent while the company crashed and burned, taking a lot of people's money with it. Bad press is bad press."

"They fired you because of your father?" His brows drew together again. "Who does that kind of thing? If we all got fired because we had lousy parents, there would be a lot of us out of a job. Including me."

"Publishing is different now," said Corrie as Jace led a second mount out of the nearby barn. "It's not like it was when I started with the Fitzgeralds and I don't know that it will ever be that way again. There's not a newspaper or news media corporation that can afford to risk their image for the dwindling advertising dollars."

"I understand taking care of the bottom line. That doesn't make it right to punish someone for their parents' mistakes."

"Lots of things in life aren't fair," said Lizzie as the other cowboy mounted his horse and came their way. "We cling to our faith and hold tight to the reins."

"And trust the good Lord to look after us, same as always," added Corrie.

"Jace, this is a family friend. Cora Lee Satterly. And Sean's niece, Elizabeth Fitzgerald."

"A pleasure, ladies." He looked toward Heath. "Are we good?"

Heath nodded. "Let's go." He tipped his hat slightly toward Corrie. Just a touch to the brim. "I'll see you later. Make yourselves at home."

He said nothing to Lizzie.

She refused to let it get to her.

She'd made mistakes. So had he. But faith and a solid work ethic had pulled her firmly into the present. She'd stayed the course, gotten her education, and now was at the helm of a teetering agricultural business worth a small fortune while he ran the large sheep ranch alongside.

A horse stamped its foot, wanting attention. Another one followed suit.

She walked to the barns, determined. She'd get to know the horses, then the finances, then the horses again. One way or another she'd do right by both.

Anger formed a burr deep in Heath's chest and hadn't let loose in the two hours it took for him and Jace Middleton to ride into the hills, ask the campers to leave, then keep watch while they did.

By the time they'd packed their camp and pulled away in a huff, he was hungry, tired, annoyed and sore. There was only one prescription to cure all of that.

His son.

"I'll tend the horses." Jace took charge once they rode into the yard. "You go get Zeke."

"Thanks, Jace." He texted Cookie, and when the cook replied that Rosina had picked up Zeke an hour before, he climbed into his Jeep and headed toward the clutch of four-room cabins between the sprawling sheep barns and the road. He pulled into Harve and Rosina Garcia's driveway. Harve had been working sheep for Sean for nearly twenty years. He and his brother Aldo had emigrated from Peru to work the sheep through the customary annual hill drives. For the local Peruvian Americans, the drive was a part of life, a tradition dating back to earlier times. Government grazing restrictions had changed things, which meant Pine Ridge had to change, too. And at no small expense, adding to current concerns.

Zeke had spotted his car from their backyard and raced his way before he came to a full stop. "Dad!"

The old knot loosened the moment Zeke jumped into his arms.

This was his reason for living, right here. This boy was his only connection to his beloved wife. And while he loved his son more than he could have ever imagined, if he'd known that Anna would be trading her life for Zeke's, Heath would have found a different way to have a family. As he held his beautiful and precocious son in his arms, that thought made him feel like a lesser man.

"Junior taught me the coolest things you've ever seen in your life!" Excitement exploded from the boy like fireworks in a night sky. "He thinks I might be the best cowboy to ever ride the Wild Wild West someday, but he says I gotta get some boots, Dad, and I told him I've been askin' for boots for a long, long time." Two hands smooshed Heath's cheeks as Zeke leaned closer. "I told him I would ask you again, because it is so very, very important." He pushed his face right up to his father's, making his voice sound squished and slightly robotic. "Can I please have a pair of real cowboy boots like you and Harve and Junior and everybody else in the world?"

Heath let his voice get all squishy, too. "I'll think about it. Good boots are pricey, and your feet grow fast. In case you hadn't noticed." He deadpanned a look that made his little boy laugh out loud. "Let's see if you were good for Rosie, okay?"

"He's always good!" Harve's wife bustled out of the door, despite the bulk of a nearly nine-month pregnancy. "And he is such a help to me, Heath. I don't bend so well right now, and Zeke is right there to get things for me when the twins need something. And a true hand with the chickens and the pigs." She beamed down at him.

"They smell." Zeke screwed up his face as Harve Junior joined them. "But Junior says if I want to be a cowboy, I've got to be a good helper and not worry about a little stink now and then."

"Junior's right. And he's a good hand on the ranch, so he knows what he's talking about."

"A good hand who needs to spend more time with his studies." Rosie leveled a firm look to her son. "Fewer sheep, more facts."

"A ranch hand doesn't need college, Mom."

"While that's true, a well-rounded ranch hand never stops learning," offered Heath mildly. "There's a big world out there, Junior."

"It's pretty big right here, sir." Frank admiration marked the teen's gaze as he indicated the lush valley and the starker cliffs surrounding it. "There's not too many things on the ranch I can't fix, things I learned from my dad. Those are skills I can take with me wherever I go. Or if I stay here in Shepherd's Crossing." He jutted his chin toward the rugged mountains climbing high to the west. "I like taking sheep upland, then bringing them back down. There's a sameness to it that suits me."

Except they wouldn't be doing that anymore, and the new grazing regulations were changing the face of ranching across the West. Where would that leave the hard-working shepherds who'd given up their lives in Peru to work at Pine Ridge and other sheep farms? Heath wasn't sure.

"I send you to school for that very reason," scolded Rosie lightly. "Because it is too easy for one to become entrenched in sameness. A rich mind entertains possibilities. And our town does not have much to offer these days," she reminded young Harve. "A failing community offers few opportunities to youth. A wise mother encourages her child to have roots but to also grow wings, my son."

"Dad!" Zeke drew the attention off Junior with that single word. "I think I'm *almost* big enough to come with you and the sheep up the tallest hills. I'm this many." He held up five little fingers. "And I've been practicing my riding on the fence rail over there." He pointed to the split rail fencing along a nearby pasture. "I'm getting really good!"

"Not yet, son." When Zeke scowled, Heath lifted him higher in his arms. "And that face won't get you anywhere. You need to be bigger to handle the sheep and the dogs and the horses. That's all there is to it. It will all happen in its own time."

He ignored Zeke's pout as he set the boy down and hooked a thumb toward the Jeep. "Car. Seat belt. Let's roll."

"Okay! Bye, Rosie-Posie!" The boy hugged Rosina but not too hard. "I can't wait to see the baby!"

"It is a feeling I share," Rosie assured him, laughing. "I'll see you next week, God willing. And after that?" She shrugged lightly. "Who knows?"

"I'll bring my dinosaurs!"

"And we'll create a habitat for them, a perfect spot for them to roam, beneath the old cottonwood tree."

"Okay!"

Zeke scrambled into his booster seat, adjusted his belt, then got down to the important matters of the day. "What's for supper?"

"Whatever Cookie came up with, but I thought I smelled beef and potatoes cooking."

"Stew?" Eyes wide, the boy wriggled in excitement. "I love stew, Dad! And cake. And ice cream. And sometimes hot dogs."

"A well-balanced diet is a boy's best friend," Heath teased as he drew closer to the main house again.

"And I get to have supper with our new company!" Zeke aimed a heart-melting grin at him through the rearview mirror. "That will be the most fun of all!"

From the boy's vantage point, maybe. Heath held a different view, but that was his problem. Not Zeke's.

"You sure do." He pulled the car around to the back parking area, and climbed out. He was just about to remind Zeke about the basic rules of behavior around women…simple things, like wiping your face, washing your hands, no barreling through the house like a young elephant, and flushing the toilet, thank you very much…

But Zeke had spotted Lizzie coming their way across the square of grass. He raced toward her like a flash. "Hey! Hey!" He skidded to a stop along the dirt walk, spattering her jeans with fine brown dust. "Oops. Sorry!"

"I've been dirty before. I expect it will happen again, my friend."

That voice. The drawl. Softened by years of education, but still enough to draw a man in, which meant he'd have to watch his step because the drawl and the beautiful woman were far too familiar.

She'd bent to talk to Zeke at his level, then looked up at Heath, smiling.

The smile gut-punched him. Was that his fault? Or hers?

She turned those rusty brown eyes on him and all he wanted was to go on listening as she spoke. Meet her gaze above that pretty smile. Since those were the last things he *could* do, he put the trip down memory lane on hold.

The kitchen gong sounded, the perfect segue into something else. Anything else. Anything that didn't remind him of old losses and broken hearts. He'd made a grievous mistake by taking things too far. Yes, they'd been young. And in love.

But he should have known better.

"There's my young helper." Cookie grinned when they walked into the kitchen, and the hulking Latino's face lit up a room when he smiled. "Where you been, little fellow? Usually you're in here, pestering me for cookies we don't mention to your father when it gets this close to supper time."

"He is a bottomless pit these days," Heath acknowledged. "And you're mighty good to him, Cookie."

"We're good to each other," the cook teased. Then he spotted Lizzie coming through the door and his grin widened. "And this young woman might have come to help with horses, but she brought reinforcements which only endears her to me more." His grin indicated Lizzie had won his heart as well. "A man can deal with a whole lotta crazy on a spread like this, but some extra help in the kitchen is appreciated. And Miz Corrie mentioned something about Kentucky ribs that made me even happier," Cookie added. "We're gonna try those right soon."

"The best way to survive on a ranch is by being nice to the cook." Lizzie gave Cookie one of those utterly sincere smiles she'd practiced on Heath years before, but this time he noticed a difference in the smile. It was older. Wiser. Not jaded, and that was a surprise. But he'd be blind not to see the touch of sadness in her gaze, which made him wonder what had put it there.

She turned toward Cookie. "Do you mind if I take a plate out back? I don't want to offend, but I want to study some things while I eat."

"We like ambition in these parts," the cook assured her. "Miz Corrie told me the same thing. And don't you be worrying about cooking for yourself in those empty rooms." He pointed a fork toward the premier horse stables. "You grab food here as needed. It don't much matter where you lay your head, the food bag's on for all."

"Thank you." Sincerity marked her voice and her gaze. "Corrie and I will appreciate that a lot. I'll go get her now." She went up the front stairs just before Jace and four other hungry stockmen strode in.

"Hey, guys!" Zeke high-fived each one, walking down the row of men with a mighty cute swagger.

"You goin' to the front of the line, little man?" asked Ben, one of the older hands. "No one here minds if you do."

"Naw." Zeke faced him, chin up. "Front of the line's for workers. My dad told me that."

"Your dad's a good man. I respect that." Ben shifted his attention to Heath. "You know I'll take your place and guide that last group into the northwest hills. I've got enough gumption in me yet."

One of the younger cowboys snort-laughed, making them all grin, but Heath focused on the older man. "It's not that you can't do it, Ben. It's that I should."

"Ain't no law sayin' that, Heath," Ben reminded him. "Things changed back in March."

March was when they'd scattered the ashes of Sean Fitzgerald across the land he'd nurtured and loved for over three decades.

"And you should be here, keeping watch. There's a lot at stake with that next clutch of sheep ready to drop. We've got to pick our battles. If we need to divide and conquer when the odds are against us, then that's what we do."

Heath started to reply as Corrie and Lizzie came down the stairs. He paused because the sight of two women in the main house lassoed the men's collective attention, and Heath was pretty sure they wouldn't hear a word he said until the shock wore off. "Guys, this is Sean's niece, Elizabeth Fitzgerald. She's here to take over the equine operation."

Two of the men looked from him to Lizzie and back, surprised. Jace gave a nod of approval, Wick snapped his fingers the way old guys do, and Ben Fister moved forward. "You've got the look of your uncle about you, lass."

His term inspired Lizzie's smile. "My grandfather called me that. My mother's father," she added. "Not the Fitzgerald side."

Heath knew that first-hand.

Ian Fitzgerald had never been good with children. He'd expected blue-ribbon equestrianship and top-notch grades from the girls. Other than that, the man had barely acknowledged his granddaughters during Heath's years at Claremorris. He hadn't thought much of it then.

The older man was bent on building an empire, and did just that, and Heath had been a little awestruck by him.

Now Heath was a father. He saw things differently, which might be why the current state of the ranch hit him hard. He wanted Pine Ridge to succeed, and he appreciated Sean's bequest, but everything had changed at the worst possible time... Could he be the father he needed to be and keep the ranch in the black when they were short on help?

"I knew Ralph Crawford, back in the day." Appreciation marked Ben's voice. "Before Sean moved north. He was a good man that never let the thought of money go to his head. A rare breed. Sean might have gotten his business savvy from Ian but his heart was all Crawford."

"Not a bad combination," said Corrie, and Heath put a hand on her shoulder.

"And this is a family friend, Cora Lee Satterly."

"I'm Wick." The man leaned forward and shook hands with both women. "Wick Williams, that is. I knowed Sean from the get-go, when he just got here and put money down on a chunk of land before anyone thought too much of it. He done all right for himself in these hills, ladies. I hope you will, too. And I'd like to say I'm sorry for your loss even though not much was said back and forth through the years."

"To have built up such an amazing business with sheep is surprising, isn't it?" Corrie asked. "It seems Sean was in the right place at the right time and everything fell into place."

"Well, it weren't sheep that built his fortune, but he

liked to say that shepherding was good for the soul," Ben told her.

"If not sheep, then what?" Lizzie asked the question of Heath, but Ben answered.

"Technology stocks. Investments. Sean got in on Silicon Valley's ground floor back when everything we take for granted today seemed like science fiction. When Ralph passed away, Sean invested his inheritance. So the ranch was built on a foundation of stock options. Not stock. But the stock's been paying the way for a good fifteen years now. Until—" Ben shifted his gaze to the equine barns. "Which puts a lot on your plate, Lizzie Fitzgerald. Something tells me you're not as cowed by the whole notion as I thought you'd be, and I can't tell you what that does for this old heart. Welcome to Pine Ridge. It'll be mighty nice to have a couple of fine women on the ranch," he added. "We've been mostly men until now, so you're a welcome addition."

"And when her sisters arrive, we'll be four women strong," said Corrie. "Although Charlotte and Melonie aren't as ranch-savvy as our Lizzie. But they're coming to help in whatever way they can."

Not because they wanted to. Heath knew that. They needed the ranch, or at least their financial share, as much as the ranch needed hands-on help right now. Sean's will had opened a window of opportunity when their father had shoveled millions of corporate dollars into off-shore accounts, leaving the three girls broke and in debt.

Pine Ridge would be co-owned by the four of them. Heath, Lizzie, Melonie and Charlotte, as long as the women put in a year working on the ranch. Sean had done it because he'd felt sorry for the massive change in their finances caused by their father's actions. But with the large outlay of cash for the equine start-up and the loss of government grazing lands, their solid financial foundation had been temporarily downgraded. If they blew it right now, the only option would be liquidation. And selling everything off would mean he'd failed his friend and mentor. That meant he couldn't fail.

"Four women in the house?" Ben scratched the back of his head, grinning. "That *will* be a change in these parts."

Unless they all ran screaming when they realized the hills of Idaho weren't exactly the lap of luxury they'd become accustomed to, thought Heath.

He glanced at Lizzie.

She was watching him. Studying his reactions. Reading him, and not looking all that impressed with what she saw.

"Dad! Isn't this like the best surprise ever?" Zeke grinned up at Lizzie, then Corrie. "And Miss Corrie says she knows how to make real good stuff and that maybe she can teach me like she did for Miss Lizzie, if she doesn't get in Cookie's way."

"I'll make way for cooking lessons," said the cook with a grin. "I might learn a thing or two myself, having a genteel Southern woman in the kitchen."

It wasn't the best surprise, but it was also out of Heath's hands. Ben saved him by addressing Zeke's comment. "It's a grand surprise, all right, and real nice to have family here. Brad," he said to one of the younger ranch hands, "are you going to fill your plate so the line moves along? You've got some hungry folks waitin'."

"Ladies first." The young cowboy indicated the food dishes. "My mama wouldn't take kindly to me going ahead of ladies."

"That's a kindness, for certain, and one I'm willing to accept." Corrie moved forward. "Thank you, Brad."

Lizzie followed her.

The men took their plates outdoors. Heath was tempted to follow them, but Zeke had other ideas. "Can we eat in here, Dad? With Lizzie and her friend?"

"*Miss* Lizzie. And Miss Corrie."

Lizzie rolled her eyes, but didn't correct him. His son. His rules. And manners mattered. Sean Fitzgerald might have worked a roughed-up patch of old farmland into a celebrated ranch, but he'd always expected manners from everyone. Heath followed his example.

"We were going to eat in the stable office," Lizzie began, but when Zeke's mouth downturned, she moved toward the big table. "But I'd like to get to know you better, too, and supper is the best time for that. Don't you think?" She sat down and smiled his way.

She'd taken the seat Zeke usually used.

The boy didn't fuss. He sat down to her right as Heath took the seat at the foot of the table. Corrie sat to his left, opposite Lizzie.

And then Zeke reached for Lizzie's hand for grace. She gripped his little hand while Corrie reached out for his right hand. That left him and Lizzie unlinked.

He was absolutely, positively not going to hold Lizzie's hand.

Lizzie seemed just as reluctant, and the only thing that saved them from a full-blown standoff was his beautiful boy. Zeke squeezed Lizzie's hand and tipped that sweet face up to her. "You've got to hold Dad's hand, okay? Just while we pray," he added, as if assuring her that she could let go soon. "Like for a minute. All right?" He gazed up for affirmation, looking not only hard but impossible to resist.

Lizzie raised her hand slightly.

He raised his, just as slowly.

And then their fingers touched.

She didn't look at him.

He didn't look at her.

But his hand wrapped around hers like it had all those years ago, feeling both right and wrong. Maybe more right than wrong, and that took him by surprise.

It might have been the quickest grace he'd ever said. Anna would have scolded him. She'd believed that taking a few minutes to thank the Lord wasn't something to be rushed, but savored.

Not tonight.

Not with Lizzie's soft, long, slim fingers tucked in his, churning up memories he'd tried so hard to forget. Tried—and failed. Because all it took was the touch of her hand and that warm, sweet smile to bring it roaring back to life once more.

Chapter Three

"Dad!" Zeke clapped a hand to his forehead as they finished Cookie's meal of thick, robust stew and fresh, warm bread. "Is it campfire night tonight? Remember? You promised."

"I did say that, yes. Wick cleaned out the fire pit earlier. So we're ready to go."

"Then this is like the best day ever!" Zeke turned Lizzie's way. "We couldn't have campfires when the weather was really bad." Wide eyes stressed the word *really* and his voice did the same. "But now we can!"

The last thing Lizzie wanted to do was elongate an already impossibly long day by going to the first campfire of the season, but when Zeke sent her an imploring look, she caved.

She and Corrie crossed the yard about an hour later, heading toward the warm, inviting glow of the wood fire. Corrie had brought a shawl, because the spring evening had taken a chill. "I haven't been to a campfire since you gals were in that equestrian group back in the day."

Neither had Lizzie. Heath Caufield and campfires hadn't been on her radar a dozen hours ago. Now they were. "I should be working. There's a lot to learn."

"Although there is much to be said for getting to know those we'll be working with," suggested Corrie. She pulled the woven shawl tighter as they approached the fire pit tucked on a broad graveled spot below the house.

Brad and Jace stood and relinquished their seats on the bench the moment they spotted the women. Lizzie started to wave them back. Grabbing a spot on the thick log would be fine for her, but Heath caught her eye.

He shook his head slightly.

Just that gentle warning to accept the offered gesture, so she did.

Zeke rounded the fire and came her way. "You came!"

"It was a hard invitation to resist, Zeke."

His grin was reward enough, but he made things even better by proffering a small brown paper bag. "Cookie brought stuff for s'mores, but I don't like them so he gave me cookies instead. Do you like cookies?" He was quick to include Corrie in his generosity as he held the bag open. "I didn't like grab them with my hands or anything so they're pretty clean."

"A pretty clean cookie sounds like the best offer I've had all day, Zeke." Lizzie had spent two days sitting in a car, driving cross-country, and she'd been studying the horse financial records for hours. The last thing she should do was add empty calories to her already messed-up daily fitness plan, but looking around the ranch, she figured her step tracker was about to get a serious daily workout. "Thank you."

"You're welcome!" He smiled up at her, eyes shining, as if sharing a cookie around the campfire was the best thing ever. When she bit into the broad double chocolate chip cookie, she couldn't disagree.

"You made a wonderful campfire even better, my friend." He giggled as he handed a cookie to Corrie, too. When she fussed over how good it was, the boy's grin grew wider.

Endearing. Joyous. Carefree.

A dear boy, a delightful child. Gazing at him, she wondered what their little boy would have been like. Would he have gotten her eyes? Heath's hair? Would he have had Heath's inner strength and the Fitzgerald writing skills? His grandmother's fine heart and gentle spirit?

Corrie laid a hand against her arm and pressed closer to whisper in Lizzie's ear. "You are wearing your heart all over your face, darlin'."

She couldn't help it. Not at this moment. And then Zeke patted her knee. "If you like Cookie's chocolate cookies, wait 'til you try the peanut butter ones with the most special chocolate frosting ever."

"They can't be as good as these." She made a face of doubt and the boy wriggled.

"I think they are!"

So sweet. So bright. Innocence and hope, a perfect blend. She met his gaze. "I do love chocolate the most."

"And potatoes."

Heath's voice brought her attention around. Three

people sat between them, creating a good distance. Enough, she'd thought.

But it could never be enough, she realized when he lifted his eyes to hers. She read the pain in his expression. For his lost wife? For his motherless child? Or was it her presence causing that angst? "I still love potatoes. I blame my Irish heritage. They haven't come up with a potato I don't enjoy." The reply was for Heath, but she kept her attention on his son.

"My dad loves 'tatoes, too." Zeke leaned against her leg, keeping back from the fire. The boy's warmth felt good against the cooling air. "I do a little bit, but mostly I like everything."

"A boy with a healthy appetite is a wonderful thing." Corrie smiled at him. "Your daddy had a great appetite when he was younger, and look how big and strong he got. I think you'll do all right, Zeke Caufield."

"You knew my dad when he was little? Like me?"

Corrie shook her head. "Not that little, but young enough. Your dad and your grandpa worked with me a long time ago."

Heath stood quickly. He motioned to Zeke, ignoring Corrie's statement. "Bedtime."

"But I'm not even a little bit tired." Zeke braced his legs and met Heath's gaze across the fire, looking like a miniature version of the strong man facing him down. "Can I stay up with Miss Lizzie and Miss Corrie for just a little bit? Pleeease?"

Heath said nothing.

He didn't argue. He didn't get bossy. He simply met the boy's gaze. In less than half a minute, the boy trudged around the fire and thrust his hand into Heath's.

"Say good-night."

"Night, everybody." Chin down, the little cowpoke walked away. He didn't fuss and didn't fight. He obeyed his dad, as if trusting him to make the right call even though he disagreed.

It felt good, watching them. And different. Their branch of the Fitzgeralds didn't win any parenting awards. If it hadn't been for Corrie's love and dedication... Lizzie leaned over and kissed Corrie's round, brown cheek. "I love you, Corrie."

Corrie kept her gaze forward, on the fire and on Heath and his son. "I love you, too. And no matter what happens here, it is good to break away from the past, Lizzie-Beth. To forge ahead."

"An Idaho ranch wasn't exactly what I had in mind," she whispered back when a handful of bleats broke the night air. "But a stable full of horses is more of a dream come true than a punishment right now." She studied the flames for drawn-out seconds. "It's an unexpected twist in a winding road, that's for sure."

"What we've got in mind and what the good Lord's got planned don't always agree, but that's what makes life interesting. Sometimes it's a collision course. Other times it's a wide, beautiful curve."

"I think our family has more experience with the collisions." A smallish log had rolled off the fire's edge. She leaned down and prodded it back into place. "Is that our destiny or our curse?"

"Neither," Corrie declared. "It's human foolishness. Your grandfather stepped on a lot of toes to build that publishing empire, and I've heard people say his father did that, too, before him. And then your daddy did the same, but he didn't have ambition. He wanted the world handed to him."

"And if it didn't happen, he stole."

"Good or bad, it all comes down to free will," Corrie said. "You see the beauty Sean created here. That's the side of the family you take for, Lizzie. The hardworking trait, passed down. All three of my girls can say that and be proud."

"Well, life's got a way of keeping us humble, so pride's not a real big deal right now. And I've got a lot of work ahead of me in the morning. There are twenty-eight horses to learn about, I need to find a herd stallion, and I've got three emails from potential foal buyers so I need to brush up on lineage so I know what I'm talking about." She stood and straightened her shirt.

In a gesture of respect, all the men stood up as well.

Cowboy code… Respect. Honor. Honesty.

She'd loved that about Heath when they were young. His strong focus, his work ethic, the way he put the animals and others first. That sharpened the disappointment when he'd never looked back to see how she'd fared. After.

He'd gone on with his life.

She'd gone on with hers.

Now here they were, working side by side. Two goals, one ranch, and a lot at stake. More than she'd thought possible until she'd faced those stables and the cowboy running them.

"I'm going to stay a bit. Chat with the men." Corrie waved her off. "Good night, darlin' girl."

"Good night." She crossed the graveled area, moved by the rugged beauty surrounding her. She hurried inside, grabbed her camera, and came back out, snapping evening pics of the men, the campfire, and Corrie's sweet face set against a Western backdrop of hills, barns and land. She'd create a photo journal of this new path, something to share or to keep for herself. Either way, she could chronicle this new opportunity in pictures.

Then she saw him, standing alone now that Zeke was tucked into bed, braced against the top rail of a fence. Heath, in profile, backlit by a full moon, a Western cover shot if ever there was one.

She took a handful of pictures, knowing the sophisticated camera would adjust for light and distance.

Then she stood there, quiet, watching him through the camera's lens. Strong, rugged, determined, and looking so lonely and lost it made her heart ache.

She lowered the camera and moved toward the door. She didn't want him to catch her studying him. Wondering about him. But when she got to the thick oak door she turned one last time.

He'd turned, too. Their eyes met. Held.

She didn't know how to break the connection. For just a moment, she wasn't sure she wanted to.

But then she did. She'd learned a few lessons over the years. To forgive, to never hold a grudge, and to make it on her own.

She didn't hate men for letting her down. Men like her father. Her grandfather. Heath. But she wasn't foolish enough to trust one again, either. A movement outside caught her eye as she crossed to the stairs leading to her rooms. Furtive and low, something skulked outside, moving toward the pasture beyond.

Too small for a wolf. Maybe too small for a coyote,

too, the creature slipped through the night, but the low profile and the stealthy manner put her on alert.

Foals could be damaged by rogue wild animals. And worried mares might have less milk for their growing babies. She couldn't afford to risk either, so she'd figure out what this was and how to handle it because she didn't need reminders about what was at stake within these barn walls.

She'd seen the spreadsheets. No sneaking creature of the night was going to ruin this for her, for the ranch or for those beautiful mares. She'd see to it.

Heath couldn't get into the busyness of lambing fast enough, if having Lizzie around messed with his head this much. There was nothing like delivering hundreds of tiny creatures to keep your mind occupied, but tonight images flooded him.

Lizzie, in the kitchen, engaging the men in conversation. Or on the porch, her long, russet hair splayed across her shoulders, smiling at his son. At the campfire, her lyrical voice and the flickering flames taking him back in time.

Heath didn't have the luxury of lingering in the past. Fatherhood required him to be fully present in today, but that reality had changed when he'd come face-to-face with Lizzie that morning.

The other reality was the massive amount of work that they'd have on their hands after Ben, Aldo and Brad headed into the hills for the last time ever.

He pushed off the rail to return to the house, and there she was, backlit by the stable lights. She stood quiet and still, with a beauty he remembered like it was yesterday. *Favor is deceitful, and beauty is vain, but a woman that feareth the Lord shall be praised...*

He used to care what the Bible said. He used to pray with his heart and soul.

Now he only went to church because he believed Zeke needed that structure, but the old verse washed over him as they locked eyes. He stood there, unable to shift his gaze while years melted away.

She broke the connection first and kept walking toward the stables.

In a weird reversal of roles, he moved toward the house. It had been different in Kentucky. She'd lived in the grand house and he'd bunked with his drunken father in the upper part of the horse barn, but he couldn't find any pleasure in the change. It felt wrong on so many levels. Lizzie Fitzgerald shouldn't be sleeping in a barn. Not now. Not ever.

And yet she was.

He cut around to the back door and slipped inside. He kicked off his shoes and moved into the bedroom he shared with his son.

Anna had made the ultimate sacrifice five and a half years before. She'd understood the dangers to herself, but refused to terminate the pregnancy. And when the resulting heart damage from the previously undiagnosed condition proved too much for her body to bear, she'd kissed him and the perfect baby boy goodbye. And then she was gone. No pain. No suffering. Just wave upon wave of immeasurable sadness.

Zeke rolled over. He brought his hand toward his mouth, an old habit from when he used to suck his thumb, but then his small brown hand relaxed against the white-cased pillow.

Heath kissed the boy's cheek. Then he went to bed, listening to the sound of his son's breathing, like balm on a wound. But when he couldn't get Lizzie's russet-toned eyes out of his mind, he realized that shrugging some things off was much harder than others.

Chapter Four

Determined. Troublemaker. Big Red. Night Shadow. Red Moon Rising.

Lizzie stared at the impressive list of stallion names, refusing to be overwhelmed.

Getting eight mares bred to top quarter horse stallions had set her uncle back a cool hundred grand. And based on their lineage, the healthy foals could pay back three times that without a single credential to their record.

That meant each one better hit the ground running, healthy and sound.

You are now responsible for a million dollars in marketable goods. She stood and faced the broad window overlooking the verdant pasture as Heath walked toward the stable the next morning. *And your goods aren't static. They're impulsive babies who run and jump and cavort. Your job is to keep them alive and unblemished.*

Her business major had prepared her for the financial scenario, but she'd assumed she'd be working with publishing spreadsheets and corporate executives, not living creatures. Despite all she knew about horses, she'd never felt less prepared in her life.

"Sticker shock?" asked Heath when he paused at the office door.

"Is it that obvious?"

"Don't get me wrong." Heath came through the door. "Sean knew what he was doing. He didn't play to lose. Ever. And his goal was to bring Saddle Up blood onto the farm one way or another, so three of those mares are bred to Saddle Up stallions. Speaking of which, this just came through the fax."

He handed her a picture of a magnificent red roan quarter horse. Red Moon Rising, with an offer of sale attached from Rising Star Ranch.

She sighed, staring. "He's gorgeous." She noted the western Nebraska ranch named in the corner of the fax. "I have a note here from Uncle Sean saying this was his top choice, and pretty sure they'd never sell. And yet—" She raised the spec sheet higher. "Here we are. How did this happen?"

"I don't know. Sean approached them over a year ago and got nowhere. Then this appears, out of the blue. Do we want him?"

The perfectly formed horse stood tall and proud, the way a stallion should. But he had a gentleness in his eye, too, an important factor on a working farm. "That's not even a question. Of course we do. But I thought we were short on money."

"Short on cash, temporarily. At least until we get things squared away with all the changes. But we're long on assets," he told her. "And since this is something Sean tried to do before he died, I think we need to follow the plan." He tapped the printed sheet in her hand. "I'm glad they decided to share. Sean could be mighty convincing when he needed to be. When it came to horses, he knew what he wanted and where to get it. I don't have the knack," he went on. "Sheep, yes. Horses, no. But Sean did. And he thought you did, too."

"Being an accomplished rider doesn't make me a breeder." She clutched the sale offer and gazed at the mares in the near pasture. "And there's no big name vet on hand to offer advice and testing like other places have. And one groomer to help me, a guy who doesn't speak horse."

"Not everyone's a whisperer, Liz."

He used to tease her about that when they were young, about her ability to work well with the horses, to understand what they wanted. Needed. "It's not whispering. It's just instinct."

"It's a gift and not everyone has it. Eric Carrington is expanding his place a little further south in the valley. He's looking at expanding his cattle breeding operation into horses. He and Sean talked about a partnership, but then—"

"Angus cattle, black and red." She pointed to the laptop computer. "His name came up in my searches. We passed his pastures on the drive in, didn't we?"

"Yes. And if you decide to cut the deal for Red Moon Rising, I'll transfer the money to the equine account. That's a mighty fine-looking horse right there. And there are three stallion stalls sitting empty at the moment. He'd pay for himself in stud fee savings in a year."

She tapped the open page with one finger, thinking,

then looked up. "A part of me feels vastly unqualified to make this call."

He waited.

"The other part feels like someone just handed me the best opportunity in the world. To make my living working with horses. Who'd have thought?" She lifted her shoulders lightly because when the bankruptcy rulings swept in, the horses, the tack, the trailers, the food…everything disappeared. And there wasn't a thing the girls could do about it.

"Then the hesitant side will tug the reins on the other side so you don't go hog wild." He glanced behind her and whistled lightly when he saw the big calendar she'd mounted on the wall. "All the auction dates for next year. You didn't waste any time."

"No time to waste if we've got foals due all summer. We want mama and baby teams to socialize together the first six months, so if I'm going to make this call, I need to get on it now."

"I'll leave you to it. Call my cell if you need anything. I'll be in the newer lambing barn up front, but I can get back here quickly." And just when she thought he was extending an olive branch, his face tightened. "Whether I like it or not, what happens in this barn can make or break thirty years of hard work and investment. And that's nothing I take lightly."

She met his gaze and kept her face flat on purpose.

She didn't punch him.

She gave herself extra points on that, because she really wanted to.

"Nor should you. Thanks for stopping by." She sat

down, dropped her eyes and reached for the phone, effectively dismissing him.

He hesitated.

She didn't look up.

And then he left, heading toward the house.

She tried not to notice how good he looked as he strode away. She tried to ignore the breadth of his shoulders in that long-sleeved blue T-shirt and how easily he moved in the faded denim jeans. He wasn't wearing fancy Western boots. He walked off in well-made, waterproof farm boots, perfect for working stock animals.

As the Rising Star Farm phone began ringing, she saw Zeke rush out of the house to meet his dad. Heath scooped him up, noogied his head, then hugged him close.

An old ache nudged her heart with a feeling of loss, but then someone at Rising Star answered the phone. She brought her attention back to the present. She hauled in a breath and introduced herself to the person on the other end, and by the time she was through her day, she'd cut a deal on an impressive stallion and set up an appointment with Carrington's ranch manager to see two mares the next day.

They might not be what she was looking for. Until she got here and met Sean's herd, she didn't know what she'd be looking for.

Now she'd had a first-hand look, and if Sean was willing to put his trust in a woman he didn't know, Heath better be all right with doing the same.

He'd said that Sean played to win. She did, too. And the only time she lost was when the outcome was taken totally out of her hands. But life went that way sometimes, and that meant you needed to straighten up, keep your chin up and pray your way through it. She'd had to do that more than once in her life, and when needed... she'd do it again.

Heath transferred farm equity funds into the equine account, and by the time he got showered and dressed for supper, the funds were out of the account. "You cut the deal with Rising Star that quickly?" he asked when Lizzie crossed the green square separating the stables a quarter hour later.

"Yes." She tipped a smile over his shoulder when Zeke spotted her and came racing their way. "I read Uncle Sean's notes on possible stallions, and he was over the moon about this one. No pun intended," she added. "If he felt that strongly about Red Moon Rising, I didn't want to take a chance they might renege on the deal. Hey, bud." She laughed when Zeke skidded to a stop and grabbed her hand. He looked up at her, she looked down at him and when they shared a smile, an old flicker of something warm and good ignited within Heath.

"They'll deliver him Thursday with all the appropriate testing and paperwork attached. He's already in the money with his foal lines, so unless something unexpected happens to him, we've got a perfect match for those next broodmares."

Zeke tugged her arm. "What is that?" he asked when she looked back down.

She made a face of question. "What is what, sweet thing?"

His smile deepened again as he tightened the grip on Lizzie's hand. "A brood thing."

"Ah." She squatted to his level, and Zeke's eyes lit up. "It's a horse who's going to have a baby. A foal. Some of the horses are pregnant and that's what we call them. Broodmares."

He clapped his other hand to his forehead, astonished. "We're going to have baby horses?"

She nodded. "Yes."

"And more baby sheep?"

"Lots of them," Heath said.

"And we have baby kittens and sometimes puppies and now Rosie-Posie is going to have a baby, too! Everyone is having babies, Dad! Isn't that so cool?"

He was about to say yes. But the pain in Lizzie's expression paused him, then he answered his son's question. "It is cool, Zeke. Having a baby is a wonderful thing, but we're going to be working like crazy for a while which means you're going to have to be a super good boy."

"Because Rosie-Posie will be busy with her baby."

"But Justine will be here to take care of you," Heath reminded him. "Jace's sister. Until Rosie's had time to recover."

"I don't even know her a little bit, Dad." Zeke sent him a glum look. "She's not like my friend or anything."

"You know Jace."

Zeke scrubbed a toe into the dirt.

"And you met Justine last year."

Zeke didn't look impressed. "I was little then. I don't even remember her and she might not know what I like to do."

"Can we tell her?" Lizzie directed the question straight to Zeke. "Can we tell her all your favorite things to do and eat and where you like to explore?"

"I can explore?" His brows lifted high. "For real?"

Lizzie stood and nodded. "Every little kid should explore things. Right?"

"Except every little kid isn't on a working ranch with animals and heavy equipment moving from dawn to dark, and sometimes after. So exploring is kept to a minimum unless you're with a grown-up."

Zeke didn't hear his father's warning. Or he chose to ignore it. "I can't wait to tell her we can go exploring! I'm gonna tell Miss Corrie and Cookie!" He raced into the house, leaving them alone on the graveled yard.

"His enthusiasm is contagious." Lizzie smiled after him.

"But unbridled enthusiasm can get him into trouble. And around here, trouble can mean danger, so please don't encourage him to test his boundaries. Usually he's tucked at Rosie and Harve's house with a little fenced yard and safe borders. Being here during a busy season will open up way too many temptations for him. Keeping him safe is my number one priority, Liz. He's all I've got."

She didn't raise her gaze to his. She kept it averted, then firmed her jaw. Swallowed. And only then did she look up, and when she did, it was to change the subject. "They'll be delivering Red by the end of the week. We might need help unloading. It's a long ride for a horse that's been a ranch cornerstone for six years with mares being brought to him. Not the other way around."

Images of rogue stallions running amok in the movies took control of his brain because when it came to Zeke and safety, worst-case scenarios always seemed to prevail. "Is that why they're selling him? We don't need a horse with behavior problems on the ranch, and why else would an established setup sell off a money-maker like him?"

"Because too many of their horses are related to him now."

Of course. He didn't run into that problem with sheep because they were market animals. Animals bred for longevity and breeding operated on a whole different cycle.

"And," she went on, "they liked Uncle Sean. Everett Yost called him one of the good guys, and we're far enough north that we're no threat to their sales numbers. He made it clear that they liked the idea of a solid Quarter Horse operation up here."

Three good reasons. Just then, the dinner bell sounded. She turned toward the house and he went with her. "The rest of the horses look all right?"

It was a lame question. He knew they looked all right because he'd been doing double duty the past six weeks. "They'll be fine once they're back on a regular grooming schedule. Stable help is in short supply, I guess. Brad's a nice guy, but he's uneasy in the stable. And that's not good," she answered.

He flushed. "Help is scarce across the board right now. It will get better once full operations are down here in the valley, but having two bands of sheep in the hills cuts us down by six men. I thought hard about sending them off." He paused on the middle step and she did, too. "But we'd paid for this year's rights, we weren't prepped for that amount of hay or pasture and it ended up really being no choice."

"Then don't second-guess it."

She'd nailed it completely because that's exactly what he'd been doing.

"We can limp along for a few weeks, can't we?"

Lambing, hay production, decreased help and a shallow pool of available people as the local population moved away in search of jobs that no longer existed in Shepherd's Crossing since Boise and Sun Valley had mushroomed in size and popularity. "Don't have much choice."

"Then that's what we do. Is that steak I smell?" She breathed deep, and there was no missing the appreciation in her eyes.

"We send the shepherds off with a steak dinner and welcome them back the same way. Tradition."

"Well, that's a tradition I can get behind," she said. "I haven't had a wood-fired steak in a long time."

"Too busy to cook?" He followed her up the steps and tried not to notice how nicely she moved. The natural grace and curves he remembered so well. Too well.

She turned at the top step and he was pretty sure she read his mind. She paused, folded her arms and held his gaze tight. He expected a scolding. But she surprised him once again and kept to the topic at hand. "Reduced circumstances put steak dinners out of reach. Lawyers don't come cheap and while a lot of the fallout rained down on the publishing company, Char, Mel and I fielded our share. So yeah, the steak smells good. Real good."

She turned and walked inside, leaving him on the step.

He glanced at the horse barn, then the house as reality hit. Sean had said Tim's girls had suffered a mighty financial blow, but Fitzgerald News Company was worth millions. Billions, maybe, for all he knew. It wasn't like he paid attention to such things. Rich was rich and the rich always seemed to get richer, one way or another.

Evidently not this time, and shame on him for assuming things. And now she was camping out in an unfurnished stable apartment that held nothing but an old bed.

He used to be a nice guy. When had he gotten so angry that he forgot how to just be a nice guy? A few phone calls and not too much money could have taken care of that little apartment, but he hadn't done so. Why? To punish her? Or because he never expected her to bunk in the barn?

The kitchen gong rang again, Cookie's signal to come now or go hungry.

He went inside, feeling a little smarter and a little stupider than he'd been before, and when he saw Corrie beam a smile at Lizzie—while she held up a bite of steak—he realized the magnitude of the family financial issues.

And then he recognized something else.

Lizzie wasn't complaining. She wasn't whining or throwing her father under the bus. She was dealing with the situation as best she could and for the second time that day he wondered about her strength.

Clearly she was no longer the teen who caved in to family pressure to keep the Fitzgerald name pristine. In light of Tim Fitzgerald's total ruination, the irony hit him fully. Tim had sent his daughter off to terminate a pregnancy to protect the family reputation, and less than a dozen years later he'd shattered that reputation beyond repair.

Zeke took a seat next to Lizzie at the wide-planked farmhouse table. He peered up at her and grinned.

She grinned back, and for just a moment, he wondered if it could always be like that.

His thumb moved to the wedding ring he still wore on his left hand, a reminder of his wife's sacrifice, and when Lizzie leaned down and whispered in Zeke's ear, making him laugh... Heath's heart slowed.

It should be Anna teasing their son. She should be here, being a mom, a wife. When Lizzie reached for Zeke's hand for grace, Heath turned away, unwilling to pray.

He pretended to join in most of the time. He took the boy to church, he stood and prayed or sat and prayed, because he wanted to set a good example.

But he didn't believe. He wasn't like those placid sheep he tended each day, following one after the other, being led along.

He was his own person. Hard work and honesty had gotten him this far. They'd get him the rest of the way.

But when Lizzie finished saying grace with his son, when she leaned down and pressed a kiss to Zeke's forehead, making him smile, Heath read the peace in her gaze, and a little part of him both wished for it and resented it at the same time.

But that was his problem. Not hers.

Chapter Five

Heath Caufield was a major problem and Lizzie wasn't sure how to fix it. The fact that her heart tipped into overdrive or slo-mo every time the man looked her way was no help at all, and she'd just determined to keep her distance when a text from him came through the next morning. There was a picture attached, of a solid, small sofa and chair, with an end table. For sale in town. Looks perfect for stable apartment. What do you think?

What was he doing? Being nice? Worth a look, she texted back. When?

Truck's running.

That made her smile, and when she looked out the window, there he was, with Zeke, standing oh-so-casual next to the running pickup truck. She waved, stuffed some cash and her phone into her pocket, and slipped her arms into her denim jacket as she walked toward the truck.

He opened the door for Zeke, then her. The little guy

climbed onto his booster seat, fastened his seat belt and grinned. "I had three pancakes for breakfast," Zeke announced. He waggled three fingers to make his point. "And they were so delicious! Miss Corrie made them because Cookie had to go shopping and Miss Corrie said she'd throw on the feedbag."

She made a face at him, then lifted a brow to Heath once he took the driver's seat. "Is Corrie trying to sound Western? Because that's a little crazy."

"She did use the term feedbag. But then she laughed, so we let it go."

"Oh, man." He turned the truck toward the road as she indicated the sheep barn. "I thought you were seeing the men off this morning."

"Five thirty a.m. Hence the empty upper pastures. We'll rotate the new mothers onto the east pasture as the lambs drop. Give that one a rest."

"I can't believe I slept through it."

"It was early." Heath tapped a finger to the center console, an old habit. "There's a spot where they cross the highway in a week, up north. We could take a ride up there to see it. They shut down traffic for a few hours and folks gather to take pictures."

"So it's really a thing here," she said, and he made a wry face.

"Less of a thing now. Fewer farms, fewer sheep, limited grazing. But Idaho hay is a rising commodity and when Sean bought land, he made sure he offset every purchase with land for hay or grazing potential. He didn't want to play the crop game. Too much risk in that for him, too weather dependent."

"A man who understood measured risk and return on investment."

"Exactly." He took a left turn into a small town. An old green painted sign used to say Shepherd's Crossing, Idaho, but a few of the letters had worn off over time.

"This is the town?" She didn't mean to sound so surprised, but she was. "Are there shops, Heath? Stores?"

"That's our church, Lizzie!" Heath shot him a look through the mirror and Zeke corrected himself. "I mean *Miss* Lizzie! That's where we go tomorrow!"

A worn stone-and-clapboard church sat tucked in a clutch of pines. It fit the setting, nestled into an alcove that allowed room for gathering outside in the grass, while a forested feel surrounded the setting. "That's a sweet church, Zeke." She shifted back toward Heath. "And is that the only church I see?"

He ground his jaw, then raised his right shoulder. "Used to be two others. And there were shops when I first got here, but even then things were slowing down. Smitty does barbering in his basement. And we've got a retired pastor at the church. He came up from Boise a bunch of years back. There's a gas station up ahead with a little store attached but I heard he's looking to sell. Or just close it up."

Empty storefronts faced each other from opposite sides of the road. A tiny post office sat proud and alive in the middle of Main Street, with a bright, fresh American flag flying atop a silver pole. The brilliant flag was the only real symbol of life along the short passage. "No deli? No food? Where does Cookie go to shop?"

"He makes the drive to Council. Or up to McCall.

And he orders things online. He's not afraid to fill the freezer with food, but the fresh stuff requires trips."

"That will make Corrie's summer garden most welcome, I expect."

"Cookie will love it. Here we are." He pulled into the address he'd put into his phone. "Let's go see what we think."

A woman opened the door and let them in. Lizzie didn't hesitate when she showed them the set. "It's perfect. I'll take it."

Zeke pushed down on the cushion closest to him as if testing it out. "Can I jump on it?" He tipped a grin up to Lizzie and she made a face at him.

"Not if you want to live, darling. Jump outside. Or on a trampoline. Not on furniture. Got it?"

He high-fived her. "Got it!"

She pulled out her money to pay but Heath stopped her. "This is on the ranch, Liz. I should have done it before you got here, and I didn't. I'm sorry."

A part of her heart melted right there, but she couldn't afford to let down her guard. "I appreciate it, Heath. Thanks."

They loaded up the loveseat and chair, then the small lamp table. And when they were driving back to the ranch, Heath angled a look her way. "She'd have taken less for the furniture. But you knew that, didn't you?"

She'd suspected as much but didn't want to take advantage of the situation. "And she needed more by the looks of things, so this works for both of us. She got a fair price and I've got a super cute set for the apartment."

"How bad is the bed up there?"

"On a scale of one to ten, we're into negative figures."

"I'll order a new mattress and box spring from Boise. It'll take a few days."

"It's not like I'm going anywhere," she answered. "And that would be nice. Thank you, Heath." The too-soft mattress was already making her hips ache when she climbed out of bed in the morning.

He started to say something, then stopped. Kept driving. As he turned down the long Pine Ridge Ranch drive, he glanced her way. "Anything else you need right away? Like a kitchen table? Chairs?"

She shook her head. "I'll eat with you guys when I can. I'm not planning on doing a lot of cooking or entertaining, but having a place to sit and a decent bed will be wonderful. And a small TV, but I can order that online."

"Don't." He rounded the stable and backed the truck up to the door closest to her apartment staircase. "Sean had one in his room. I'll bring it over. We can mount it on the wall easy enough."

"That would be nice, Heath. Real nice." She faced him over the hood of the truck. She wasn't sure what inspired this kindness, but she welcomed it. "Thank you. Again."

Jace came around the corner just then. He and Heath hauled the furniture up the stairs, and only nicked the painted walls twice. When they got the three pieces settled, Heath looked around. "That's better. Isn't it?"

She nodded. And when they showed up twenty minutes later with the television and mounted it on the wall, she realized he was really trying, because the last thing he had right now was time.

"Done." He grinned at Jace. "And with no extra holes in the wall."

"That's because I'm here helping," Jace answered. "Lizzie, you should be all set. I wrote down the password and account for the ranch's channel service. If you have to update anything, you've got full access."

"Sweet." She taped the code to the kitchenette wall. "That way I don't lose it."

"Dad! Can I stay with Miss Lizzie for a little while? Just a tiny while? Like this much?" Zeke held his thumb and forefinger up to show a thin space. "I'll be so good."

"Lizzie's got horses to tend."

"But I'm letting them all out to graze, and then cleaning stalls, so he's welcome to hang out with me. He might be able to spread fresh straw when I'm done."

"You don't mind? You sure? Because he can tag along with us. That's what he usually does on Saturdays."

"I'd love the company," she replied as she exchanged grins with the boy. "I think we should get our work done, then see if Corrie's got cookies in the kitchen. Because I know she brought along some of her signature macadamia nuts in case she couldn't find them up here. And grits."

"I haven't had grits in a long, long time." Heath looked up at her, and they both knew why he hadn't had grits in a long, long time. Her heart went tight. She wondered if his did, too, but then she put a hand on Zeke's shoulder.

"You come with me, kiddo. You can hang in the main hall while I open the stalls. Okay?"

"Okay!" He looked so excited to be there. To be with her. Hang out with her. He chattered as he worked, a distinct difference from his quieter father. By the time they were done, it was well past lunchtime.

"Kid, we've skipped lunch."

"And I am so hungry," he assured her. "Like maybe starving, my Lizzie."

My Lizzie?

It made her smile and she couldn't bring herself to correct him. "Let's go rustle up some grub, cowboy."

"You talk funny!"

It probably did sound odd to the little boy, her drawl at war with an imitation Western twang. She shut the door to the center barn and crouched, just a little. "Race you to the house?"

"Yes!" He sprinted off with eggbeater legs, kicking up dust across the dirt while Lizzie pretended to be catching him.

"I'm getting closer," she called with a burst of speed. "I'm—"

"I won!" He pivoted on the top step of the porch and laughed, then jumped into her arms. "I must be superfast, my Lizzie!"

He was super in a lot of ways. Supercute, supersweet and quickly finding his way into her heart. Was that because she was transferring old emotions for new ones?

One look into Zeke's big brown eyes said no.

He was cementing his own place in her heart. She'd faced Heath with the realization that she had to harden her heart to him, but when he pulled out his secret weapon, a motherless boy...

She hugged Zeke and set him down.

She needed to keep her distance. It was hard enough

to be living here with her first love. It was nearly impossible with his beautiful son.

She didn't go through the barn door when she headed back to the stables after lunch. She rounded it instead and came to a quick stop.

Last night's creature was creeping toward a stand of trees and an old shed.

Not a wolf. Nor a coyote. The surreptitious creature was a tattered dog with a matted coat. The medium-sized canine slipped along the edge of the trees with its head hanging low as if tired.

She whistled softly. "Hey, boy."

The dog whipped its head around, then hurried to the shed and out of sight.

She started to chase after it, but common sense prevailed. Instead, she nipped dog food from the sheep dog bin in the front barn and set a cache of food and water along the walk bordering the back of the barn. She'd tempt the little fellow in with food and kindness. And then, maybe…a bath.

A "notice me" type pickup truck pulled into the yard on Thursday, hauling a quad horse trailer. The coating of road dust did nothing to diminish the truck's wide wheel base and total muscle look. The driver pulled up in front of the house, stopped the truck and climbed out.

"He's here." Corrie was standing behind her in the stable barn. "Let's go meet this fellow."

"Red Moon Rising?"

Corrie winked. "I meant the cowboy. But the horse is probably good-looking, too."

Lizzie grinned and led the way. As she drew close,

she didn't miss the light of appreciation in the truck driver's eyes. And she wasn't immune to the fact that he was ridiculously handsome. He strode forward and stuck out a hand. "I'm Everett Yost," he said as he gave her hand a firm but easy grip. "The younger one. They've always shortened it to 'Ev' to make the distinction between me and my dad. And you've got to be a Fitzgerald because you look like your uncle."

"Lizzie Fitzgerald." She shook his hand firmly. "A good trip, I hope?"

"Fine. We put up the one night and I don't think Red loved being penned, but when he gets a load of this…" He raked the mare-filled pasture an easy nod of approval. "He'll adjust. How long you been breeding horses, Lizzie?"

"A week," she told him.

He laughed. And then he stopped laughing when he saw she wasn't kidding. "You serious?"

"I've run horses. I grew up on a Kentucky horse farm, but we didn't talk breeding at our house around impressionable young ladies."

He laughed again, understanding.

"Riding, racing and deportment were the topics of the day, but having said that, I've done my homework."

He looked skeptical and amused.

"To get this right," she told him as she motioned to the trailer. "My uncle trusted me to do this and not mess it up. And he said if he could bring one of your stallions on board and begin there, he could die a happy man."

"Well, I'm sorry we didn't cut the deal quicker, then," said Ev. "No one realized he was that bad off, and when we did, it was too late. I met him a couple of times as he was traveling through Nebraska, checking stock. No matter where he was he'd always find a Quarter Horse farm and drop in. See what they had. How they were doing. This was a dream of his." He thrust his chin toward the equine facilities. "He said he didn't need it crazy big like some of those Texas spreads. But he wanted to grow it big enough so that the name Fitzgerald and Quarter Horse made a solid pairing."

"And the pressure mounts," Lizzie muttered under her breath as Ev unlatched the door. He moved inside, murmuring to the big roan horse, and when he came out backwards, with a lead in his hand, Lizzie took in a deep breath and held it.

"You approve." Ev smiled when he saw her face. "He's a beauty, isn't he?"

"Way beyond that," she answered. "Shall we introduce him to the ladies one by one? Or just walk him into the pasture?"

"He's been with a herd all his life. He'd think it strange to be separated."

"Then let's go." She took the lead and led the way to the first gate. She paused the horse, moved forward and drew the gate open.

He didn't rush the gate. He waited like the gentleman he was, and when she walked him inside, he seemed to take in his surroundings with slow, long looks. Then he entered the pasture with strong, full steps, tossed his mane, flicked his tail and stomped his right hoof twice.

And the ladies all turned his way.

"Oh, man. He's an attention seeker." Lizzie watched as the big horse stood fairly still while the mares came toward him. "And he got their attention, all right."

"You'll want to keep a close eye these first days, make sure there's no seniority issues. Horses have a pecking order like most creatures, and if you've got a couple of highfalutin mares, they might challenge him for the lead. But mostly Red just takes the lead and the ladies are content to follow." He winked at her, then grinned, and she couldn't help but laugh back.

"So. This is Red Moon Rising."

Heath's deep voice surprised her. She turned as he crossed the last few feet to reach them. "It is. Heath Caufield, ranch manager, this is Ev Yost. The younger one," she added with a smile.

Everett extended his hand.

Heath didn't hesitate. He took the other man's hand in a quick handshake, but then released it quickly. Too quickly. As if dismissing him.

"Ev, you've got to be hungry," said Lizzie. "It's past lunchtime. Come on in and we'll grab something. I'd like to hear more about Red. His likes and dislikes, his habits. I read all the stuff you guys have online and what your father sent along, but I don't want to make any stupid novice mistakes."

"Food and conversation sounds perfect, Lizzie. And fresh coffee would round things off. My to-go cup was fresh six hours ago, but I didn't want to extend Red's trip any longer than I had to."

"That stop-and-go stuff can be hard on trailered stock. Corrie, can you keep an eye on Red for a little bit? Or would you rather take Everett inside for food and I'll watch the horses?"

"I've got my phone." Corrie patted her pocket. "If

there's a problem, I'll call right off. But he seems like a gentle giant."

"He is," said Everett. "My dad and I hand-raised him from birth, so giving him up was not an easy decision. But we've got two up-and-coming stallions with distinct genetics and we need to mix things up a little."

"Figuring out broad-based genetics versus the strength of family ties is a breeder's trick."

"You have been studying." He laughed down at her. "Well done."

If she thought Heath's jaw couldn't grow tighter, she was wrong. She moved toward the house, then turned. "Heath. Are you coming in?"

"Work to do," he said curtly.

"All right." She kept moving. Everett fell into step beside her.

"You guys have a big undertaking here. I checked the online stats. The sheep numbers alone would keep a man up at night."

"My uncle may have bitten off more than we can chew," she answered. "But if we can ride the current wave until the shepherds are all back in the valley, I think it can work. We just don't worry about mundane things like sleep."

He laughed, reached out and pulled open the screen door for her. "I hear you. Taking this drive was my way of catching a breath. I love my family, but a day or two apart now and again isn't a bad thing."

"It makes the reunion that much better."

"Got that right." He grinned down at her, then followed her inside, letting the door ease shut behind them.

* * *

"You might want to think about losing the frown now and then. Just a suggestion, of course," Corrie noted as Heath followed Lizzie and Everett Yost's progress to the house. "The occasional smile. Conversation instead of grunts. All the things that separate us from the monkeys, Heath."

"I don't need advice. I need more ranch hands and longer days and perfect weather for the next four weeks so the first hay gets in under cover and these lambs hit the ground healthy. It's easy to laugh when everything's going right." He thrust his jaw toward Ev Yost and Lizzie as they went up the steps. And when the Yost guy caught the door *and* Lizzie's attention right there on his porch, Heath was pretty sure the guy needed to be punched for no other reason than that Heath wanted to wail on something. A flirting cowboy fit the bill perfectly.

"Or when one is at peace with himself and the Lord. With his place in the world."

"Don't lecture me, Corrie."

She aimed a look of warning his way because nobody bossed Corrie around. Ever.

He sighed. "Sorry. I'm tired. I feel like I'm spinning in circles. And that's not your fault."

"Sometimes we spin in circles because we've misplaced our direction. When we can't see our way forward we tend to run in place."

That's how he felt, but how could he fix it? Could it be fixed?

His phone buzzed a message from Jace. "Gotta get back to the lambing shed."

"I'll keep watch here."

He didn't look at the house as he retraced his steps to the front barn. He didn't think about Yost flirting with Lizzie. He refused to imagine her laughing with him over a slapped-together lunch. But he hoped—really hoped—that the Nebraska rancher would get on his way before supper. He was glad they'd trailered the big horse north, saving Lizzie the trip, but the jovial cowboy made Heath look too deep into his heart and soul because Heath hadn't been able to laugh like that in a long time. Something about having Lizzie here, joining in the dance of ranch chores and campfire evenings, made him wish he could.

And that felt plain disloyal to Anna.

Chapter Six

Red Moon Rising seemed quite at ease in his new surroundings, and Everett Yost climbed back into his big rig for the trip back to western Nebraska, but not before asking for Lizzie's number.

"You have it," she reminded him. "On the paperwork."

"Not the ranch number." He grinned down at her and tipped his hat, just so. "*Your* number."

"At the moment they're one and the same," she told him honestly. "Right now I'm pretty much eating, sleeping and drinking ranch stuff."

"Is it getting to you?" he asked nicely. "It can, you know."

She glanced toward the lambing shed and didn't try to mask the concern in her voice. "No, I'm doing something I love and maybe helping this place stay special, the way my uncle wanted. Plus I'm spreading my wings in a way I never thought possible as a publishing executive. I'm pretty sure all of this happened for a reason."

"Well, then, I wish you the best, Lizzie." He slanted a sweet smile her way. "At least until Caufield gets a clue."

She hoped she didn't blush, but with her pale skin, it wasn't easy to hide. "Have a safe trip home. And thank you, Ev." She raised her hand toward the equine pasture. "You and your father."

"Will do."

He pulled away, made a wide U-turn in the barnyard and headed for the road.

He'd nailed her interest in Heath. Was she that obvious? Still deep in thought, she relieved Corrie at the stables, pulled out her phone and scrolled through her contacts. And when her sister Melonie answered, she did what she'd always done: she spilled her guts. The only thing missing was the plate of cookies or brownies they usually shared during conversations like this. She found a fun-size Snickers bar in her uncle's desk, and felt like she'd just discovered gold as she relayed the past week to Mel.

"Heath is running the ranch?" Melonie's voice arched in a true Southern drawl. "That is the very definition of impossible, Liz."

"Clearly not."

"Why didn't you tell me this last week? I could have been on the next plane."

"You had cable TV producers coming into town and I didn't want you messing up what could be influential professional contacts just to come up here and hold my hand. You'll be here soon enough. You're already taking time away from your boyfriend and your media profile to be here. It's not like the situation is about to change, Mel. You tie up your loose ends, then head north."

Mel had been working as the on-site interior decorator for Fitzgerald Publishing's popular *Hearthside*

Home magazine. The final issue would be complete in the next week or so, then Mel would follow Lizzie to Idaho. But Mel longed to launch her own HGTV-type show. Taking a year off to secure her part of the ranch would thicken her pocketbook with the inheritance but thin her career profile. "A year in the mountains wasn't exactly in your plans and I didn't want to mess up your last weeks of work."

"We look out for each other. The four of us," Mel reminded her. "You. Me. Char and Corrie. That's how it's always been. And the boyfriend downsized me two weeks ago."

"What? Charlotte and I were already picking out bridesmaid gowns behind your back. Really ugly ones, too. He dumped you? What a—"

"Dumped like a concrete block in the East River, darling, once he realized that my fortune was gone and the magazine right along with it. But don't call him names. You'll regret it later because I'm fine with it. Although I must admit I was not quite as calm and low-key when it first happened."

"I am calling him names. In my head."

Mel laughed. "Better to realize this sooner rather than later."

"Still, I'm sorry that he hurt you, Mel. Because you deserve the best."

"Ditto. So… Are you crushing on Heath? All over again?"

"No. Of course not." She knew better. They'd crashed and burned once. Once was enough. Wasn't it?

"Do you need me to tell you what a bad idea that is?"

"No, because it's not happening. Leave it, Mel. I've got this."

"Of course you do, honey," said Mel in about as unconvinced a tone as there could be. "Why is he still single?"

"Widowed."

"Oh." Mel's voice changed completely. "Oh, gosh, Liz. I'm sorry to hear that. So what's the plan? How do we handle this? What do you need from me? And I can seriously get on a plane first thing tomorrow if it will help."

She would, too, which was why Lizzie had held off on calling. "Nope, I'm good. Just busy and tired and trying not to mess up."

"As if."

Lizzie stayed quiet. She had messed up in the past. A lot. But she'd used her faith, brains and work ethic to move on.

"Should I warn Charlotte?"

"Fill her in as needed. I didn't want to worry her while she was studying for her certification." Charlotte had been scheduled to take her veterinary licensing exam the past week. Her goal was to pass the exam and apply to the state of Idaho for a temporary right to practice for the coming year.

"I will. She's decided to skip the graduation hoopla, Lizzie."

"Why?" Charlotte had worked for over seven years to earn her veterinary degree. "She's got to do it, Mel. She deserves to have that moment and get handed her diploma. I'll talk to her."

"I wouldn't, Liz." Mel paused for several seconds before she went on. "She doesn't see the point. I told her I'd come up to Cornell for the ceremony, but she said the sooner we get to Idaho, the sooner we get out of Idaho."

"Idaho isn't that bad," she began and Mel snorted.

"Save the sales job for next January, darling, when we're in the throes of a mountain blizzard. Anyway, Char wants to skip it. It's not like there'll be proud parents cheering her on. She's ready to get on with her professional life. You can annoy her about it if you'd like, but I'm leaving it alone."

While it seemed wrong to ignore the graduation ceremonies, Lizzie understood her sister's reticence. "Mega college loans and the urge to move past this year's craziness would have tipped me the same way. I won't push. But we'll celebrate here once you've both arrived."

"Are we wrong to do this?" Mel asked. "To take on this challenge to inherit Uncle Sean's ranch when we didn't even know him? Does that seem greedy to you?"

"We weren't allowed to know him, so that's not our fault," answered Lizzie. "Considering the fallout from Daddy's choices, I'm okay with being out of the limelight for a while. And Shepherd's Crossing is definitely off the beaten path. I get to work with horses all day and manage the business side of things without too much interference from Heath, mostly because he's got lambs dropping."

"I bet they're the cutest things ever. And maybe we can develop a woolens side business linked to the ranch's sheep output. Natural fibers are all the rage right now." The marketer in Mel jumped right on board. "Idaho's the perfect spot for something like that, don't you think?"

The thought would never have occurred to Lizzie. "That's why you're the decorator and I'm in the stables. Oops, gotta go, my mare app is signaling. I'll see you in a week or two. I love you, Mel."

"Love you, too, Liz."

She hurried to the stable area, but didn't approach the laboring horse. Commotion could delay the mare's progress. She slipped into the center stable and crossed to the office just as Heath did the same thing from the opposite end. He held up his phone. "Looks like it's go time for Clampett's Girl."

"I didn't know you had the app, too."

"It made sense." He moved her way. "Are you watching from a distance?"

"As much as I'd love to cheer her on, that would be a stupid move on my part, so yes." She opened the office door and switched on the lights. She turned on the office monitors while Heath brewed coffee. When he had a cup made, he added cream and sugar and brought it to her. "That smells perfect." She breathed in the scent. Rich. Full. Real coffee, the kind she loved. "From the looks of her, this might be a while."

"Lots of coffee pods." He pulled up a chair once his coffee was made and took a seat.

"Who's in the lambing barn?"

"Wick. Jace is catching some sleep. He'll holler if he needs me."

"Or I can page you if you're needed here," she suggested, then paused. Looked at him. "You're not sure I can handle this."

He denied that quickly. "That's not why I'm here. I don't know anyone more comfortable around horses than you, Liz. It was like you were born to do this kind of thing, but while we're both good with horses, neither one of us knows a lot about breeding them. Although with other animals it generally goes smooth on its own, so I expect this will, too."

She pointed to a stack of books and printed articles. "I may have read up on a few things."

"I know." He acknowledged that with a sip of his coffee. "But I need to learn, too, and the best way to do that is to be here. I won't get in your way. And yeah, I've seen a few mares foal over the years, but there wasn't this much riding on it. So this is different."

How could she argue with that? "Okay."

He dozed off twenty minutes in. Tucked into the wide office chair, his chin dropped onto his chest and his breathing changed.

He looked...vulnerable. That wasn't a word she'd normally associate with a strong man like Heath, but it fit the moment. She watched the monitor, played solitaire on her phone, and when things began moving along two hours later, she nudged him awake. "Hey. Wake up. We're getting close."

He shot upright, frowned, then seemed to remember what he was doing. "I fell asleep?"

"A quick nap," she told him. "Needed, I expect."

He looked at his watch and groaned. "Over two hours. I shouldn't have sat down."

"Well, all you missed was some flank staring, walking and bodily functions. But now we've got a foal presenting. Let's walk down to the outer corridor in case she needs help. But make sure your phone is on vibrate. I want a quiet birth. No distractions."

"All right." She wasn't sure if he took direction from her that easily because he felt guilty about the nap or because he wanted her to feel in charge. Either option worked. They crossed to the south-facing stables and slipped down the hall where they could follow the process through their phones but be close enough to intervene if needed. Lizzie hoped it wouldn't be needed.

Thirty-seven minutes later a perfect sorrel filly was born. Wide-eyed and long-legged, the newborn horse blinked, peeking out from the clean bed of straw. "She's a pretty little thing, Liz."

"Watch the mom," Lizzie spoke softly as she moved around the foaling pen. "New moms can get protective and spook easy."

"And with a lot more force behind it than a ewe," he whispered back, but they didn't need to worry. Clampett's Girl tended her baby, took a long drink, then cleaned her foal again.

Lizzie pulled out a checklist once they closed the stall door. "Done. I'm going to bunk here so I can keep an eye on things."

She was going to rest here? On the floor? "Won't the app wake you upstairs in the apartment?"

"I want to be close enough to check her every hour for the first few." She set her phone and propped herself in a corner outside the stall.

It felt wrong to leave her there, which was silly because he'd spent many a night in the lambing barns. But this wasn't him. It was Lizzie. And when she stuck a ridiculously small pillow behind her head, he wanted to snatch it up, send her to bed and offer to watch the horse for her.

She gazed up at him from her spot, looking so much like the girl she'd been twelve years before. But different, too. "It's my job, Heath." She kept her voice quiet. Matter-of-fact. And quite professional. "People don't inherit a quarter share of a ranch worth millions without putting in some time. I'll see you tomorrow."

She was right. He knew that.

But walking away from her, down that hall, through the door into the cold spring night, was one of the toughest things he'd done in a long time. He did it because it was the right thing to do. But he hated every minute of it.

Lizzie stirred, scowled at her phone, then closed her eyes.

She'd checked the foal twice. The first time she'd been sleeping, curled up against her mother. The next time she was nursing, and that was only thirty minutes before.

What woke her?

She didn't know. That fuzzy stray dog, maybe? She hadn't seen it in days, but something was feasting on the food dish she'd put behind the barn. She could only hope it was the stray brindle dog.

The sound came again and she recognized the noise instantly. The bleat of a sheep in trouble. Not that she had any experience with sheep before this week, but no one could survive a week on a sheep ranch and not hear the various sounds of the ewe. Happy. Playful. Sad. Worried.

And this one sounded very, very worried.

She stood, stretched and walked the length of the barn hall separating the north-and south-facing stalls. A horse was walking her way, clomping quietly along and behind the horse was a very unhappy sheep. "Aldo?"

The bronze-skinned man turned toward her voice. Across his lap were discontented twin lambs. They bawled softly to their mother and she replied in kind, only louder and with more force behind every bleat.

"What happened?"

"Somehow this one got in with the others and went into the hills. And then…" He dropped his gaze to the twins. "There were three, but we did not realize what was happening until it was too late."

"But you saved two," she reasoned, moving closer.

"It should have been all three," Aldo professed. He sounded sad, as if he'd failed. "We should have known she was nearly due, but her mark had faded and she blended herself in. Until this."

"Aldo." Heath appeared from the lambing shed. "Bring them into the near end, I've got a stall ready."

"She can't just go out into the lambing shed with the other new mothers?"

"We'll want to monitor what's happening. She's been through a lot, to take that long walk into the hills, then deliver in the cold. Lambs are hearty as a rule, but if she lost one, then conditions were rough enough to cause havoc already. She's nervous right now and I don't want her to spook the other sheep. Why were you up? Has something gone wrong with the foal?"

He probably didn't mean to sound so gruff. He was tired. She was tired. And Aldo had taken a crazy night-time ride by the light of a nearly full moon. "I heard a sheep in trouble and came to check it out."

"I was going to call you and have you meet us with the truck when we got to the road," Aldo told them as they got nearer to the shed. "But in the end, it was just as quick to ride them in the last half mile."

"You were in the worst place for this to happen," said Heath. He reached up and withdrew a lamb, then held the little creature close to his chest. "No easy way up. No easy way down."

"That's how it hits sometimes." Aldo climbed down, then lifted the second lamb from the saddle, easing it into his arms.

"I can put your horse up for you, Aldo," said Lizzie.

The men turned, surprised.

"So you don't have to do it," she went on. "You've had a long night."

"You have a good heart, Lizzie." Aldo smiled at her, but refused her offer. "I'll take the horse back up straightaway. By the time I get there, they will have started for the next hill."

"And by hill, he might mean mountain," added Heath. "Wick dozed off about an hour back. I'll keep an eye out here. Thanks for bringing them down."

He set the first lamb into the bed of clean straw. Aldo set the second one right next to it. "Both ewes. Pretty little girls. It was a ram we lost."

The mama sheep answered the babies' plaintive calls with a sharp cry, then dodged into the stall. She circled the babies, tending to them with her tongue, then her voice.

She was worried.

The babies were worried.

And as Lizzie gazed at the tiny twin sheep, she felt pretty worried herself.

"You need sleep," Heath told her. "Unfortunately that's been in short supply tonight. They should be fine, but we'll watch for any problems."

"Perhaps tomorrow night we all shall sleep soundly." Aldo climbed back into the saddle and tipped his round-edged hat slightly. "Here is to sleep and an uneventful night. What's left of it."

Lizzie's phone buzzed just then. "Mother and baby calling, barn number three."

She started to walk away.

Heath called her name.

She turned around.

"Thanks for checking on what you heard. That's solid, Liz."

She wished his praise didn't mean a lot, but it did. No way she was about to let him know that, though. She tipped her head and offered a careless wave. "All in a day's work." Or a night's work, she thought as she re-entered the horse barn.

Stable sounds surrounded her. Horses breathing. An occasional snort. And then the sounds of Clampett's Girl caring for her newborn foal.

The mothering thing came so naturally to animals. At least it seemed to. Were humans different? Were they too smart to trust instinct and love?

She wasn't sure, but there were times when she thought so. Times when she wondered how different her life might have been if she and Heath had defied her family and run off to a justice of the peace when she was seventeen. Was it fear that had kept her from doing that? Or had she been ashamed of disappointing her father and grandfather?

She paused outside the mare's stall and peeked in. All was well. And this time when she curled up on the chilled floor to rest, nothing woke her until the morning sun rose a few hours later.

Chapter Seven

Sean's lawyer pulled up to the house about the time Heath would have liked a nap on Saturday afternoon.

Obviously the nap wasn't about to happen. Sean had decreed that Mack Grayson should go over the will with each beneficiary personally. Sean liked a personal touch as long as *he* wasn't required to do it. He made contacts because he needed them to build the ranch, but by nature he was a loner. That kept Sean away from the little town more often than not. Had he even noticed the town's steep decline over the past several years?

Possibly not.

Heath glanced back, wanting to check on the unexpected mother in the first lambing barn, but time was money for Mack and everyone else trying to eke out a living in Shepherd's Crossing. Keeping him waiting would be plain rude. "Hey, Mack."

"Heath." Mack stuck out a hand, looking every inch the cowboy he was, despite the impressive law degree. "How you holding up?"

"Fine, Mack. Just fine."

"Right." Mack sized him up. "Nothing a half day's sleep wouldn't cure. Is Elizabeth around?"

He hadn't heard anyone call Lizzie Elizabeth in a long time. "She's in the house."

"When are the others coming north?"

"Soon, I'm told." He pulled the screen door wide for Mack, then followed him in. "Melonie is finishing up her job at one of the Fitzgerald magazines and Charlotte's about to graduate from veterinary school."

"A vet on hand?" Mack's brows rose in appreciation. "Handy turn of events. Still, having a house full of women around is going to be different. You up for it?"

"Do I have a choice?"

"Nope."

"Well, then." Heath crossed to the great room. "Let's get this done."

Lizzie wasn't in the great room even though he'd texted her.

Corrie came out from the kitchen. He motioned Mack over. "Mack Grayson, this is Corrie Satterly. She raised the Fitzgerald sisters after they lost their mother."

"I've heard only good things, Mrs. Satterly."

"Ms. Satterly," she told him firmly. "But just Corrie will do nicely." She turned back toward Heath. "Lizzie's not here?"

"Not yet." He checked the clock, then his watch. Both read the same time, making her ten minutes late.

Irritation snaked a line beneath his collar and up his neck. Maybe being late was fashionable in the publishing world. But here on the ranch, no one wasted time, especially this time of year.

He looked at Corrie. "Do you know what's keep-ing her?"

She headed toward the door as she answered. "She was ready half an hour ago. I'll go check."

She was ready? Then where was she? A momen-tary unease niggled him. What if she wasn't all right? What if something had happened? He started to cross the room just as Lizzie walked through the front door. She looked fine.

Real fine, he noted, but he wouldn't dwell on that.

He was about to lambaste her for keeping them wait-ing when she pointed behind her. "The ewe, the one that delivered in the hills." She paused to catch her breath, but the worry on her face clued him in. "I went to check on her and something's wrong. Very wrong."

He hurried through the door, and down the steps with Lizzie on his heels. He barked a message to Harve over the pager and raced to the foremost barn.

He should have checked on her before. If anything happened to her, it was on him, and him alone. He ran into the barn, his mind racing through various possi-bilities. Lizzie followed.

Harve appeared from the other direction.

The diagnosis was clear and dangerous the moment he spotted the downed ewe. "Hypocalcemia," Heath told Harve as he knelt beside the ailing sheep.

Harve disappeared and returned quickly with a small leather case and a bottle. "You administer, I'll hold."

Within seconds Heath began the IV drip into the ewe's jugular vein while Harve held the life-giving bottle of glucose and calcium above. Once they had the fluid dripping, Heath looked up. "This is going to take a while—it's got to go in slowly. Can someone tell Mack?"

Corrie answered while Lizzie watched the ewe with grave concern. "I'll go."

Within minutes the ewe was showing signs of recovery. She blinked, then opened her eyes with a renewed interest in life. He turned to thank Liz for her intervention as Mack and Corrie came up alongside her.

"Necessary change of venue," said Mack as he withdrew an envelope of papers from his Western-styled briefcase. "If you're going to be on the ranch, what better place to get the lowdown than the barn, saving an ewe's life?"

He handed Lizzie a copy of the will, then opened his to read out loud.

And when he began reading, Heath heard the sound of Sean Fitzgerald's voice rang through the words.

"I like things my way," Mack began. "That's not always a blessing, and when I found out I wasn't going to make it through this final battle, I did some thinking. Quiet thinking and out-loud thinking, and here's where we're at. The legal mumbo-jumbo will be squared away below. Mack Grayson has assured me of that, but here's my message to all four of you: Life's short.

No matter what you've been through, what rivers you've crossed or grass-crawling snakes you've avoided (especially the two-legged kind pretending to be family or friends) I want you to see Pine Ridge Ranch as a fresh start, a new beginning in a land wild and free and stunningly beautiful.

A land a man can get lost in and a woman can call home.

I don't know if you'll love it. I want someone to love it, and if it's family, that's good. But if not, then Heath can buy you out because he's the closest thing I've got to a son. He knows the sheep. He knows my heart.

Lizzie, I don't know you or your sisters, but I know horses and Heath says you do, too. I started something I'm not going to finish. I hate that. A marine doesn't start something and leave it go. We work, plan, strive and wrap up a mission. Every time. But not this time, and I'm leaving it to you to either make it work or sell it off. The good Lord has his own timing. My life is drawing down, but you and your sisters, your lives are just beginning, and if a share of Pine Ridge helps launch you gals, well, that's a job well done.

Two tips: Don't sweat the small stuff. Life sends plenty of big worries, the small ones don't merit your time.

Second tip: Don't waste time. Seasons come and go, and it's a rhythm. You mess up the rhythm, you mess up the year.

I'm leaving the rest for Mack to handle, but I must add this: I don't know you ladies. Never had a real chance to meet you or know you, and that's a mistake I can never fix. But I can give you a piece of my dream. If it's not what you thought, well, give it back, and that's okay. But a smart woman gives things a chance and there's something about horses and lambs and shepherds and the Good Book and all that goes with it. All I can ask is that you give it your best shot, and your forgiveness for not being the uncle I should have been all along.

Sean Michael Fitzgerald

Heath forced down the lump forming beneath his Adam's apple, because Sean's message hit home, even more since Lizzie appeared on the ranch.

"She is looking much better," Harve noted as the twin lambs bleated from the adjoining stall. Hearing them, the ewe raised her head in concern. "I'll keep an eye on her," Harve continued. "You go back to finish up. Crisis averted."

"Because of Liz." Heath stood and crossed the pen to where Lizzie was standing. "You saved her life, and possibly the lives of those two babies. If we'd waited, we might have lost her." He looked her in the eye. "Thank you."

She didn't look at him. She trained her attention on the ewe and spoke softly. "A sick mother should never be left alone. A little tender loving care goes a long way when needed."

He nodded, but she tossed him a look as she moved away. A look of regret and disappointment. In him? It sure felt like it.

Then Corrie looped her arm through Liz's like she'd done for as long as Heath remembered. "Mothers and young ones need tending, surely as the sun rises in the morning. Seeing to them has been one of the great joys of my life. And it's good to see this extends to all God's creatures, Lizzie-Beth."

Heath watched them go from his spot in the stall.

"She's kind of handy to have around, I'd say."

He'd forgotten about Mack. He slapped a hand to the nape of his neck and frowned. "She's got a way with horses and it's no secret we needed some help with that."

"Hmm." Mack left it at that as he closed up his leather bag. "I'll go over the details with Lizzie up at the house. Then I'll come back and meet with the other sisters as they arrive."

"Thanks, Mack."

"No problem."

Harve frowned at him once Mack had left. "You know I've got this and Wick's up front." He meant the foremost lambing shed.

Heath moved out of the stall as Harve stepped back in. "I'm going to have a look around. Just to see."

Harve pressed his lips tight, gaze down.

There was nothing to see at the moment, and the reason he was avoiding the house was to avoid that look. The one he'd glimpsed in Lizzie's gaze. Because maybe if he'd been a better man back then, things would be different now.

"Dad!" Zeke knew not to be loud around the sheep, but the excitement in his voice resounded through the mock whisper. "Look what happened. Come see!"

When Heath spotted a tiny white tooth in a sealed plastic bag, he hauled Zeke up into his arms and hugged him tight.

Second-guessing the past was stupid when his present was so vitally alive—and missing a first tooth. "That's awesome, dude."

"I know! Now I have to put it under my pillow

and see what happens. So the Tooth Fairy will come. Right?"

"Umm. Sure. That's what we'll do. Want me to put it in my pocket? Keep it safe for you?"

"Yes, sir!" Zeke's grin didn't just warm his heart. It owned it. "Can we go show everyone? Cookie said they'll all be so happy for me!"

For Zeke he'd do anything, even facing down those old regrets, but when they got to the house, Lizzie had gone back to the stables. When Zeke pestered to go see her, Corrie bent low. "I think she's sleeping, little man. She had a long night and she was pretty tuckered out. How about if Dad takes a picture and you can show her in the morning?"

His lower lip thrust out. "But I really wanted her to see it tonight. Before the Tooth Fairy takes it away."

"We could wait until tomorrow night to put it under your pillow," suggested Heath. "Then you can show Lizzie in the morning."

"The Tooth Fairy won't mind?" That thought made his eyes go round. "She can come tomorrow night instead?"

"Absolutely, partner."

"Then let's do that." Zeke thrust his hand into Heath's. "I don't mind waiting, Dad. Because I want Lizzie—"

Heath arched a brow.

"*Miss* Lizzie to be so happy for me, too," he corrected himself. "Because that makes everything special."

Corrie smiled. And Harve's silence in the barn punctuated the air, making him wonder why they didn't just come out and say what they were thinking.

Because you'll get defensive and overreact.

He'd been doing both for too long. But with so many plates spinning in the air, he wasn't sure how to stop. Take a breath. Be a nice guy again.

But if this many people were tiptoeing around him, he needed to wise up. And as soon as he could take a deep breath, he'd do just that.

"Liz?"

Lizzie scrunched her pillow into a tighter ball and rolled over, but the annoying voice sounded again.

"Liz? Are you awake? It's Heath."

Did he think she didn't recognize his voice? She jammed the pillow over her face for a few seconds before tossing it aside and creeping to the door. "Of course I wasn't awake," she whispered when she opened the door. "It's three-thirty in the morning. No one is awake by choice at this hour, Heath. Except you."

"Rosie is in labor," he explained. "Harve wants me to wait with him at the hospital but I need someone to watch Zeke."

"Zeke, who is sound asleep right now?" She yawned. "You woke me up to ask me to watch a sleeping child?"

"He'll be up in a few hours, and I figured it was smarter to talk to someone rather than leave a note. Listen, never mind…" He began to back away. "I can wake the little guy and take him along."

"Don't be ridiculous. Of course I'll watch him. What are you waiting for?" She motioned to the stairs. "Go keep your friends company as they welcome their child into the world." She didn't say what she was thinking, that she'd have given anything to have that kind of support from him twelve years ago.

She'd thought she'd dealt with that time of sadness. Maybe being here, with Heath, stirred a pot that had been simmering all these years.

"Thanks." He started away, then turned back. "Rosie's lost babies in the past so they're both kind of scared. More than most, I expect."

Oh, her heart.

To hear the emotion in his voice over someone else's sadness—and nothing for their own. She had to tamp down an emotional surge before she said too much. "Go."

He took the stairs quickly but quietly. The soft click of the stable door marked his exit.

She tiptoed back into the room, grabbed her laptop and slipped downstairs. She peeked into Girlie's stall.

All was well.

She crossed the chilled grass and welcomed the warmth of the big house once she got inside. She made a quick cup of coffee, then curled up in a wide-backed chair, opened her laptop and tried to crunch figures.

Despite her efforts, all she could see was Heath's focus and concentration as he labored to save a ewe's life. One ewe, out of a few thousand.

Was the ewe that important? Clearly she was.

She opened a new doc file and began again, starting with the ewe's mistaken trail ride, into the hills. And how a dedicated shepherd rode through the night to bring mother and children home. She didn't make Heath the focus. She used Aldo for that, the small, tan-skinned shepherd, putting the needs of the animals foremost.

By the time she was done, she had a solid article about a true cowboy, the kind of thing that showed the Western heart, beating true.

It read differently than her previous stories. More depth. More emotion. Was that because of the circumstance or the cowboys? Both…and maybe her, too.

The patter of footsteps came her way just before seven o'clock. "Miss Lizzie?" Zeke slid to a stop at the end of the short hall linking the front of the big house to the back wing. "Is my dad out here?"

"He's not," she replied as she set the computer aside. "He's with Rosie and Harve because they think the baby's about to be born. So Daddy asked me to keep an eye on you. Okay?"

"The baby might be born today?" His eyes went wide when he lifted two dark, little brows. His teeth flashed white in a bright grin, revealing a tiny new gap. "This might be the best day ever! First, there's this." He opened his mouth extra wide and grinned, showing off the empty front space. "I wanted to show you last night, but Dad said you needed to get some sleep."

She smiled at the boy. "He was right, so thank you both. Did you put it under your pillow?"

He shook his head, surprising her. "I wanted you to see it, and if the fairy tooked it away, you would never ever get to see it. But you can see it today and then we can put it under my pillow tonight. Okay?"

"More than okay," she assured him. "And thank you so much for thinking of me. That was really nice of you to do, Zeke-man."

"Well, Daddy and I both kinda did it."

His innocent words made her heart leap. She tamped it down quickly. "You hungry?"

He shook his head.

"Thirsty?"

"Can I have chocolate milk?"

She had no idea if Cookie kept chocolate milk on hand, but she'd seen chocolate syrup in the fridge. "Sure can."

"And maybe toast," he added. He followed her into the kitchen and pulled himself up onto one of the tall stools. She had to stop herself from cautioning him to not to fall. He handled the climb and the balance with the ease of an expert.

"Cinnamon sugar toast?"

"Yes!" He giggled. "My favorites!"

"Glad to oblige, my friend." She made the toast and used the hand-held frother to mix his chocolate milk, filling the glass with creamy bubbles. When she handed it to him, his eyes went round.

"It's like a milk shake." He whispered the words as he sipped the milk. "You should tell my dad how to make it this good, I bet he doesn't even know! You can help him!"

She wasn't sure his dad would welcome her advice, but she agreed. "I'll tell him. So what are you and I going to do today? After we check the new mama sheep, of course."

"I think we're supposed to go on a horseback ride." He peered up at the calendar with a scrunched brow. "Do I get to stay here all day?"

"You do. Rosie won't be watching you for a while because she'll be busy with the baby."

"You can't leave babies alone," he assured her. "When I'm with Rosie-Posie, I can't do too much because she has to watch 'Lencia's babies now. They're so little and they just crawl around and mess up my toys. Even if I put the toys on the couch, they can reach them now."

"Two babies?"

He made a grumpy face and nodded.

"I bet they're cute," she went on as she brewed fresh coffee.

"They kinda smell bad sometimes, but they smile at me when I make stuff for them. Then they wreck it," he added. "But on this day it's just you and me doin' stuff." He looked up, expectant. "Like riding a horse together. That's something we could do!" Anticipation brightened his eyes.

"Do you have a helmet?"

He nodded.

"Then we're on, my friend. After breakfast. And after we check the mama sheep. Honey's Money is a good mount and they didn't take her into the hills." Honey was a placid but bright-moving ranch horse. Old enough to be trustworthy and young enough to work the milling sheep as needed.

He drew those little brows tight, as if concerned. "It's a ewe, Miss Lizzie. A mama sheep is always a ewe." His tone wasn't impertinent, but he sure sounded like he might be doubting her intelligence, so she leaned in and met him eye-to-eye.

"A ewe can still be a mama sheep. The terms can be synonymous if the sheep has had a baby. So she's a ewe..." She lifted a brow and held his gaze to make her point. "But she's also a mother or mama sheep. And where I come from, little boys don't correct their elders."

"Their what?" He frowned, surprised.

"Grown-ups. Little boys listen and learn, and they don't boss grown-ups around."

"Oh." Guilt made him cringe. "My dad says that, too."

"Your dad and I are in complete agreement. Once you're done, let's head to the barn."

He chugged his chocolate milk in seconds and grabbed the rest of his toast. "I can eat this on the way. Come on!" He grabbed her hand in his.

And held an instant part of her heart, as well.

"I love helping with the farm," he told her, skipping alongside once they cleared the steps. "I love big, huge barns and horsies and all of it. But mostly I love the sheep and the little lambs. They make me smile."

"Me, too."

He peered up, interested. "Did you have a horse when you were little, Miss Lizzie?"

She had. A big, beautiful bay mare that sensed her every move. A marvelous jumper, a sterling competitor. Gone now, like all the rest. She swallowed around a lump in her throat and nodded. "I did. Her name was Maeve and she was my special friend."

"That's a funny name for a horse."

"I suppose you think Honey's Money is normal?"

His expression said it was.

"I lived on an Irish farm and a lot of the horses had Irish names." She didn't call Claremorris home. The expansive holding hadn't been home to her in decades, but she'd missed working the horse barn. Feeding, tending, grooming, riding. She hadn't realized how much until she'd stepped into her current position, a chance that felt like home. A real home with a real job.

Zeke released her hand and raced into the barn. She started to chase after him, then realized the boy knew his way around better than she did. He paused at the right stall, stepped up on a rail, and peered in. "One happy sheep!" he announced in an excited but soft voice. "And two little lambs!"

The discontented cries of the lambs had changed to quiet bleats of satisfaction overnight. The ewe appeared better. One hundred percent improved. She watched the babies snuggle in against their mother's abundant udder as they dozed off.

Sweet contentment had replaced angst and worry.

Successful mother. Satisfied babies. The dream come true that didn't always come out that way.

"I think that baby is so happy."

Zeke's little voice broke her mental musings. "Why's that, my friend?"

"Well, she's got a mama to snuggle her." His matter-of-fact tone was belied by the longing marking his face and his gray-blue eyes. "I think my mama used to snuggle me just like that. When I was little," he added.

The hunger in his gaze softened the part of her heart she'd put on hold long ago. "I'm sure she did."

"My dad misses her sometimes." His voice turned more pragmatic again. "He gets that funny look when I talk about her, so then I don't talk about her so much. Can we ride now?"

They sure could. Anything to get out of talking about lost mothers and sad children. She'd lived the scenario, losing her mother when she was just shy of six years old, but Zeke had one big difference. His father loved him. Doted on him.

Tim Fitzgerald loved Tim Fitzgerald. He'd never pretended his girls meant much. In return, the three sisters had grown up between Corrie's loving kindness and their grandparents' somewhat aristocratic affection. It could have been so much worse, she knew, but she'd learned that wealth and status didn't replace love and that was a valuable lesson.

She helped Zeke down from the rail. "Let's get Honey ready, shall we?"

"Sure!"

She snugged the boy in front of her once the horse was saddled and headed across the adjacent field.

Rugged hills became mountains to the north and northwest. The wide valley continued beyond the ranch, in the direction of Shepherd's Crossing. As they moved uphill, she spotted other homes, other farms, sporadically spaced, and when they got to an intermediate ledge, the distant image of a town came into view. From here, she couldn't see the decay, the flaking paint, the listing shutters. From here the town offered an image of what it had been before times got hard. Small. Compact. Cozy.

The valley splayed green and lush as the spring greening moved up the hills. Flat land spread from side to side, and the curve of a creek or small river marked an almost central path with mountains to their back.

The beauty of the land lay different than Kentucky and light years from Louisville.

Her phone buzzed in her pocket. She withdrew it carefully, keeping a snug hold on Zeke. No baby yet, maybe C-section. I know I shouldn't worry, but I am. Thanks for watching little man.

"Is that from my dad? Did Rosie-Posie have the baby?"

She kept the details to herself and tried to sound relaxed. "Not yet, but they think it will be soon."

Zeke turned his head. "Rosie-Posie says we can pray anywhere." His voice and expression turned serious. "It's not just for goin' to church and stuff, so maybe you and me can pray for her and for the baby and for my frog that got stepped on last week. Because I miss my froggie a lot. Okay?"

"Very okay."

She let him lead the prayer, and when he was done, he looked back up at her. "You're apposed to say 'amen'," he reminded her.

"Amen." She smiled down at him, and then, on impulse, she leaned her cheek down, against his. "God bless you, little man."

He leaned his cheek into hers, then shifted again. "Did you bring some snacks? My dad always has snacks in his bag."

She hadn't considered such a thing. "No. Sorry. But we can head back and see what Cookie's up to."

"Today is his day off."

"Corrie, then. And maybe we can do something in the kitchen together. Would you like that?" She angled the horse along the ridge edge, then down an easy grade trail. "Cookies?"

"I love cookies!"

"And I like making cookies. I've been making them since I was a little girl. Corrie taught me."

"Well, she's very smart."

Lizzie smiled, and as Zeke relaxed against her, her heart eased a little more. It felt good to hold the boy, talk with him, laugh with him.

She hadn't expected that. How natural this would seem, despite the awkwardness of the situation.

"Thank you for bringing me on a ride." Zeke sounded peaceful, clearly comfortable and wonderfully content. "It's my favorite thing, Miss Lizzie."

Having grown up on a horse farm, she understood that completely. "Mine, too." She'd longed for that kind of tranquil therapy for years. How much it had meant to saddle up Maeve and hit the ground running.

Maybe because she had been naive then.

As she hit the flats, she encouraged the horse to a gentle lope. Mane flying, Honey cantered her way across the unfenced pasture like a master. Not too fast, not too slow, enough to make Zeke laugh with delight while she held him snug with one arm.

When she slowed the horse to a cooling walk, Zeke squealed softly. "I love going so fast, Miss Lizzie. This was the best ride ever!"

She'd had a lot of sweet rides in her youth. She'd brought home many a ribbon and trophy as a young equestrian. But Zeke was right. Holding him on the saddle and letting the gentle mare fly free might have been the sweetest ride she'd ever taken.

Chapter Eight

The sight of Zeke in Lizzie's arms, curled on the couch in the great room, made Heath stop short later that afternoon.

His breath caught somewhere in the center of his chest. His heart winced, then continued beating.

She looked beautiful, holding his son, as both slept. Her lashes lay dark against her pale skin.

And Zeke's lashes lay black against more coppery tones while his brown face was tucked beneath hers.

The peaceful scene looked natural.

It wasn't.

He knew that. His son was a total blessing despite the grievous result of Anna's pregnancy. He'd been conceived in love...

His conscience gave him a sharp mental kick.

That first baby had been conceived in love, too. A younger love, fierce in its beauty and excitement. As he watched Lizzie snuggle Zeke in sweet repose, he realized a marked difference.

He'd married Anna. He'd gone about things the right

way that time. He'd made her his wife in front of God and a small gathering at the Holy Grace of God Church in the village.

He'd made no such vow to Lizzie. He'd let her father and grandfather browbeat him into leaving while she'd ended the pregnancy. Anguish had begun his journey north once Sean Fitzgerald contacted him, and anger had taken over about halfway to Idaho.

And yet—

If he hadn't been strong enough to fight for the girl, was the outcome more his fault than he'd been willing to believe back then?

Lizzie's eyes opened.

His heart paused. His mind raced back, over the years. She'd been pretty back then.

She was beautiful now. She blinked slowly, saw him, and her gaze clouded. Then she seemed to remember Zeke and her arms folded around him in a protective gesture. "Is he still sleeping?" She whispered the words, stirring more old memories.

Heath nodded.

She shifted slightly and adjusted the curled-up boy as she did. When Heath reached for him, she shook her head. "Don't disturb him, he's comfortable. We had an early morning and a busy day," she went on, and Heath couldn't help but notice how she cradled the five-year-old against her chest. "I got schooled in sheep, then I schooled him in cookies, horses and chocolate milk bubbles. A good day, all in all. How is Rosina doing?"

He sat along the edge of the rugged sofa table, perfect for propping feet after a long day, or holding a mug of coffee. "They ended up doing the C-section, but the baby's safe and sound." He paused. "And tiny. I forgot how small babies really are." He let his gaze rest on Zeke for a few seconds. "Anyway, she's beautiful. Rosie's doing all right, and Harve looked shell-shocked. But happy. So happy, both of them. She'll be home in a couple of days which seems really quick for a procedure like that. But then sheep recover from C-sections pretty quickly, so maybe I'm being overprotective."

Her smile faded. She sat more upright and indicated Zeke with a glance. "On second thought, can you take him, please? I need to get back to work."

Her voice had been soft and lyrical. Now it was clipped. "Sure." He lifted the boy to his chest. "Thanks for watching him, Liz."

"Glad to help."

Was she? It'd seemed like it, and then…not so much. He tucked Zeke into his bed, yawned, and wished he could join the little guy, but there were things to do. Sleep would have to wait.

He walked outside, hands in his pockets. Seeing Rosie in labor, then seeing baby Johanna in her father's arms, thrust him back in time. Anna had been a scheduled C-section to spare her heart the rigors of labor. She'd wakened long enough to see Zeke. To hold him. To smile at her son and bless him before he was whisked off to the NICU.

She'd lingered for three days, in and out of a semiconscious state. And then she'd slipped away forever. Johanna wasn't in the NICU. At over seven pounds, she was a full-term, beautiful little girl with clenched fists and a button nose, but seeing her brought so much flooding back. And then, walking in, spotting his son curled in Lizzie's arms.

He headed to the lambing shed to relieve Wick. Corrie would call him when Zeke woke up. After a snack, she'd noted, as she packed fresh cookies into a zipped bag for him.

"Hey, boss." Wick had been bent over a stall wall, monitoring a fresh delivery. He straightened, rubbed the small of his back, but kept smiling. "Harve and Rosie are doing all right, I hear?"

"You hear right. Mother, baby and aging father."

Wick laughed. "Nothing like a baby to keep you young. And it's real nice to see them welcome this little girl after so long. And this little mama just presented triplets so we should red-string this one." He motioned to a ewe with a single lamb behind him. "And gift her a daughter so no one has to fight for food. If she takes it on, that is."

"I'll keep an eye on them to make sure she takes." Most sheep would accept an orphan lamb, but not all. "I'll give the baby a colostrum bottle before we shift her over." He scanned the tape markers on the stall doors, indicators of what had happened on the last shift. He whistled softly. "You've been busy."

"We're in the thick of it now, but I just fed and you should get a breather for a little while."

"I've got coffee." He set his insulated cup onto a small shelf close by. "And a fistful of cookies. I'm good."

Wick washed up in the barn sink before he went off to rest. Heath warmed a bottle slightly. He slipped into the pen, picked a female lamb and fed her the bottle. Then he marked her ear before offering her to the mother down the aisle.

The ewe had been resting comfortably, her baby at her side. She brought her head around when he deposited the little lamb alongside the day-old baby ram. Then he backed away.

The baby seemed confused. She bleated, turned and bleated again.

Her biological mother's voice answered from down the walkway. Then the new ewe leaned back and sniffed at her. She sniffed again, then looked around as if wondering how this had occurred.

Then she stood. The moment of truth had arrived. Would she clean up this newborn and feed her? Or would she chase her off to protect her original baby?

The lamb bleated again, as if pleading her case.

The older ewe nudged her with her nose. And then she began cleaning her, working the lamb's surface with her tongue, letting the newborn know it would be all right.

His mind went straight back to Lizzie, cuddling Zeke on the couch. Could a woman accept another person's child as readily? And how could a parent risk a bad pairing? Zeke was his responsibility. Would anyone else be able to love him like Heath did?

Anna would scold you and tell you to get over yourself. To get real.

The mental reminder was right. Anna had a way of setting him straight when he let worry take hold. She'd had faith in God and confidence in him when he had precious little in himself.

"Dad!" Zeke came through the lambing barn with a

broad, open grin. "I had so much fun today! My Lizzie is the best babysitter in the whole world and she was so excited about my tooth!" He grinned wide to show off the gap. "It was like the best day ever!"

There was no denying the naked joy on his son's face. His grin. His excitement. "What did you guys do that tuckered you out so much?" he asked. "When I got home from the hospital, you were sacked out on the couch."

"Rosie's baby!" The little guy slapped a hand to his forehead in an almost comical move. "I almost forgot and we've been waiting so long!"

"The baby is beautiful, she's little but not as little as you were when you were born, and her name is Johanna."

"Jo-Jo." He shortened the name immediately. "Miss Lizzie made a card with me, and we're going to pick some flowers for Rosie-Posie and the baby. Just to make them smile when they come home."

"That's a great idea." And nothing he'd have thought of personally. He'd already ordered a bouquet of flowers to be delivered later in the week. He hadn't thought of personalizing it and making Zeke a part of the gift. But Lizzie had. "What else did you guys do?"

"Went on the best ride ever," Zeke told him. "I wanted to ride one of the new horses, but Miss Lizzie said no...but then she got Honey's Money all ready and we went up into the hills."

The hills?

"We went so high we could see the skinny top on the church and the old silos."

Which meant they'd gone beyond the soft green grasses and into the rockier outcropping to be able to see Shepherd's Crossing.

"And then she rode so fast across the grass that it was like flying, Dad! Like a real cowboy! And Corrie made cookies and grilled cheese and we cleaned stables and I fell asleep."

He zeroed in on one term. Flying.

Lizzie loved speed.

She was fearless around horses and just as courageous up top, but to run a horse with Zeke on board?

Anger thrummed along his spine until his ears rang. He bit it back. It wasn't Zeke he needed to scold. It was Lizzie, and as soon as Zeke was tucked in for the night, he'd have a word with her. She could do what she liked on her own. Her skills made that a non-issue.

But when it came to Zeke, Heath's word was law and Lizzie Fitzgerald needed to understand that.

Don't dwell on the negatives in life. Focus on the positives, the good things, the blessings surrounding you. The past can be a good advisor but a bad ruler. Don't let it pull you down.

Lizzie needed the mental reminder as she worked a mare in the far field bordering the hills. She'd disappointed herself as a teen, but faith had saved her midway through college. She'd moved on from the past and worked hard to adopt Paul's message to the Philippians. *"Finally, brethren, whatsoever things are true, whatsoever things are honest, whatsoever things are just, whatsoever things are pure, whatsoever things are lovely, whatsoever things are of good report; if there be any virtue, and if there be any praise, think on these things."*

She'd adopted this verse as her family and their business crumbled around her. She worked hard to keep a positive attitude. But facing Heath dredged up her old choices. Her loss. So when he strode her way looking way grumpier than any man should that evening, she squared her shoulders. He could be grumpy all he wanted. That was his right. But no way would he be allowed to take it out on her.

"We need to talk." He stopped a few feet from her, as if preparing for battle, a battle she wasn't about to have.

"About me needing a stable hand that's accomplished at riding? Perfect. I'll start looking first thing Monday."

His brows drew down. "I got the text you sent about that, but that's not why I'm here."

"Then…why?" She kept her voice cool and her face relaxed.

"You took Zeke into the hills today."

His topic surprised her. "Yes. Of course. On Honey's Money."

"And you had her run with him on her back?"

And there it was, the sound of a hovering parent, micromanaging every tiny aspect of a kid's life. She'd seen plenty of that among her millennial friends. She hadn't expected to see it from Heath, a four-season cowboy with a strong work ethic. "Yet what other be so glorious to see? A horse, mane flying, running free." She refused to flinch beneath his dark gaze. "Your words, cowboy."

"I wrote that poem a long time ago, Liz." Hands braced on his hips, he scowled down at her and she returned the favor by staying cool and calm.

"A lifetime, Heath. That's how long ago it was."

"Listen, you did me a favor today, and I'm grateful."

"And yet, oddly, your tone of voice belies your words."

His frown deepened. "Zeke's my son. We play by my rules. If you're going to be here for a year—"

"Not *if*, Heath. I *am* here for a year, and probably longer because not only am I *good* at working horses—" she drew a little closer just to underscore her point "—I *love* working them. And I've got the business degree and acumen to make it work. And if you question my judgment about what I do with Zeke, then you need to find someone else to help watch him because no one—" she stepped forward again "—sets my rules except me. I've made it on my own for a long time and I'll continue to do so long after this initial year is up. So this is what you need to think about. If you leave that sweet boy in my care, I'll do as I think best. If that means riding into the hills and cantering through the grass, I'll do it again." She started to pivot but stopped when he said her name.

"You'd do it again?" She hadn't thought he could stand any taller, but he did. And then he folded his arms. "Over my dead body."

"Whatever it takes, Heath." She lifted her gaze and locked eyes with him in the fading light. "What form of torture is it to raise a boy on a beautiful ranch like Pine Ridge and deny him the chance to run a horse?" She met his anger with a steady voice. An even countenance. "There's almost nothing as wonderful as being up top a horse, Heath Caufield, and a cowboy like you should know that." She reached out and tapped his chest, just once. "Unless you've forgotten that, too."

And then she walked away.

Chapter Nine

The church bell began to toll a five-minute reminder the next morning, an old Shepherd's Crossing tradition. When folks lived in town, the tolling bell reminded them to step lively. Heath had just stepped out of the pickup truck when the bells began to chime.

"Yay!" Zeke threw his arms into the air. "We're here for the bells, Dad! I get so happy hearing the bells ring. And Cookie's chocolate cake makes me happy, too. But not as happy as riding with Miss Lizzie." Zeke amended his statement with a glance back, over his shoulder. "That was like the best ever."

"Ezekiel—" Talking about this now wouldn't be a good idea. He'd already decided to quietly let the subject go and make sure Justine understood the rules when she stepped in to watch Zeke the coming week.

But Zeke was on a roll and the caution in Heath's voice added no restraint. "She snuggled me so tight, and it was like having a mom, laughing and holding on to me so nothing would ever happen to me. And she said it was okay to miss my mom, because she misses her mom, too."

Holding him so tight? Missing his mom?

Heath's throat went tight. Zeke never talked about Anna. He never referred to missing his mother, but he'd shared that emotion yesterday. With Lizzie.

Zeke had started up the church steps but Heath called him back. "You had fun with Lizzie? Miss Lizzie," he corrected himself.

"It was awesome." Blue-gray eyes in a dusky face held his gaze and his heart. "When I go to school I'm going to tell all the kids about riding Honey's Money with Miss Lizzie."

Great. He'd spent five years raising the boy on his own, losing sleep and balancing things like a tightrope walker. And Lizzie breezed into town and won the kid's heart in less than two weeks.

It was like that for you, too. Back in the day. Remember? It took no time at all for you to lose your heart to her. "I expect they'll like hearing it."

"Me, too." Zeke reached for Heath's hand and held it. "But first I'll tell them that my dad is the best cowboy ever. Okay?"

Oh, man…

The boy's trust and devotion were wonderful things, but had Heath earned them? Did he deserve them?

Some days, yes. Others…not so much. And now he'd lambasted Lizzie for something he probably should have been doing with Zeke all along. Not racing the boy across fields, of course, but letting him experience the joy of being in the saddle, safe and secure, going faster than an old plodding horse would take him. "Very okay.

And next time we go riding, I'll go a little faster. All right?"

"Yes!"

He owed Lizzie an apology. Another one. And it didn't take a math whiz to understand that if he needed to apologize this often, he was the common denominator in the problems.

He spotted Lizzie and Corrie sitting in the front of the sparsely populated church as he walked through the door. She wore a vest made from soft faux fur, trimmed in white, and her hair lay rich against the paler colors. Ivory sleeves covered her arms against the chilled April air, and when she stood, she brushed her hair back, behind her shoulder. Then she glanced back.

She spotted him, but didn't let her gaze linger. Not after he'd been such a moron the night before.

No, she dropped her eyes to Zeke and he hurried her way as if drawn, and Heath could do nothing but follow him to the front pew.

Zeke scrambled into place. He grinned up at her, then his father, then Lizzie again, as if being tucked between them was a treat. And when the elderly pastor began the short service, Zeke pretended to read out of Lizzie's book of prayer. And word by word, Lizzie helped him, tapping the words with one trim finger.

The aging pianist sounded the notes for a final hymn, but before the congregation could begin, the pastor raised a hand. "I need to say a few words before we go," he announced from the three steps leading to the sanctuary.

The pianist looked faintly annoyed but stopped playing. The small congregation grew quiet.

"You all know I've been having some health issues this year." He glanced around the church as people nodded.

"And that winter is tough on me like it is on some other old folks in the area. So here it is." He splayed his hands and gazed out at the thin clutch of people who'd made it a priority to come to church, and half a dozen of them were from Pine Ridge Ranch. "I'll be leaving Shepherd's Crossing in a few weeks. I'm going back to Boise, to live with my daughter. I wish I didn't have to do this," he told them. "Being here has meant a great deal to me, and I hope it's been good for all of us. But there's too much for an old man like me to do here, and that's the truth of it. I'll see you for a couple more weeks, and then…" He tried to smile but then his jaw quivered slightly and he stopped trying. "We'll say our goodbyes." He paused for several long seconds, then sighed. "The thing is…there won't be anyone coming to take my place."

Heath saw the congregation glance around nervously.

"There's not enough money to pay a proper wage, and even clergy needs to eat. I'm sorry. I truly am," he went on, then folded his hands tight across his middle. "We'll have to close the church."

"But not the bells, right, Dad?" Zeke might have thought he was whispering the words, but he wasn't. "We can still listen to the bells on Sunday, right?"

The whole church stayed silent. Waiting for his answer? Waiting for someone to protest? To make things right?

He clutched Zeke's hand, because how could he answer such a question when he had no answers himself?

Then he stooped low. "I don't know, Zeke. I really don't know."

Zeke stared up at him, then lifted his eyes to where the bell tower stood above the front entrance. His gaze darkened and when old Ella Potts began banging on the piano with more zest than talent, Zeke didn't move, apparently wondering about the bells he loved so much. And Heath had absolutely no idea what to tell him.

The aged pastor was standing at the door when Heath came through with Zeke. Lizzie had threaded her way through the people, and when he got to the door, she'd disappeared from view. But as he approached the minister, the old man proffered a hand his way. "Can I have a minute, Heath?"

Zeke clung to Heath's right hand. He looked sad, and so did the pastor. No church. No pastor. No services. What kind of town were they left with? Was this what he wanted for his son? "I'm sorry you're not doing well, Pastor."

"Age catches up with most, one way or another," Reverend Sparks said. "I can't keep breath to preach like I should or pray like I should, and that's no good for me or the people. And with the church so small and getting smaller—" His voice faded. "And the town down on just about everything… Only a few dozen show up on Sundays now."

He was right, but the thought of no church in town didn't sit right with Heath, even if the only reason he came was the three-and-a-half foot boy by his side. "The town needs a church. Doesn't it?"

"The town needs God," replied the old man softly. "A building's just a building. A town steeped in the faith of our fathers can stand strong against adversity. But a town divided, with everyone going their own way, well, that's different, isn't it? When we serve ourselves and money, there's not a lot of room left for God."

A town divided.

Apt words for Shepherd's Crossing.

And he was as bad as any, taking care of his son, Sean's ranch, the sheep, and having little to do with the town or the people except as needed. He'd never seen that as a bad thing, but no church? No school? Not even a general store to grab a sandwich and a conversation on a rainy afternoon.

"You're a town leader now," the pastor continued. "Folks might want a meeting about what to do with the church. It's old and needs work, but the volunteer fire department is always looking for practice fires to hone their skills."

Burn the church? His gut clenched. "You can't be serious."

"This falling-down wreck isn't the church." The reverend pointed to Heath and Zeke, then to the thinning cloud of dust the other cars had left behind. "The people are the church. Without them, four square walls aren't much use. The church isn't in there, son. It's here in you. And them. In us."

The pastor leaving. Sean's death. Grazing rights revoked. Heath was surrounded by change. Too much, too fast, too soon. He wouldn't have thought of himself as an introvert, but right now he'd like to hole up at the ranch, take care of his own and let the world pass them by. But that attitude was what had gotten them into this mess in the first place. So maybe there was a message in the multiple blows.

"Do you need help getting ready, Reverend?"

"June'll see to it," he replied. "That's my daughter. She'll be here shortly after Memorial Day. I'll say my goodbyes to those that come the next few weeks. And then lock the door." He sighed, glanced at the church, then the town, and walked away on quiet feet.

A locked church.

An empty town.

A dusty street that saw little traffic.

"Surrounded by the rich, ignoring the poor." Lizzie's quiet observation interrupted his thoughts. He wasn't sure where she'd come from, but her words hit their mark. "This is a very Robin Hood–style place you've got here."

"Lizzie—"

She lifted her phone up. "My barn app's alerting me. I wanted to catch you in case your phone was turned off for service. Gotta run." She hurried to her SUV, got in and headed back toward Pine Ridge with Corrie by her side.

"Is Lizzie mad at us, Dad? At you and me?" Zeke peered up at him, eyes wide.

"No, son." He could say this honestly as he opened Zeke's door and helped the boy in. "She's not one bit mad at you. For anything."

"Well, then it might be you in big trouble," Zeke offered seriously, "'cause I think she was mad at somebody, Dad. And we're the only people here."

"We'll fix it when we get home. And I'm going to

leave you with Cookie this afternoon because Lizzie and I have to take care of a horse having a baby."

"And then I can peek at the baby when it's done?" Eagerness lifted the worry from his tone.

"You make it sound like we're cooking a turkey, not delivering a foal, but yes, you can come look. As long as you're quiet."

"I will be!"

Jace was exiting the first barn as Zeke scrambled out of the rear seat. He moved Heath's way and paused. "Two things, and you're not going to like either one of them so let me apologize first."

Jace's troubled look underscored the words.

"Justine isn't available to watch the little guy like we planned. She got an offer of a paid internship in Seattle and can't turn it down so she's staying in Seattle for at least six weeks. She tried calling you but your cell went straight to voice mail and your mailbox is full. She feels terrible because she knows this leaves you in a lurch, but the offer just came through."

He'd turned his phone off before church, and hadn't noticed the missed call when he turned it back on. "She's sure, Jace? Because this puts us in a spot we can't afford to be in." He'd managed to insult Lizzie's child care abilities, Cookie wouldn't take kindly to non-stop child duty and Corrie hadn't come north to play nanny. Although she'd be a great one.

"I know. But wait, Heath. It gets worse."

He watched his friend struggle for words, and Heath was pretty sure he didn't want to hear whatever Jace was going to say next.

"I'm leaving."

Heath swallowed hard. Jace was great on the ranch, but ranching wasn't his primary job. He was a skilled carpenter: he'd overseen the building of the last two barns and he'd honed his reputation on Pine Ridge properties, but with the area's diminishing population, there weren't enough jobs to keep him busy. And he was Heath's closest friend.

"I love working here and living here," Jace went on. His gaze wandered the ranch, then lingered on the hills beyond. "My family helped build this town over a hundred years ago, and there weren't too many black ranchers in these parts. Or anywhere. But things have gone downhill and I've got to go where there's work. I'm going to sell my parents' place and use that money to pay off Justine's schooling and stake my business."

His parents had passed away just over a year apart when Justine started college three years before. "You going to Sun Valley?"

"Where else?"

The rising fortunes of the picturesque central valley had drawn a lofty tourism trade while home values pitched up. Folks in Sun Valley would have the means to hire a guy like Jace and pay him what he was worth.

"I've looked the situation over every which way, but it seems like the only option on the table right about now. It'll take some time to sell our place," he added. "There aren't folks lined up to buy houses around here, so plan on me being here at least a month. Maybe more. I'm sorry, Heath." Jace tipped his cowboy hat back slightly. "This wasn't how I saw things going. We've been friends for a dozen years, and I never thought it would go down like this but my hands are tied."

They'd had plans as younger men. Thoughts about how to resuscitate the town, how to bring back jobs and hope. But the plans went on hold as the ranch grew. Sean's vision and dreams kept them both busy, and they'd forged ahead without seeing the whole picture. Now it was too late.

"I get it, Jace. You know I do. A man's got to have work and you're too good a builder to spend your life running sheep."

"I like working the ranch well enough. I'd like to have my own spread someday, a Middleton ranch like my great-grandpa had. That was always my dream." Jace shrugged. "But I'm meant to hold a hammer and run a saw, and I knew that from the time my daddy taught me everything he'd learned. It's not even just wanting to do it. It's *needing* to do it. I just never thought I'd be doing it away from here."

Heath understood completely. It wasn't about the money or the power of heading up a high-priced property. It was about taking the right trail to get where you were going.

Lizzie texted just then. Maybe labor, maybe not. Nothing much happening. Will keep you posted.

OK, he texted back,

"I'll turn the established pairs onto the meadow." Once a ewe established her little family with strong nursing instincts, they were turned onto a select nearby pasture to eat, grow and socialize, making room for more newborn lambs. Head down, Jace moved toward the lambing shed.

Heath turned toward the stables. Lizzie didn't need him if the horse wasn't laboring, and he had plenty to do, but he owed her an apology for his outburst the day before. She'd put a light in his son's eyes, and he'd squelched things by hitting the panic button. Now he had to eat his words because Rosie wouldn't be able to watch Zeke for weeks.

He texted Cookie to keep an eye on Zeke for the time being. That meant the little guy had to stay inside on a brilliant spring day because Cookie had jobs to do.

Guilt rose within him but that had become more normal than not. Did all single parents face these dilemmas? He wouldn't know because he'd become very good at insulating himself. Just like Sean.

He walked into the barn, crossed to the office wing and tapped on Lizzie's door. She turned, surprised, then pointed up toward the monitor on the wall. "Nothing much happening. Didn't you get my text?"

"I did." He walked into the room, shoved his hands into his pockets, then pulled them right back out again. "I didn't come because of the mare. I came to apologize."

Apologize? She stood, faced him, then folded her arms. "I'm listening."

Gorgeous eyes gazed into hers, as if searching.

"I was out of line yesterday and I'm sorry."

She lifted a brow slightly but stayed quiet because he was right. He was out of line and no one got to treat her that way. Ever.

"I should have been glad you took Zeke for a ride. I know your skills, I know your instincts, I know you. I let old buttons get pushed and that was plain stupid."

Still she waited, unwilling to offer him help or absolution.

"It's been crazy busy here, not just since Sean died but since he got sick. I haven't had time to do things I should with Zeke, and Rosie had her hands full. She was pregnant and watching Zeke and a set of twins."

"Zeke told me about the twins. I think he felt trapped because Rosie was busy and he couldn't do too much outside."

"Rosie said as much. I just figured it would all work out in time, but it didn't. It was winter and then Sean started to go downhill. That increased the workload on me, but I did it at the expense of my son. Now I'm not sure how to undo any of it."

"Delegate?"

He brought his chin up quickly.

"You trust the people working with you to handle vital things, but when it comes to Zeke, fear gets in the way. Trust more and worry less," she told him.

"Easier said than done."

She laughed. He scowled, and that only made her laugh more. "You know those birds of the air? The fish in the sea? Those sparrows that God cares for every single day? Be more like them," she suggested. "Trust. Reach out. There is life beyond Pine Ridge Ranch, just like there was life beyond Fitzgerald News. It's a question of exploring it. Then embracing it."

She glanced up at the monitor, saw nothing of note, and eased a hip onto the office desk. "Zeke loves being on the ranch. He's a born cowboy. But he could use some time with his daddy to figure out how to be the best cowboy he can be. And if you can't take him with you off the ranch because time is short right now, make him your sidekick. When it's safe. It will do you both good. And while I appreciate the apology…" She moved a step closer, determined to make her point. "Nobody gets to go off on me like that, Heath. Ever. Don't do it again."

If her reprimand surprised him, he didn't show it. "I won't. Most of the time." He sent her a rueful grin, a look she remembered like it was yesterday, the kind of grin that stole a young girl's heart. "I get stupid about Zeke sometimes."

"Loving your child isn't stupid. It's how it's supposed to be. Every kid in the world should have at least one parent who loves them."

Sympathy softened his jaw. His gaze. "Your father's a moron, Lizzie. And selfish. I'm sorry he messed you girls up."

"We're educated. We're smart. We'll be okay. But he cost over a thousand people their jobs and their pensions while he lives the life of a rich man in Dubai on stolen capital. That's indefensible. And he got away with it." She frowned. "I honestly don't know how he lives with himself."

"And that's why Sean named you three women in the will. He couldn't believe what his brother did to you. How he left the three of you holding the bag and some pretty stiff college loans for Charlotte and Mel."

She was tired of rehashing her father's misdeeds. "Just be glad you ended up working for this Fitzgerald brother. That he gave you a chance. Because I can see you love this place, Heath."

"It saved me." He turned his gaze outward. "I owe Sean and I owe this ranch, and no one expected him to get sick. To die. So the fact that he left me part of all this humbles me. And challenges me. So yeah." He stood, tall and strong, shoulders back. "I love it. And I have to do whatever it takes to continue its success."

"That's when I call on my faith," she told him quietly. "To give me the strength I need."

He looked at her. Right at her. And he didn't blink an eye. "The work of human hands has gotten me a whole lot farther than some intangible belief system. Diving in, getting things done, staying the course."

"Except that you were just in church with me a couple of hours ago. Somehow this doesn't compute."

"I always take Zeke to church. His mother isn't here to do it, so I do it in her place. She'd have wanted me to. It was important to her."

But not to him.

The ring he still wore on his left hand gleamed brighter when a stray sunbeam hit the corner of the office window. It made a perfect reminder for Lizzie.

Heath didn't do change well. He depended on himself and few others, and most assuredly not God.

She depended on God for everything. He'd been with her throughout the dark days after her father discovered her pregnancy. The shunning she'd received from her illustrious grandfather. And He'd been with her when she'd called on Heath for help, and Heath had ignored her pleas.

She folded her hands lightly in her lap. "I don't know where I'd be today without my faith, Heath. It's been my mainstay when people let me down. When man failed me, God stood watch. I'm sorry it hasn't been that way for you because I remember when you used to go to church every Sunday and pray for your father."

"A fat lot of good that did me."

She heard the pain in his voice. She understood how hard it was to grow up happy when parents fail in their job of simply loving their children. She'd had money and stature to fall back on.

Heath had a drunken father in a dirty stable apartment.

She wouldn't argue with him. Or try and convince him. He needed to find his own path back to faith, on his own terms. But she could pray for him to find the peace and joy God wanted for him. The quiet contentment she wanted for him.

His phone buzzed a text. He read it and moved to the door. "Jace needs a hand."

Would he go get Zeke and let the little fellow pal around in the sheep barn? Or was he expecting others to take charge and keep Zeke under lock and key for the duration?

"I'll keep you apprised of what's going on here."

"I'd appreciate it." And before she could make a face behind his back, he turned. "Not because I don't trust you to do it, Liz. But so I don't thoroughly mess up if I have to step up to the plate someday."

"A good plan. See you later."

He cut across the grass to the house to throw some work clothes on.

She stared up at the cloudless sky, wondering how anyone could live here and not see the beauty of God's creation. Or believe in God Himself.

Could she help Heath? Or would drawing close to him again simply draw her into his work-first world?

She didn't know, but when he came out of the house

and headed to the sheep barn without Zeke, she was disappointed.

Sure, there was risk on a ranch. There was risk everywhere. But if Heath used all his time working solo instead of bringing his little boy with him whenever possible, he wasn't just building a ranch. He was building a wall between father and son, a wall that didn't need to exist except when fear grabbed hold and wouldn't let go.

And that might be the worst wall of all.

Chapter Ten

Heath returned to the stables when she texted him in the late afternoon. "I got your message. How's she doing?"

"We've got hooves showing."

"That's quick. And she's handling it well?"

"This isn't her first rodeo," replied Lizzie as she jotted notes into the electronic notebook. She'd set up a small table around the corner from the foaling mare. It held a tall iced tea in a plastic bottle and a container of Corrie's homemade cookies, the closest she'd come to food all day. "She's had two other successful foals. And one stillbirth."

Heath had been watching the monitor above him. He stopped watching and turned her way. "Sean bought a horse with a thirty-three percent failure rating?"

Lizzie's heart went tight. So did her hands. And when she found the breath to address his statement she kept her voice soft on purpose. "I don't think the horse considered it a failure. I think she saw it as a loss, Heath."

Her reply flustered him. Good.

"I don't mean she failed, that was a stupid way to put it. We have lamb losses. Their percentages get higher if the weather turns, or if we get an attack of scours. There are so many factors that affect newborns that we're constantly watching during lambing season. But with a horse it's one foal every two years and when you lose one out of three, that's a higher percentage than Sean would have normally entertained."

He made sense but that didn't erase the sting of the word "failure." "Let's just say they might not have been forthcoming about the stillbirth. I found it accidentally when I was examining records. Maybe Uncle Sean only saw what they wanted him to see. Or maybe he wanted her to have another chance. A happier one."

He seemed to miss the latter part of her statement and bore directly into the first half. "They falsified records?"

"It wasn't in the paperwork so unless they told him verbally, then yes. By omission," she added. "But right now let's focus on them."

A nose appeared between the two thick hooves, and within twenty minutes they had a blue roan colt on the ground, one of the most majestic colts she'd ever seen.

"Oh, he's a stunner." Lizzie breathed the words, watching. "A classic beauty. And with a lineage that puts him into a class all his own. So maybe Uncle Sean did know about the lost foal." She leaned on the adjoining stall gate, watching the pair bond. "But he saw Josie's potential and bought her anyway."

"That's a big chance to take on a whole lot of investment," said Heath, but then his next words eased the sting. "And well worth every penny. Like I said before, you and Sean have an eye for horses. And an ear. I'm making a pledge right now that I won't interfere with your decisions. Mostly."

"And I'll promise to ignore you as needed. Mostly."

She tipped a smile up his way, then paused.

Their eyes met. Held. Lingered.

His gaze dropped to her mouth. Stayed there. And then he reached out one finger to her cheek. Just one. He traced the curve of her cheek with that one finger as if remembering. Or maybe reminding himself of what they'd had way back when.

The sound of the stable door clicking shut pulled them apart, and when Corrie turned down the alley with Zeke, Lizzie was studiously watching mother and baby, which was what she should have been doing all along.

She turned to welcome Heath's son and focused on the boy's excitement. "Hey, little man. The baby is here and he's beautiful."

"I'm so happy he's here!" Zeke kept his voice quiet. He peeked into the stall when Heath lifted him into his arms. "Isn't he like the coolest baby horse ever?"

"He is a rare beauty," noted Corrie, but she sent Lizzie a sharp look. A look that Lizzie refused to acknowledge. "He might be your second-generation stallion if you keep him. That color alone is worth a fair price."

"We'll see how he musters up, but yes." Lizzie hung back with them so they wouldn't spook the mother. "He's a looker."

"He sure is. I'm going up to take care of some overdue office work up front," Heath said. He faced Corrie. "Are you okay with Zeke for a while?"

Corrie shook her head. "Unfortunately, no. We've had a nice afternoon, but Cookie and I are laying plans for the vegetable garden. But I'll see you both at supper."

He started to turn toward Lizzie. The mare whinnied, a reminder that Lizzie was on the job, too. "Well, bud, you'll have to tag along with me."

Zeke pressed a kiss to his father's cheek. "I love that, Dad!"

Heath's expression relaxed. "Me, too. We'll see you ladies later."

"Wonderful." Corrie smiled, but when he was out of sight, she turned to Lizzie with a more thoughtful expression. "You guard your head. He guards his heart." She drawled the words intentionally. "How can this possibly work, darlin'?"

"There's nothing to work," Lizzie told her.

Corrie sniffed. "You couldn't fool me then, you can't fool me now. And it's not that I don't understand the attraction. Heath Caufield is a fine man. And he carries himself tall and strong, but there's a world of hurtin' in those big blue eyes and you've had enough of that, I think."

"Corrie…"

Corrie raised both hands up, palms out. "I'm not interfering."

"Mmm-hmm." Lizzie drew the wheelbarrow closer for stall cleaning.

"But I'm not afraid to protect my own, Lizzie-Beth. I might have failed in that before. I don't aim to fail now."

Concern drew Corrie's brows together and Lizzie knew the sincerity of the sweet nanny's words. But she wasn't a wayward teen any longer. "I'm all grown up, Corrie. And pretty independent."

"Tell this old woman something I don't know."

Lizzie grinned and looped an arm around Corrie's shoulders in a half hug. "You're not old. You're seasoned. And I'd be lying to say there isn't an attraction. The kid is a total bonus. But I will never settle for less than the whole thing again, Corrie. Faith, hope and love. Heath's so mad at God and life that whatever faith he had is gone and he wears his wedding ring like a badge of honor. I decided a long time ago that I'll never take second place again. And I meant it."

"So we wait and see while we work here. Maybe the good Lord has brought us to Idaho to make a difference. Your uncle's generosity has opened a door for us. Perhaps there's a way to open a door for others."

Lizzie envisioned the worn-out town, the thinning population and the problems surrounding them. "I don't know how, Corrie."

"Then we pray for vision." Corrie squeezed her hand lightly. "The little man and I made spoon bread to go with supper. If we bring some Southern cooking and hospitality into the deep north, it's bound to have some kind of effect. It can't hurt anything more than it's already hurting."

Southern cooking.

Hospitality.

Lizzie worked those thoughts around in her head once Corrie went back to the house.

How could people work together if they never came together? And what brought most people out?

Weddings and funerals.

Since there wasn't a wedding in the plans, she sought Heath out that evening, once Zeke was in bed. "Got a minute?"

"Before I fall asleep?" He'd been checking something on his phone. He put it away. "Yes."

"You said Uncle Sean was cremated."

"He wanted his ashes returned to the ranch he loved. Yes."

"Is there a memorial?"

He frowned. "A what?"

"A grave. A marker. Something to commemorate his life."

"I think the ranch is a pretty big marker. Don't you?"

"No." The night had taken a strong dip in temperature so she pulled her hoodie closer. "Uncle Sean was a decorated marine. He was awarded the Navy Cross and a Purple Heart. He saved three men from an ambush and took a bullet to the leg while dragging them, one at a time, to safety. The farm is a great legacy. But a memorial is a better reminder of that sacrifice."

He took her words seriously. "I've never thought of that. You mean like put a place in the cemetery? For us to buy a plot?"

She shook her head. "Why not right here on the land he loved?"

"Listen, this is a great idea, it really is, but I don't have time to organize something like this during lambing. I wouldn't even know how to."

"I'll do it."

He still looked hesitant, but Lizzie pressed her point. "It's the right thing to do, Heath."

"It is. I'm just embarrassed we didn't think of it ourselves."

"And now we did. Zeke and I will get on it first thing tomorrow."

"About Zeke—"

"Yes?"

He worked his jaw slightly. "Do you mind helping with him the next few weeks?"

She should refuse. Heath was way too protective and she found that stifling and fairly annoying. But he was caught in a jam. He'd done the responsible thing and had arranged child care, then got thwarted at the last minute. She couldn't fault him for that. "I'll help as I'm able. Between you and me and Corrie, we should be able to keep one five-year-old out of mischief for a while."

He covered her hands with one of his, the one sporting a plain gold band. "Thanks, Liz."

She kept her smile light and her tone easy. "That's what friends are for." She withdrew her hands from his and headed for the stables, but first she checked the dog food dish out back.

More food was gone, but there was no sign of the bedraggled dog. She whistled lightly, hoping it would come but nothing moved in the growing darkness.

At least the little dog was getting regular meals. She understood Heath's concern about animals and disease control, but kindness mattered, too.

So the food dish stayed right where it was.

Chapter Eleven

Two hundred and forty-three lambs and they weren't half done, but their results were promising, and that was a weight off Heath's shoulders.

His phone rang midmorning. He glanced down, chose to ignore the call and shoved the phone back into his pocket.

"Melos again?" asked Jace.

Heath grunted. A sheep farmer from farther down the valley wanted to raise a ruckus over the change in grazing rights.

Heath didn't have time for a ruckus, and he'd said that outright, but Blake Melos was persistent. "They're having a meeting tomorrow night. Who's got time to have meetings this time of year?" he asked.

Jace kept cleaning lambing stalls to prepare for the next wave. "If you want to have a neighbor, you've got to be a neighbor."

Heath growled but Jace was good at ignoring his growls. Today was no exception. "Like it or not, you don't exist in a vacuum here. Pine Ridge Ranch isn't an entity unto itself. It's part of something bigger. A town. A community. And if no one starts caring about that, then what do we have left?" The sound of the pitchfork hitting concrete punctuated his point. "Every fix begins somewhere. Getting together with these people is a smart thing to do. Sean lived on his own for a lot of reasons," Jace reminded him. "But he probably should have reached out more. And Carrington, with his monster-sized spread, flying in and out on his private landing strip." Jace waved toward south where Eric Carrington was developing a celebrated Angus cattle operation with his family's pharmaceutical fortune. "If the big players on the board ignore the good of the community, pretty soon there is no community."

Which was what they were facing now.

Jace was right. He didn't have to like being involved in this group of angry ranchers, but it was the right thing to do. He texted Blake a quick message. I'll be there.

Then he pushed the phone back into his pocket.

"I'll go with you," said Jace. "Wick will be on barn duty then. And Lizzie should go, too."

"It's got nothing to do with horses."

"And everything to do with joining forces. Like it or not, she's part of the force."

That was another problem, because he did like it. He liked it a lot. She didn't let him get so caught up in himself or the ranch that he couldn't see beyond it, and that hadn't happened in—

So long that he couldn't remember. He'd been putting his shoulder to the wheel since setting foot on Pine Ridge soil, but maybe it wasn't a question of working harder. Maybe it came down to working smarter.

Corrie had been with Zeke that morning. Lizzie was taking the afternoon as long as the remaining mares stayed quiet. He walked up to the house midafternoon. Zeke should be napping and he'd have a few minutes of quiet time with Lizzie.

That thought made him walk a little quicker, but when he kicked off his barn boots and came through to the kitchen, Zeke wasn't napping. He was perched on one of the tall stools, making a cake. With Lizzie. And the sight of them, laughing together, daubing frosting onto the cake, softened another corner of his heart.

"Did I miss someone's birthday?" he asked.

Zeke slipped off the tall stool as if he were a much bigger kid and dashed toward his father. "Nope. Lizzie and me—"

"Lizzie and I." The two adults corrected him in unison, and then they smiled. At the same time. At one another, with the miniature cowboy grinning between them, almost as if it was supposed to be that way.

"Lizzie and I," Zeke corrected himself, sounding bored with the effort. He beamed at his father. Frosting smeared his shirt and the back of his hands. "My Lizzie said we're making a cake just acause."

"*Because*," she told him. "Because we can and we thought everyone would really, really love cake."

"Because it's so delicious! Right, Dad?"

Heath reached out and swiped a finger along the edge of the frosting bowl and tasted it. "It is amazingly delicious."

"And now Zeke is going to decorate the cake," said Lizzie. She held up a plastic cone half-filled with frosting. "Remember how we practiced? Hold the bag tight with one hand and squeeze with the other."

"I will." He scrambled back to his seat, grinning.

"Don't lick your fingers like I did," warned Heath. "You're fixing this for other folks to eat, so you've got to be careful."

Lizzie didn't mention that Zeke may have already licked his fingers a time or two. "Blake Melos called the house phone twice. He left two messages. Which means he's probably calling your cell and you're ignoring him."

"Was ignoring him," he corrected her. "I texted him that I'd be at the meeting, although the diminished grazing bill is a done deal. I don't see the good in talking it to death. Not when we're so bogged down in work right here."

She handed Zeke a bottle of spring-colored sprinkles that Heath was pretty sure were a new addition to the kitchen, because Cookie wasn't a sprinkle kind of guy.

"I've been here a long time now," he went on, "and most folks here mind their own business."

"Which could explain the failing town," she noted as she watched Zeke's attempts to squiggle frosting onto the cake. "I've never lived in a small town, but I'm pretty sure folks are supposed to rally together when things are rough. Aren't they?"

"You've got big game hunting and tourism on one side of this issue and failing sheep farms on the other. Beef is taking over and that lessens the effect of anything the sheep ranchers might say and hay's battling it out with potatoes as the top crop. Why get into a war we can't win?"

"Because maybe the other ranches don't have the

means to switch things up and need that hill grazing to survive. This place is well-established and had money for a solid start. Not everyone has that option." She was guiding Zeke's hand to keep at least some of the frosting on the cake, but shifted those pretty eyes up to him. "If no one's producing market lambs for the West Coast, you've got a lot of disappointed customers. A lot of ethnic celebrations use lamb as part of their festivities. Pointing out the beneficial factors to the governor might not be a bad idea. I'd be glad to write the letter for you."

He tensed instantly. "I can write my own letter."

"So why use the journalist to help?" She made a face of pretend surprise. "My bad."

"My Lizzie helped me write a letter, Dad." Zeke kept on dotting the white-frosted cake with yellow blobs. "She's a good teacher."

His Lizzie? Heath drew his brows down, good and tight. "You mean Miss Lizzie."

"Well, I keep forgetting that part, and I like saying my Lizzie." Zeke flashed a smile at Lizzie and leaned his dark head against Liz's side. "She teaches me lots of things. Like how to write letters. So maybe you should let her help you, too." He beamed a smile up at Liz, then pointed to the far end of the table. "That's my first letter, Dad! And it's for you!"

Heath crossed to the table and picked up the sheet of paper. He read it, then turned back to her. To Zeke. "You helped him write this?"

"I helped him with spelling." Lizzie bumped shoulders with the boy. "I was working on my things while he was working on his. Didn't he do a marvelous job?"

"It's beautiful." Heath stared at the paper, then his son. He didn't want to get emotional over something so simple, but he did because his kid had just written him a letter. "I don't know what to say, Zeke. Thank you."

"It says *I Love You Dad*," Zeke declared from his spot on the stool. "And I do! I love you this much!" He spread his arms, but forgot to set the bag down. Suntoned frosting dribbled onto the floor.

"Oops." Lizzie grabbed a couple of paper towels while Heath picked up a washcloth. They both bent to clean up the mess, a swirl of neon gold soaking into their respective wipes.

And then their hands touched.

Paused.

"Liz." Heath didn't just say her name. He whispered it in a voice that begged a question, a question with no answers. He covered her hand with his, and whispered her name again.

She raised her eyes.

The look of him. His scent, the messed up hair, the ruggedness of a man unafraid to work the land long hours, day into night...

Did she lean closer?

Did he?

She didn't know, but the temptation drew her in.

She pulled back quickly.

What was she thinking? Doing? She knew better.

"Our young helper made a little mess?" Corrie's cheerful voice severed the moment. "Heath, you'll need hot water and drops of dish soap to get the grease off the floor. We don't want anyone slipping, and I've just been over to see Rosie and that new baby." Corrie laid a hand to her chest as if to swoon, Southern woman to the max. "My heart, my heart, to hold one that small, and so perfect. I told them about the ceremony we'd like to do for Sean's marker at the end of the month. Land sakes, she was excited. They'd like to wait for the men to come out of the hills, but that's a long way off. When I mentioned Memorial Day, both she and Harve thought that was a good idea."

"Good." Lizzie didn't look at Corrie. She didn't look at Heath, either. She didn't dare, because what would she see?

She didn't know, and wasn't sure she wanted to know.

He'd stood up when Corrie walked in. He crossed to the sink, rinsed out the cloth, then heated it with hotter water and a little soap. He cleaned up the spill thoroughly, then tossed the cloth into a laundry room hamper before he grabbed a sandwich from the tray in the fridge.

Nothing in his manner suggested they'd shared anything other than a wipe-the-spot moment.

"You're okay with the pest for a while more?"

His teasing made Zeke grin.

"We've got some errands to run, so yes. We're double-teaming the memorial project."

"After his nap?" Heath asked.

"My Lizzie says I'm getting too big for naps." Zeke drew his brow into a frown so much like Heath's, it made Lizzie smile.

"Corrie's advice," said Lizzie. "And I never argue with Corrie." She shared a smile with the older woman. "Not when it comes to raising wonderful kids. And I believe my exact words were that you won't be needing a nap every day," she corrected him. "Because you'll be off to school soon and there are no naps in school."

"That's four months away. And little kids need their sleep."

"'Zactly, Dad." Zeke offered his father a sage look. "But big kids don't hardly need them at all. And 'member how you said I'm a big kid now? When I turned five?"

Heath looked trapped by his own words, and Lizzie kind of liked that. "I think the grown-ups around you will take it day by day. Flexibility is good. And right now we need to finish this cake, my friend, and get out of Cookie's way. He's due back from the market any minute."

"Okay!"

She'd made a pretty picture standing there, a smudge of white frosting on her right cheek. She'd tucked her hair up in some kind of clip, and the pale, freckled skin of her arm, curved around Zeke but not touching him, showed a protective instinct that surprised him but shouldn't because he'd known her gentle heart for years.

He set a ladder up along the back of the barn farthest from the house. Winter winds had loosened shingles on a lean-to addition, and heavy rain and winds were predicted. Damp conditions played havoc with newborn lambs. He pulled old shingles and tossed them into the bed of a pickup below, but no matter how hard he worked, he couldn't unravel the mix of threads running through his head.

Landowners had largely ignored the town, and as online services and shopping improved, they'd gone into Shepherd's Crossing for little more than church and to pay the taxes. Then the local government had made it possible to pay taxes online, so for the past couple of years now a click of a button took care of that.

He wanted to help.

Not just help.

He wanted to fix things, to make it better. And to do that, he needed help. Or maybe just needed to be a help. Tomorrow's meeting might be a good place to start.

It felt odd to include others on Pine Ridge business, but it no longer felt wrong, and that was a step forward.

An out-of-place sound grabbed his attention. A dog, he thought, where no dog should be. He stood up, peering left, then right.

The sound came again, fainter this time, moving away from the sheep and the lambs.

He saw nothing, but stray dogs were a rarity here. They posed a danger to sheep. A malicious dog could wreak havoc with a flock. The Maremma sheepdog hadn't barked, and all seemed well in the nursing pasture. They'd moved the sheep and lambs up one field that morning to avoid soggy ground following the rain, and all seemed calm.

His thumb went to the ring finger on his left hand, the reminder of what he'd had and lost. As it did, Lizzie's SUV pulled away from the house, with Zeke in the back seat.

He wasn't sure if his heart ached or stretched just then, but it did something it hadn't done in a long while. It opened. It opened to the thought of opportunities he'd never expected and didn't know he'd want until Lizzie had stepped foot on the ranch.

He slipped the ring into his pocket, then pushed the odd feeling away. His hand would grow accustomed to not having a ring in time. And he needed to be open to the changes around him. *All* the changes, he reminded himself.

"Need help up there?" Jace asked from below.

"I wouldn't say no."

Jace climbed the ladder quickly. "Wick's in the barn, Harve texted me that he's going stir-crazy already, and we can get this done this afternoon if we double-team it."

He literally didn't know what he'd do without Jace when the man left, because there was nothing Jace couldn't put his hand to on the ranch. "Let's do it."

By the time they finished stripping the shingles, the wind had shifted. A rim of dark clouds edged the western horizon, meaning they better move quickly.

"You cut, I'll shingle," said Jace, and Heath didn't argue. They worked in tandem, heads down, as the storm front approached, so when the sound of a tractor came out of nowhere two hours later, Heath stood.

Lizzie and Zeke were rumbling up the farm lane leading south. He was on her lap, holding the steering wheel of the small, older tractor, and she was guiding the rig with her hands over his.

Zeke looked up, saw Heath and tried to stand while the tractor kept moving forward. "Dad! Look at me! I'm driving a tractor!"

He didn't think. He didn't pause. He climbed down the ladder. He hit the ground running, and when he raced around the edge of the barn, he doubled his pace to get in front of the tractor up the gentle grade. He squared himself in the path, held up one hand and said "Stop."

Lizzie stopped.

She stared at him and rolled her eyes, but she stopped. Of course the other option would be to run him over, and the flash in her eyes indicated it might have crossed her mind.

"Come here." He moved to the tractor's side and reached for Zeke.

"But I'm riding with my Lizzie." Zeke looked surprised and pretty indignant. "We are going to see what's at the top of the hill and then make pictures of what we see from up there."

"You could have taken a four-by-four with seatbelts," Heath scolded her. "You could have walked. You could have made a choice that put my son's safety first, Liz. But you didn't."

She locked eyes with him.

He'd infuriated her. He saw that.

But then he saw something else, something worse. Pity.

He didn't think he could get angrier, but he did.

He didn't need her pity or her sympathy. He was fine. Just fine. She was the one out of line.

He hauled Zeke into his arms and strode back to the house. Zeke cried all the way. He cried for Lizzie. He cried for his tractor ride, sounding like the tired boy he had to be.

He took him into the house, tucked him into bed, then ignored Zeke's anger until the boy fell into a troubled sleep.

Corrie said nothing to him. Not one word. But her silence spoke volumes.

Cookie arched a brow, but he stayed quiet, too.

Why was Heath the bad guy in all this? Why did everyone think they would be better at raising his child than he was?

He stomped back to the roof once Zeke fell asleep.

"Oh, you are in it now, my friend." Jace muttered the words as Heath began handing him full-sized shingles. "I expect folks all the way in town heard that child carrying on, and the poor sheep were racing this way and that, wondering what the ruckus was about."

"They were not." He knew how important it was to keep sheep calm. They were placid creatures, but once riled, they tended to stay upset.

"Perhaps racing is too strong a term, but you got their attention. You know that was one of the things I loved about my daddy," Jace continued. He waved the hammer toward the farm lane. "He'd set me right up on that tractor seat and talk to me while he worked. He showed me every little thing there was to know about working a farm, riding herd, running equipment. I don't remember an age where I wasn't part of his work detail, so when he died in that mudslide, it was like a part of me died, too. But I don't have a view in these parts that doesn't remind me of him. In the hills, on a roof, in a pew each and every Sunday or framing walls. Jason Middleton might not have lived as long as we would have liked, but he lived every minute he had, teaching me and Justine how to do things. And when he wasn't able to be there, my mama wasn't afraid to take the reins and do the same thing."

A part of Heath wanted Jace to shut up. Another part knew he was right.

"You got mad at God a long time ago," Jace noted. He didn't stop hammering, and the pneumatic gun shot nails with a steady ping! ping! ping! as Heath laid shingles. "Anna knew it. Yeah, she talked to me about it," he said when Heath gave him a sharp look. "She prayed for you. I expect Lizzie'll pray for you, too. In time." He bent low again, nailing shingles with quick precision. "If she doesn't kill you first."

They finished the roof in silence.

Lizzie had told him to delegate. He hadn't listened, not really. And it wasn't just where Zeke was concerned, although that was a major issue.

He was turning into a micromanager, not trusting folks to do their jobs and that was no way to run a busy ranch. Overseeing was one thing.

Being a bossy jerk was quite another.

I will not kill him.
I will not kill him.
I will not—

Lizzie ran the pledge through her head while she drove the tractor back to the equipment shed.

The little guy had been perfectly safe in her arms on the wide-seated tractor. She'd learned to run tractor in Kentucky, not because she needed to learn that stuff. That was what farm staff was for on a sprawl like Claremorris.

She'd learned it because she loved working the land and working with horses, because showing, riding and caring for horses was part of her Celtic blood, and because she was born to it, just like she was born to run a business. God had gifted her with both talents.

Did Heath know this? Or was he assuming a green-horn was taking his kid on a death-defying adventure?

The hammering on the roof stopped as she parked the tractor. She crossed to the stables. She wasn't ready to have a face-off with Heath. In the peace of the horse barn she could work, think and pray.

And then she'd kill him.

That thought cheered her as she rounded the stable, but she hadn't paused to peek around the corner and her quick approach startled the scruffy dog.

It jumped up, barked twice and raced off toward the walk-in shed at the back of the first horse pasture. It darted out of sight like it had done before and she rued the lost opportunity to coax the dog closer.

"Was that a stray dog?"

She hadn't heard Heath approach, and she wasn't all that pleased with him so his tough tone of voice didn't sit well. "Not a stray anymore."

He glanced to the food and water dish, then surprised her because he didn't scold. He sighed. "It's different here, Liz."

Right, cowboy. Tell me something I don't know.

"Sheep view dogs as wolves. The Border collies and the Maremmas are raised with them. That's why we keep them in the field, not in the house. They're here to do a very important job as guardians. But stray dogs can make sheep crazy, and crazy sheep lose lambs. They stop feeding, they get nervous, and that nervousness spreads through a flock. It's not that I'm against being nice to animals. It's that the wrong dog can mess up a flock real quick. We'll have to catch that one." He thrust his chin toward the shed. "And there's a lot to lose if he starts bothering the horses. Had you considered that?"

Of course she had, hence the coaxing. But he wasn't scolding. He was…talking. And that eased the edge off her earlier ire. "Catch him and do what with him?"

Heath frowned. "We could start with a bath."

She almost smiled. "I noticed that, too."

"And then take it from there. How long have you been feeding him?"

"A while," she admitted.

"Ah." He smiled then, a true smile, the kind she knew and loved back in Kentucky. "Listen, Liz…"

She waited.

He rocked back on his heels and rubbed his jaw like he always did when he thought too hard. "I shouldn't have interfered with you and Zeke. I just—"

"Get scared to death over things you can't control and lash out irrationally?"

"I was going to say I overreact when I get worried, but your take works, too."

She thrust her hands into her pockets as the cold front rolled in. "You are embarrassing yourself and me when you act like that. It's got to stop."

He didn't deny it. But he didn't look happy, either.

"Is this how you treat Rosie when she cares for Zeke? As if she's incapable of handling a busy five-year-old?"

"I would if she pulled dangerous stunts with my son involved. She doesn't. Nor would she."

Lizzie raised a hand to thwart him. "First of all, learning to ride with an expert rider isn't exactly letting the boy set off fireworks or juggle steak knives.

And seeing the workings of machinery first-hand, for a little guy who loves Mega Machines and constantly asks to watch it on his tablet, is a no-brainer. If you were giving him a tractor ride, I suppose it would be all right?"

"I'm his father."

"Except you're busy, you've taken on a huge responsibility here, you're short on help and you've got more irons in the fire than a beef ranch branding party. Let's cut to the chase. You don't trust me. But it's not just me, Heath," she added, facing him. "It's everyone, except my uncle, maybe. And he's gone."

He flinched.

"You didn't used to be this untrusting and get angry over things. I don't know this Heath Caufield." She pointed to him. "But I know one thing. The other Heath Caufield was one of the best men I ever had the privilege to know. I'd like to see that one more often."

He stared beyond her to the deepening twilight, made denser by the dense clouds. "I didn't know you could drive a tractor."

She arched one brow, waiting.

"I saw you driving, then Zeke stood up and all I could see was him tumbling down, falling beneath the equipment. Being crushed."

She frowned. "That's a glass half-empty if I ever heard it."

A tiny muscle in his jaw twitched slightly. "He's the only thing I have, Lizzie. The thought of anything happening to him makes me a little crazy."

A little? She did a slow count to ten. Only made it to five, but it was enough to keep from smacking him upside the head. For the moment.

She didn't apologize for taking Zeke on the tractor.

She didn't commiserate with the depths of Heath's worry, either.

She understood his words. They pained her, to think how much he thought of his child with Anna, but then, Zeke was real to him. Their tiny boy, Matthew, hadn't existed in Heath's realm. He'd been a fleeting thought.

Not to her.

To her he'd been real. So very real.

She pivoted and walked away before she said too much. "Liz."

She didn't turn. She refused to turn, because then he'd see the sheen of tears. The quivering jaw.

He hadn't cared then. Pretending to care now would get them nowhere, so why push him to sympathy?

She kept walking, head high, and if she swiped her hands to her eyes once or twice, he wouldn't know it. Because when she glanced back as she moved through the broad barn door, he was halfway to the house. And he didn't look back.

Chapter Twelve

Alone in a house full of people.

The thought hit Heath when he found Liz on the side porch the next morning. He'd had thirteen hours to consider her words. The truth in them frustrated him.

She'd curled up on the side-porch swing. Her laptop lay perched on her knees and a hot, steaming mug of coffee sat on the rustic wooden table alongside the swing. The cool air lifted the steam like one of those holiday coffee commercials. He didn't ask. Didn't hesitate. He plunked himself down on the end of the swing, and braced his arms on his legs. The action made the laptop teeter.

She reached out to right it. So did he. And this time, when their eyes met, he wanted them to go right on meeting. Like maybe forever. He studied her while she studied him right back, and when he spoke, it was almost like talking with his old friend again. "You're right about Zeke. And about me. And the faith thing you called me out on."

She opened her mouth to speak, but he shook his

head. "I've messed up. I've done good things, too, but I'm not afraid to own up to my mistakes. I did wrong by you years ago, and I've never forgiven myself for that. All this time, it's sat there, niggling me, and I wasn't man enough to come to you and say I'm sorry for letting things get out of hand. If I'd been a stronger man, you wouldn't have been put in that position. It was wrong of me, and I apologize, Liz. Please forgive me." He wasn't sure what he wanted her to say, or what he expected, but his action was thwarted by a really cute kid.

"Dad?" Zeke bounded out the side door with all the enthusiasm a new day had to offer. "Miss Corrie said I can carry a special thing for Uncle Sean's ceremony, like a real important thing with his name on it! Isn't that awesome? I've got to practice marching right now!" He flew down the stairs, picked up a stick, and with the stick held high in front of him, he began a solemn march across the gravel, back and forth.

"That's perfect, son." Heath turned back toward Liz. She wasn't looking at him.

She was watching Zeke as if her heart and soul were bound in his actions. As she watched, a single tear left a pale gleam down her right cheek. "Liz."

He reached over to wipe away the tear.

She didn't let him. She swiped it away herself, and kept her attention on Zeke. "Consider yourself forgiven, Heath. There were two of us involved—"

"I was older…"

She interrupted him swiftly. "Regardless. Plenty of blame to go around. But thank you for your kind words."

She slipped off the swing and tucked the laptop beneath her left arm. "What about Zeke?"

Her quick and almost curt reaction wasn't what he wanted, but it was probably what he deserved. He stood and answered her question. "I'd consider it a real favor if you'd help keep an eye on him with me. He's already told me that he loves Rosie-Posie but he's never going back there because he likes it when his Lizzie takes care of him. So that's going to be an interesting hurdle to handle in a few weeks' time."

"It won't be that huge a hurdle." She indicated the marching boy with a quick glance and a soft smile, a smile that made Heath wish there was room for him in that smile, too. "It's not like I'm going anyplace, so it doesn't have to be a standoff. It can simply be a change of venue."

"How'd you get good at this?" He motioned toward Zeke. "Knowing how to handle kids, how to work with them. It doesn't come naturally to everyone."

"That's easy." She looked at him this time, the trace of tears gone. "I watched Corrie raise Charlotte and Mel. I saw her take them under her wing, two little girls who would have no memory of their mother, and she just helped them blossom into the amazing women they are today. A part of me has always wanted to be like Corrie. Strong. Courageous. Invincible."

"Well, it works. You sure are good with him." He reached out and drew the screen door open for her. "I'm grateful, Liz. When I'm not being a jerk."

She wanted to drink in the scent of him. Soap-and-water fresh, nothing fancy. Cotton, just washed. A few hours into the rising heat of the day and that would change, but for now it heightened her senses.

"How about some breakfast, buddy?" Heath called back to Zeke as he held the door wide.

"With my Lizzie? Yes!" Zeke tossed his stick along the edge of the steps and climbed the stairs quickly. "Cookie said he was making oatmeal, and I don't even like it one little bit, but I think he was teasing because you know what I smell?" He laughed up at them, grabbing a hand from each. "Pancakes! With chocolate chips, I think!"

Zeke's hand gripped hers. Heath was holding his son's other hand, and here they were, joined by a child like they were so many years ago, young lovers, impetuous, not looking down the long road of life.

It shouldn't feel right, but it did, as if the second chance she never thought she'd wanted lay here, right here, in the hills of Western Idaho.

Was she being silly?

One glance toward Heath said maybe not, because he was noting their joined hands, too. And smiling.

"I'm so starvin'!" Zeke pulled them forward, then released their hands. "I'll race you to the kitchen!" He darted off, knowing he wasn't supposed to run in the house, but the pancake-scented air was too much of a draw.

Her hand felt suddenly empty, holding nothing but air, and just as she realized that, Heath's hand covered hers. Clasped it. And then he drew it up gently. "My hand remembers your hand, Lizzie. Like it wasn't all that long ago. Like it's here and now."

He'd asked for forgiveness moments ago. Not for abandoning her, but for creating a child with her. Did he not understand that of the two, being forsaken was far worse than being loved? Maybe to him it hadn't been true love. She'd learned that men often speak of love when what they wanted was a physical relationship. And Heath, for all his wonderful strengths, had given up on faith. That was a deal breaker, right there.

She withdrew her hand gently. "Our here and now is a whole different thing, though, isn't it? We've grown up. Moved on. But for an accident of timing, we would have no idea what the other one was doing at this point. It's good that we still work well together," she went on, but then she hooked a thumb in Zeke's direction. "Over most things." She tucked the computer under one arm and picked up her coffee with the other. "I think I'll catch up on things at the barn. Check and see if our little friend has made a reappearance."

She started to move off, but Heath braced a hand against the wall, blocking her in. "What if the timing isn't accidental?" He didn't give her much space, and right then, gazing up, space was the last thing she wanted. "What if this is our destiny, Liz?"

Liz didn't believe in destiny. She believed in faith, in choices, both good and bad. After a lifetime filled with broken promises, she'd learned that actions spoke way louder than words, and Heath's actions said two things: he'd loved his wife and his beautiful son, and he'd been able to disregard their baby as an inconvenience. So be it.

That might be a maturity thing, or a character flaw, she wasn't sure which, but she was sure of one thing: she never wanted to take a chance on it again. "In a life rife with coincidences, this is simply another one, Heath. Let's not make it more than it is, okay?"

She moved by him, greeted the incoming stockmen with a smile and walked toward the stables.

"So what did you two do today?" Heath broached the question carefully so that Lizzie wouldn't feel like he was checking up on her that night.

Zeke hugged him around the legs and pointed toward the ranch driveway. "We took flowers to Rosie-Posie, we saw baby Jo-Jo and we gave out papers to a lot of people in their mailboxes and we hope we don't get in big, deep trouble. Is that right?" he called to Lizzie across the farmyard driveway.

"That is one hundred percent correct. And we practiced rhyming words and numbers and letter sounds and fishies in the creek and habitats. And mucked stalls and watched for signs of labor and saw none."

"Dad." Zeke reached up to be held and Heath hauled him up, into his arms. He was getting big for this, but Heath wanted to grab every chance he could to show the boy his love. Growth and independence would make this a no-deal soon enough. Too soon, Heath decided as Zeke did that smushy face thing he liked so well. "Did you know that everything has a habitat thing? Like our house and our farm is our habitat thing, and for fish it's a water thing, and for toads it's a shady thing."

Heath tested the boy's understanding with a question. "What does habitat mean?"

"It's where things live, silly!" Zeke crowed that he knew something his father didn't. "So where we can live is our habitat thing! Isn't that so cool? I think God makes it that way on purpose, don't you think so, my Lizzie?"

"Absolutely. He's pretty smart, that God."

"And like when it gets really cold out, I can put on a coat. And some mittens."

"That's adapting. That means you can change your behavior to fit the situation and make the best of it."

"So God made us so we can change!" Zeke bumped knuckles with Heath. "That's like so perfect!"

"It's hard to argue his logic." Heath said the words softly, and when Lizzie leaned forward to rub noses with his son, a longing gaped open inside the father. A longing so deep and wide, he wondered how he hadn't noticed it before.

"It is, therefore I won't argue because Zeke Caufield is an amazingly smart little boy."

Zeke laughed and leaned forward from Heath's arms. He grabbed Lizzie in a hug, and there they were, meshed together, him, Lizzie and Zeke, in a group hug he hadn't sought, but thoroughly enjoyed. "So what were you guys putting in mailboxes, therefore breaking federal law?"

Liz looked downright guilty. "I know we're not supposed to do it, but I couldn't think of another way right now, at least not until I get an email list of neighbors."

"And you need this because..."

"I think the best way of facing the town's troubles is raising awareness and opening the conversation."

"Isn't that what tonight's meeting is for?"

Zeke spotted the growing kittens near the first barn and squirmed to get down. "Dad, I'm gonna go play with the kitties. My Lizzie says it's one of my jobs on the ranch, 'kay?"

"Very okay." He set him down and watched as Zeke

raced across the gravel. The kittens were bigger and faster than they were a few weeks prior. And instead of running from the boy, the kittens chased toward him to play. "They're not crazy cats anymore. When did this happen?" he wondered out loud.

"We play with them every day, at least two times, so they won't go feral," Lizzie answered. "And I think Mrs. Hathaway needs a kitten. She mentioned it when we stopped by her place."

Old Mrs. Hathaway was an eccentric and fairly grumpy widow whose husband had governed a big spread of land north of Pine Ridge Ranch. The elderly woman lived in a decaying mansion-styled house a little closer to the Payette National Forest. He didn't know her, but then, he didn't know much of anyone if he didn't see them at church services. And it wasn't like he stayed to talk. Not with so much work to be done.

"She mentioned a mice problem, and I told her we've got kittens here. Would you have a problem with her taking one or two?"

"Anything that cuts down rodent populations is all right by me. How did you run into her?"

"She was getting the mail when we pulled up to leave a flyer about the memorial service. She didn't look well and we helped her back up to the porch."

"Then we took her some food," said Zeke from his spot with the kitties. "She said that was a—" He struggled for the word, then aimed his attention to Lizzie. "What did she say?"

"It was a thoughtful thing to do."

"Oh, yeah!" He grinned. "So that was nice. Wasn't it, Dad?"

"Real nice." He tipped the brim of his cowboy hat up slightly. "Mrs. Hathaway isn't exactly hurting for money as far as I know. She's kind of a recluse…"

"Lot of that going around these hills," said Lizzie, and he couldn't deny it.

"She was hungry? Like for real?"

"I don't think she's healthy enough to cook for herself. Or maybe it's a strength thing, because her appetite was solid. But she's thin and seems lonely."

"I haven't seen her at Sunday services."

"And I don't expect anyone's been checking on her." Sympathy brought her brows together. "That's the worst part of this town decline, Heath. No one's checking on anyone. How sad is that?"

It was sad. Sadder yet was needing Lizzie to point him in the right direction.

"I think I like this little fellow the very best, Dad!" Zeke's enthusiastic callout broke the moment. "Maybe orange kitties would be best in our barn habitat!"

"Orange rocks." Lizzie started to cross toward the barn as Rosie and Harve walked their way, pushing an old-style buggy, the image of a happy family.

He wanted that, he realized as they drew closer. He hadn't thought of the option in years, but now, with Lizzie on the ranch, making a difference in Zeke's life and his, he didn't just think about it.

He longed for it.

Harve was beaming.

Rosie looked happy. So happy. And when the baby peeped a tiny sound from the buggy, Lizzie came back their way. "Is this her first walk?" she asked, smiling.

"Her very first." Rosie reached in and lifted the tiny girl. "We wanted to show her the beautiful ranch on which she lives. How blessed we are to be part of all this, to be here, in America. To have this new beginning."

The baby shut her eyes tight against the light. And then she brought one perfect and tiny fist to her mouth in a move he remembered like it was yesterday, from the time he and Zeke had fumbled their way through those first grief-filled months.

"We wanted her first walk to be over here because we wanted to ask you a question." Harve directed his attention to Heath as he laid an arm around Rosie's shoulders. "We would like you to be godfather to Johanna. It would honor us greatly if you would accept this. Sean gave us the opportunity to work here, and you have worked side by side with me and Aldo from the beginning. It would be our pleasure to have you stand with us at her christening."

"Not Aldo?" Heath was pretty sure his voice might have squeaked in surprise because this was a big deal. "Will his feelings be hurt?"

"Aldo is in full agreement," Rosie told him. She adjusted the baby to her shoulder and rocked her gently. "He is Harve Junior's godfather and we would all like you to be a guiding force in our daughter's life. My sister Amina is coming midsummer. She will be Johanna's godmother, so we'll have the service then."

A godparent.

Never had he been asked to do such a thing, nor had he considered it, but he accepted the offer quickly. "I'm the one who's honored," he told them. He thrust out a hand, then gave Harve a half hug instead, thumping him on the back. "I'm so happy for you guys, so yes, I'd love this. Thank you for asking. For thinking of me. Just—" He was blabbering, but he couldn't seem to stop. "Thank you."

"Rosie-Posie, the kitties are nice now? See?" Zeke waved from his spot near the barn. "We're making them nice so they can find happy homes to live in. Isn't that a great idea?"

"It is, my friend." Rosie smiled his way, but kept the newborn away from the kitties and grubby hands. "It is the best of ideas. Yours, I take it." She addressed Lizzie and smiled when she nodded. "It is good for this little man to have new influences in his life. I regret that our home has been so busy with babies this past year that I have not been able to do things I would like to do with Ezekiel."

"He told me about the twins. That's a lot to handle."

"Their mother has much conflict with the world. With her family. There is no love between Valencia's mother and Valencia, so she is no help with those precious babies." Concern darkened Rosie's eyes. "Valencia speaks of moving away, then staying, then moving. But where she would go, a single mother with two in arms, we do not know." She exchanged a look of worry with Harve. "So we pray. We watch those babies and we pray. For now they are with a friend as I recover. But then, who knows?"

The baby squirmed. She opened her mouth in a soundless cry that would not be soundless for long.

Rosie tucked her back into the buggy. "We shall walk with swifter feet, I think."

Heath watched them go. The sounds of Zeke and the kittens gave a sense of normalcy to an abnormal situation. "I had no idea things were like that. Valencia's situation with her mother."

"There's a lot we don't see when we are so focused on one thing." Lizzie jutted her chin toward the town. "Can it be fixed? Or is it too late? That might be something you and the other bigwigs around here need to ask yourselves."

"I'm not a bigwig," Heath protested, but when she indicated the beautiful spread of Pine Ridge with a quiet look, he rescinded the words. "I'm not some great community leader, Liz. I'm a cowboy who was raised by a drunken father and a mother who disappeared a long time ago. I'm not exactly a model citizen."

"Then you'd better hone your skills, or you'll have no community to speak of. And I don't see that as a great way to raise your son. Do you?"

She walked away, leaving him with more questions than answers while Zeke played nearby.

His son.

Baby Johanna.

Valencia's babies.

What would life be like for these sweet youngsters if everything fell apart around them?

Dude, it's already fallen apart. The question is, can it be put back together? Is there enough left to work with?

As Zeke squealed laughter at kitty antics, reality hit him square. If the entire town dissolved, could he justify raising his son here? Should he? Was the ranch enough?

That thought sobered him further.

He didn't like spending time going to stupid meetings or blabbing about change. But instead of being a reluctant participant, he'd go to the evening meeting with goals in mind. How to approach the state government to reconsider the grazing rights issue...and how to help the town recover.

Making himself part of the town could be a good first step. He only hoped it wasn't too little, too late.

"Well, go big or stay home," drawled Jace about four hours later. He shot a grin toward Heath. "Committee chairperson? And you said yes?"

"Only because I know I've got letter-writing help on hand," answered Heath. He looked at Liz through the rearview mirror. "If the offer still stands."

"It does. And it was nice to meet all those farmers and ranchers. But almost no one from town, even though these problems have an effect on all of us."

"The town's pretty empty," offered Heath.

Jace turned her way. "The town had more people living in it when I was growing up here. They've torn down a few old houses and boarded up some others. It could use a facelift, for sure, but with no one to live in the houses, what would be the point?"

"My sister will see the point," said Lizzie. She jotted a note into her phone. "Melonie sees potential in the simplest things. So what aspects of a town do we need? For survival?"

"Jobs." Heath spoke first. "If there are no jobs, there is no survival."

"How do we create jobs out of nothing?" asked Jace.

"Well only the good Lord can do that," answered

Lizzie, but she made another note. "Stores. Shops. Services. Church renovation."

"Lack of investment capital," replied Heath. He sounded flat. "Who wants to invest funds in a high-risk venture with little potential?"

"No one," answered Jace, but Lizzie made them think with her next statement.

"You're talking like men."

The two men exchanged blank looks.

"You've got to get to the heart of the matter. If people have reason to love a town, they fight for it. It's not about opportunity only. It's about emotion. Compassion. People helping people."

"Where was she ten years ago?" wondered Jace. "Because we might have had a shot then."

"We've got a shot now," she replied. "You should have seen people's faces when Zeke and I brought the flyer around about Uncle Sean's memorial. If you get to the heart of the matter, you get results. That's all I'm saying."

"It will be a wonderful memorial." Heath met her gaze once more. "And we're grateful that you and Corrie have taken it on. But I don't know how you turn a one-day prayer service into a movement."

"It's real nice of you and Corrie to do this, Lizzie." Jace turned and smiled her way again.

They didn't see the potential.

Lizzie did.

She and Corrie spent the next two weeks working and chatting with people. She supervised two more foals and kept the stray dog's food dish full. On rainy days she tucked it beneath a covered bench to keep the food dry, and by the end of the two weeks, the little dog seemed stronger. Still a mess…but rounder, and less furtive. Corrie proved to be a great emissary and Zeke got to know the layout of the town. The current lambing season was quieting down, in time for haying season to begin as the sun sloped higher in the northern sky.

The last Sunday in May was Reverend Sparks's final day on the pulpit. A subdued group of people filled the church. Before the opening prayer he gazed around the church, from person to person and smiled. "If we'd gotten this kind of turnout more regularly, we'd be staying open!"

Some folks squirmed, but most offered wry smiles, and when he completed the service, he shook hands, one by one, outside. When he got to Lizzie's hand, he held it a little bit longer. "You're beginning to make a difference, Miss Fitzgerald."

"Call me Lizzie."

His smile deepened. "I'll see you tomorrow for the memorial service, and I want to thank you for asking me to officiate. It is an honor to stand tall at a military service. My dad served. And my brother. It means a lot to our family."

He squeezed her hand lightly, and moved on to the next person.

Zeke grabbed her other hand. "Are we baking the cakes today? For real?"

"Cakes and shortcakes because Miss Corrie got a great deal on strawberries."

"I love them so much!"

So did Lizzie. "And you can be our kitchen helper, okay? Although…" She withdrew her phone as her app signaled. "Well, it might be just you and Corrie and Cookie in the kitchen. It looks like we're having foal number five today." Corrie had just joined them and Lizzie held up the app. "I'm abandoning the kitchen in favor of the foaling stall."

Corrie accepted that like she accepted most anything. "No matter. Rosie is cooking, and Cookie and I can handle everything else with the help of our young friend here."

"And I'm making the cupcakes. Right? Because being a kitchen helper is a real important job."

"That it is," Corrie told him.

Mrs. Hathaway came their way and put out a hand to Corrie. "I don't believe I know you."

"I don't believe you do." Corrie took the old woman's hand gently. "Corrie Satterly. I'm helping out at Pine Ridge Ranch."

"Are you the cleaning lady?" Mrs. Hathaway asked.

Lizzie's cheeks went red. She was pretty sure her mouth dropped open and she was just about to leap to Corrie's defense, when Corrie laughed and tucked the old woman's arm through hers. "I do my share of that, for certain." She smiled and the old woman smiled, too. Kind of. "I help out with this and that and you know how it is with a barn full of men. They are always needing something, aren't they?"

"I expect there's truth in that." Mrs. Hathaway motioned to her car. "Do you mind walking an old woman over? My feet don't like to listen to my head the way they used to."

Corrie walked her over as Heath crossed the churchyard for Zeke. "I've never seen Gilda Hathaway in church. Or talking to people."

"She thought Corrie was our cleaning woman, Heath."

He winced. "Sean used to call Gilda an old bat. She didn't have a kind word to say about anything or anyone and holed herself up in that great old house and let it dissolve around her. He offered to buy some of her land and she offered to call the sheriff, so he wasn't too pleased with her. Having her come down to the service is about as out of character as you can get. Call me if you need help in the horse barn."

"You're cutting hay today."

"All this week. Watching the forecast and hoping nothing breaks down." He walked her to her SUV. "It was nice to have the reverend bless the farmers and ranchers. To hear him talk about the everyday people. The simple folk."

"Jesus didn't recruit prominent men to do his work, Heath." She leaned back against the car and gazed up at him. "Fishermen. Tradesmen. A tax collector, a repugnant profession even then." She smiled at his expression of agreement. "His father was a carpenter. His friends and followers worked with their hands. When you talk about not being a community leader, you're wrong. You're exactly the type of leader Shepherd's Crossing needs. I'm just hoping you'll turn out to be one of many."

"It's not a one-man job, that's for sure."

"Which is why we reach out to others." She opened her car door. "It's a start."

"It is." He glanced around at the number of people still there, saying their goodbyes to the pastor. "Because

I've never seen this many people darken the doors of this church. Not even on Christmas and Easter."

"Sometimes the greatest good comes out of the worst circumstance. See you at home."

At home.

He watched her pull away and realized what he wanted. What he needed.

He needed her. He needed her by his side, keeping him focused, keeping him grounded.

He'd loved her as a young man. Watching her car pull away, he realized he loved her now, too.

The aged pastor was still shaking hands.

His gentle words of blessing had touched Heath's heart.

He thought about that as Zeke scrambled into his car seat in the truck and fastened his seat belt.

Was there a God for real? Did He exist? Did He have a heart for humankind, the way the pastor said? Or was it all silly feel-good talk to keep people in line, like the easygoing sheep, one plodding after the other, rarely thinking for themselves?

He didn't know, but seeing the light of faith in Lizzie's eyes and Corrie's bearing, for the first time in a long time, he wanted to know.

"Dad. I'm so 'cited about today, I'm so 'cited to be a kitchen helper with Miss Corrie and my Lizzie!" Tangible joy lit Zeke's face. "And then I get to march with my plaque thing tomorrow! I will be the best marcher, ever, Dad. The best!"

"I know you will, son." He aimed a smile at his beautiful boy through the rearview mirror. "And I can't wait to see it."

"Me, either!" The boy wriggled with all the anticipation of youth. "And my Lizzie will be so proud of me." He grinned again, and Heath saw what was missing. What had been missing, for so long.

He'd grown up without a mother, and that emptiness had left a gaping hole in so much of what he did. Zeke had no memories of a mother, of that softer side of encouragement. The warmth. The glee.

And Lizzie had grown up the same way, her mother gone far too soon. But she'd had Corrie's love and devotion. The strength and wisdom of a good woman, guiding all three girls along the way.

Better than anyone, Lizzie would be able to lovingly accept his son as her own.

His thumb went to his empty ring finger, and this time it didn't feel naked. It felt right, like it was supposed to be that way.

Anna would want him to move on. He knew that. She'd want what was best for their son and for him, and what was best for them was Lizzie. Now he needed to do whatever it took to convince the lady in question.

She wanted faith, hope and love. His job was to make sure she got all three.

Chapter Thirteen

A small army of vehicles snaked their way up the Pine Ridge Ranch drive Memorial Day morning. Car after car worked their way toward the barnyard, then parked along the barn's edges as if finding a spot along a small-town street. As the minutes ticked closer to ten o'clock, the yard and the graveled drive filled with people. More people than Heath thought lived in a five-mile radius.

"About time someone's doing something to remember this man." Gilda Hathaway came forward. She'd looked unhappy when he first met her a dozen years before. She looked just as unhappy now. "I had my differences with Sean Fitzgerald, but then I've had my differences with most everyone. Where will this begin? Here?" She indicated the grassy slope. "In the house?" She swept the steps a fierce look, then brought it back to Heath. "In the barn?"

There was no time to reply because a somewhat hunched older gentleman offered his hearty hello as he came up beside her.

"I met Sean some thirty years back," he said, after

greeting Gilda and Heath. "That was when he first come to these parts, and while I'm sorry the men in the hills can't be here, I wanted to come and pay my respects." His voice rasped as if short on air, but his eyes gleamed with gentle wisdom. "Sean wanted this place to sit up and take notice, and we won't ever forget that. Not all wanted to listen and he wasn't a time waster."

Heath understood the truth in that. Sean valued time and industry.

"He gave out his share of good advice, too," the old fellow continued, "and I wasn't afraid or too proud to take it." He offered a gnarled, arthritic hand to Heath. Would it hurt the old-timer to shake his hand? Heath had no idea. Using a gentle touch, he accepted the hand with care.

"Name's Boone Webster," the aged man told him. Shocks of gray hair peeked out from beneath a cowboy hat that had seen better days two decades back. "I spent my share of time on a lot of farms and ranches in my day. When my hands worked."

"Boone's old but he makes a mean pot of venison stew," Gilda announced to anyone who would listen, and by that time, there were a few dozen folks closing in on them. She didn't break a smile, but she seemed almost approving, and Heath was pretty sure the old-timer blushed. "He's got a heart for doin' good, for all the good that's done him."

"Now, Gilda. You said you wouldn't fuss today," Boone reminded her in a gentler tone than she probably deserved. "Today we're respecting the dead and rejoicing the living. Remember?" He nodded across the yard and the old woman followed his look to a group of locals. Ben, Jace, Aldo and a few other ranch hands rounded out the group.

"I remember, all right."

"Well, good."

"Glad to be here, Heath!" called one woman as Gilda and Boone moved on.

"Harve, good to see you! Congratulations on your new daughter!" Blake Melos's younger sister had spotted Harve and Rosina coming their way.

Seven old men came in military uniform. Three of them unfurled flags, and three others carried long guns.

Folks were greeting one another all around him, like a potluck gathering, and when Eric Carrington and two of the other big landowners joined the group, Heath saw the brilliance in the moment. Lizzie's brilliance.

He turned as she and Corrie approached the porch stairs. "You reached out to all these people to put this together."

"Zeke and I informed people of the date and time, with a message about Sean's service and his love for Idaho. Their hearts did the rest."

"Theirs and yours." Gazing down, he glimpsed what the future could be like with this woman. He'd known it a dozen years before, but he'd been too young to understand the full implications.

Now he did. Lizzie didn't back down. She never gave up. She moved forward, saying what she meant, and meaning what she said.

"Are you the gal who put this in my mailbox?" A middle-aged woman came close.

Lizzie met her with a welcoming smile. "Guilty as charged."

"Well, it was like old times, walkin' out there and findin' somethin' to read again," the woman declared. "Like when the weekly arrived in the old days. I'd grab that up and read it front to back to see what was going on, especially in the winter. During rough snows it was about the only way to stay in contact with people before the snow plows got commissioned. I forgot how much I missed that until I found that paper in my box. And so well-written, too!"

Lizzie's smile grew. "I do love writing," she confessed to the woman. "And every little town could use its own paper, couldn't it?"

"Just to see what's what," the woman agreed. "Nothin' too big or fancy. Just enough."

Lizzie moved to the top step. She raised a hand, and when folks noticed, they got quiet. Zeke had slipped out the side door. When he spotted Lizzie, he moved her way and tucked himself beneath her left arm, close to her heart...and she snugged that arm right around him in welcome, confirming what Heath had figured out.

She belonged here. With him. With his son. In Heath's arms, day and night. Now his job would be to convince her of that.

"We want to thank you for coming today." She smiled at the gathering of people and they smiled right back. "I didn't know my uncle Sean, but the memories you emailed to us painted a picture of a wonderful man who left us too soon. While Uncle Sean wanted his ashes sprinkled on the land he loved so well, we decided that there should be a place to remember him." She pointed to a spot between the house and the road. "He liked shade, so we picked a favorite group of trees. He liked sun, so the garden faces southwest. He was born a Southerner, and while Southern plants don't transplant well to Idaho, woodcrafts do, so the benches in the garden are from Kentucky. But more than anything, my uncle Sean loved God and his country. He loved Idaho. The beauty of the valley and the majesty of the mountains. We see it here in his house. On this ranch. And in the kind of job he did every single day. From the battlefield where he risked his life to save others and here, where he opened the doors of opportunity to others." She smiled at Harve, Rosie and Aldo, then gave a slight pause before she went on. "Anger and division kept our family at odds a long time. Our hope is that this memorial today, on a day when we remember those who've served our country, becomes one that brings family, friends and this sweet town back together." She looked down. "Zeke. Are you ready?"

His son nodded and Lizzie handed him the plaque to carry.

The elderly honor guard took their places. Flags in hand, guns shouldered, they began the solemn walk to the driveway's curve.

When they got to the curve they veered left, toward a small copse of trees. There was no casket flag to fold. There were no ashes to scatter. But as they set the flags into newly installed flag holders, the freshly landscaped site took on a new meaning.

It wasn't the patch of flowers the women had tucked in front of a few trees.

It wasn't the two rustic benches inviting quiet repose.

With the flags in place, and a single bagpiper standing by while seven old fellows stood at attention, Heath began to see new possibilities out of old realities.

Reverend Sparks was there to lead them in prayer, but he'd asked Heath to say a few words in remembrance, enough to remind people who Sean was. What he meant to him, Ben, Aldo and Harve. To Jace and Wick. To so many.

He shifted slightly to the right and faced the crowd. "I'm keeping this short, like Sean liked," he promised. That garnered a few smiles. "But also to the point, because Sean respected that, too.

"Sean Fitzgerald was a good man. He took care of his own, and he reached out to find the best folks to do the job to make his dream come true. When you look around Pine Ridge, you can see he did exactly that. But he wanted more," Heath told the people. He met a few looks of surprise, then adjusted his meaning. "Not for himself. For the town. The people in it. He ran out of time, and he'd be the first to admit he might have back-burnered it too long. Today, I'd like to see that change." He met the eyes of Eric Carrington and two other wealthy landowners who were rarely seen around town. "Big spreads are nice, but if we don't work together to save this town, *our town*—" he stressed the words gently "—we could regret it. I think most of us have had enough regrets in our lives. Something to think on, anyway, while we pray together."

He linked hands with Lizzie on one side and Zeke on the other, and when the aged pastor led them in prayer, a flicker of hope began within him. Not a big, burning flame. Nothing so grandiose. Just enough to recall Lizzie's words, how everything had to begin somewhere.

Three old soldiers stepped forward. Aiming high, they shot seven volleys into the clear blue sky, marking the moment.

He hadn't had a lot of time to mourn when Anna died. There was too much to do, and Zeke did enough crying for both of them.

And he'd held back tears during Sean's final days and his passing because Sean had entrusted him with a huge job. Tears had no place at such moments. He didn't want his dear friend and mentor to spend his last earthly moments worrying about the ranch.

But today, tears slipped down his cheeks.

Not too many, and he dashed them away, but enough to know that maybe he'd grown a bigger, better heart somewhere along the way.

Lizzie hadn't known Sean, but she clutched a wad of tissues to swipe tears away as she watched the solemn military salute.

And then one lone bagpiper stepped forward to play "Amazing Grace."

The poignant notes of the familiar tune…with the row of aged men standing at attention, their love for God and country so obvious…

His throat choked up all over again.

Then Lizzie left him no choice. She leaned her head against his arm. He put his left arm around her shoulders and pulled her closer, then leaned down to kiss her forehead.

He didn't care if people saw.

He didn't care what some might think.

He thought of what she'd missed all her life, the love and care of parents who cherished her.

Could she be happy here?

She lifted watery eyes to his and the moment she did, he knew his answer.

Yes.

She could love him again. Would love him again. It was written in her heartfelt gaze, through the sheen of sorrow.

Zeke tugged on his sleeve. He looked down into a little face lined with worry. Zeke reached up and Heath scooped him into his arms.

He held him in one arm and Lizzie in the other, and for the first time in a long time, Heath was pretty sure everything was going to be all right.

Lizzie had just finished up in the stables when Heath came her way a few hours later. "Has everyone gone home?"

He nodded. "Even the few old timers that hung around, just wanting to chat. Wick drove the last couple home. And Lizzie…" He moved closer, and his look…

Lizzie was pretty sure she could get lost in that look if they shared all three blessings. Faith, hope and love.

"I wanted to thank you."

He laid strong hands on her shoulders in a gentle grip and held her gaze. "You saw what needed to be done and you did it. You reached out and people responded. Having this service today made a difference. It brought people together that I haven't seen in years."

"Let's not get carried away," she began, but he paused her with a finger to her mouth.

"Why not?"

Her heart began to beat harder. Faster.

He stepped closer. "Maybe just a little carried away." He smiled down at her as his eyes went from her eyes to her lips...and back again. "Like this." He leaned down and paused just shy of her mouth, waiting for her to close the distance.

Lizzie didn't make him wait. She rose up on tiptoe to touch her mouth to his, and when he gathered her into his arms, a rush of sweet emotion grabbed hold.

She'd loved him once. Probably never stopped. And now...

"Liz." He pressed kisses to her cheek, her ear, her hair. "You've made a difference, Lizzie. Not just to me, but to my son, to this ranch, and maybe to the town." He stopped talking long enough to kiss her again. Then he paused and dropped his forehead to hers. "I can't let you go again, Liz. Not now, not ever. I want you to stay here, with me. With Zeke. I want us to be a family, Liz. I want to court you like I should have done years ago."

She started to speak but stopped when a long, drawn-out whine pierced the air.

They both paused, listening.

The whine came again, fainter this time.

"The dog." Lizzie pulled back and raced for the door. Heath followed.

She didn't burst through the back door. She opened it carefully, not wanting to scare the animal. She crept out, with Heath behind her, and searched the pasture with her eyes.

The yowl came again, long and slow as if begging for help.

And then the dog appeared at the edge of the shed. She started their way, then paused, panting.

They navigated over the split rail fence and ran toward the dog. Normally it would have ducked away into hiding.

Not this time. This time the roughed-up pooch stayed right there, waiting.

Lizzie moved right in. Heath caught her arm. "An animal in pain might bite. Let me get her."

Lizzie pulled off the hoodie she'd had tied around her waist. "Wrap her in this. She's shaking, Heath."

He bent over the dog, wrapped her in the soft jacket and lifted her into his arms as if he carried something precious and beautiful. Not a sad, dirty, matted canine. "Let's get her up to the house."

"Not the barn?"

He shook his head quickly. "I think she's going to need some warmth and TLC, Lizzie. She's very pregnant and seems to be going into labor."

"She's having puppies?"

He nodded, grim. "Let's see if we can get her cleaned up some. There might not be time for that, though."

She moved up the steps ahead of him as his phone alarm went off. The dog jumped in his arms, frightened by the sudden noise. He held her close while Lizzie drew a bath in the laundry room sink.

His phone buzzed again. He frowned, hit Decline, and helped hold the weak dog as Lizzie sluiced warm water through the nasty fur. When the dog let out a yelp, Lizzie put the hand sprayer down. "Let's let her rest now. We got the worst of it. Are there flea meds in the barn?"

"Yes. Good thought. Cookie would not approve of fleas in his work area. I'll have one of the men bring them in." He held up his phone in apology. "The meeting that Carrington scheduled is today. It's in fifteen minutes. I don't know how long I'll be, but I know he's got an early flight back to the East Coast." He looked from her to the dog and back. "I don't want to leave you with this, but I don't want to miss this chance to talk with these guys, either."

"Strike while the iron's hot," she told him. "You go and figure out what can be done to help the town and—"

The back screen door slapped shut and Zeke barreled their way. He skidded to a stop and plugged his nose. "Something is really smelly around here." He looked from his father to Lizzie, then spotted the wet dog. He moved closer, intrigued, but didn't let go of his nose. "That is a weird dog, my Lizzie."

"A sick dog," said Heath. He bent low. "I don't want you to go near her, okay? We think she's going to have babies."

"Puppies?" His voice pitched up. His eyebrows did, too. "In the house? We never have puppies in the house. I can't even believe that we're going to have puppies in the house."

Cookie had followed him through the door and when he cleared his throat with meaning, Lizzie was pretty sure he couldn't believe it, either. She put a finger to her lips and indicated the worn-out dog with a look.

Zeke clapped a hand over his mouth. "I forgot to use my inside voice." He made a face of regret. "Maybe we should just whisper around the doggie, right? Like this." He whispered so softly that Lizzie didn't have a clue what he was saying.

"I think just a soft voice works. We want her to get used to our voices, so she's not afraid to come into the house."

"Can we keep the puppies? Like here, with us and we can have a dog just for me?" Hopeful, he peered up at his father, but Heath shook his head.

"Zeke, I can't answer that right now. I don't know how this will all turn out. She's not healthy. She's been neglected a long time, so things might not go okay with the puppies. Let's wait and see, okay?"

Zeke's lower lip stuck out. "'Cept when you say wait and see it means no, Dad. It always just means no." He folded his arms and stood stubborn as a mule in a stare-down with his father. "I don't know why I can't have one animal for me when you have like a gazillion all over the place."

Heath's phone buzzed once more. He made a wry face and put the phone away. "On that note…" He bent and kissed Zeke's forehead. "Be good. We'll discuss this later. I've got a meeting to go to. If it's all right with Lizzie, you can help with the dog, but you've got to keep your voice soft, okay? This dog isn't used to people and she sure isn't accustomed to busy little boys." He aimed a look at Lizzie, over Zeke's head. "I'll be back as quick as I can."

"Corrie's on her way back from Rosie's place. Her calm head in a crazy storm mentality is just what we need right now." She dropped her gaze to Zeke and Heath seemed to catch her meaning.

He nodded and left quickly.

"Can I pet her?"

Lizzie shook her head. "Not just yet. She might get nippy. But there is one very important, maybe most important thing you can do, Zeke."

His frown had deepened substantially as she spoke, but it disappeared when she said, "You can name this dog. How can we take care of a little mama dog with no name?"

He grinned, elated with this new assignment. "I don't even know what names to think of!" He kept his voice toned down and his smile in place, but he'd had a long day already and Lizzie knew that could change.

"Well, it's a girl, so we need a girl's name."

"Not Clifford."

She shook her head, because reading about the big red dog's antics was one of Zeke's favorite pastimes. "Definitely a boy's name. Let's go through the alphabet," she suggested. "Addie. Abby. Bria. Belle. Betsy."

"That's it!" Zeke whispered up to her, excited. "Betsy! I think it's the best name ever for a dog that's not so big, right? A name all her own."

Oh, Zeke…

So precious.

So sweet.

And needing a mother to love him. To laugh with him. Challenge him. The thought of that shared kiss didn't just sweep over her. It enveloped her, like a warm blanket on a chilled night.

Zeke yawned once, then yawned again. "I really wish I could just have a dog all my own. I would share him with you." He looked up at Lizzie. "I wouldn't hog him all by myself. But I could play with him a lot. He would be my friend."

Lizzie knew what he meant. The farm had several working dogs, but they weren't allowed to follow a little guy around and go on boy adventures, and there were no children around to play with. "I didn't have a dog, either. We'll talk to your dad later, okay? First, we have to make sure the puppies arrive and that they're all right."

"He'll say no. He says no to everything." Zeke stood, scowled and yawned again, clearly worn with the busy day. And when he got tired, he got grumpy.

"Why don't you take a rest," she suggested softly. "If the puppies start arriving, I'll come get you, okay?"

"I'm not even a little bit tired." He yawned again, punctuating the declaration.

She hid a smile. "You don't have to sleep, darling. Maybe just a rest and a cookie."

"All my favorite cookies are gone." He sighed as if the world had just crumbled around him. "Maybe I'll get one anyway."

"Okay."

She heard him in the kitchen, then the nearby bathroom. She stroked the dog's head, murmuring sweet words of comfort, right up until she heard the scream followed by a solid thud.

Her heart stopped, but the adrenaline punch pumped it right into high gear. As she burst through the door onto the side porch, her heart ground to a halt again because there was Zeke, the beloved boy, lying on the ground.

And he wasn't moving.

Chapter Fourteen

While one volunteer EMT cared for Zeke, a second one addressed the gathered crew of Pine Ridge Ranch. "We've called for the chopper," he explained. "We want him at a level-one trauma hospital, just in case he needs additional services."

"Additional services?" Lizzie gripped his arm. "What does that mean?"

"It's concussion protocol. Some are worse than others and having skilled hands and equipment on hand is clutch. I hear it coming." He pointed south as the sound of the chopper grew. "Let's get him transported and they'll take it from there. With a head trauma like this, we don't want to waste time."

Head trauma.

Zeke.

Lizzie's hands shook. Her fingertips buzzed.

"How far up the tree was he?" the medic asked, and Lizzie had to shake her head.

"I don't know. I was inside and he was going to take a rest. I heard the scream as he fell. I—"

Her voice was lost in the growing noise as the chopper descended into the fresh-cut hayfield nearby. Medics hurried their way, lugging necessary equipment at a dead run.

How had this happened in the space of a few short minutes?

"Zeke." Heath sank to the ground on the other side of the inert child. Anguish darkened his face while worry clouded his eyes.

She hadn't heard him arrive. The sound of his Jeep had been shrouded by the chopper noise.

The first EMT made way for the new arrivals. She approached Heath. "We've got concussion symptoms, Heath. Possibly a broken wrist. They're going to fly him to Boise."

"Am I going to lose him?"

Heath's voice held more than fear. It held the stark reality of life and death. Guilt and sorrow fought for dominance within Lizzie.

"Kids get concussions all the time," she told him. "But he needs care and observation, all of which they can give him. There's so little up here to work with."

They'd immobilized Zeke's little body on some kind of a board.

The sight of the child, lying still and quiet against the hard surface, shattered Lizzie's heart again. He should be kicking and screaming at the thought of being trussed up, but he wasn't.

He couldn't because she'd been too distracted to watch him properly.

"You'll have to drive to the hospital, Heath. There's

no room in the chopper. I already checked. Are you okay to drive?"

Of course he wasn't.

Tears filled his eyes. Worry darkened his face. The guy was totally over the top and it was one hundred percent her fault.

"I can drive." She reached for his keys, determined. She'd messed up. It was her job to see it through.

"I'll drive myself."

Lizzie started to protest, but Heath was already moving away. She chased after him. "Let me drive. You're in no condition to—"

"Tell everyone I'll call to let them know what's going on."

He started the engine, turned the car around, and was heading down the driveway as the rescue chopper roared back to life.

And then they were gone, the beat of the chopper blades leaving a dull thudding noise as the copter headed south.

She stared after the chopper, then Heath's car, then the helicopter again as it faded from sight.

She couldn't stay here, waiting. Heath might not want her with him, but she couldn't stay hours away while that blessed child fought for his life.

"Corrie." She turned as Corrie came up next to her. "I've got to go."

Corrie didn't pretend to hide her concern. "I know, Lizzie-Beth. I know. But do you think it's best, darlin'?"

"Twelve years ago I lay in a strange room, in a strange hospital, all alone while my baby passed away. I can't risk Heath being alone right now. He's got every reason in the world to hate me for risking his son," she admitted, "but I can't leave him there alone. I've got to go to the hospital, Corrie."

"Then we go." Corrie turned toward the house to collect what she'd need.

Lizzie jutted her chin toward the house. "The dog. Betsy. We can't leave her alone."

"I'd forgotten."

Lizzie hurried into the house to retrieve her keys and purse. "You stay here. Stay with her, okay?"

"But…"

"Please?" She grabbed her keys and tucked her purse over her arm. "Don't leave her to have those babies alone. Okay?"

"You'll be all right?" Concern shaded Corrie's tone, but understanding shone in her eyes.

"I will." Lizzie started the engine, then faced her sweet mentor. "Because I have to be."

"We will be praying for all. Drive safely."

"I will."

She turned south on the two-lane, determined. Heath might hate her for this tragic accident. She would deal with that as needed. But she understood the grief of facing loss all alone. No way was she about to let Heath… her hard-working, imperfect beloved…endure the same thing.

Zeke.

Heath's heart pounded as he hurried through the ER doors. He sprinted to the desk, gave Zeke's name, and raced down the hall once he had directions.

"And you are?" A middle-aged woman blocked his way to Zeke's curtained cubicle.

"His father. Are you his nurse?"

The woman pierced him with a look before she sighed, pretending offense. "I'm his doctor. You did well sending him by chopper even though it's a pricey form of taxi. We did a quick scan and see nothing really bad."

"But he's unconscious, isn't he?"

She drew the curtain back so Heath could see. "Sleeping now. And he might sleep all day. It's the brain's defense against injury so the body can concentrate on healing. He's got a broken wrist that we've splinted," she explained softly as she moved into the small, curtained room. "You'll need to have him see an orthopedic doctor in about three days. Do you have an ortho near your home?"

They had next to nothing near the ranch, he realized anew.

What if Zeke had died because there was no medical help nearby?

She must have mistaken his hesitation for confusion because she made a quick note before looking up again. "Never mind, I'll give you a few names. You might have to travel an hour or so but if there's ice cream involved at the end of the trip, it's not so bad. All in all I'd say he's a pretty fortunate boy."

"How is falling from a tree considered fortunate?"

She brushed that off as she wrote something else in a hand-held computer. "Having trees to climb. Places to explore. Things to do. These days too many kids are inside, playing on devices. Boys and girls should have adventurous spirits, shouldn't they? Unless we want to raise them in a bubble."

He stared at her, then Zeke. "Right now the bubble sounds good," he admitted and the doctor laughed.

"I bet it does, but this will give him stories to tell later on. It does bear caution, though. Once a kid has had a concussion, the likelihood for another one is elevated. Just keep that in mind, but don't curtail his curiosity because of it. I'll be back in a little while, but so far, so good. There's a very uncomfortable chair right here." She pointed to it and made a face. "Unfortunately that's all we've got available. The nurses will keep checking in."

"I don't care about the chair. As long as he's going to be all right, I'm fine."

The doctor left. Five minutes later, the curtain opened again. He looked up, expecting to see a nurse, but it wasn't a nurse.

It was Lizzie.

She stood at the curtain's edge, watching Zeke, then winced when Zeke winced. "How is he?"

"The doctor said he's going to be fine. But he might be sleeping here for hours." He stood up and crossed to her. "Did you drive here on your own?"

"Like you did. Yes."

Because he'd been too crazed to have her drive along. What was the matter with him? "I should have just brought you with me," he told her. "I wasn't thinking. All I could think of was that chopper, whisking my boy away and no one would be here to greet him. None of his family, that is. So I rushed away, but we should have come together. I'm sorry."

"It's all right." But it wasn't all right, because it was her responsibility to watch the little guy and she'd failed. Failed miserably. "As long as he's going to be okay. Are you sure about that?" If she felt as guilt-stricken as she looked, she was feeling really bad right now, and that wasn't fair.

"Doctor's words," he assured her. "The EMT was right about the broken wrist. It will put a dent in his summer activities, but it's fixable."

"Good. Good." She reached out a hand to Zeke's shoulder. Tears filled her eyes, and a few slipped over.

"Liz."

"I'm fine, really." She sniffled and he grabbed a few tissues from a small box and thrust them her way. "You know what they say. It's all right to cry after the emergency. Not during."

"You've never been much of a crier, Liz. Ever."

"Well, there's some truth in that. I suppose it depends on the situation," she finished as she swiped her cheeks. "This guy's worth a few tears."

"Aren't all kids?"

This time she raised her head. She stared at him as if he'd grown two heads. A flash of anger, or maybe disappointment, changed her expression, and then she faced him, dead-on. "Yes, Heath. All kids should be loved, cherished, cared for and mourned. Regardless of the circumstances surrounding them."

"Lizzie—" He started to move her way, confused, but she held up a hand. He stopped.

"Don't 'Lizzie' me. Where were you twelve years ago when your first son passed away? Where were you when I was in that wretched little hospital, trying to save Matthew's life, and failed? Where were you when I begged for help, for you to come and stand by me as I miscarried? Because I understand your love for Zeke, Heath. I really do. But where was this love when our tiny baby died? Because I sure could have used a dose of it back then."

Her words shell-shocked him.

He stared at her, unable to digest and believe what he was hearing. "You didn't end our pregnancy on purpose?"

She recoiled as if slapped, then started to move away.

He stepped in her way. "Liz, talk to me. Please. I had no idea that you didn't end the pregnancy. Your father and grandfather told me they'd sent you off to have it terminated so you wouldn't mess up your freshman year at Yale."

"And you believed them?"

He hadn't thought she could look more disappointed and disillusioned, but he was wrong. So wrong, because the minute she said the words, he realized the truth. Lizzie—his Lizzie—wouldn't have done such a thing, so why had he believed their lies? Because he was guilt-stricken over what happened?

He'd figure that out later. Right now he needed to talk to her. Sort this out. Beg forgiveness. "There was no way to get in touch with you. I tried. They'd taken your phone and no one would give me any information. Including Corrie. When Sean called me and offered me a job up here, I came north to start a new life. Liz, I'm sorry. So dreadfully, horribly sorry. I don't even know what to say to you right now to make this better because I can't make it better."

* * *

He looked penitent. And sad. Concern drew his brows together, and he looked as if he really cared, but she knew better. "I called you. When things went bad, I called you, over and over. You didn't answer and you didn't return my messages. I faced losing that baby, *our* baby, all by myself, and I lost a part of myself with him. No." She stepped back when Heath made a move to embrace her. "Don't touch me. I thought I knew you, Heath."

"Lizzie, you did. You do." He kept his voice soft to match hers as Zeke slept on.

"The young man I fell in love with would never have believed I could do such a thing. He would never accept the idea that I would terminate a life."

He started to move forward again, but she slipped to the side, and out of the cubicle.

She wouldn't let him see her break down.

She wouldn't let him have the chance to offer words of comfort now because she'd needed them *then*. She'd needed them so badly that her heart broke for lack of it.

She crossed the ER, then the parking lot, then climbed into her car.

She'd meant to stay with him while Zeke mended, but she couldn't. Not now.

He probably thought his excuse was understandable, but it wasn't. Weeks had passed from when she was sent away to when the pregnancy failed. He could have—

She steered toward the road as her conscience kicked into high gear.

Could have what? He was thrown out with nothing but the clothes he had. Where would he be now if Sean hadn't offered him help? And how did Sean know to offer that help?

Corrie.

She drove back toward the ranch, and used the two-hour drive to frame the questions she had for Corrie, starting with how Heath had gotten his job at Pine Ridge Ranch...

And why Corrie had kept it a secret all these years.

Chapter Fifteen

Corrie was on the side porch when Lizzie parked her SUV alongside the house. She exited the car, slammed the door and pounded up the steps. She faced Corrie, the only mother figure she'd known for over twenty-five years, and threw down the gauntlet. "You knew Heath was here all along, didn't you?"

Corrie faced her from the wide-seated rocker. She studied Lizzie for a long, slow moment, then nodded. "I asked Sean to give him a chance. I told him what happened and how your father and grandfather had thrown him out with nothing. No paycheck, no chance to gather things, no chance to say goodbye to you. Absolutely nothing, all because he had the audacity to fall in love with you. That's the kind of men they were, and Heath's own father wasn't one bit better." She sighed and folded her hands into her lap.

"Sean was different. He'd always been different. He took the money he'd inherited and invested it. Then he spent years working the land, working here, to build something unique. Something so far away from publishing that the wheeling and dealing of Fitzgerald News Company couldn't touch him. I figured if Heath had a chance to see what a real man stands for, it would be good for him. And it would give you a chance to grow up a little."

She'd made these decisions without telling Liz. Without giving her a choice. Pressure-cooker anger built inside her. "You never told me. And you never told him about Matthew. He thought I terminated the pregnancy on purpose."

Corrie didn't back down and didn't look one bit guilty. "Isn't that a thing in itself? That he'd believe lies like that back then? Because he shouldn't have believed them, Lizzie. I expect he knows that now."

"You could have told me where he was."

Corrie frowned. "I could have. But to what end? He needed to grow up. He needed to see what a good man does, how a good man stands by his family in thick and thin. You were giving Matthew up for adoption, you'd made that decision and it was a noble one. And then circumstances took it all out of our hands when that tiny fellow went home to God. And there isn't a day that goes by that I don't imagine sitting in heaven one day, rockin' that boy and telling him what a wonderful mother and father he had. Just in case he doesn't know it. I'll share Beulah Land with him and your sweet mama. May God forgive me my mistakes, but then the good Lord knows the reasons for them. And that's for certain."

"I needed him, Corrie," she pressed. "When that baby passed from me, I needed Heath there. With me. By my side. And you thwarted that." She couldn't believe the words as she said them, that her beloved Corrie, the woman who'd loved her all along, who'd come to her side when called, didn't tell her where Heath was.

Corrie stood and faced her. Regret and unshed tears marked her face. "You'd called him. You'd called him over and over and he didn't come. He didn't call back. And you were in such anguish and pain that I had to decide what was best for you. I couldn't help baby Matthew. And I'd done what I thought best and helpful for Heath, by having Sean offer him a job, but when he didn't have the courtesy to answer your phone calls or return your messages, I got angry. Angry at him for not making himself available the way he should have. Angry at him for putting you in that situation. From that day on I never contacted Sean or checked on Heath until we drove up this driveway. And that's the truth of the matter."

She stood strong and solid, a woman of compassion and commitment, a woman who'd stood by the three daughters in her care no matter what.

But the thought that one phone call might have changed everything soured Lizzie's heart. She turned and went down the stairs. She crossed the yard, entered the first barn and brought Honey's Money into the prep area.

She saddled her with quick hands and no mind to where she'd go or what she'd do. Just mind enough to know that she thought better on horseback.

She led the horse into the yard.

Corrie was no longer on the porch. No one was about. No matter.

She climbed into the saddle and let the horse walk an easy pace toward the ridge. Once they were in the mowed field, she let the mare have her head and they ran. They ran across the freshly mowed hay lot, across the lower ridge, wide and flat, until the ridge dipped down. She slowed the horse and followed the descent until she found herself in the middle of the failing town.

The old pastor was just leaving the church. He saw her on horseback and stared, surprised. Then he chuckled low and waved her over.

What choice did she have?

The last thing she wanted to do was talk to anyone, and yet the path had brought her here, into the center of town. She dismounted, caught the reins, and walked his way. "I didn't mean to startle you."

"It was a start, for sure," the old man laughed. "I haven't seen anyone ride a horse into town in years, and then it was scarce enough. There are hitching posts right over there. You see 'em?"

She turned and noticed the trio of posts up the road apiece. "An odd place for them, isn't it?"

"Not odd, considering the post office and general store used to stand right there. The Middletons have pictures of it, nothing all that grand, but solid like they used to build them. And Western-looking with a wide porch, all covered so the lady shoppers would be all right while the farmer husbands had to load grain from the back in the rain, snow and sun. They did right by the ladies, wantin' to take care of them first in those days. It's a cowboy way, and a good one."

He held a set of boxes in his hands. She tied Honey's Money to the hitching post and put out her hands. "May I help you, Reverend?"

"I won't say no," he told her. "I'm heading back to

my place." He motioned north. "Standin' in one place bothers my hip. Once it's in motion, it's right enough, but standin' still makes it act up."

"I don't mind a walk."

They walked side by side, toward the far end of town. "You said last week that you're retiring again, which means you retired before. Correct?"

"Twice." The admission seemed to amuse him. "I can't seem to stay still, and I hoped coming here would make a difference. To the town, to the people. It's been on a downward trend for a while, losing folks to other places, towns with jobs. I kept thinking that if we could just start the ball rolling the other way, and gather momentum, we could catch the remaining pieces before it all falls apart."

"But it didn't work out that way," she observed, and he turned her way quickly, surprising her.

"But it did!" he exclaimed, smiling. "Not in the manner I expected, but then that's the way of things, isn't it? The good Lord sees beyond the bends in the road while we humans see the straight and narrow.

"So it's working fine, don't you think?" he asked her and when she looked surprised, he angled his chin toward her, then the town. "You're here. You've got other family heading this way. You got Heath to meet up with the other ranchers in town, now there's a solid group of stubborn men determined to go their own ways. And I haven't seen attendance at church or a memorial service like we had this weekend, so something's working, young lady. Something filled with faith and hope, and I think part of that is you. And Miss Corrie that came along with you. When I heard that Eric Carrington took some time away from his fancy horses and cattle to talk with regular folks, that was a big step in the right direction from where I'm standing. Oh, there's change brewing, Miss Lizzie Fitzgerald. And you're in the thick of it. Now if we can have folks learn to forgive and forget. To move on and not hold grudges." He swept the faltering town a long, slow look. "Well, that's my prayer right there."

They paused outside the square, worn rectory, the last building at the north end of town.

"For a long time folks in the Crossing have been going their own way, not sharing words or the Word. God's word, that is, about loving and caring and sacrifice and forgiving. But you and the boy, going house to house, inviting folks in, well…"

A winsome smile deepened the crinkles edging his eyes. "You got it started, and I'm only sorry I won't be here to see it all change, but that will take time and a man my age doesn't take time lightly." He winked, still smiling. "My daughter's due to pick me up tomorrow, but I'm glad I got a chance to thank you for that nice service today. And for being here. It makes me see how there is a season for everything, like the Good Book says. Your season is upon us."

He shook her hand, and for a quick moment, she didn't want to let go because the old fellow's wisdom struck a chord within her. Loving. Forgiving. God's word.

She'd never considered that her messages hadn't reached Heath. Messages always got through, eventually. Didn't they?

Reverend Sparks moved to the house, just as the church bells chimed the six o'clock hour.

The last toll trailed off softly. A zephyr breeze lifted upper leaves in a rustling whisper. She breathed in clean air, with the bright blue sky above and beyond the rugged peaks of mountains.

Then she thought of that woman at Uncle Sean's service, so happy to get a bit of news, of how one small flyer had brought neighbors and friends together.

A town worth fighting for.

She turned Honey's Money around and re-mounted, studying the layout of the mostly empty buildings as she went by. As she scanned them, the potential opportunity gleamed beneath shoddy exteriors. Shepherd's Crossing was a chance to start fresh, and make a difference in another way she knew well: a paper. Simple, to-the-point good reporting to reconnect the small town to its near neighbors.

But first, there was a mother dog who needed love and attention and Lizzie was determined she'd get it. By the time she got the horse settled, light was fading, but the two-story ranch home glowed from within. And inside, Betsy was presenting the world with tiny reddish gold puppies, and Lizzie sat right there, alongside the whelping box Cookie had brought in from the barn, and softly cheered her on.

Chapter Sixteen

Zeke's overnight stay at St. Alphonso's gave Heath plenty of time to think. And then berate himself. And then think again. And in between all that thinking, he did some first-class praying, the way he had when he was a kid.

How had this happened? How had everything gone so completely astray twelve years ago? Lizzie had spent all that time thinking he didn't care enough to come to her. To help her. To be with her.

He'd have done anything to help her. Then. And now. She must think him to be the worst loser to ever walk the planet, and yet—

She didn't. She'd come to the ranch calm and gentle. Ready to move on. He'd been the angry one, the defensive jerk, and all because he believed the lies he'd been fed like a stray dog grabs morsels of food.

Shame bit deep. Real deep. And the doctor had been correct, the chair he'd bunked in overnight was about the least comfortable piece of furniture known to man. But today was a new day. His boy was recovering. And

Lizzie…well. One way or another he was going to convince her to give him a chance. To give *them* a chance.

"Your little fellow's going to be just fine," the doctor told Heath when she came into the cubicle to discharge them. "I've written down the name of that orthopedist in McCall. He'll set the wrist and cast it, and by midsummer Zeke will be right as rain. Everything was fixable, and that's a good thing."

Relief flowed through Heath as she handed him the discharge papers. He only wished his history with Lizzie could be mended that easily.

Zeke wasn't in the best of moods. When Heath had to help him with his seat belt latch because the boy's left hand couldn't maneuver the buckle, Zeke's lower lip stuck out. "I wish I never climbed that stupid old tree. It was a dumb thing to do and I'm never, ever, ever going to climb a tree again."

Heath saw the choice before him, plain as day.

He could agree with the kid and offer his son a measure of safety…

Or he could let Zeke grow up, encouraged to explore the world around him.

He chose the latter and kept his voice easy. "Hey, cowboy, climbing the tree wasn't the problem."

"It wasn't?" Zeke peered up at him, perplexed.

"Nope." Heath slid into the front seat and smiled at his boy through the rearview mirror. "Letting go was the problem. Next time you climb the tree, hang on tighter, okay? I climbed a lot of trees in my time, and it's a good thing for a cowboy to know. In case you get chased by a cougar or something."

The likelihood of that was about zero, but Zeke's

brows shot up. "So it's really good to know how to climb a tree?"

"On my honor." He pulled onto the road and considered his words as he drove north.

He hadn't been honorable with Lizzie.

He'd let things go too far, then he'd left. Sure, they'd tossed him out, but what if he'd stayed and fought for the right to be with her? What kind of difference could that have made?

Eric Carrington had told the rest of the major landowners that he thought their efforts to revitalize the town were too little, too late. He'd made his view clear at that quick meeting the previous day, and Eric could be right.

But did the same thing apply here? Could he make things up to Lizzie or was it too little, too late? The thought of her losing that baby all alone—

His throat choked and his gut clenched tight when he considered the years he'd spent believing the worst. What kind of a man did that?

He'd be the right kind of man this time. The kind she'd deserved all along.

He pulled into the driveway and parked the car. Corrie bustled out of the house. Relief brightened her dark features and a wide smile echoed his relief that Zeke was going to be all right. "There's our boy! And doesn't Cookie have all of your favorite foods waiting inside because we're that excited to have you back! How are you doing?" She bent low to ask the question as Jace and Ben hurried their way.

But no Lizzie.

"My arm hurts." Zeke climbed out of the car and

leaned against Heath's leg. He sounded tired. He looked tired, too. "And my head hurts. But not as much as yesterday," he added. Then his profile brightened as he pointed inside. "Did Betsy have her puppies?" he asked. "That's all I kept dreaming about in the hospital, a chance to see little puppies. Are they so very tiny?"

"Come see."

Zeke swung about when he heard Lizzie's voice and his face lit up when he saw her holding the back door open. "My Lizzie!"

Zeke raced her way, even though he'd been told no running for at least a few days. Obviously that didn't count where Lizzie was concerned.

He threw his good arm around her. She cuddled him as if he was her own, and Heath's heart thudded all over again. She'd never had the chance to hold their baby. Nurse him. Sing to him. Rock him. She'd never had a moment of that sweet time while he'd had the pleasure of Zeke by his side for years.

How bitter that must have seemed when she first arrived. And yet she'd shown nothing but kindness and caring to his son.

"You have to be quiet." She put a finger to her lips as Heath moved their way. "Betsy is tired, but she's being a very good mom and good moms like their babies looked after. So no loud noises, okay?"

"Okay." He whispered the word, but then pumped Lizzie's hand with his good one, clearly excited. "I can't wait to see them!"

They crossed into the laundry room. Betsy was stretched out on a thick, old blanket with a row of puppies nuzzling along her side.

"They are so very itsy-bitsy!" Zeke's voice started loud, then he reduced it, remembering. "I mean like the tiniest ever," he whispered, as if shocked. "Lambs aren't tiny like this."

"Much bigger," Heath agreed. He palmed his son's head. "All animals are different."

"They're so cute, but how come none of them have curly hair like Betsy?" Zeke asked as he squatted low. He began to look up and couldn't hide a slight wince.

Lizzie had squatted down alongside him. She saw the wince and smoothed a soft hand across his brow. "The curls will come," Lizzie assured him. "As they get bigger. You can have more puppy time later," she went on gently. "Go rest, and make Cookie feel good by sampling all the stuff he made just for you."

The big cook came up behind them just then. "Hey, little man. Welcome home." And when he gathered Zeke into his big, beefy arms, Heath realized something anew. Sean had built a community here on the ranch. People who cared and looked out for one another.

Now they needed to do the same for the town. But he didn't want to face that task alone. He wanted—

Lizzie smiled as Cookie carried Zeke into the kitchen to tempt the boy with culinary delights. Then she turned, realized Heath was looking at her, and the smile faded.

What could he say to bring the smile back? To bridge a gap that stretched so wide?

Wishing he'd practiced the words on the long drive home, he stayed in the doorway. "The puppies are doing okay? They look really good, Liz."

Chin down, she stroked Betsy with one hand. "These

four seem fine. There was one that didn't make it. So sweet. So perfect. But she never took a breath."

He'd lost pups from the farm dogs before. Lambs, too. And each time he felt like he'd failed them somehow. "Liz—"

Regret drew her mouth down. She released a softly drawn breath as she continued to comfort the dog. "I buried her beneath the roses. I thought it would be a good spot."

"A real good spot." He ventured forward, unsure what to say, but knowing he had to say something, to open the conversation about their tiny son somehow. He drew closer, close enough to see the light shimmering along strands of her pretty hair. Close enough that a hint of vanilla and spice came his way. And then he restarted the conversation the only way he knew how, with an apology that came way too late, but was necessary, nonetheless. "I'm sorry, Liz." He paused and took a breath around the lump in his throat. "I'm sorry we lost him. And I'm sorry I wasn't there for you when you needed me. So sorry."

He didn't say "her," like he would have if he was talking about the puppy.

He was talking about their son.

"I never got your messages," he went on. "That old phone of mine broke on the way north and I didn't bother replacing it for a few months. And they tried to load all my old stuff onto the new phone, but coverage up here wasn't all that great back then. Neither were the phones. It's no excuse, I know, but I don't want you to think I'd have ever ignored you. I'd have come, Lizzie. If I'd known. I'm just real sorry it all came down that way."

She took a deep breath and faced him, at long last ready to talk. "I am, too. My heart broke that day because there was absolutely nothing I could do, Heath. And I'd have done anything to save him."

A tear trickled down her left cheek. Then her right one. He reached out and caught the tears with his hand in a touch so sweet and gentle it made her want to cry more. Not less. But the time for tears was over. She took a deep breath and said what she needed to say. "I'm sorry it got all messed up. Sorry about all the lies and secrets. I hate that kind of thing. I think that's why I jumped at this opportunity so quickly. To get out of the offices and into a barn. Horses don't lie. They don't cheat. They don't steal. To run an operation like we've got here is such a total blessing after being surrounded by my father's crimes. So Uncle Sean's timing was perfect. In so many ways."

She'd tipped her gaze down to the dog, but now she locked eyes with Heath.

He moved closer to her. So close she could smell the remnants of hospital soap on his hands and sweet creamed coffee on his breath. "I want to make a home here, Heath. On this ranch. In this town. Maybe I'll buy one of those little bungalows in town and fix it up, sweet and simple. And I can be the eccentric spinster lady who writes a little paper once a week. Just enough to bring folks together."

"I like the staying part." He sat down next to her

as Betsy cared for her four busy babies. "But not the house in town."

"No?" She turned and met his gaze, and he was pretty sure her eyes twinkled into his. "Do you have a better idea, cowboy?"

He raised one hand up to caress her hair, her neck, her cheek. "I believe I do. And it involves a ring and a promise and a little boy who loves you already. But not nearly as much as I do, Liz." He took her mouth and kissed her lightly, then not so lightly. When he finally drew back, he left his forehead touching hers. "It's about us. And that's how I want it to stay. If you'll give me another chance, that is. I'd like to have the chance to court you properly."

"And quickly?" she wondered, smiling.

He laughed and kissed her again. "Quick works for me."

He pulled her into his arms for an awkward but beautiful hug, a hug she'd been missing for so long. Too long. "It sounds perfect to me, Liz."

She met his smile with one of her own, then leaned her head against his broad, strong shoulder as the sated puppies dozed off, one by one. "It certainly does."

Epilogue

Lizzie finished tacking tiny twinkle lights around the second front window while Heath and Zeke hung a festive ornament in each pane.

"I've never seen anything so pretty in all my life, my Lizzie!" Zeke started to launch himself into her lap, but Heath caught him.

"Gentle with Mom, remember? There's a baby growing inside her."

"And it's so tiny right now," Zeke acknowledged because they'd been talking about this for weeks. "But in the spring it will be big enough to get born and be my brother or sister!"

"Which is exactly why we're all gathering out here tonight," announced Lizzie as the rest of the family and friends began to gather in the great room. "Zeke is going to tell us if this baby's a boy or a girl by eating a cupcake. If the filling is pink, then the baby's a girl. If it's blue…"

"Then it's a brother!" Zeke ran in a circle, because that was the kind of thing brothers did. And when the entire family and a host of friends had gathered with glasses of punch to toast the newest Caufield, Zeke took a bite of the cupcake.

He stared at it, then held it up for everyone to see. "I'm gonna have a sister, just like Jo-Jo!"

"A girl!"

"Oh, Lizzie." Corrie didn't wait for others to have a turn. She grabbed Lizzie into a hug and held on tight. "I am so happy for you, my precious girl."

"I know." Lizzie hugged her back as Heath tucked an arm around her waist.

"We've got something else to say," he announced as Charlotte and Melonie drew closer to Lizzie.

"We've picked out a name for our little girl."

Everyone got quiet.

"We're naming her to honor the person who has stood by us, all of us—" Lizzie indicated Mel and Charlotte "—all our lives. In about four months you're all going to meet Coralee Caufield."

"You are naming that baby for me?" Corrie's eyes grew wide, then filled with tears. "You don't have to do that, you know. It's a fine name for an old Southern woman like myself, but—"

"It is the perfect name," Lizzie told her. "Stop fussing and be blessed. We couldn't name our little one after anyone better, and if she turns out to be a strong, gracious, faithful woman like her Grandma Corrie, then we'll be the happiest parents ever."

Tears slipped down Corrie's cheeks. Then Lizzie's. But before Charlotte and Mel could join in, Corrie stepped back. "Well, now, this is not the time for tears, Fitzgeralds! This is a time to celebrate so much good this past year." She reached back and lifted her little cup of punch and raised it high. "To new life. New chances. And to a baby, born in a manger, in a land unknown, I say Alleluia!"

A chorus of Alleluias rang out around them, and when Heath was finally able to grab a quiet moment with Lizzie, nearly two hours had passed. He put his arms around her from behind and laid his hands over their growing child. "Happy, Mrs. Caufield?"

"The happiest."

He kissed her cheek, then offered a sweet kiss to her mouth. "Thank you for making this the best Christmas ever."

She'd come to Idaho wanting to make the best of things, but never expecting to *have* the best of things.

But God knew. Through the winding and changing and uprising, he knew.

She leaned back against him, happier than she'd ever dreamed possible, then tipped her face up for his kiss, a kiss she wanted to enjoy forever as tiny lights twinkled around them. "The first of many, my love."

* * * * *

HILL COUNTRY REUNION

Myra Johnson

Remembering all the special pets whose unconditional love has made a difference in my life, and dedicated to the caring veterinarians who have helped to keep our pets healthy.

With thanks once again to my dear friend and Love Inspired Historical author Janet Dean for her insightful advice during the early planning stages of this story. You never fail to get me thinking in new directions!

My grace is sufficient for thee:
for my strength is made perfect in weakness.
—2 Corinthians 12:9

Chapter One

Saturday mornings at Diana's Donuts typically brought brisk business, but today had gotten just plain ridiculous. Must be the hint of fall in the late-September air, because Diana Matthews couldn't brew coffee fast enough, and the steady flow of customers had all but cleaned out the bakery case.

"Here you go, Alan, a half caf and a blueberry muffin. Sorry we ran out of crullers." With a friendly but frazzled smile, Diana handed Juniper Bluff's local insurance agent his change, then swiveled toward the kitchen. "Kimberly, how are those scones coming?"

"Five more minutes," came her assistant's shout.

A crusty farmer, one of Diana's regulars, plopped his empty coffee mug on the counter. "Di, honey, how about a refill?"

"How many times do I have to tell you, LeRoy? It's *Diana*." Her smile tightened as she poured. She'd never cared much for the nickname—or being called anybody's "honey"—at least not since the person who'd once used such endearments had vanished from her life.

"But, Di, your doughnuts are to *die for*. Get it?" LeRoy laughed at his own play on words.

She widened her grin to disguise an annoyed eye roll.

Her apron pocket vibrated with a call on her cell phone. The display showed her dad's number. "Ethan," she called to the freckled teenager who bused tables on Saturdays, "cover the register for me. I need to take this call."

While Ethan scurried around to help the next customer, Diana slipped into her office. "Hey, Dad, how's it going with Aunt Jennie?"

"All packed and ready to go. We should get to the care center around noon. Any chance you can meet us there?"

Diana's heart warmed in anticipation. Mom and Dad had driven over to San Antonio yesterday to move Dad's aunt into an assisted-living facility on the outskirts of Juniper Bluff. "I'll try, but we're crazy-busy today. On top of everything else, Nora, my part-time counter girl, called in sick."

"Uh-oh. Well, get there when you can. Aunt Jennie's been asking about you, and you know you're her favorite great-niece."

"Yeah, right," Diana said with a chuckle. "Only because I bribe her with cream-filled chocolate doughnuts." She peeked through the miniblinds to see how Ethan was faring. "Give Aunt Jennie my love, and tell her I'll see her real soon."

Clicking off, she hurried out in time to help Ethan fill an order for four lattes to go, along with the last two apple fritters.

"I'll take over here," she said. "Looks like some tables need clearing." As Ethan grabbed a dish tub and cleaning cloth, Diana gave her attention to the next customer.

"Mornin', Diana." Doc Ingram, Juniper Bluff's long-time veterinarian, slid some bills across the counter. "Need two regular coffees and—" he frowned toward the bakery case "—two of whatever you've got left."

"Sorry, we've been swamped today. If you can hang on a sec, Kimberly's about to bring out some fresh-baked cinnamon-raisin scones." Diana reached behind her for two ceramic mugs bearing the pink Diana's Donuts logo. "Who's the other coffee for?" She looked past the doc for a glimpse of his companion.

A familiar face beneath close-cropped brown hair grinned hesitantly back at her. "Hello, Di."

Both mugs crashed to the tile floor. Diana gasped and skittered backward as hot coffee splashed her bare ankles between her sneakers and jeans cuffs.

Kimberly had just stepped through from the kitchen with a tray of scones. "Diana, are you okay?"

"I'm fine." Teeth clenched, eyes lowered, Diana snatched a wet cloth from the workstation and swiped at her legs. No way could she risk another glance at the man standing next to Doc Ingram. It couldn't be. It simply *could not be* Tripp Willoughby.

Kimberly shoved the tray of scones into the display case, then grabbed a broom and dustpan. "You take care of the customers. I'll get this cleaned up."

Murmuring her thanks, Diana bent over the sink to rinse out the coffee-stained cloth, using those few moments to compose herself. After drying her hands, she squared her shoulders and turned. With studied slowness, she let her gaze drift upward to the face of the man she'd never expected to see again.

Concern etched the hard planes of Tripp's features. "Sorry for taking you by surprise like that. Sure you're okay?"

"Of course. My goodness, Tripp, what's it been—ten years? Twelve?" As if she didn't recall the exact day, hour and minute he'd told her it was over between them. Flicking at a wayward strand of hair, trimmed to shoulder length now instead of the waist-long braid she'd worn through college, Diana wondered if she looked as different to him as he did to her.

"Been a while, hasn't it?" At least he had the decency to show a little remorse. Shame-faced guilt would have suited the occasion even better.

One elbow propped on the napkin dispenser, Doc Ingram arched a gray-flecked brow. "What am I missing here? You two know each other?"

"We, um, met in college." With a shaky laugh, Diana edged away. "Let me try again with those coffees."

Kimberly had most of the spill mopped up. Their backs to the customers, she nudged Diana. "Lucy, you got some 'splainin' to do."

"Cool it, Kim. Go bake more muffins or something." After filling two new mugs, Diana carefully set them on the front counter. She smiled stiffly at Tripp. "First coffee and pastry is on the house. Care for one of our fresh-baked scones?"

"Thanks, but I'll stick with just coffee." He scanned the menu board behind Diana's head. "Unless I could have one of those Greek yogurts instead?"

Pursing her lips, she wondered when the guy who used to inhale junk food like it was going out of style decided to eat healthy. "Sure. Plain, berry or lemon?"

"Plain, thanks. Any chance you have soy milk for the coffee?"

"On the condiments bar to your right." Diana retrieved a yogurt from the cooler, then turned her attention to Doc Ingram. "How about a warm, buttery scone for you, Doc—or have you gone health-nut on me, too?"

A bemused look in his eye, the vet quirked a grin. "I'll take two, thanks. Need some carbs to tide me over for my farm calls."

"Great. Y'all find a table and I'll bring your scones right out." Diana took Doc Ingram's payment and handed him a receipt.

When another customer stepped up to the counter, it was all Diana could do to tear her gaze from Tripp's retreating back. She hurriedly filled a coffee order, then snatched two scones from the display case.

Kimberly had just returned from disposing of the shattered mugs. "You're looking a little freaked out. Want me to deliver those?"

"No—actually, yes. I think I'm getting a headache."

"Hope you didn't catch Nora's bug." Kimberly leaned closer and squinted, then wiggled her brows. "Nope, looks more like a bad case of blast-from-the-past blues. I'm warning you, soon as things slow down around here, you are telling me everything you know about our good-looking newcomer."

While Kimberly took the scones out to Doc Ingram's table, Diana made sure the other customers had been served. The steady flow seemed to have tapered off, so she took advantage of the lull to clean up the workstation.

And to eavesdrop. Even with all the other conversations droning around her, she had no trouble homing in on Kimberly's voice as the perky bakery assistant chatted it up with Doc Ingram and Tripp.

"So you're new in town?" Kimberly was saying. "Didn't catch your name."

"Tripp. Tripp Willoughby." His rich baritone was still as silky-smooth as Diana remembered. "Just moved here a couple days ago."

Oh, great. He was *living* in Juniper Bluff now? Stomach flipping, Diana squeezed her eyes shut.

"Tripp's taking over the small-animal side of my practice," Doc Ingram explained. "Now I'll be able to focus entirely on horses and cattle, like I've been hoping to do for a while."

"So it's *Doctor* Willoughby—cool!" Kimberly bubbled. "My little dachshund's about due for her yearly checkup. I'll be sure to make an appointment."

Diana scoured the coffee stains around the sink drain and hoped she hadn't flirted quite so overtly when her former high school classmate Seth Austin would stop in before he and Christina got engaged last year. Now they were happily married and expecting twins.

While Diana remained depressingly single.

Of your own choosing, she reminded herself. She hadn't exactly been dateless since things ended with Tripp, but no relationship since had made it past the superficial level.

She dared a glance across the shop. Kimberly had moved on from Tripp's table to pour coffee refills for other customers. Without other distractions, and without being obvious, Diana could observe the man who'd unceremoniously broken her heart the fall of her senior year in college—and just when she'd been so certain they had something special going on.

Apparently, she'd completely misread Tripp's signals, and everything she'd imagined about sharing a future with him was just that—all in her imagination.

Was it only Tripp's imagination, or was Diana staring a hole through the side of his head? He didn't dare shift his gaze to find out.

He'd sure gotten an eyeful when he'd stepped through the door earlier. Diana Matthews was every bit as beautiful as he remembered. Yep, even without the waist-length dark brown braid he used to love weaving his fingers through. The fresh herbal scent of the shampoo she'd always used still lingered in his memory.

What had he gone and done, accepting Robert Ingram's offer of a partnership in his veterinary practice—and when Tripp *knew* Juniper Bluff was Diana's hometown?

Okay, so he'd wrongly assumed Diana would be married, with 2.5 kids and living somewhere far, far away from here by now. Hadn't his sister told him only a few months after the breakup that Diana was seeing someone else?

Besides, he couldn't pass up this opportunity to get out of the big city and leave behind the pressures of a huge practice where he was one of fourteen vets on staff and rarely got to see the same patient twice in a row.

"Coffee okay?" Robert's question, laced with friendly concern, interrupted Tripp's thoughts.

"Yeah. Fine." Not the coffee fanatic he used to be, he stirred in another splash of soy milk and hoped his stomach would settle quickly.

"Had no idea you knew Diana. Small world, huh?"

"Yeah."

Robert polished off the last two bites of his scones, then drained his coffee mug. "Need anything else before we head back to the clinic?"

"I'm good, thanks." Pushing back his chair, Tripp avoided so much as a glance in Diana's direction, scared to death of what he'd see in her eyes. After how he'd left things, she had every right to despise him.

He'd just hoped, after all these years, she might have forgiven and forgotten.

Like he could ever forget her. Or forgive himself.

Outside, he inhaled a bolstering breath of sunwarmed Texas air and followed Robert to the white dually pickup with Ingram Veterinary Hospital and the clinic phone number emblazoned across both sides.

As they neared the clinic on the south edge of town, Robert broke the silence that had settled between them. "Ready to hold down the fort while I head out on some calls?"

"No problem." Tripp mentally reviewed the smallanimal appointments scheduled for the rest of the morning. It should be a slow and easy first day on the job.

Robert pulled in behind the long, gray-brick clinic building and shut off the engine. He angled Tripp a curious grin. "You always this talkative?"

With a self-conscious chuckle, Tripp shook his head. "Guess I'm still recovering from the shock of running into Diana."

"I'm getting the impression y'all were way more than just college friends."

"Yeah." Tripp sighed. "We were."

"Well, she's still single, and so are you, right?" Quirking a grin, Robert shoved open his door. "And

Diana's Donuts is the best place in town to get your morning cup of java."

Tripp sat in the pickup a moment longer while his new partner's words sank in. Could it be more than mere coincidence that had landed him in Juniper Bluff? Was this God's way of fixing the worst mistake Tripp had ever made in his crazy, mixed-up life?

Noticing Robert already had the back door to the clinic unlocked, Tripp scrambled from the pickup. Not a good idea to flake out on his first day. While Robert geared up for his farm calls, Tripp grabbed a lab coat on his way to check in with Yolanda, the salt-and-pepper-haired receptionist.

"Good, you're back." Yolanda nodded to the waiting area. "Mrs. Cox just got here for her ten a.m. appointment—Schatzi's annual checkup and shots. Plus, we've got two walk-ins. Sue Ellen Jamison's cat needs to be dewormed, and Carl Vasquez's German shepherd tangled with a coyote last night."

Tripp smiled toward the pet owners. "Bring Mr. Vasquez and his dog to exam room one. Apologize to Mrs. Cox for the delay, and tell Ms. Jamison we'll work her in as soon as we can."

Two hectic but gratifying hours later, he scanned the empty waiting area. Yes—all caught up, and none too soon. It was lunchtime, and his stomach was growling louder than Sue Ellen Jamison's angry cat.

"I heard that," Yolanda said with a snicker. She made a notation in a patient file, then tucked it into a slot on the shelf behind her. "By the way, Sue Ellen said to tell you nobody's ever gotten Cleopatra to take her medicine as easily as you did."

Tripp rubbed the teeth marks on his left thumb. "Then I'd hate to see the last vet who tried."

"That would be Doc Ingram, and he has the scars to prove it." Yolanda shut down the computer, scooped up her shoulder bag and started turning off lights. "Truth is, I think Cleopatra had a whole lot to do with convincing the doc it was time to bring a small-animal vet on board."

"Well, there was no mention of a psychopathic Siamese in the paperwork I signed." Chuckling, Tripp followed the receptionist out the rear door. They said their goodbyes, and Tripp climbed into his SUV. Time to grab a sandwich and some groceries and head home.

With only a couple of days between his last day at his former practice and coming to Juniper Bluff, Tripp hadn't had much time to settle in. Robert Ingram had made arrangements for Tripp to stay at a place outside of town called Serenity Hills Guest Ranch. One of their staff cabins was currently vacant, and for a bachelor like Tripp, the single bedroom, small living area and kitchenette would serve him just fine until either the owners kicked him out or he found a place closer to the clinic.

As he waited for his to-go order at the supermarket deli, another advantage of living so far out of town occurred to him: a much smaller likelihood of accidentally running into Diana. Despite what Robert had hinted about the possibility of their getting back together, Tripp figured he'd long ago blown his chances.

Anyway, hadn't he pretty much convinced himself marriage and family weren't for him? Something much more ominous than hunger pangs could be blamed for the rumblings in his abdomen. Sure, the Crohn's might be well controlled most of the time, but flare-ups were inevitable. And how, in good conscience, could Tripp ever risk passing on this possibly genetic and sometimes excruciatingly painful disease to any children in his future?

Business at the doughnut shop generally slowed as lunchtime approached, which meant Diana could turn things over to Kimberly and get away for a while. Still shaken by the unexpected encounter with Tripp, she needed a break before her runaway emotions got the best of her—*and* before her nosy assistant had a chance to pepper her with more questions.

Figuring her parents would be too busy helping Aunt Jennie move in to think about lunch, she filled a small white bag with her great-aunt's favorite doughnuts, then texted her mom with an offer to run by the supermarket deli and pick up sandwiches.

At the supermarket, a line of customers waited at the deli counter, so she picked up a sandwich menu and joined the queue.

While she studied the menu, someone paused beside her. "I hear the ham-and-Swiss is really good."

The page nearly fell from her hand. "Tripp."

"Yep, it's still me." His lopsided grin made her stomach dip. He held up a bulging deli bag. "Guess great minds think alike."

Or not. Diana forced a smile. "Just moved in and you're already discovering all the popular eateries in Juniper Bluff. When you're ready to try Mexican, I recommend Casa Luis."

An odd look crossed Tripp's face. "Thanks, I'll keep it in mind."

"Oh, I forgot. You're on some kind of health kick these days."

"You could say so." Tripp glanced away. "Well, don't let me keep you. Have a good afternoon, Diana."

"Yeah, you, too." The line moved, and Diana took a giant step forward. She was so ready to end this conversation.

"Diana?"

She winced, then turned and met Tripp's steady gaze. "Yes?"

"I just wanted to say how good it is to see you again. Your own business and everything—that's…really great. I'm happy for you."

At the pensive look in his eyes, the corner of her heart that had been frozen all these years melted a tiny bit. "Thanks. I'm glad to know you're doing well, too. I hope you'll be very happy in Juniper Bluff."

"I think I will be. The slower pace is already a welcome change."

"Funny," Diana mused with a twist to her lips, "I didn't think anything could lure you from your big-city lifestyle."

Tripp shrugged. "Maybe that was true…once."

"Well, I guess a lot can change in twelve years."

"Yeah, a lot can change." The words came out on a sigh. After a moment's pause, he offered a parting smile and strode away.

Lost in trying to figure out what this new Tripp Willoughby was all about, Diana jumped when the deli clerk called her name. "Oh, hi, Stan. Yes, I'd like two Reubens, an egg salad on whole wheat and a ham-and-Swiss on rye, light on the mustard."

She added a gallon of fresh-brewed iced tea to her

order, then selected a large bag of chips. Fifteen minutes later, she was on her way to the assisted-living center.

By the time she arrived, she'd regained a semblance of composure. At the reception desk she asked for directions to Aunt Jennie's quarters, then followed the signs to apartment 18C. The door stood open, and her great-aunt beamed from the opposite end of a small dinette.

Aunt Jennie stretched out her arms. "Come around here and give me a big ol' hug!"

Diana dropped the deli and doughnut bags onto the table, then scooped the petite ninety-two-year-old into a gentle but enthusiastic embrace. "I'm so glad you're finally here!"

Aunt Jennie patted Diana's cheek as she knelt on the carpet beside her chair. In a conspiratorial whisper, she asked, "Did you remember my favorite doughnuts?"

"Right here." Diana slid the smallest bag closer. Rising, she swept her gaze around the room. "Oh, good, you brought some of your own things to make it feel more like home."

"Yes, but it was very sad leaving my comfy little house and garden." The elderly woman's lips turned down with remorse. "Even harder to give up my sweet little Ginger-dog."

"I know, and I'm so sorry." Diana had known Aunt Jennie wouldn't be allowed to bring her lovable corgi to the new apartment. Aunt Jennie's next-door neighbor Mrs. Doudtman had taken Ginger, saying she'd be a great playmate for her two shelties.

"She'll adjust, honey, just like I will." Aunt Jennie patted Diana's arm.

Her great-aunt might be putting up a brave front, but the wistful look in her eyes every time she mentioned

Ginger's name brought a lump to Diana's throat. She'd have offered to keep Ginger herself, but she already shared her two-bedroom cottage with three cats, a lop-eared rabbit and a parakeet. Besides, her tiny backyard wasn't fenced, so a dog was out of the question. Ginger was too prissy to last long as a farm dog, which meant Diana's parents weren't able to take her, either.

But Diana did have an idea she hoped to implement soon. She'd begun investigating programs where volunteers brought pets to visit shut-ins, and if things worked out, she planned to establish a group right here in Juniper Bluff.

Thinking about pets brought to mind an unexpected complication. Unless Diana wanted to drive the extra miles to a veterinary clinic in a neighboring town, anytime her menagerie needed health care, she'd have no choice but to make an appointment with Tripp.

Chapter Two

Nothing like fresh country air to sweep away the mental cobwebs. A plate of scrambled eggs and toast in one hand, a glass of almond milk in the other, Tripp eased into a red retro-style metal lawn chair and propped one bare foot on the porch rail. He couldn't ask for a more relaxing start to a Sunday morning.

For now, at least, it remained quiet. Not long after he'd arrived to start moving in on Friday, Serenity Hills Guest Ranch was invaded by a vanload of excited kids. Tripp's landlord, Seth Austin, had apologized for not giving him a heads-up about Camp Serenity, a program the ranch participated in for disadvantaged children. Turned out this was one of their camping weekends.

The clop-clop of horses' hooves drew Tripp's attention to the tree-shaded lane. Moments later Seth Austin ambled into view with his towheaded young son, Joseph, each of them leading a horse.

"Mornin'." While his son continued on, Seth halted in front of Tripp's cabin. "Getting settled in okay?"

Tripp swallowed a bite of toast before replying. "Close. Got a few more things to unpack."

"Any problems, feel free to holler." Seth patted his horse's neck. "Just taking horses out to pasture. Didn't mean to disturb you."

"Not at all. I grew up in the city, but my grandparents used to have horses. Nice being around them again."

"Anytime you're up for a trail ride, I'm happy to oblige. In fact," Seth said with a nod behind him toward the barn, "we'll be taking several campers out for one more ride this afternoon before they head back to San Antonio. You're welcome to come along."

"Thanks, I'll think about it."

"Oh, and my wife and kids are going into town for Sunday school and church this morning. Christina would be happy to introduce you around."

Tripp chewed his lip. Juniper Bluff was a small town. How likely was it that Diana went to the same church? Nope, not quite ready to risk running into her again. "Maybe next time, after I get a little more organized."

"Sure thing." Seth clucked to his horse and continued along the lane. "Let me know if you're interested in that trail ride."

"I will. Thanks."

While Tripp finished breakfast, the nickering of horses, birdcalls from the treetops and the scent of cedar in the air lulled him into the deepest sense of relaxation he'd felt since before he started veterinary school. Man, did he need this! After a couple of debilitating flare-ups within the last several months, his doctor had warned him that if he didn't significantly reduce his stress level, keeping the Crohn's under control would be next to impossible.

From beyond the trees came the sounds of doors banging and children's laughter. The campers must be up and about. Tripp took the commotion as his cue to go inside.

As he set his breakfast dishes in the sink, his cell phone rang. The display showed his little sister, Brooke's name and number. "Hey, sis."

"Hey, yourself. All moved in yet?" Much more a morning person than Tripp would ever be, she sounded way too perky for 6 a.m. California time.

"Getting there. How's it going with Mom?"

Brooke's long sigh drained all the lightness from her tone. "Not so good, Tripp. She's trying hard to be positive, but the dialysis routine is wearing her down."

Tripp sank into the nearest chair and massaged his eye sockets. Fighting kidney disease for the past few years, their mom seemed closer than ever to losing the battle. "How's Dad handling it?"

"He's struggling. Yesterday I caught him behind the garage crying his eyes out."

The image of his father breaking down brought a catch to Tripp's throat. "I'm glad they moved out there with you, but I feel bad I can't be of more help." As the only family member who'd tested close enough to be a potential match for kidney donation, he felt even worse. The Crohn's made him ineligible. "Maybe I should have transferred to a vet clinic near you in Los Angeles instead of staying here in Texas."

"No, Tripp, you'd hate it here. I would never have relocated to LA if not for Jeff—and then right when I thought the jerk was about to propose—" A gulp left the rest of her statement unspoken. "Tripp, I'm sorry. Our situations were totally different."

"It's okay. I get it." But he could have done without

the reminder of how he'd ended things with Diana. Best to change the subject. "You still like your job, right?"

"Definitely." A smile had returned to her voice. "Getting promoted to accounts manager for an advertising firm has been my dream since college. So whenever I start fixating on…other things… I remind myself of the story of Joseph in the Bible where he tells his brothers, 'You intended to harm me, but God intended it for good.'" Her tone softened. "You need to believe that, too."

"Yeah, most days I try." The thing was, Tripp had never wanted to hurt Diana, not in a million years. His Crohn's diagnosis had hit him hard, though, and he felt he had to come to grips with it on his own before even considering bringing that kind of baggage into a relationship. During those difficult early months of two steps forward, one step back, as he learned to live with the disease, he'd convinced himself he'd done Diana a kindness by letting her go.

"Hey, bro, I really called to find out how you're doing. Do you like the new clinic?"

"Nice people, a lot less stress. I think it'll be a good fit." *Except for one tiny detail.* "Uh, Brooke?" Back to the subject he didn't seem able to avoid. "Did you happen to remember Juniper Bluff is where Diana Matthews is from?"

"Diana—oh, wow! It's been so long I'd forgotten." A concerned pause hung between them. "Does she still live there? Have you seen her?"

"Yes, and yes. She runs her own bakery and coffee shop, Diana's Donuts. My new partner took me there for coffee yesterday."

"Yikes. Was it ridiculously awkward?"

"You could say so." Their second encounter at the supermarket deli hadn't been much easier.

"Maybe this is your chance to clear the air. I still can't believe you never told her *why* you ended things. Do you have any idea how hard it was for me to keep your secret?"

"I know. It wasn't fair." He plowed his fingers through his hair. "But she's got her own life now. After all this time, what if telling her the truth only hurts her more?"

"Or...what if it gives you two a chance to fall in love all over again?"

Tripp hadn't so much as hinted that Diana was still single, and now he wasn't about to. Seemed like the perfect time to end the call, before his sister went any more hopelessly romantic on him. "How about you tend to your own love life and let me tend to mine." Dismal as it was. "Bye, sis. Give Mom and Dad hugs for me."

Later, as he arranged socks and T-shirts in the chest of drawers, his hand grazed the small velveteen box he'd never been able to part with, its contents an ever-present reminder of what he'd given up. He opened the lid for one more longing look at the classically elegant diamond ring nestled inside, while his sister's parting words played through his mind. What if he and Diana really could find their way back to each other?

And how many more regrets would he carry through life if he didn't try?

Closing the shop after the early Sunday morning coffee-and-doughnuts rush, Diana almost decided to skip church. Why risk running into Tripp again in case he tagged along with Doc Ingram?

But the past was the past, and she was a big girl now. Anyway, Juniper Bluff was too small a town to avoid Tripp for long—seeing him twice in the same day had proven as much—and she refused to rearrange her life on his account.

Even so, when Doc Ingram and his wife arrived without Tripp in tow, Diana relaxed slightly. She offered a friendly nod but couldn't help wondering how much Tripp had revealed about their shared history.

Leaving the sanctuary after worship, Diana spotted Christina Austin, pregnant with twins and already showing. Her service dog, Gracie, stood faithfully at her side. The gentle golden retriever, who helped Christina deal with the aftereffects of the traumatic brain injury she'd suffered in a car accident a few years ago, reminded Diana yet again how an animal's love and devotion could make a positive difference in someone's life.

She ambled over to say hello. "Hey, lady, how are things at the ranch?"

Christina turned with a cheery smile. She held the hand of her seven-year-old stepdaughter, Eva. "It's another Camp Serenity weekend. Need I say more?"

"Ah. That explains your handsome hubby's absence. Did Joseph stay home, too?"

"No, he's around here somewhere." Christina's glance swept the crowded foyer. "He had a question about his pony for Doc Ingram."

Eva looped one arm around Gracie's neck. "I have a pony now, too," she told Diana. "Her name's Candy."

"Wow, that's great!" Diana knelt to tweak Eva's pale yellow curls. "Can I come see her sometime?"

"Sure. We're gonna do a trail ride with the campers after lunch. Wanna come with us?"

Diana hadn't had much time lately to take her own horse out on the trail, and the weather today would be perfect. She pushed to her feet. "What time are y'all heading out?"

"They'll saddle up around one thirty," Christina replied. "Seth can always use an extra hand to keep those energetic campers in line." She patted her pregnant belly. "And I'm not much help these days, especially if it involves getting on a horse."

"It does sound fun." Diana checked her watch. She could easily grab a bite for lunch, run out to her parents' ranch to load Mona in the horse trailer and make it out to Serenity Hills in time for the ride. "Okay, count me in."

By one o'clock she'd stowed her saddle and other gear in the tack compartment of her dad's one-horse trailer, already hitched to his pickup. Mona, her copper penny bay mare, looked eager for a change of scenery and pranced into the trailer with her head held high.

"Hope you settle down before we get there," Diana said as she clipped the trailer tie to Mona's halter. "I don't need any extra drama this weekend." Seeing Tripp Willoughby walk into her doughnut shop yesterday was about all the drama she could handle for the next, oh, fifty years or so.

At Serenity Hills, Seth Austin and his stable hands already had several horses saddled and tied to the corral fence. Waving to him as she passed, Diana pulled into a parking area next to the barn.

As she stepped around to the rear of the horse trailer, Seth ambled over and offered a friendly hug. "Christina said you'd probably join us. Need some help with Mona?"

"I'm fine." Diana grinned toward the camp counselors struggling to buckle riding helmets onto the heads of several rambunctious campers. "Anyway, looks like you've got your hands full over there."

"That's the truth. Two more hours and we'll have peace and quiet again." Seth exaggerated a look of fatigue, but Diana knew how much he enjoyed the arrangement he and his grandparents, Bryan and Marie Peterson, had made with the San Antonio–based philanthropic organization that sponsored Camp Serenity. Besides saving the family from having to sell the guest ranch, the camp provided fun and adventure for kids who might otherwise never have the chance to get out of the city, much less to learn about horses and riding.

Diana unlatched the trailer door, and Seth gave her a hand lowering the ramp. Sidling into the trailer, Diana clipped a lead rope to Mona's halter and prepared to back her down the ramp. Apparently, the drive over had only heightened the mare's excitement. "Easy, girl."

"She's lookin' kind of feisty." Seth laid a steadying hand on Mona's rump.

"No kidding." Diana barely got her toe out of the way in time to keep from getting stomped on. "Maybe I'll take her over to the round pen and see if I can settle her down some."

Seth returned to his campers while Diana walked Mona to the round pen. Standing in the center of the fifty-foot-diameter pen, Diana used a lunge whip to send her horse into a trot around the perimeter. When Mona began to settle down after a few circuits, Diana wasn't quite so concerned about getting tossed on her keister somewhere out on the trail.

At the horse trailer, she buckled on Mona's saddle

and bridle and mounted up as Seth started her way leading his trail riders. Immediately behind him were Joseph on Spot and Eva riding her new palomino pony.

One hand gripping the reins and saddle horn, the little girl grinned and waved. "Hey, Miss Diana! You came!"

"Sure did, hon. Is this Candy? She's adorable!"

Eva beamed. "You can ride next to me, okay?"

"Love to." Diana prepared to fall in step.

Then, as she glanced back toward the other riders in the lineup, a familiar pair of crystal-blue eyes locked gazes with her—*Tripp*.

She froze, her jaw going slack, while Tripp Willoughby drew closer and closer.

"Miss Diana," Eva called, "hurry and catch up."

She snapped her mouth shut. Nudging Mona with her boot heels, she reined the horse around and trotted up next to Eva. When she could find her voice, she said, "Hey, Seth, what's with the, um, new volunteer?"

Straining to look past her over his shoulder, Seth grinned. "Oh, you mean Doc Ingram's new partner? He's just along for the ride. We're renting him one of the staff cabins."

"So he's…he's living *here*?" Her voice climbed an octave. "On your ranch?"

"Yep. Sorry I didn't get a chance to introduce you. Remind me when we get back later."

Diana grimaced. "That's okay. We've already met."

Diana was riding with them? Great. And Tripp assumed living out at Serenity Hills would mean fewer unexpected encounters with the woman he'd never gotten out of his heart.

Could this move to Juniper Bluff get any more complicated?

Maybe if he made sure to stay at the rear of the line, he could spare them both more discomfort.

And yet...man, she looked good on the back of a horse! He'd seen Diana in boots and jeans plenty of times, even gone riding with her when they used to spend weekends now and then at his grandparents' place outside Austin. The passage of time had only made her more beautiful, and though he did miss the long hair, her shorter, perkier ponytail poking out beneath a tan felt Stetson added a certain amount of sass.

Not that she didn't have plenty already. The look she'd shot him a few moments ago was one hundred percent sass. Although in that split second of recognition, Tripp had definitely glimpsed something else in her expression, and it looked a whole lot like panic. Considering he'd had the same reaction to their third unplanned meeting in less than two days, he ought to know.

Noticing his poky old cow horse was falling behind, he gave the beast a gentle kick. "Git up, Tex. No backing out now. Might as well see this through."

The trail meandered past a small lake and picnic area, then up a rocky slope shaded by cedars and live oaks. The hills should have been teeming with birds and animals, but with the campers laughing and howling like wild animals themselves, any expectations Tripp had about observing wildlife soon vanished.

He was too busy watching Diana anyway. And making sure to keep a nice, safe distance between them. Once or twice on the way up the hillside, she scrunched up her shoulders as if she could feel his eyes on her, but she never looked back.

Soon the trail opened into a meadow tufted with brown grass. Up ahead, Seth angled right, leading the riders in a wide circle as they changed directions for the return to the barn. In another few strides, Diana would be riding directly toward Tripp. His pulse ratcheted up a good twenty beats per minute. Would she say anything? Would she even look at him?

"Hi, Tripp." She spoke. Even smiled. At least he thought so. With her face shaded by the hat and a pair of sporty sunglasses, it was hard to be sure. "Enjoying the ride?"

He had about three seconds before their paths would diverge. "Yeah, can't beat this weather."

"Mmm-hmm." The quirk of her mouth told him exactly how lame his reply had sounded.

When she rode on by and he was once again bringing up the rear, he let out a frustrated sigh. Brooke was right—eventually he needed to be honest with Diana about why he'd broken things off. Maybe if she knew the truth, she'd forgive him.

If only he could count on forgiveness being her *only* response. The whole point of *not* telling her in the first place was so she wouldn't stick by him out of pity or obligation. If they did have any chance of starting over—if Diana would even give him the time of day after how he'd hurt her—he wasn't about to risk a "sympathy relationship" by playing the Crohn's card.

Up ahead, a flicker of motion caught Tripp's eye—a startled deer bounding into the woods. In the same instant, Diana's horse shied and skittered sideways. Tripp swallowed a gasp as Diana landed hard in a clump of dry grass.

"Hold up, everyone," Seth shouted as he wheeled

his horse around. He instructed those nearest Diana to move their horses a safe distance away.

Tripp wasn't waiting. He urged Tex forward, swinging out of the saddle the moment he drew even with Diana. He knelt beside her, resisting the impulse to physically check her for broken bones. "You okay?"

"Stupid horse. I knew she was way too full of herself." Diana sat up and rubbed her hip, then groaned as she snatched up her mangled sunglasses. "There goes fifty bucks down the drain."

Tripp couldn't care less about the glasses. "Take it slow. You might be hurt worse than you think."

"Stop looking at me like I'm one of your patients." Diana's hat lay an arm's reach away. She slapped it onto her head, then cautiously pushed to her feet. Brushing dead grass off her jeans, she scowled at Tripp. "I'm fine, I promise. The worst damage is to my ego."

Seth rode over, leading Diana's horse. "Here you go." He snickered as he handed her the reins. "Guess y'all should have taken a little longer in the round pen."

"Guess *you* should keep your opinions to yourself, cowboy." Diana's sharp tone didn't match the teasing twinkle in her eye, which reassured Tripp she really was unhurt.

Her horse still looked a little skittish, so Tripp kept a firm grip on the mare's bridle while Diana climbed into the saddle. Once she'd settled, he looked around for his own mount. Tex hadn't wandered far, seeming content to munch on grass and ignore the commotion. Back in the saddle, Tripp decided he'd risk Diana's scorn and ride next to her in case her horse acted up again.

By then, the other riders had continued on, leaving

Tripp and Diana at the back of the line. Exhaling loudly, she glanced over. "Thanks for coming to my rescue."

He cocked his head and grinned. "Yeah, it brought back memories."

"Oh, please. Don't you dare bring up the time at your grandparents' when my horse threw me into the water trough."

At least she was smiling—a good sign. "That had to be a softer landing than today."

"No kidding. My hip's going to be a zillion shades of purple by this time tomorrow." Diana sat straighter and cleared her throat. "We should catch up with the others. I still need to go visit my aunt this afternoon."

"Aunt Jennie's in town?"

She looked surprised he'd remembered the great-aunt she'd always been so fond of. "Yes, as of yesterday." Briefly, Diana told him about moving Aunt Jennie into the assisted-living center. "I'm just sorry she had to give up her dog. Juniper Bluff really needs a therapy pets program."

"If you need help starting one—"

"Got it covered." Diana clucked to her horse. "Let's go, Mona. We're getting left behind."

Then Tripp was the one left behind, since the old trail horse was content to plod along at a snail's pace. Just when he thought things were relaxing between him and Diana, she'd shut him down. Was there any hope at all they could come through this as friends?

Was he crazy to hope for more?

Chapter Three

Returning to the barn after the ride, Tripp clipped Tex to the cross ties at the far end of the barn aisle and loosened the saddle cinch.

Seth moved down the line to check on the campers, then stopped next to Tripp. "So you and Diana know each other?"

"Small world, huh?" Tripp managed a quick laugh. "She and my sister were college roomies." It was the truth. Just not all of it.

Hiking a brow, Seth tipped back his Stetson. "Yeah, that totally explains why you two are walking on eggshells around each other."

"This goes in the tack room, right?" Tripp hefted the heavy saddle off Tex's back.

"I'll take care of it." With a nod toward the barn door, Seth cast Tripp a knowing grin. "She's limping a bit after that fall, so I'm sure she'd appreciate some help with her horse."

Shoulders slumping, Tripp handed over the saddle. The sooner he and Diana could put this awkward phase behind them, the better. Squinting against the afternoon sun, he traipsed out of the barn, hauled in a deep breath and headed for Diana's trailer.

She'd just gotten the horse loaded and grimaced as she stepped off the ramp, clearly favoring her bruised hip.

Tripp hurried over. "Here, let me give you a hand."

"That's okay, I've got it." Turning, she bent to lift the ramp, then groaned beneath the weight.

"Sure you do." Ignoring her refusal, Tripp donated his muscles to the cause. Together they hoisted the ramp into position and secured the latches.

Diana stepped back, dusting off her hands. "Thanks. Again."

"My pleasure." Tripp shifted his stance. "Look, Di—"

"I prefer Diana, if you don't mind."

"Sorry. *Diana*." She wasn't about to make this any easier. "It's pretty clear my being here is making you uncomfortable, and I just wanted to say I'm sorry. If I'd known you were still in Juniper Bluff—"

"What? You'd have turned down Doc Ingram's partnership?" Her withering stare made him flinch. "Yes, this is a small town, but it's plenty big for both of us."

He bristled. "I'm trying to apologize. We were having a nice conversation for a few minutes there on the trail, and I was hoping—"

"That we could be friends? Let bygones be bygones?" Diana brushed past him and marched around to the driver's side of the pickup. "Sure, Tripp," she called over her shoulder. "Don't even think twice about it. It's all in the past."

Catching up, Tripp blocked her from opening the door. "First of all, quit finishing my sentences for me. Second, I get it. I hurt you, and I'll regret it to my dying day. Third, yes, I would like it very much if we could start over as friends." He let out a long, slow sigh and hoped his desperate half smile would win her over. "Please."

Her throat shifted. She crossed her arms. "You're right," she murmured, "and I'm sorry. I don't like this tension between us any better than you do."

"Thank you." A part of him really, *really* wanted to take her in his arms for a hug, but he figured that might be pushing things. Besides, he was afraid once he held her again, he'd never be able to let go.

She didn't give him the chance anyway. After tossing her hat across to the other seat, she jumped in behind the steering wheel. "Need to get going. See you around."

"Yeah." Tripp stepped back as she yanked the door closed. "See you around."

Diana could not leave Serenity Hills quickly enough. And there was nothing the least bit *serene* about her departure. She could see Tripp sincerely felt bad about barging back into her life. But *friendship*, after she'd thought they were on the verge of making a lifetime commitment? The fact that it still hurt so much only proved the depth of the feelings she once had for him.

Once? All right, *still*. Every man she'd dated since had the misfortune of being held to the standard set by Tripp Willoughby. Either the guy wasn't funny, smart, kind or romantic enough, or if he happened to meet all those criteria, there remained the chance he'd dump Diana just like Tripp had. It was a lose-lose proposition any way she looked at it.

Arriving at her dad's ranch, she returned Mona to the pasture, then backed the horse trailer into its spot next to the garage. Before she could get it unhitched, her dad came out to help.

"Have a good time?" he asked.

"It was fun—until Mona spooked and I hit the ground."

"Uh-oh. You okay?"

"I'll live." Stooped over the trailer hitch, she could pretend her hip was the only thing bothering her.

When they'd moved the trailer tongue onto a cinder block, she thanked her dad and forestalled more questions by saying she needed to get home and change before going over to see Aunt Jennie. She just hoped to have her emotions a little more under control by then.

An hour later, with freshly washed, finger-combed hair and wearing a clean pair of jeans with a purple peasant top, Diana tapped on the door of her great-aunt's tiny apartment. A soft "Coming, dear" and shuffling feet preceded the click of the doorknob. The door swung open, and Aunt Jennie welcomed Diana with a cheery smile and a warm hug.

Diana stepped into the cozy sitting room. Her great-aunt's plush blue recliner and favorite antique end table added a homey touch. "Looks like Mom and Dad got you all settled. It's a lovely apartment."

"Yes, it's quite comfortable, and the people here are as nice as can be." Aunt Jennie sighed as she eased into the recliner. "Only one thing could make it better."

"I know—you miss Ginger. Tell you what," Diana said as she plopped onto the love seat. "One day this week I'll take you over to my house and you can hug on my critters."

"Oh, that would be wonderful." A bright smile lit

Aunt Jennie's face. "Do you still have all three of those spoiled-rotten cats? And the rabbit, too?"

"Sure do. Plus a stray parakeet I found fluttering around the bird feeder last spring. He's made himself right at home, and he knows how to show those cats who's boss."

As Diana described her menagerie, she itched to get rolling with her plans for a therapy pets program. Not only would it make Aunt Jennie's transition a little easier, but pet visits could bring a spark of life and laughter to the other residents, as well.

The next morning, Diana awoke to a blaring clock radio and an overweight gray-striped tabby sitting on her chest. She slapped the off button on the radio while shoving the cat to one side. "Okay, okay, Tiger, I'm awake."

Midnight and Lucinda, the tomcat's partners in crime, paced across Diana's feet, all apparently near starvation, if their plaintive mews could be believed.

The hardest part of owning a doughnut shop? The 4:00 a.m. wake-up call. And Diana had stayed up entirely too late last night downloading information and application forms for starting a therapy pets program. Tossing back the covers, she stumbled to the bathroom and splashed water on her face, then saw to her pets before sitting down to her own breakfast.

By 4:50 she was out the door. At the shop, she helped Kimberly start batches of doughnuts, muffins, scones and apple fritters, then set up the coffeemakers. At one minute before six, she flipped the Closed sign to Open and unlocked the door.

After the early-morning rush ended, she helped Kimberly get more pastries in the oven, then made herself a café mocha latte and carried it to her office. Logging in to her email account, she hoped to have a response from the therapy pet organization she'd contacted about sponsoring a chapter in Juniper Bluff.

And she did. Agnes Kraus, a representative from Visiting Pet Pals, asked Diana to call at her earliest convenience. Adrenaline pumping, she dialed the number immediately.

"Yes, Diana, it's good to hear from you," Mrs. Kraus said. "We're delighted you want to launch a program in Juniper Bluff." Papers rustled. "I'm looking at your application right now. I see you want to focus on dog owners initially. How are you doing with potential volunteers?"

Diana chewed her lip. "No commitments yet, but I have some acquaintances in mind. I was planning to get going on that over the next few days."

"You do understand each dog must have basic obedience certification? Plus, we require a minimum of eight sign-ups before I can make the trip to evaluate the animals and conduct a training session specific to therapy pets."

"Yes, ma'am," Diana said, quickly jotting reminders. "I have your list of requirements right here in front of me. Once I have my volunteers, how soon could we be evaluated?"

Mrs. Kraus paused, the sound of clicking computer keys filling the silence. "My fall schedule is filling up, so the earliest date would be the second Saturday of November. That would give you about six weeks to get your team together."

Diana clicked open her own calendar and counted

off the weeks. She'd hoped to hold the first official pet visit at the assisted-living center as a surprise for Aunt Jennie's birthday, a few days before Thanksgiving. It just might be doable—provided she could come up with eight qualified dog owners.

"Pencil me in," she told Mrs. Kraus. "I'll do everything possible to be ready by then."

She'd just hung up when Kimberly tapped on the door. "Diana, you might want to see this."

Diana pushed back her chair and stood. "Please don't tell me the oven conked out again."

"No, the oven's working like a champ. It's…something else." Kimberly led the way out to the alley and over to the Dumpster. She pointed into the shadows. "See back there by the wall?"

Muted whimpers wrenched Diana's heart moments before she glimpsed the scrawny mother cat and four newborn kittens nestled inside a crumbling cardboard box. "Oh, dear, you poor things!"

"We can't leave them back there," Kimberly said. "This is trash pickup day. They could be crushed."

Diana edged away, afraid of frightening the cat into running off somewhere even less safe. "Can you keep an eye on things while I run over to the supermarket for some cat food? Maybe I can lure her out and then…" She shrugged. "I'll figure out something."

Half an hour later, Tiger's favorite Shrimp-and-Salmon Delight had the mama cat's nose working overtime. Within five minutes, Diana had made a new friend. While mama dined, Diana and Kimberly transferred the kittens from their dingy hiding place into a sturdier, towel-lined crate. The mama cat climbed in with her kittens, and Diana carried them to her office.

When she checked on them later, snuggled in their box next to the filing cabinet and emitting soft, rumbling purrs, she realized she was already growing attached.

Kimberly peeked in. "How's the little family?"

Diana leaned down to scratch the mama cat behind the ears. "Fine for now, but they can't stay here, and there's no way I can take them home with me." She looked hopefully at her assistant. "Any chance—"

"Uh-uh, no way!" Kimberly held up both hands. "Olivia despises cats."

"Yeah, I forgot." The little dachshund definitely was not cat-friendly.

"Doc Ingram's new partner seems really nice. Maybe he could help find them a home."

Diana's lips flattened. She'd already let that idea zip right on past. Too bad it was the only one that made sense. Juniper Bluff wasn't big enough to have its own animal shelter—the nearest one was over in Fredericksburg—and even so, Diana had no confidence they could find a home for a scrawny mother cat with kittens.

"Okay, Ms. Matthews, no more stalling." Pulling a side chair closer, Kimberly plopped down directly in front of Diana. "What are you not telling me about our handsome new small-animal vet?"

Breath catching in her throat, Diana tipped forward, head in her hands. She was *so* not ready to relive the worst day of her life.

Kimberly set her hand on Diana's shoulder. "Honey, tell me! Did that guy hurt you somehow?"

Heaving a sigh, Diana straightened. "If effectively ripping out my heart, stomping on it with combat boots and dousing it in hydrochloric acid counts, then yes, he hurt me really, really bad."

Kimberly's mouth fell open. "When? How?"

Steeling herself, Diana gave her assistant a condensed version of the facts—how her college apartment mate Brooke Willoughby had invited her along on a weekend visit home to Austin. There, she met Brooke's older brother, Tripp, a veterinary student at Texas A&M. The attraction was immediate, and the more time they spent together, the deeper in love Diana had fallen.

Until the phone call that ended it all. Tripp had caught her between classes—called her cell phone, of all things! The jerk didn't even have the nerve to break it to her in person.

I'm sorry, Di, but... I need to cancel our plans for this weekend.

Tripp, I'm on my way to an economics test. Can I call you back in an hour?

He'd paused too long, a warning in itself. *I need to say this now. About us. This...* A pained swallow. *It's just not working.*

Not working? Her heart had turned stone-cold with dread. *What are you telling me?*

I think we need to slow down a bit, maybe take a break. I'm under a lot of pressure with my vet studies and...other things. It's...complicated.

"I thought he cared for me the same way," Diana said, brushing a tear from her cheek. "But I guess I was wrong."

Kimberly scowled. "He really used the 'it's complicated' line? Next time he comes in, I will personally lace his coffee with Tabasco sauce."

Something between a laugh and a sob burst from Diana's throat. "Hold that thought. I may still need his help finding homes for these kittens."

"Are you sure? Because if a guy had treated me like that, I'd have trouble being in the same county with him, let alone the same room."

Diana thought back to the trail ride yesterday and Tripp's attempt at an apology. He'd seemed sincere, and really, twelve years had passed. Holding a grudge after all this time certainly didn't speak well of her as a Christian. Besides, if Tripp *had* been the right guy for her, wouldn't God have kept them together somehow? As it was, she'd only hurt herself by letting the fear of having her heart broken again shut down every other relationship she'd had a chance for since then.

Time to put her own words from yesterday into practice and let bygones be bygones. She gathered up her purse and car keys, then hefted the cat box. "The shop's yours for an hour or two, Kim. I'm headed to the animal clinic."

Kimberly followed her to the back door, holding it open as Diana stepped into the alley. "Are you sure you want to do this?"

"Not in the least."

On his lunch break at the clinic, Tripp had just set a bowl of chicken-and-rice soup in the microwave when Yolanda peeked in.

"We have a walk-in," she said. "Stray cat with newborn kittens. Can you take a look?"

"Sure." His next appointment wasn't until three o'clock anyway, so plenty of time to warm up his soup later.

Yolanda pointed him to exam room two and handed him a folder. "This client's a regular—has several pets of her own. If there's a stray within twenty miles of Juniper Bluff, somehow it finds its way to her."

"A real animal lover, huh?" Tripp could relate.

Then he read the name on the folder tab, and his heart thudded to the pit of his empty stomach. "Diana?"

"Yes, Diana Matthews. Same gal from Diana's Donuts."

"I know." Oh, boy, did he!

The receptionist hesitated, probably confused by the pained look on Tripp's face. "You need me to stay, or can I go to lunch?"

"No, go ahead. I've got it from here." Hauling in a breath, he stepped into the exam room. "Hey, Di…ana."

Her arched brow said she'd caught his near slip of the tongue. "Thanks for working me in. I didn't have anyplace else I could take these kitties."

Kitties. Tripp couldn't help grinning at the tender way she spoke the word. Or the compassionate gleam in her eyes as she stroked the purring mother cat. Laying the folder on the counter, he cast an appraising eye over the scrawny mother cat, a yellow tabby who'd obviously been surviving on her own for a while. The kittens, probably not more than two or three days old, looked healthy enough, but unless their mother got better care so she could feed them, they wouldn't last long.

"Well?" Diana caressed the mother cat's ears. "Can you help me with them?"

"First thing we need to do is get the mother started on some vitamins and quality food." Stethoscope in his ears, Tripp listened to the cat's heart and lungs, then gently palpated her from neck to tail for any signs of growths or infection. The worst he found was matted fur and a small cut on one shoulder, probably from a fight.

The cat wouldn't like what he had to do next, but he needed to take her temperature, check for worms and take a blood sample. Turned out she was a lot more co-operative than Sue Ellen Jamison's Siamese. After setting aside the specimens, Tripp jotted some notes in the file. "The initial results will only take a few minutes. Do you mind waiting?"

"That's fine." Diana's expression remained neutral, but her tone suggested it had taken every ounce of will-power to bring the cats to Tripp.

With a quick smile, he excused himself and slipped down the hall to the lab. When he returned, he found Diana seated on the padded bench with the cat box in her lap.

"You get why I can't keep you," she murmured as she tenderly stroked the mother cat. "I would if I could—" Noticing Tripp, she straightened abruptly and cleared her throat. "What did you find?"

"No visible evidence of worms, and no problems I could see from preliminary tests. I'll have to send samples to our outside lab for a more complete report. That'll take two or three days." Tripp came around the exam table and sat down at the other end of the bench. With the tip of one finger, he rubbed a sleeping kitten's soft, fuzzy belly. "I gather you want help finding homes for these little critters."

Lips in a twist, Diana nodded. "Guess you've seen from my file that I already have a houseful. To borrow a phrase, there's no more room at the inn."

"You always had a soft heart for animals. Remember the baby squirrel—"

"It was so tiny." A tender smile stole across Diana's face. Just as quickly, it vanished. She cleared her throat.

"If you can keep the cat and her babies here, I'll put up adoption flyers around town. And I'll cover the vet bill and boarding costs."

"No problem. Since you're a regular, I'm sure we can cut you a deal." Tripp winked. "Or maybe barter vet services for coffee and pastries?"

Diana's eyebrows shot up. "You'd do that?"

"Considering Doc Ingram's affinity for your scones, I think we could twist his arm."

The mother cat was purring loudly now, the sound appearing to have a calming effect on Diana. She glanced up at Tripp. "I appreciate this. More than you know."

Tripp felt like he could sit there all day, basking in the warmth of Diana's presence. Man, how he'd missed this woman! All the years apart seemed to melt away like ice cream on a hot sidewalk, along with all the reasons Tripp had used to justify their breakup.

Maybe…maybe they really could start again. He'd been feeling better every day since getting out of the city. Yes, it had only been a few days now, but his health could only go uphill from here, right? Anyway, in the years since his diagnosis he'd heard of lots of people with Crohn's who went on to live normal, healthy lives, even raised families. Was it possible he'd been too quick to give up on his own chance at happiness?

Diana's sharp sigh brought him back to the present. "I didn't realize how late it was. I need to get back to the shop." She slid the cat box onto the bench between her and Tripp, then stood, her hand lingering on the mother cat's head. With a tentative glance at Tripp, she said, "You'll take good care of them, right?"

"Of course, the very best." He rose as well and picked

up the box. "Want to walk back with me and see the kennel where they'll be staying?"

"No, that's okay. I should make this a clean break." She winced, and Tripp could guess exactly where her thoughts had taken her.

"Diana…"

"Gotta run." Her perky smile was back in place. "Tell Doc Ingram y'all can drop in anytime to collect on your coffee and doughnuts. Bye!"

Her brusque departure left him feeling like he'd just been sideswiped by a semi.

And also shocked him back to reality. He had no business entertaining thoughts of rekindling what he and Diana had once shared. She might give lip service to the possibility of starting over as friends, but the flicker of hurt in her eyes made him wonder if she'd ever fully forgive him.

Diana tried hard not to call the clinic every day to check on the mother cat and her babies. Even though Tripp had called a couple of days later to report that mama cat was healthy and her kittens were thriving, Diana couldn't help being concerned. She'd already prepared adopt-a-kitten flyers to post around town as soon as the kittens were old enough to leave their mother.

In the meantime, she spent most of her spare time working out details for the therapy pets program. She still needed to enlist her volunteers, but working all day at the doughnut shop didn't leave much time for recruitment efforts. It was the first week of October, and unless Diana had her volunteers lined up and ready by the end of the month, she'd have to postpone Agnes Kraus's evaluation and training visit. Time to speed things up, and tonight's service committee meeting at church might be her best chance.

Around midafternoon, a couple of Main Street business owners stopped in for coffee. Diana cheerfully filled their orders, and the customers had barely sat down at a window table when Tripp and Doc Ingram breezed in.

"Good afternoon, gentlemen. What can I get for you?" Diana tried to keep her attention on Doc Ingram, but her eyes kept betraying her with darting glances at Tripp. The last time she'd actually seen him was at church last Sunday, and then only in passing. Seth and Christina had kept him occupied as they introduced him to the pastor and other acquaintances.

"Two coffees, for starters." Doc palmed his Stetson. "Then I'd like to bend your ear about catering an open house for us at the clinic."

"Sure. Meet me at the corner table over there and you can tell me all about it." Diana filled two mugs, then a third one for herself. As she set the mugs on a tray, she remembered Tripp had asked for soy milk on his first visit, so she filled a small ceramic pitcher. Still wearing her pink Diana's Donuts apron over her T-shirt and jeans, she carried the tray to the table.

As she distributed the mugs and handed Tripp the container of soy milk, his smile conveyed both appreciation and surprise. "Thanks," he murmured in the mellow tone that once set her heart racing.

And apparently still did, if the heat rising up her cheeks meant anything.

She straightened her apron and took the chair on the other side of Doc Ingram. "So. About your open house. When is it, and what's the occasion?"

"If it's not too short notice, I'm thinking next Sunday afternoon, say from two to four," the doc answered. "It'll be a welcome party for Tripp here, a chance for the community to drop in and meet him."

"Sounds fun." With a smile and nod in Tripp's direction, Diana pulled a pen and notepad from her apron pocket and jotted down the date. "What would you like to serve?"

"Thought I'd leave the menu in your capable hands." Doc chuckled. "Consider it part of Tripp's bartering agreement for seeing to those cats you dropped off last week."

Tripp caught Diana's eye and mouthed, *Not my idea.*

Something she should have guessed. Tripp had never been much of a socializer. If they went out with friends, there would be only one or two other couples. If someone hosted a party, Tripp would steer Diana to the less noisy perimeter, and he was always ready to say their goodbyes long before Diana had run out of conversation.

She gave a mental shrug. One more indication they weren't right for each other.

"I was teasing about the cat thing," Doc Ingram said. "Planned on doing this anyway, so I'm more than glad to pay."

"No, it's perfectly all right. A deal's a deal." Diana tapped the pen against her lips as she considered what to serve. "We can do coffee, doughnuts, minimuffins… and maybe some cranberry punch for the kids."

"Great. I'll start getting the word out." As Doc Ingram took a sip of his coffee, his cell phone chirped. Reading a text, he grimaced. "Horse down with colic at the Hendersons'. Gotta skedaddle. Hate to strand you, Tripp, but the Henderson ranch is clear the opposite direction from the clinic."

"No problem," Tripp said. "I'll find my own way back."

Halfway to the door, the doc halted and snapped his fingers, a mischievous look curling his lips. "Hey, since your appointment calendar's clear for the rest of the day, why don't you hang out here? Y'all can hash out the open house menu together."

Suddenly nervous, Diana arched a brow. But with only a few customers and Kimberly covering the counter, she didn't have an obvious reason to excuse herself. She offered Tripp an empathetic smile. "So…an open house, huh?"

He hiked one shoulder. "Like I said, not my idea."

"It's a small-town thing. People like to get to know the folks they're doing business with."

"That's one part of this job I already appreciate. People are way more relaxed and friendly than at the Austin clinic I came from."

Something in Tripp's tone evoked a pang of concern. "I thought opening your own big-city vet practice had always been your goal."

"I thought so, too…at first." His jaw edged sideways. He sat forward as if on the verge of saying more, but then he abruptly stood and picked up his mug. "Think I could trade this for a glass of water?"

"Keep your seat. I'll get it." Diana bustled over to the counter and signaled Kimberly.

Handing Diana a glass of ice water, Kimberly wiggled her brows. "Looks like y'all are having a real nice chat over there. Mending some fences?"

Diana hesitated, wondering the same thing herself. Her tone became wistful as she murmured, "Maybe we are."

* * *

Tripp tried not to stare as Diana sauntered back to the table with his water. Since his first glimpse two Saturdays ago, he couldn't get enough of looking at her. The way she walked. The way her long, tapered fingers held her horse's reins or caressed those tiny kittens. The way she flicked a loose strand of hair out of her eyes or tossed her perky ponytail.

She set the glass in front of him, then shifted from foot to foot. "Unless you have more thoughts about Sunday's menu, I should probably get back to work."

"Right." Biting back a smile, Tripp nodded toward the only other two customers in the shop. "I can see you're super busy right now."

She rolled her eyes, another endearing gesture he recalled all too well from when they were dating. "Well... I do have a few things to catch up on in the office. I *am* the owner, after all."

"Of course, sorry. I'll just finish up here and be on my way."

Nodding, Diana started to turn away, then swiveled to face him again. "But how will you get back to the clinic?"

Tripp shrugged. "It's only a mile or two. I can hoof it."

Just then, Diana's blond assistant bustled over. She carried a square white box with a cellophane lid. "Diana, can you run these pastries over to Alan's insurance office? They're for his staff meeting in the morning."

Suspicion clouded Diana's expression. "But Alan usually comes by early on Wednesday mornings to pick up his order."

"I know, but he's always so rushed, and I've got this

batch fresh out of the oven, so I thought, why not save him the trip?"

Smiling to himself, Tripp watched the play of emotions across Diana's face—confusion, consternation, then the clear realization that Kimberly was playing her. Arms crossed, Diana glared at her assistant. "And is there some pressing reason *you* can't drop them off?"

"I have more muffins in the oven." Kimberly held the box out to Diana. "You can take Alan his pastries, then give Doc Willoughby a ride to the clinic."

Talk about obvious! Tripp took another swallow of water and pushed back his chair. "I told you, Diana, I can walk. Don't put yourself out on my account."

"Oh, she wouldn't be," Kimberly gushed. "This is perfect, Diana. While you're there, you can visit your kitties." Winking, she added, "You *know* you want to."

Diana chewed her lip. "Well, I *would* like to see how they're doing." Relaxing her stance, she took the box from Kimberly, then glanced uncertainly at Tripp. "You wouldn't mind?"

He wasn't particularly happy about being set up, but spending more time with Diana? That he didn't mind in the least. "You're welcome to visit anytime."

Ten minutes later, he waited in Diana's SUV outside the Alan Glazer Insurance Agency while Diana delivered the pastries.

Returning to the car, she frowned as she climbed in behind the wheel. "That was awkward."

"Problems?" Tripp asked.

"I had to reassure Alan we weren't trying to pawn off last weekend's stale leftovers." Mouth in a twist, she looked like she blamed Tripp for the awkwardness.

Didn't she get this was all Kimberly's doing? Tripp was just an innocent bystander.

Okay, not exactly innocent. Apparently, there was no statute of limitations for breaking someone's heart. Tripp doubted Diana would have yielded to Kimberly's ploy if not for the chance of visiting the kittens.

So he'd take what he could get. In the meantime, he'd keep chipping away at the gigantic wall Diana had erected around her heart.

They arrived at the clinic a few minutes later. As Tripp led the way through the rear entrance, the three dogs they were boarding for vacationers started yipping.

"It's just me, fellas." Tripp opened the door to the dog kennel wing, and the noise grew louder. "Calm down, okay? Suppertime isn't for another couple of hours."

Hands over her ears, Diana grimaced. "This is why I have cats."

"Wimp." Tripp grinned and shut the door. "I think you'll find the feline quarters a bit quieter."

He showed Diana along a short corridor and into a room with two tiers of spacious cat kennels along one wall. Most of the kennels were vacant, except for the upper kennel on the near end with the mother cat and kittens, and at the other, a cat recuperating from minor surgery. Opposite the kennels stood a large tank with colorful tropical fish lazily swimming about.

Eyes widening, Diana glanced around briefly, then strode over to peek at the kittens, snuggled up to their mother on a snowy fleece pad. "Wow, I had no idea how plush your kennels were."

Tripp had been quite impressed as well when Doc Ingram gave him the tour. "You've never been back here before?"

"No, my parents or a neighbor always take care of my pets when I'm away." She poked her fingers through the grate to scratch the mother cat behind the ears.

"You can open the door," Tripp said, stepping closer. "Here, let me." He reached for the latch at the same moment she did. When his hand closed over hers, she flinched. He knew he should back off, but he let his hand linger.

Diana's breath quickened. "Tripp…"

"Sorry." Throat raspy, he dropped his hand to his side and edged away, giving Diana space to open the kennel door. When she leaned in to love on the cat and kittens, the mother cat's purring could be heard clear across the room.

Maybe the sound would drown out the pounding of Tripp's pulse. Yep, he was just plain crazy for thinking he could keep things platonic, when everything in him wanted to fight to win Diana back. But until he felt ready to confide in her about the real reason they'd broken up, he didn't dare try.

"They're growing so fast." Diana turned from the kennel, a serene smile replacing the tension of moments ago. "The kittens' eyes should open soon, and then they'll start getting playful."

Glad for the distraction from his going-nowhere train of thought, Tripp grinned. "Kittens are fun. It's cute when they act like miniature wild beasts on the hunt."

"Still wish I could keep them, or at least one of the kittens." Latching the kennel, Diana stiffened her shoulders. "But, alas, I must be strong and resist temptation."

Tripp released a nervous chuckle as he opened the door to the corridor. "Thanks again for the lift. I'm sure you've got a million other things to do."

"It was worth the extra trouble to spend some time with the kitties." Diana paused in the doorway, her cheeks reddening. "I didn't mean that the way it sounded."

A barely suppressed sigh caught in Tripp's throat. "It's okay. I totally get it."

"Do you?" Diana gave her head a quick shake. "Because I'm not sure I do." Stepping into the hallway, she swiveled to face the wall, her gaze fixed on a poster depicting the life cycle of fleas. "I'm trying, Tripp. Really trying to deal with having you back in my life. I'm working on letting go of the past, but this—this *friendship* thing isn't always as easy as I'd like it to be."

Tripp swallowed over the thickness in his throat. "Believe me, Diana, if I could go back and change the way I handled things, I would. Breaking up with you was the last thing I wanted to do."

She tossed a pain-filled glance over her shoulder. "Obviously not, since your career apparently became a much higher priority."

"That isn't how it was. I mean, yes, my vet studies were pretty demanding back then, but—" Palming his forehead, Tripp silenced himself before he revealed more than he was ready to. Besides, his belly had just issued an unpleasant warning. He inhaled and tried again. "I messed up, okay? And I realize no amount of apologizing is going to make up for it. But I still care about you, Di. I never stopped caring."

Her chin quivered. At least she hadn't smacked him for calling her Di. "God's been working with me on this forgiveness thing for quite a while now, and I'm making progress, I promise." Turning toward the exit, she blew out a distracted breath. "But now, I really do have to go."

Tripp followed her out to her car. Grasping for even one more minute with her, he blurted, "How's it going with the therapy pets thing?"

"Slow but sure. I'm hoping to get some support from our church's service committee tonight." Diana fished in her purse for her car keys.

"I started to tell you the other day, I worked with a therapy pets group during my veterinary internship. If there's anything I can do to help—" The moment the words left his mouth, he could tell he'd overstepped.

"Thanks, but I've got everything under control." With a brisk nod, Diana climbed into her car.

Watching her drive away, Tripp wondered if there'd ever come a time when she wouldn't look at him through eyes clouded by the past.

Leaving the clinic, Diana suffered a twinge of guilt at how abruptly she'd rejected Tripp's offer of help. It was just way too soon to involve him in her life any more than necessary. Besides, the therapy pets project was her idea. She didn't need Tripp, or anyone else, waltzing in and taking over.

After wrapping up end-of-the-day office work at the doughnut shop, she hurried home to feed her menagerie and warm up a microwave dinner for herself, then drove over to the church. Pastor Terry had just opened the meeting as Diana slid into one of the last empty chairs at the conference table. She scribbled a few notes while the other members reported on completed and current service projects, but mostly her mind raced with thoughts of how to persuade the committee to consider adopting her therapy pets venture as a church outreach.

When her turn finally came, she opened her file

folder of notes and cleared her throat. "I know this is a little different from the service projects we've done in the past, but I believe it could bless not only the recipients but anyone who volunteers, as well."

She went on to talk about her great-aunt's move to the assisted-living center and how hard it was for Aunt Jennie to part with her precious corgi. "That's what gave me the idea, so I've done a lot of research and have contacted a therapy pets organization about starting a group right here in Juniper Bluff."

As she described the requirements and training process, a few heads began to nod around the table, while other committee members looked skeptical.

"It sounds good in principle," a woman across the table said. "But if having a friendly, well-behaved dog isn't good enough...sorry, but I don't have the time or the money to invest in obedience training."

Others voiced similar thoughts. Only two people expressed interest, saying their dogs had completed basic obedience classes and asking Diana to keep them posted as plans progressed. When Pastor Terry asked for a motion to table the discussion until their November meeting, Diana's heart sank. As slow as this committee operated, even if they did decide to get behind the plan as one of their service projects, it would likely be the first of the year or later before Diana could expect to see any action.

Anyway, by the end of the meeting, the committee had jumped on someone's suggestion to put Christmas care packages together for the Camp Serenity kids. Diana reluctantly agreed the idea made more sense for the committee as a whole, but she couldn't help feeling discouraged.

After the meeting adjourned, Pastor Terry stopped Diana on her way to her car. "Sorry about the lack of support for your therapy pets project. Have you thought about putting up some flyers at the vet clinic? I'm sure Doc Ingram and his new partner would be happy to help spread the word."

Diana had to admit the pastor was right. What better place to connect with pet owners than a veterinary clinic? "Thanks, I'll think about it."

"You might consider *praying* about it," Pastor Terry said with a knowing smile. At her questioning look, he continued, "I heard through the grapevine that there might be a bit of history between you and Juniper Bluff's newest resident. Anytime you'd like to talk…"

Heaving a sigh, Diana leaned against her car door. "It's true, Tripp and I dated in college, and it didn't end well. The day he walked into my doughnut shop and I found out he'd moved to Juniper Bluff, I felt blindsided."

"Because you still have feelings for him." It was a statement, not a question.

"No. Yes. I don't know!" A growl rumbling in her throat, Diana tipped her head to gaze into the starry sky. "It's been twelve years. I should have been over him a long time ago."

"But since you aren't…" Pastor Terry lifted one shoulder. "Maybe your heart is trying to tell you something."

It was a thought Diana couldn't quite bring herself to entertain. She turned slowly and pulled open her car door. "I just don't want to make the same mistake twice."

The pastor chuckled. "Then I repeat my earlier advice. *Pray.*"

Giving a meek nod, Diana climbed into her car. "I will, Pastor. Thanks."

Chapter Four

It was Sunday before Tripp saw Diana again, which was about five days longer than he'd have liked. But he couldn't bring himself to pop in at the doughnut shop and disconcert her any more than he already had.

As he joined Robert Ingram and his family in church that morning, he glimpsed Diana across the sanctuary. He looked forward to even a brief moment to say hello after the service, but by the time he made it out to the foyer, she'd disappeared.

"You'll see her this afternoon at the open house," Robert said as if reading Tripp's thoughts.

Tripp shrugged. "If she hasn't already delegated the catering job to her assistant."

"Diana has too much pride in her business reputation. Don't worry. She'll be there." With an elbow to Tripp's ribs, Robert motioned toward the double doors. "Better get a move on. Emily'll have a conniption if we let Sunday dinner get cold."

Tripp had to admit, everyone in Juniper Bluff—with one notable exception—had made him feel warmly welcomed. The Austins and Petersons out at Serenity Hills had extended several invitations to join them for supper at the main house, and Tripp had quickly learned he'd be a fool to turn down one of Marie Peterson's home-cooked meals. Today would be his second time to have Sunday dinner with the Ingrams, and if last week's pot roast was any indication, Emily's cooking could compete with Marie's any day.

One problem, though—if he wanted to continue accepting these invitations, he'd eventually have to say something about the Crohn's. He'd already earned a few concerned glances from his hostesses after discreetly leaving some of the more troublesome foods untouched.

It happened again at lunch when Emily Ingram tried to load his plate with her crispy fried chicken and a green salad teeming with raw veggies. Just thinking about what those foods could do to his system gave him a belly cramp.

Emily frowned as she returned a huge chicken thigh to the platter. "Surely you can eat more than one teensy piece of white meat. You're not much more than skin and bones, young man."

True, he'd dropped several pounds in the years since his diagnosis, but he was eating healthier than ever. He'd learned which foods caused him problems, though, and if he wanted to avoid a flare-up, he had to be picky. "It all looks delicious, but I'm saving plenty of room for your baked squash casserole. Robert told me it's his favorite."

The compliment seemed to mollify her, even more so when Tripp asked for a second and then a third helping of the tasty dish. He'd learned long ago that steamed or baked veggies were his friends, so he figured he'd better eat as much as he could so he wouldn't be tempted by Diana's pastries at the open house.

After helping with the kitchen cleanup, Tripp left for the clinic with Robert so they could open up for Diana. A few minutes later, she arrived with Kimberly and a teenage boy Tripp remembered seeing at the doughnut shop. Tripp stayed out of the way as they arranged baked goods, coffee urns and a cold beverage dispenser on cloth-covered tables set up in the reception area. As Tripp watched them work with practiced efficiency, his admiration for Diana grew even stronger. She really had done well for herself here in Juniper Bluff—and was probably a lot happier living among her hometown family and friends than she would have been if things had worked out between them. Even without his health issues, Tripp's long hours completing his veterinary degree, followed by an even heavier schedule working at a big-city vet clinic, meant they'd have enjoyed precious little time together as newlyweds.

Newlyweds. Exactly what he'd expected them to be twelve years ago.

Until the Crohn's.

Sometimes he got downright angry with God for allowing this disease into his life. Even angrier that it had compelled him to give up the woman he loved. He'd tried hard to learn from the example of Saint Paul, to be content with his circumstances and accept whatever God wanted him to learn from his own "thorn in the flesh."

Then again, God had brought him to Juniper Bluff— surely not to torture him with an almost daily reminder of what might have been. Even if the only reason was so that Tripp could set things right with Diana, he'd do his best and be grateful for the opportunity.

Watching Diana at work, he hadn't noticed how deeply he'd sank into his musings until Robert came over and stood right in front of him. "Excuse me, Doc Willoughby, but this is *your* day. Time to smile and mingle."

"Sorry, got distracted."

"Obviously." With a wry grin, Robert steered Tripp over to a cluster of middle-aged women chatting near the coffee urn.

One of them was Sue Ellen Jamison, whose cat Cleopatra had done a number on Tripp's hand his first day at the clinic. "Look, girls, here's Doc Willoughby now," Sue Ellen chirped. "My Cleo's new favorite vet, and mine, too!"

"Now, Sue Ellen," Robert said, "you're gonna hurt my feelings if you keep talking like that."

Tripp offered polite greetings to Sue Ellen and her friends and tried to ignore their flirtatious winks. They were all old enough to be his mother anyway, which reminded him he needed to give Brooke a call later and find out how Mom was doing.

Stifling a pang of worry, he let his gaze stray to where Diana served punch and pastries to a few of the children who'd arrived with their parents.

She glanced up briefly. When their eyes met, her hand faltered and she overfilled a punch cup. With a startled gasp, she grabbed some napkins to mop up the spill.

Robert's firm grip bit into Tripp's shoulder. "Why don't you get it over with and go talk to her?"

Tripp shot his partner a mock glare. "With friends like you—"

"—the world would be a happier place. Just do it already." Grinning mischievously, Robert gave Tripp a not-so-gentle shove.

He barely kept himself from tripping. Diana's smirk said she'd noticed. By the time he made his way across the crowded reception area, she'd poured him a cup of punch. Their fingertips grazed as she handed it to him.

He sipped gratefully, the tangy cranberry concoction soothing his dry throat. "This is really good. Thanks."

Her gaze slid to just below the level of his chin, and she hiked a brow. "Wow, a tie and everything. Dressing to impress?"

"Just trying to look professional." Tripp had debated about wearing a sports coat and was glad he'd decided not to. The ladies wore their Sunday best, but jeans, boots and open-neck shirts seemed to be the wardrobe of choice for the younger males of the community, no matter what day of the week.

"Well, you look very nice." Diana offered him a plate and napkin. "Care for a pastry? You're the guest of honor, after all."

"Don't remind me." Knowing he shouldn't—and wouldn't—eat it, out of politeness Tripp chose a blueberry minimuffin and set it on his plate. He smiled and nodded as Sue Ellen and her friends crossed in front of him for coffee refills.

"Just breathe," Diana murmured as she filled punch cups for two youngsters. "Only one hour and forty-three minutes to go."

"You're all heart." It was encouraging to think Diana felt comfortable enough to joke with him, but Tripp suspected the jibes were only her self-defense mechanism kicking in.

For the next hour and a half, the continual ebb and flow of guests diverted Tripp's attention, a good thing since the ground beneath his feet never felt totally stable with Diana nearby.

By the time four o'clock rolled around, most of the guests had said their goodbyes. Tripp shook hands with the last family to depart and said he looked forward to meeting their pets very soon. Even though he'd relaxed a bit as the warm welcomes flowed over him, he whistled a sigh of relief that the open house was finally over.

Turning from the door, he saw Diana and her helpers starting to pack up the leftover pastries. Diana pointed to the plate he'd set down earlier with his uneaten minimuffin. "Want this now, or should I add it to the other goodies I'm boxing up for you?"

A boxful of sugar-laden doughnuts and muffins was the last thing Tripp needed, but he figured Seth Austin's kids would appreciate the treats. He ambled over to the table. "Guess I got too busy visiting to eat."

"It was a nice turnout. You'll be the talk of the town for weeks." Diana closed the lid on the box, then began gathering up the remaining plates and napkins.

"Anything I can do to help?"

Diana cast him a dismissive glance and kept working. "No, thanks. We've got it handled."

He couldn't help feeling stung by her refusal. With a tight smile, he backed away.

He hadn't taken two steps when his cell phone vibrated in his pants pocket. Reading his sister's name on the display, he pressed the answer icon. "Hey, Brooke, I was going to call you later."

"Tripp, I've got bad news. Mom's been admitted to the hospital."

* * *

Moments after Tripp answered his cell phone, the sudden change in his expression made Diana's heart clench. Twisting sideways, shoulders hunched, he looked as if he'd been caught off guard by disturbing news.

Kimberly returned from emptying the coffee urn. She paused next to Diana. "Is Tripp okay?"

"Not sure." Diana gnawed on her lower lip. This appeared to be much more serious than someone's pet needing emergency treatment.

"Maybe you should find out. He looks pretty upset."

Diana wasn't so sure Tripp would welcome her intrusion. Glancing around, she hoped to enlist Doc Ingram's help but then remembered seeing him escort a couple of older ladies out to their car.

Tripp spoke a few more words into his phone, then disconnected. Still facing away, he heaved a shaky breath.

Diana couldn't restrain herself a moment longer. She scurried around the serving table, stopping just short of laying a hand on Tripp's arm. "Is—is there anything I can do?"

He seemed surprised to see her standing there. His Adam's apple bobbed with a pained swallow. "That was Brooke. My mom's in the hospital."

"Oh, no! What happened?" Diana had sweet memories of Peggy Willoughby, the soft-spoken woman who had welcomed her into their family like a daughter.

"Mom has kidney disease. It was causing some heart problems, so they hospitalized her to get things under control."

"Kidney disease? Tripp, I had no idea."

"It's been going on for a while. That's why Brooke got my folks to move out to California, so she could help with Mom's care."

Diana hadn't even known Brooke was living in California now. After college, they'd lost touch. At a loss for words, she motioned toward a row of chairs. "Sit down. Let me get you some water or something."

"No, thanks." Groaning, he pressed a hand to his side. "I think I just need to get out of here."

"Tripp—"

Before Diana could say more, he pushed through the inner door and marched down the hallway. His thudding footsteps faded, and moments later, the rear door slammed.

Kimberly, who'd continued quietly packing up their catering supplies, sidled over. "I couldn't help overhearing. Sounds like his mom's pretty sick."

"I feel horrible for him. For his whole family."

"Guess you got pretty close to them, before…"

Diana nodded. "I loved them all, very much. After we broke up, it felt like I'd lost them, too."

Doc Ingram returned through the front entrance, his expression grim. "Caught Tripp as he was leaving. Said he wasn't feeling well and to apologize for taking off so quickly without thanking you again."

"Our pleasure," Kimberly answered when Diana couldn't seem to find her voice. "We'll just finish up here and be on our way."

Brushing aside her troubled thoughts, Diana joined Kimberly and Ethan in loading their catering supplies onto a rolling cart. Twenty minutes later, Diana parked in the alley behind the doughnut shop, and shortly after they'd carried everything inside.

"Ethan and I can put all this stuff away," Kimberly offered. "Go home. You look beat."

Diana couldn't deny she was exhausted, both physically and emotionally. Maintaining her composure around Tripp made everything harder, and the heartbreaking news about his mother only added to her distress.

She gave Kimberly a grateful hug. "Offer accepted. I'll come in extra early in the morning to help you with the doughnuts."

Back in her car, Diana started for home. Before she'd driven two blocks, she had a flashback to the pained look on Tripp's face in the moments before he'd left the clinic. He'd never been the type to burden others with his personal problems, and now she pictured him alone in his cabin, racked with worry while he waited for more news from his sister.

At the next intersection, with no traffic in either direction, Diana braked and rested her head on the steering wheel. Her conscience was telling her to go to him, but her heart resisted. *What should I do, God?*

Her conscience spoke a little louder, which she took as God's direction to put her misgivings aside and do the right thing. If she were a stranger in a new community, she'd certainly be grateful for the support of an old friend at a time like this.

Old friend. After what they'd meant to each other—what she'd *believed* they'd meant to each other—could she really bear to settle for friendship?

Did she have a choice?

With a resigned sigh, Diana flipped on her turn signal. Two right turns took her back toward town. She passed the square, then turned left onto the farm road leading to Serenity Hills. She couldn't be sure he'd gone straight to his cabin, but if he hadn't, she'd wait for him.

Arriving at the guest ranch, she followed the lane around to the staff cabins. When she spotted Tripp's dark green SUV, she suffered a moment of panic—could she really do this?

Before she could change her mind, Tripp stepped onto the porch. He still wore his dress shirt, the sleeves rolled up to his elbows and his tie hanging loose from his open collar.

As she pulled up beside his car, his eyes widened in surprise. He came down the steps to meet her. "Diana, what are you doing here?"

Nudging the door closed with her hip, she crossed her arms and forced herself to meet his gaze. "I couldn't stop worrying about…your mom."

"She'd appreciate knowing that." Tripp ducked his head. "I do, too."

Diana narrowed her gaze. "You didn't tell Doc Ingram about your mom, did you?"

Guilt furrowing his brow, Tripp glanced away with a shrug. "I will, when I know more."

"This is so like you, Tripp, always holding things in." Sarcasm riddled her tone. "So what are you planning to do in the meantime? Pull your 'Mr. Cool' routine and go on about your business like nothing's wrong?"

"If you drove all the way out here to lecture me—"

"I drove all the way out here because I thought you could use a friend."

Jaw muscles bunched, he stared at her for a full second. "Yeah," he said, his voice husky. "Guess maybe I could." He plowed stiff fingers through his hair. "Sorry, it's been kind of a roller-coaster day."

"For both of us." This time she didn't hold back from touching his arm. "Your mom will always be special to me. I hope you know that."

"I do. I wish—" Tripp squeezed his eyes shut, then shook his head as if trying to clear it. "Never mind. Just…thanks for coming. It means a lot."

Diana wondered what he'd been about to say but decided she might be better off not knowing. She nodded toward the two red chairs on the porch. "Since I'm here, maybe we could sit for a while and work on this friendship thing?"

Tripp answered with a soft chuckle. "I'd like that."

Sitting on the porch with Diana was nice…real nice. Tripp had never in a million years anticipated her showing up like this, offering friendship and, at least figuratively, a shoulder to lean on while he waited for word about his mother.

Diana gazed toward a nearby pasture where two mares grazed. "Did Brooke say when to expect more news?"

"She promised to call back after they get Mom stabilized." Tripp spoke with more confidence than he felt. Each setback seemed worse than the one before, and he worried how much longer he'd have his mom around.

"I hate that she's going through this." Diana's fists knotted on the armrests. "Isn't there anything they can do? Maybe a kidney transplant or something?"

"It's not that simple. Blood type, tissue matching—a lot of things have to come together for a kidney donation to be successful."

"And no one in your family was a match?"

"We all got tested, but…it didn't work out." The familiar lump of regret landed hard in the pit of Tripp's belly. He stood and paced to the porch rail. Glancing back at Diana, he pasted on a smile. "Mind if we talk about something else? Tell me how your therapy pets project is going."

Her shoulders sagged. "Things aren't moving as quickly as I'd hoped." She told him about the cool reception from the church committee members, then added hesitantly, "I was planning to ask you today if I could post flyers at the clinic, until..."

Sidestepping the subject of his mother's illness, Tripp said, "Sure, of course you can. I told you I'd help any way I could." He returned to his chair. Forearms braced on his knees, he continued thoughtfully, "Obedience certification is usually the biggest hurdle. Once we get some interested dog owners, we can find a trainer and schedule the classes. Then it's just a matter of—"

"Tripp."

He met her tight-lipped stare.

"I only asked you about posting flyers, not to take charge of *my* project."

Straightening, he cleared his throat. "Didn't mean to. Guess I got a little carried away."

Diana faced forward. "I'm a little touchy, I suppose."

She didn't have to spell it out. He lifted his hands in a gesture of surrender. "Really sorry, okay? This is me backing off."

"And now you're just mocking me." Her voice trembled the tiniest bit, the pitiful sound tying knots around Tripp's heart.

"I'd never mock you, Diana. I care—" He cut himself off before he said too much.

For a microsecond he thought he glimpsed a spark

of hope in her eyes, before she covered it with an indifferent shrug. "This is silly. You said you've had experience working with therapy pets, and since I have no idea what I'm doing, I'd be a fool to refuse your help."

He wanted so badly to take her hand, to tell her how incredibly cute she looked with that conciliatory pout on her lips. His voice fell to just above a whisper. "Whatever you need, just ask."

With a sharp exhale, she muttered, "Thank you."

Several minutes of silence passed while the warm afternoon breeze swept away the remnants of their quarrel. Tripp chose to concentrate on the fact that Diana was here and speaking to him at all, which meant there had to be some hope for them, right? How many times had he prayed for this chance to clear the air between them, to somehow make up for the hurt he'd caused?

Tell her.

His inner voice just wouldn't shut up. But he couldn't tell her, not yet. Not until their connection as friends in the present overshadowed the heartbreak of the past.

"You're right," Diana said, interrupting his thoughts.

He shot her a startled glance. "I am? About what?"

"Obedience classes. How soon do you think we could set something up?"

Smiling to himself, Tripp tried to keep any hint of smugness out of his tone. Her use of the word *we* wasn't lost on him. "I'll make some calls first thing in the morning."

"Great. I'll get on my computer and work on those flyers tonight. As soon as business slows down at the shop tomorrow, I'll bring them by."

"Or…maybe we could meet somewhere for lunch?" Tripp figured he was expecting too much, but he couldn't stop himself from asking. "By then, I might have some answers for you about a dog trainer."

Diana appeared to be thinking over his suggestion. At least she hadn't given him an outright no. "The supermarket deli has an outdoor café. Would twelve thirty work for you?"

Tripp couldn't believe she'd agreed. "Sounds good."

Checking her watch, Diana sighed. "I should go. My *kids* will be wanting their supper." She pushed up from the chair. "When you hear from Brooke again, would you give me a call?"

"Of course."

"Promise me? I don't care if it's the middle of the night. I'd like to know."

Tripp crossed his heart. "I promise." He followed her down the porch steps. "Diana?"

She turned. "Yes?"

"Thanks."

Her brusque nod told him he didn't have to explain. "See you tomorrow."

Seconds later, she drove away, leaving Tripp with a bittersweet ache in his chest.

Too anxious about his mother to think about supper, Tripp made do with scrambled eggs and a slice of Canadian bacon. For the next hour or two, he tried to distract himself by reading up on the latest heartworm preventatives. When Brooke hadn't called by 10 p.m., his frustration got the best of him. He grabbed his cell phone off the lamp table and rang Brooke's number.

"Tripp, sorry for not calling sooner." She sounded tired.

"I've been going crazy. How's Mom?"

"Hold on a sec. I'm stepping into the corridor." The ambient sounds coming through the phone grew louder—indistinct voices, random beeps, the rattle of wheels across tile. "Okay, I can talk now. They got Mom's blood pressure stabilized about an hour ago."

"Thank God!" Tripp ran his hand across his eyes.

"We're not out of the woods yet. This was pretty serious." Brooke's voice faltered. "Tripp, the doctor said we need to be prepared."

A knot lodged in Tripp's throat. "Prepared?"

"Mom's weakening. Even if they found a kidney donor tomorrow, it wouldn't help. Her health has deteriorated too much."

For the millionth time, Tripp blamed the Crohn's that made him ineligible to give his mother a kidney. Barely able to speak the words, he asked, "How long?"

"The doctor won't commit to a timetable. He says it all depends on how well she rallies after this setback."

Tripp stood and paced the small sitting area. "Should I fly out there? I can leave in the morning—"

"No, Tripp." Brooke released a long sigh. "If you come now, it would only reinforce to both Mom and Dad that we're expecting the worst. I want to keep their hopes up for as long as we can."

Her logic made sense, but Tripp hated having his family so far away at a time like this. "All right, but if you even suspect—" He had to swallow hard before continuing. "Just don't wait till the last minute, okay? I want to be there."

"I promise. You're coming for Thanksgiving anyway, right? That's only a few weeks away."

"Yeah, that's still the plan." Except at this point, that felt like forever.

His dad's voice sounded in the background. "Is that Tripp? Let me talk to him."

Brooke passed the phone to their father, and for the next few minutes Tripp did his best to keep his tone light and his words encouraging. He could tell Dad was struggling equally hard to stay positive.

By the time the call ended, a stomach cramp warned Tripp he was on the edge of a flare-up. Usually he achieved the quickest stress reduction from focused breathing while meditating on Scripture. The verse he turned to most often came from 2 Corinthians 12, the Lord's words to Paul: "My grace is sufficient for thee, for my strength is made perfect in weakness."

Tonight, though, God's grace seemed beyond reach. "Why, God?" he shouted to the empty room. "If not for this stupid disease, my mom would have one of my kidneys and her health back, Diana and I would be happily married, and You and I would be having an entirely different conversation."

Silence answered him. He collapsed into the chair, pressed his hands to his stomach, and tried to deep-breathe the cramp into submission.

Diana. He'd promised to let her know after he heard from Brooke.

All at once, the idea of hearing Diana's voice again seemed the only answer to his misery. He picked up his cell phone, thankful he'd had the foresight to copy her personal number from the clinic files into his contact list. It had been a spur-of-the-moment decision, and extremely presumptuous, since at the time he hadn't envisioned she'd ever welcome a call from him except concerning veterinary business.

She answered almost before the first ring. "Tripp?"

"You must have had your thumb on the answer button."

"Practically. I was sitting here watching the late news and hoping you'd call." Her concern warmed him briefly, until he reminded himself she only wanted to know about his mother. "What's the latest?"

He opened his mouth to tell her, but the words stuck in his throat.

"Tripp, are you there?"

"Yeah, sorry," he choked out. "Mom's past the crisis." *This time.*

Diana released a relieved sigh. "Are you planning to fly out there?"

"No, not right away." He explained Brooke's reasoning and mentioned his Thanksgiving holiday plans. "In the meantime, it looks like all we can do is wait."

"And pray," Diana said softly. "Never discount the power of prayer."

Massaging his forehead, he muttered, "I'm, uh, having a little trouble in the prayer department these days."

"Oh, Tripp, I understand. I know how hard it can be when God..." The empathy in her tone shifted toward regret. "Well, when He doesn't let things turn out like we hope."

A swallow jammed his throat closed. "Diana—"

"The point is to keep praying," she rushed on, "even when it seems like God isn't listening. We have to believe He cares, or nothing in life would make sense."

Little in Tripp's life did at the moment, but he kept the thought to himself. "Maybe you'd say a few prayers for my mom?"

"Of course. I'll pray for all of you."

"Thanks." The pain in Tripp's abdomen had eased slightly. "It's late. I should let you go."

294 Hill Country Reunion

"Will you be okay?"

He wondered what she'd say if he said no. But the one thing he didn't want from her—had *never* wanted from her—was pity. "Just talking to you has helped a lot."

"I'm glad," she said, a smile returning to her voice. "Anyway, things are bound to look brighter in the morning. A good night's sleep always makes a difference."

After saying goodbye, Tripp washed down his evening meds with a glass of almond milk and hoped Diana was right about a good night's sleep. Unfortunately, he didn't foresee the likelihood.

Chapter Five

On Monday morning, while Kimberly kept the bakery case replenished with fresh doughnuts and other goodies, Diana brewed coffee and filled orders…and glanced at the clock about every five minutes.

"Expecting a visit from the queen?" Grinning, Kimberly set a tray of muffins in the display case.

"What— *Ow!*" Diana shook off the hot coffee she'd just dribbled on her hand. Trying to take care of a customer while checking the time *and* responding to her nosy assistant was a recipe for trouble.

Kimberly handed Diana a paper towel. "Seriously, you've been preoccupied all morning. What gives?"

"Didn't get much sleep last night." With a noncommittal shrug, Diana set two to-go coffee cups, sugar and creamer packets, and two blueberry scones in a cardboard tray. "Here you go, Kelly."

Kelly Nesbit, the nurse from the pharmacy's urgent care clinic, slid her debit card into the chip reader. "Too much going on? I heard you're starting up a therapy pets group."

"That's definitely been on my mind."

"Among other things," Kimberly muttered with a smirk.

Diana shot her assistant a get-lost glare.

"Try lavender essential oil on your pillow," Kelly suggested. "A couple of drops work wonders when you can't relax."

"Thanks, I'll remember that." Diana tucked Kelly's receipt and some napkins onto the tray.

"And keep me posted about your group. I've got a sweet rescue dog I think would make a great therapy pet."

Diana perked up. While waiting to hear from Tripp last night, she'd finished designing and printing out copies of her informational flyer. She'd placed a few on the counter and handed one to Kelly. "I'm working with Visiting Pet Pals. This explains some of their requirements. My cell number's at the bottom, so give me a call if you'd like to get involved."

"I will." Giving a nod, Kelly added the flyer to her coffee tray, then hurried out.

With another glance at the time, Diana stifled a groan. Still an hour and twenty minutes before she was supposed to meet Tripp for lunch. As distraught as he'd been yesterday, would he even remember their plans, much less that he'd promised to make inquiries about dog trainers? She considered calling him at the clinic with a friendly reminder but quickly trashed the thought. As much as the therapy pets project meant to her, it was nothing compared to what Tripp's family was going through.

Business slowed again as folks returned to their offices and shops. While Diana tidied the coffee service area, Kimberly consolidated the remaining doughnuts and pastries at the front of the display case.

Finishing, Kimberly peeled off her food prep gloves and dropped them in the trash. She gave Diana's shoulder a friendly poke. "Take off, why don't you? I can tell you're chomping at the bit to get out of here."

Diana grimaced. It was past eleven thirty now. She could brood just as easily sitting outside the supermarket deli as she could finding busywork at the doughnut shop—*and* she wouldn't have to fend off Kimberly's prying questions. She slipped out of her apron. "Thanks, I do have some…errands to run."

Kimberly winked. "If you happen to run into Doc Willoughby, give him my regards."

With a disbelieving glance toward the ceiling, Diana hung up her apron and marched to the office to grab her purse.

By noon she'd ordered an iced green tea and carried it to one of the umbrella-shaded tables outside the deli. From there, she had a good view of both the parking lot and the supermarket entrance. She also laid her cell phone on the table in case Tripp called or texted.

Then, annoyed with herself, she jammed the phone back into her purse and shifted her chair sideways. What had gotten into her, letting herself get so keyed up about seeing Tripp again? There was nothing between them, and this wasn't a date. Why should she—

Her cell phone chimed. She dove for her purse. Reading Tripp's name on the phone's display screen, she took a deep breath before answering. "Hi. Are you on your way?"

"I'm stuck at the clinic," Tripp said. "Last-minute appointment. Afraid I can't make it for lunch, after all."

"Oh." Diana clamped her teeth together to stifle an unexpected wave of disappointment. "Okay, then. Guess we'll talk later."

"Sure. But I wanted to tell you I did get hold of a dog trainer this morning."

"That's great. Thank you." Gazing across the parking lot, Diana sighed. "I... I figured the therapy pets thing might be the furthest thing from your mind this morning."

Tripp uttered a weak chuckle. "Actually, it's helping to keep my mind off other things—which I really need right now."

"Then I'm glad to be of assistance." Diana reached into her purse for a pen and a scrap of paper. "If you have the dog trainer's number..."

"Actually, I wondered if you'd be free later this afternoon. I thought we could drive over to the pet shop where he works in Fredericksburg and meet with him in person."

"You really don't have to do that, Tripp. I can take it from here."

"You'd be doing me a favor if you let me tag along." His tone softened. "Like I said, I need the distraction."

How could she refuse? After a quick review of her schedule, Diana agreed, and Tripp offered to pick her up at the doughnut shop around three thirty. They said goodbye, and Diana returned to the deli to pick up a salad to go—although the thought of lunching alone at her desk evoked an empty feeling in the pit of her stomach that was far more disconcerting than hunger pangs.

About time you admitted it, she told herself. *You were actually looking forward to having lunch with Tripp.*

Well, she'd have her chance to spend time with him

later when they drove to Fredericksburg. Except she'd better keep her priorities straight and remember this outing was strictly business.

Back at work, though, she found herself doing too much clock watching. At three twenty, she turned the shop over to Kimberly and stepped out the front door to wait for Tripp.

He'd just driven up. Climbing into the passenger seat of his SUV, she said, "You're early."

"So are you," he answered with a grin. "Ready to head over to the pet shop?"

"Let's go." Diana buckled her seat belt and slid on the cheap new pair of sunglasses she'd bought after the horseback riding fiasco. "By the way, I brought some flyers for you to take back to the clinic—that is, if it's still okay."

"Absolutely."

Tripp fell silent as he headed toward the highway, and Diana was having trouble coming up with scintillating travel conversation.

Then Tripp broke the silence with a long sigh. "I just wanted to say... I mean, if I got a little emotional last night..."

Diana glanced over, noting the embarrassed twist to his lips. "You had every right," she said. "I can't even imagine how worried you must be."

"Still, I shouldn't have burdened you with my problems."

Annoyance tightened Diana's chest. This was Tripp being Tripp, so why should she be surprised? "It's no burden. That's what friends are for."

He met her gaze with an uncertain smile before returning his attention to the road. "You're right. Thanks."

A few minutes later, they arrived at the pet store. Tripp asked one of the clerks to page Sean, and shortly a shaggy-haired young man in a blue T-shirt came up and introduced himself.

"Hi, Sean. Tripp Willoughby. We spoke on the phone this morning." Tripp offered a handshake.

"Oh, yeah, about the obedience classes for the therapy pets thing." With a polite smile in Diana's direction, Sean addressed Tripp. "Ready to set up a schedule?"

Diana tamped down a pang of irritation. She stepped forward and extended her own hand. "I'm still recruiting my volunteers," she stated. "I just need some information I can give them about your availability, fees and such."

Sean tugged on the ends of a leather leash dangling from his neck. Clearly getting the message that this was Diana's project, he motioned her toward some offices at the far end of the checkout counters. Tripp seemed to have grasped the point, too, letting Diana lead the way.

Squeezing between a cluttered desk and a tall filing cabinet, Sean shuffled through a drawer and brought out a trifold brochure. "This describes what my four-week basic obedience classes cover. Unless your volunteers want to join one of our nightly classes here at the store, my only availability for off-site training would be Sunday afternoons. You'd just need to arrange for a facility."

Diana nodded thoughtfully. "I'll work on that. Can you tentatively put us on your calendar for the next four Sundays? This all needs to be completed by the first week of November."

"Dr. Willoughby mentioned that." Sean flipped pages in a desk planner and began marking off Sunday afternoons. "Okay, just let me know in the next few days if this is a go."

With sign-up instructions and several of Sean's brochures in hand, Tripp and Diana left the pet store. They hadn't traveled far before Diana's initial optimism faded. "None of this matters if I can't come up with enough dog owners to participate."

Tripp reached across the console to gently touch her hand. "You're not getting discouraged, are you?"

Her first instinct was to pull away, but she realized she didn't want to. She'd forgotten how nice it felt when she and Tripp used to hold hands.

Or maybe she hadn't forgotten at all. As if with a will of their own, her fingers entwined with his. She blinked rapidly, unable to tear her eyes away from the sight of his manly, sun-bronzed hand wrapped so tenderly around her much smaller, paler one.

Tripp slid his hand free and grasped the steering wheel. He cleared his throat roughly. "I mean…it's a worthy cause. Once your recruitment flyers start circulating, you shouldn't have any trouble lining up volunteers."

"I—I hope you're right." Tucking the hand he'd touched firmly into her lap, Diana sat straighter. She'd overreacted, clearly. Tripp had only meant to reassure her, and now they were both fighting embarrassment.

To ease the tension, Diana mentioned how the flyers she'd given out this morning at the doughnut shop had already garnered interest. Besides Kelly, three other customers had said they might be calling for more information.

"There you go," Tripp said, as if her success were a

foregone conclusion. "You'll have the minimum number of sign-ups in no time."

With a shaky smile, Diana turned toward the window. She appreciated Tripp's help and encouragement,
but to work this closely with him? She wasn't so sure
her heart could withstand the emotional chaos.

Tripp returned Diana to her car behind the doughnut
shop, then headed out to his cabin. But all that evening,
he couldn't get his mind off the way her hand had felt
in his. The moment had seemed so natural, so right.

But also very, very wrong. Much as his heart was
urging him to pick up where they'd left off all those
years ago, he couldn't rush this. They both needed time
to adjust to the "new normal" of being near each other
again.

Finishing his first appointment the next morning,
he escorted Vince Mussell and his overgrown mutt out
to the reception desk. "Darby's vaccines are good for
three years," Tripp explained. "Yolanda will give you
his new rabies tag, and I'll call in a couple of days with
the heartworm test results."

"Thanks, Doc." Vince stroked the dog's big, brown
head. "This boy may not be so pretty to look at, but
he's a cuddler. He means the world to Janice and me."

"He is a sweetheart." Best guess, Darby was part
Labrador, with maybe some shepherd and bloodhound
mixed in. "Say, would you and your wife consider volunteering with Darby as a therapy pet? He looks like
a good candidate."

Vince's forehead creased. "Therapy pet? What exactly is that?"

Tripp handed Vince one of Diana's flyers. "This will explain. Do you know Diana Matthews?"

"Oh, sure, from the doughnut shop. Sweet girl." A thoughtful frown twisting his lips, Vince perused the flyer. "Hmm, I'll show this to Janice. Looks interesting."

Before the day ended, Tripp had handed out flyers to the owners of every canine patient he'd seen that looked even halfway suitable for Diana's program. He couldn't completely rule out a dog that exhibited extreme nervousness at a veterinary appointment, because the animal might be perfectly fine in less stressful social situations. It would be up to the therapy pets evaluator to make the final decision.

Would it be too soon to let Diana know about the positive responses? He could wait and call after he got back to the cabin, or he could casually drop in at the doughnut shop, using the excuse that he'd like to replenish his supply of the flyers.

The longing to see Diana again, even if only as a friend, won out. Leaving the clinic, he headed into town and parked in front of the doughnut shop, only to be reminded it closed at four. The disappointment forcing the air from his lungs seemed way out of proportion, but he couldn't help himself.

He'd just about accepted the inevitability of not seeing Diana again until tomorrow when his cell phone rang. Diana's name on the display kicked his pulse into high gear. The sensible part of his brain shouted at him to get his eagerness under control before he answered, but he ignored it. "Diana, hi. I was just thinking about—"

"Tripp, I need help." The panic in her voice hit him

like a bucket of ice water. "It's my cat Tiger. I don't know what's wrong."

Professionalism taking over, Tripp tightened his grip on the phone. "What are the symptoms?"

"Retching, coughing, wheezing and he acts like his stomach hurts." Diana gave a shaky sniff. "I'm sorry for bothering you, but the clinic number went to the answering service and I was too scared to wait for a callback."

"It's okay. I'm still in town, and I can head straight back to the clinic. Can you meet me there with Tiger?"

"I'll be there in five minutes."

"Don't rush. Better to be safe—" Too late. The line went dead.

Tripp tossed the phone onto the seat, then backed out of the parking space and aimed his SUV in the direction of the clinic. He suspected Diana's cat had an impacted hair ball, which could be life threatening without immediate treatment.

Arriving at the clinic, he spotted Diana waiting on the front step, her arms wrapped protectively around a bulky blue cat carrier. Tripp parked next to Diana's car, then hurried to unlock the clinic. He showed Diana to the first exam room, where she helped him coax the hefty striped tomcat out of the crate.

A cursory exam reaffirmed Tripp's suspicions. He shared them with Diana. "To be certain, I need to sedate him and get some X-rays. Then we're probably talking surgery."

She nodded and wiped away a tear. "Do whatever you need to."

An hour and a half later, Tripp had successfully removed the obstruction. Knowing Diana would be anxious for news, he found her in the waiting room. "Tiger did great. He's sleeping off the anesthesia. Want to see him?"

"Yes!" She held his forearm in a death grip as he showed her into the surgery suite, where Tiger lay sleeping in a padded kennel. "Oh, my poor kitty," she murmured, stroking his paw. With a glance at Tripp, she asked, "How soon before he can come home?"

"Since you have other cats, it might be better if I kept him here for a few days while the incision heals." At her look of dismay, Tripp added, "I'll take good care of him, I promise."

"I know. It's just that…" Diana covered her mouth to stifle a sob.

Instinctively, Tripp pulled her into his arms—and instantly knew it was a mistake, because holding her like this was bringing back all kinds of memories. As he strove for the wherewithal to release her, she pressed closer, her face buried in the hollow space beneath his collarbone.

Then, just as quickly, she shuddered and pulled away. "Sorry, didn't mean to fall apart like that." Using the back of her hand, she brushed wetness from her cheeks and returned her attention to the cat. "Tiger's been with me the longest of all my pets. If I lost him, I don't know what I'd do."

A coldness seeped in to fill the emptiness Diana had left behind. Finding the breath to speak, Tripp willed calm detachment into his tone. "I told you, he'll be fine. Once he's ready to go home, I'll give you some pointers on how to keep this from happening again."

"Good, thanks." Diana glanced at her watch. "Wow, is it really after seven? No wonder my stomach's growling."

Caught up in doing his job, Tripp hadn't even thought about food. Now, Diana's reminder brought an answering rumble from his own abdomen. The banana he'd downed for an afternoon snack had long since worn off, but he wouldn't leave the clinic while Tiger was still in recovery. "Go get some dinner. I'll keep an eye on Tiger."

Diana chewed her lip. "Well, I do need to check on my other kids. Can I bring you back something?"

"Thanks, but I'll grab a snack from the fridge. Anyway, don't you have to be up early to open the shop?" Tripp nodded toward the door. "Go home. We'll be fine here."

Halfway down the corridor, Diana halted and spun around. "Tripp?"

"Yeah?"

"Thank you." With a quick but meaningful smile, she hurried out.

One shoulder braced against the door frame, Tripp suppressed a sigh of longing. Every minute he spent in Diana's company only made him want her more. He'd been crazy about her in college, all set to pop the question before...

Nope, not going there. It was no use dwelling on might-have-beens. He'd made a good life for himself in spite of everything, and so had Diana. If—and it was a big *if*—there was still the slightest hope of a future together, their relationship would have to be based on who they were now, not the starry-eyed romantics they'd been twelve years ago.

But would Diana ever be ready to give him—*them*—another chance at love?

* * *

Diana had no idea what she would have done if Tripp hadn't answered her panicked call. Doc Ingram, busy as he'd been while running the practice single-handedly, wouldn't have been quite so easy to reach in such an emergency.

Thank You, God. Thank You for sending Tripp back into my life, exactly when I needed him.

Because he was an excellent vet, that's all. Smart and kind and dedicated—

"Face it, girl," she murmured to herself as she spread fresh bedding in Alice's crate, "he's still the same man you fell in love with back in college."

The same...but also different. Different in ways Diana had yet to comprehend. Yes, apparently, he paid a lot more attention to a healthy diet than he ever had when they were together. But he also seemed more mature, more grounded, more...jaded?

No, *jaded* was too strong a word. *Resigned*, maybe, as if making the best of some painful disappointment in his life.

Painful disappointment? Diana slapped her forehead, startling the parakeet. "Sorry, Sparky." She placated him with an apple slice while wondering how Tripp could possibly regret the breakup as much as she did.

He'd been the one to call things off. *He* was the one who, with one cowardly phone call, had destroyed their dreams for a future together.

Turning her attention to preparing supper for the mewing cats circling her ankles, she thrust aside any thoughts of letting Tripp off the hook. There was no argument about his veterinary skills, nor the fact that Diana probably wasn't going to get this therapy pets program off the ground without his help. But she absolutely would not let herself fall for him again.

Right. Like the fool she was, she'd gone all weepy and fallen into his arms. It galled her now to recall how naturally the moment had happened. Until she'd come to her senses anyway.

"Professional," she told Lucinda and Midnight as she set bowls of salmon-flavored cat food in front of them. "I've *got* to keep this relationship strictly professional."

After warming a microwave dinner for herself, Diana carried it to the sofa and flipped on the TV. By the time she finished her meal, both cats had curled up next to her, and since Tiger usually claimed her lap, she missed him all the more. She glanced at her cell phone lying on the end table. Would Tripp mind if she called to check on Tiger?

Deciding Tiger was *her* cat and it didn't matter if Tripp minded—he was a *professional*, after all—she picked up the phone.

"Hi, Diana." His silky-smooth voice sounded cheerful but tired.

And totally discombobulated her. "Hi. I, uh…wondered how Tiger's doing."

"He's still a little groggy but in no pain. I'll make sure he has a restful night."

It only then occurred to Diana that Tripp meant to spend the night at the clinic, and guilt niggled about not taking him some supper. On the other hand, he was probably used to this sort of thing. Still, she couldn't stop herself from asking, "Did you find something to eat?"

He hesitated a couple of seconds too long. "A little."

"What, exactly?"

"Yolanda left some pita chips and hummus in the snack room."

"Tripp! That's not supper." Diana cringed at the up-surge of concern swelling her chest. "You should have let me bring you something."

"I'm a big boy. I'll survive." His tone grew edgy. "You've got enough on your mind. I don't need you worrying about me."

"But I do—" She clamped her mouth shut. *Way to keep it professional, Matthews.* "I mean, if not for me, you'd have had a relaxing evening and a decent meal. I just…feel bad about that."

"Well, don't. As soon as I check Tiger one more time, I'm running over to the supermarket to pick up something and bring it back." A weary laugh sounded in Diana's ear. "This is what I signed up for, Di. I love my work, and I'd do the same for any of my patients."

"Oh." She didn't know whether to feel relieved or of-fended. Worse, he'd called her Di again, which stirred up all kinds of other emotions she'd rather not deal with. "Well…thank you."

"Get some sleep. I'll call you in the morning with a report."

Clicking off, Diana had a feeling she was in for yet another sleepless night.

She couldn't have been more right. Staring at her re-flection in the bathroom mirror the next morning, she wished she could blame her dark circles and bloodshot eyes on worrying about Tiger, because the truth was a lot harder to deal with. During the little sleep she'd got-ten, her dreams had been invaded by Tripp—his eyes, his smile, his arms gently enfolding her as she leaned into his solid chest.

"What am I going to do?" she said aloud to the frazzled woman in the mirror. Her life had been humming along perfectly fine until Tripp Willoughby showed up. Now everything was—

She waved her hands in a gesture of futility. No time to sort through it all now. The doughnut shop awaited. And so did a giant-sized mug of supercaffeinated coffee.

Work definitely proved a panacea for getting her mind off Tripp. Temporarily, at least. Once the early birds had been served, Diana returned to her office to catch up on some bookkeeping and paperwork.

A few minutes after nine, the business line rang. "Diana's Donuts, Diana speaking."

"Hi, Diana. It's Yolanda from Ingram Veterinary Hospital. Dr. Willoughby wanted me to let you know how Tiger's doing this morning."

Diana flinched. It didn't get much more professional than having the receptionist do the calling. "Yes, how is he?"

"Just fine. Tiger is eating and drinking well and generally on the mend. Doc says Tiger should be ready to rejoin your little family in another couple of days."

"That's wonderful. Thank you." Closing her eyes briefly, Diana took a quick breath. "And thank Dr. Willoughby, too."

Chapter Six

Juniper Bluff might be a small town, but the animal clinic drew plenty of business from the surrounding area, and Tripp's appointment calendar stayed comfortably full. According to Yolanda, they were also getting several new patients as word spread that Doc Ingram had taken on a partner.

Over his lunch hour on Friday, Tripp took a few minutes to look in on his surgical patients—a neutered Pomeranian, a Lab mix with a benign tumor and of course Diana's cat Tiger. The old tomcat's incision seemed to be healing well, and Tripp decided it would be safe to send him home this afternoon. He started to the front desk to ask Yolanda to make the call, then thought better of it. All week long, he'd taken the coward's way out and had his receptionist report to Diana about Tiger's progress. His convoluted logic had him believing if Diana really wanted to talk to him, she'd say so—or, better yet, show up at the clinic wearing the megawatt smile that had always been his undoing.

He was almost glad she hadn't, because he wasn't

sure how much longer he could hide the feelings her nearness had rekindled.

Their personal issues aside, he wanted to find out where things stood with the obedience classes. If she needed more help recruiting volunteers, he'd gladly step up his own efforts—anything to help her be ready for the early-November evaluation.

With a tight-lipped groan, he backtracked to his office and closed the door. He placed the call on his cell phone, knowing she'd see his name on her cell's display. That way, she could choose to answer...or not.

Three rings later, she picked up. "Hi, Tripp." Shyness, and maybe a teensy bit of accusation, tinged her tone. "It's been a while."

"Yeah, I've stayed pretty busy this week." Technically true, but a lame excuse nonetheless. "Thought you might be ready to take your boy home today."

"Yes, definitely! I'll pick him up as soon as we close this afternoon."

Her burst of enthusiasm made Tripp annoyingly envious of the tabby. "Great. So I'll see you shortly after four?"

"I'll be there." All business again, she continued, "By the way, thanks for referring so many of your patients. I've gotten several inquiries this week."

"I'm glad." He cleared his throat. "Any takers for Sean's obedience class?"

"Possibly. Still need to confirm with some phone calls."

"If I can help..."

"I'll let you know." With a crisp goodbye, she ended the conversation.

Naturally this *would* be the one afternoon when

Tripp didn't have a full slate of appointments. After giving a squirming puppy its first round of vaccinations, then explaining to the new owner of a kitten why investing in a scratching post was a much more humane option than declawing, Tripp had little more to occupy himself than catching up on his veterinary journals.

At long last, four o'clock rolled around. With one eye on the front door, Tripp tried to look busy reorganizing magazines in the reception area while Yolanda completed the daily computer entries and filing.

The superobservant receptionist wasn't fooled, though. "I was going to clock out as soon as I finish up here, but if you need a chaperone, I could stick around." She winked. "Of course, I'd expect to be paid double overtime."

"In your dreams." Giving up his pretense, Tripp folded his arms on the counter. "I can assure you, there won't be anything happening here requiring a chaperone."

"Too bad." Yolanda stood across from him to straighten the three remaining therapy pets flyers. She tapped a violet acrylic nail on Diana's name. "Anyone can see you two were meant for each other. Why you are both fighting it so hard is beyond my understanding."

Mine, too, Tripp didn't say aloud. "Too much water under the bridge. Let's leave it at that."

The rumble of tires on pavement drew Tripp's attention to the front windows. With a threatening glance at Yolanda, he strode to the door and held it open as Diana came up the steps. The cat carrier tucked under one arm, she smiled up at him. It wasn't exactly a thrilled-to-see-you smile, but he'd take it.

"I don't have much time," she said, bustling past him

into the waiting room. "I need to return a call from my Visiting Pet Pals contact."

"No problems, I hope."

"I don't think so. She probably wants to make sure everything is still on track." With a quick greeting to Yolanda, Diana set the cat carrier on the floor next to the counter. She fingered the three remaining therapy pets flyers. "This is all you have left?"

Tripp came up beside her. "I've been meaning to ask you for more, but I kept getting sidetracked."

"Yes," Diana said stiffly, "you mentioned you've been busy."

Yolanda patted several file folders into a neat stack. "These can wait until Monday. I'm calling it a day." She took her purse from a desk drawer and stepped from behind the counter. "Nice seeing you, Diana. Take care!" With a pointed look at Tripp, she reminded him to lock up on his way out.

Moments later, the back door banged. Alone with Diana, Tripp whooshed out a breath. "I guess we should get Tiger so you can be on your way and make that call."

"Right." Diana bent to pick up the carrier at the same moment Tripp did, and their heads bumped. "Oh, sorry!"

"No harm done." Rubbing his forehead, Tripp stepped back and let Diana get the carrier. He showed her down the hall to the room where cats were boarded.

Stepping inside, Diana gave a happy gasp and rushed over to where the stray mother cat and kittens were kenneled. "Oh, look how much they've grown!"

"They're doing great. Won't be long until these little guys are ready for their forever homes." Tripp nodded toward a kennel at the far end of the room. "Tiger's down this way."

As Diana approached, the old cat mewed and rubbed against the mesh. "Aw, glad to see me, fella? I've missed you."

Tripp released the latch, and after Diana had given Tiger some hugs and kisses, he helped her ease him into the cat carrier. "I've got some postsurgical instructions up front for you with notes about hair ball prevention."

Diana grimaced. "I'm sure you've got a hefty bill for me, too."

"No hurry. Talk to Yolanda about it next week." They started toward the front. "Anyway, I figure you qualify for our multi-pet discount."

"No kidding." Reaching the reception area, Diana paused and turned. "I'd better get going. Still need to get my notes in order before I call the Visiting Pet Pals lady."

"You'll let me know how it goes, I hope?" Tripp stepped behind the counter to find Tiger's file and retrieve the information sheets he'd prepared.

Tucking the papers into her purse, Diana gnawed her lower lip. "Actually, with your therapy pets experience, I could probably use your advice and moral support for this conversation. I don't want to give Agnes Kraus any reason whatsoever to deny my application."

Tripp's pulse quickened. "Whatever you need."

After a thoughtful pause, Diana asked, "How do you feel about pizza?"

Tripp did some quick mental calculations about his food intake so far this week. He'd been pretty sensible about his choices, and pizza generally wasn't a problem, provided he skipped the spicy or high-fat toppings.

"I actually love pizza," he said, then offered a crooked grin. "Is this a dinner invitation, perchance?"

"If you're buying." Diana wiggled her brows. "Because after I pay my vet bill, you're going to be a lot richer than I am."

"All right, you're on." Too stunned to question Diana's openness to spending the evening with him, he jotted down the name of the pizza place she suggested. "I'll close up shop here and call in the order. Be at your place around six?"

"Great. See you then."

Later, as Tripp placed the call to order their pizza, he wondered what kind of emotional torture he'd just set himself up for.

With Tiger curled up on the sofa cushion beside her, Diana firmly but lovingly instructed Midnight and Lucinda to give him some space. Once the other cats had settled, one on an armchair and the other on a plush ottoman, Diana spread her notes across the coffee table in preparation for her conversation with Mrs. Kraus.

Seeing everything laid out in front of her—seeing her germ of an idea come to fruition after weeks of dreaming and planning—made everything all the more real.

"It's happening, Tiger," she squealed. "I can't wait for Tripp—"

Tripp? Since when was *he* the first person she thought of sharing this moment with? Fists clenched against her mouth, Diana trembled from the shock of how easily the past had converged on the present. She and Tripp had once shared every joy and disappointment, each one a milestone along their journey toward lasting love…until the final disappointment that had shattered her dreams forever.

The doorbell rang, and Diana jumped. She had to get her feelings under control, or Tripp would see the turmoil written all over her face. Tearing the elastic band from her ponytail, she shook out her hair, then stood and straightened her shirt and jeans. There had been no time to change out of the clothes she'd worn at work all day, and a faint aroma of coffee lingered.

Too bad. This certainly wasn't a *date*, which meant she had no excuse for suddenly being so concerned about her appearance. With a steadying breath, she walked casually to the front door. As she pulled it open, enticing smells of crispy crust and flavorful toppings surrounded her.

And of course Tripp stood there wearing a boyish grin and looking as handsome as ever. "Hi. Hope you like chicken with spinach and artichoke hearts."

"Wow, you went gourmet." Diana showed him into the kitchen. "I've got the oven set on warm. We can eat after I talk to Mrs. Kraus."

"I was hoping to get here in time." Tripp slid the pizza box onto an oven shelf, then straightened to face Diana. He looked as if he wanted to take her hand but at the last second dropped his arms to his sides. "Nervous?"

"A little." She checked her watch and whistled out a breath. "Guess I'd better make that call."

Returning to the sofa and her table full of notes and lists, Diana picked up her cell phone and dialed Agnes Kraus's number. With a tight-lipped glance at Tripp, she put the call on Speaker and laid the phone on the coffee table.

"Good evening, Diana," the woman greeted. "This won't take long. I just need a quick update on your progress."

"I've had a very productive week. Eleven dog owners have expressed interest, and we're working now on the obedience qualifications."

"Excellent. Remember, to complete your chapter certification, we will need copies of the dogs' health records, verification of obedience training and documentation from the assisted-living center stating their agreement to participate."

Tripp was already perusing Diana's checklist. He silently passed it to her.

"Yes, ma'am," she said, scanning the page. "Everything's in process. I've already been in touch with the center, and they're anxious to get the program going."

"Very well, then. Keep me posted, and unless I hear otherwise, I'll see you the second Saturday of November for evaluation and volunteer training."

"Looking forward to it." Saying goodbye, Diana released her pent-up breath.

Tripp gave her knee a quick pat. "You did great."

"Thanks. Crazy, but this is almost more nerve-racking than when I applied for my small-business loan to open the doughnut shop."

"Not crazy when it's something you care so much about."

"I do care. This is all for Aunt Jennie." Diana rose to check on the pizza. "My own grandmother—Aunt Jennie's sister—died before I was born, so she's always filled that spot in my life."

"I remember," Tripp said, following her to the

kitchen. "Your great-aunt's a very special lady. I know how much you love her."

His understanding tone brought a catch to Diana's chest. She cleared her throat. "Guess we should eat this pizza before it turns to rubber. What would you like to drink? I have decaf iced tea, diet cola or lemon-lime."

"Iced tea, please. Point me to the cupboard and I'll get plates."

As Diana filled two glasses, she became acutely aware of Tripp moving around behind her, making himself at home in her kitchen. *This is how it should have been*, a wistful voice whispered in her head, *the two of us, a comfortable, old married couple making a home together.*

She swallowed over the lump in her throat and carried the drinks to the table. Tripp had already served slices of pizza onto their plates. Like the gentleman he'd always been, he pulled out Diana's chair for her—which did nothing to mitigate the cozy, homelike ambience. When he asked if he could offer grace and hesitantly reached for Diana's hand, she said a silent prayer of her own that God would get her through the rest of this evening in one piece.

Focusing on the reason for Tripp's visit might be her only saving grace. They ate in silence for a few minutes, and then Diana said, "Forgot to tell you. I asked Pastor Terry about holding obedience classes at the church, and he got the okay for us to use the back lawn on Sunday afternoons, provided the owners do any necessary cleanups."

Tripp helped himself to another slice of pizza, then slanted his head with a curious look. "It occurred to me that you're making arrangements for all these dog owners to join your program, but you don't have a dog yourself."

"I guess it is kind of weird," Diana said with a laugh. "I love dogs, but cats are a little less demanding. Besides, I don't have a fenced yard, and with the long hours I work at the shop, I'd feel bad leaving a dog cooped up in the house all day."

"Makes sense. And makes me admire you all the more for what you're doing."

Diana's cheeks warmed. "If Aunt Jennie hadn't had to give Ginger away, I'd probably never have gotten involved with this project." Her voice dropping to a murmur, she added, "Nobody should be deprived of that kind of unconditional love and companionship."

"I agree," Tripp said huskily. He stared at his half-eaten pizza slice. "Di...if I could undo the past, make up for how I hurt you—"

"Don't say it, Tripp. We're not going there tonight. And never again, okay?" It was the only way Diana could bear being this close to him. "That was then, this is now, and all that matters is the people we are today."

Tripp slowly lifted his gaze to meet hers, and in the depths of those intense blue eyes, Diana saw something that rocked her to her core. "If you believe that," he began hesitantly, "then do you think we could start over?"

Her heart stammered. "Start over?"

With a tender smile, Tripp took her hand. "Please. Give me a chance to get it right this time."

Nearly choking on her emotions, Diana clutched his hand with both of hers. "You've got to know how scary this is for me. My heart won't survive getting broken again."

A long, slow sigh escaped Tripp's lips. "As far as it's in my power, I promise that won't happen."

His choice of words struck a subtle warning note in Diana's brain, but she was too caught up in the moment to care. This was Tripp, the man she'd fallen in love with all those years ago and still cared for despite all her efforts to put him out of her heart. Could this really be God offering them a second chance at happiness? If so, she couldn't let it slip away.

Tripp was too elated to do or say anything but bask in the moment. The time would come eventually for him to confide in Diana about the Crohn's, but for now, he wanted to just *be*—him and his girl, sharing pizza and conversation, and laying out the plans for her therapy pets project.

Their project. Because he felt more a part of it—more a part of Diana's life—than he'd imagined possible barely three weeks ago.

After clearing away the supper dishes, they moved to the sofa, where they divided up the list of potential volunteers and began placing calls. By eight forty-five, they had six sign-ups for the obedience class. Three other owners said their dogs had already earned basic obedience certificates, and the remaining two on the list had decided the program wasn't right for them.

Diana tapped her pen against her chin. "That leaves us with nine strong possibilities, and we only need eight to qualify with Visiting Pet Pals." She grinned at Tripp. "I think this just might work."

"I *know* it will." Resting against the sofa cushions, Tripp nonchalantly draped his arm along the back. When Diana scooted a fraction of an inch closer, he took it as permission to lower his arm to her shoulders.

At first contact, they both stiffened briefly. Diana cast him a nervous glance, then slowly relaxed against him.

This was nice—*too* nice. The warmth spreading through Tripp's chest told him he needed to do the responsible thing and say good-night. Still, he couldn't resist allowing himself a few more minutes of this simple pleasure while his thoughts drifted to a future where having Diana next to him like this was an everyday occurrence.

Hearing Diana's grandfather clock begin its nine o'clock chime, Tripp reluctantly pushed aside the lanky black cat that had crawled onto his lap earlier. "Sorry, Midnight, but I need to go."

Diana sat forward, careful not to disturb Tiger curled up next to her. "Watch out for Alice," she told Tripp with a nod toward the lop-eared rabbit sniffing his shoe.

Tripp reached down to stroke the rabbit's velvety-soft fur. "You should find out if Visiting Pet Pals would accept Alice in the program. The group I worked with during my internship allowed dogs, rabbits, guinea pigs and birds."

"I hadn't thought of that. Next time I talk to Agnes, I'll ask." Diana rose along with Tripp and walked him to the door. "Thanks again for bringing the pizza, and for all your help."

"My pleasure." Tripp paused on the front step, fingers tucked into the pockets of his khakis. Diana looked so beautiful standing there, brown eyes shimmering and her thick, dark hair haloed by the entryway chandelier. He suffered a nearly irresistible compulsion to kiss her but knew it was way too soon for such a move. Instead, he asked, "I guess you'll be busy tomorrow at the doughnut shop?"

"We close at two on Saturdays, but then I need to catch up on bookkeeping and supply orders."

"And afterward?"

Diana cast him a regretful frown. "I promised Aunt Jennie a visit. As crazy as things have been lately, I haven't gotten by to see her as often as I'd hoped."

"I'm sure she understands. Give her my best, will you? I still remember how sweet she was to me back when..." Grimacing, Tripp left the words unsaid.

After a moment's hesitation, Diana suggested, "Why don't you come along? Aunt Jennie would love to see you again."

Tripp brightened. "Are you sure?"

"So long as you promise not to say anything about our therapy pets project. Remember, I'm planning this as a surprise for Aunt Jennie's birthday next month."

"My lips are sealed." Tripp made a zipping motion across his mouth.

Diana promised to call when she finished work so that Tripp could meet her at the assisted-living center. With more bounce in his step than he'd had three hours ago, he climbed into his SUV for the drive to the cabin.

He'd barely gotten out of town when his cell phone rang. His first thought was that Diana was already calling to say she'd changed her mind about tomorrow— about *everything* they'd said about making a fresh start. He answered without looking at the display. "Hey, Diana, it's fine if you'd rather—"

"Diana?" His sister's surprised laugh collided with his eardrum. "What have I missed here, bro?"

"None of your business." Cringing, Tripp tapped the speaker icon and set the phone on the console. Then his stomach knotted. When he'd spoken with Brooke a couple of days ago, they'd just brought Mom home from the hospital. *Please, Lord, not another setback.* "What's up? Is Mom okay?"

"That's why I'm calling. Got a few minutes?"

Tripp couldn't tell from Brooke's tone whether her news was good or bad. Either way, he'd rather not risk an accident. "I'm on the road. Hang on while I find somewhere to pull over."

Around the next bend, his headlights swept across the turn-in to someone's ranch. He pulled in at an angle, then shifted into Park. Moving the phone closer, he drew air through tight lips. "Okay, talk to me."

"Don't panic. Mom's still holding her own. It's just—" Brooke's voice trembled. "The doctor says it's time to seriously consider hospice."

The knot in Tripp's belly swelled to boulder-sized. He lowered his forehead to the steering wheel. "That means…"

"Yes, Tripp, Mom's winding down." Brooke heaved a long, weary sigh. "We knew this time would come."

Yeah, but Tripp had prayed it would be much, much later. He straightened and massaged his temple. "What do you need me to do, sis?"

"I've emailed you some information from the hospice people. Look it over and get back to me if you have any questions. And, Tripp?"

"Yeah?"

"Quit beating yourself up about this. It isn't your fault."

A fact he acknowledged intellectually, but it still made him want to punch something.

Brooke's tone softened. "Have you told Diana yet?"

"Not yet."

"You need to. You owe it to her…and to yourself."

"I will. Soon. But we're just now getting closer again—"

"Tripp, really? That's wonderful! *And*," she added sternly, "all the more reason you need to be honest with her about why you broke up."

He wouldn't deny it. "When the time is right—I promise. If this really is our second chance, I'm not going to mess things up."

"You'd better not, because twelve years ago I was really counting on having Diana as a sister-in-law, and now you've got my hopes up again."

"Brooke—"

"I'm serious, Tripp. And just think what this would mean to Mom. You know how much she loved Diana. She'd be over-the-moon thrilled if you two got back together."

Tripp pressed one hand hard against an annoying cramp in his abdomen. "Slow down, okay? Diana's barely stopped looking at me like a bug she'd like to squash. 'Back together' is still a ways off."

"But no longer out of the realm of possibility. That's the main thing."

"If you say so." Headlights flashed in Tripp's side mirror as a vehicle slowed behind him. A right-turn signal indicated the driver planned to turn into the drive where Tripp was parked. "Gotta go, Brooke. I'll take a look at the hospice info and get back to you tomorrow. In the meantime, please don't let on to Mom and Dad about Diana. Let me see where this is going first."

"I hear you. Just don't wait too long."

Not if he could help it—for his mother's sake, certainly. But also because he needed to settle the matter in his own mind and heart.

Chapter Seven

A few minutes after three on Saturday afternoon, Diana phoned Tripp to say she was wrapping things up at the doughnut shop and about to head over to the assisted-living center. He sounded relieved to hear from her…but in a way that suggested he had a million other things on his mind. Now, as he trudged up the front walk, the distant look in his eyes confirmed her suspicions. Something definitely troubled him, and she prayed it wasn't more upsetting news about his mother.

Tripp offered a tired smile as he drew closer. "Hope I didn't keep you waiting long."

"Just got here myself." Diana tilted her head. "If you'd rather not—"

"No, it's fine. I've been looking forward to this." Tripp stepped around her to get the door. "Looks like a nice facility. Has your aunt adjusted well?"

The edge to his voice told her he was forcing small talk. Maybe later he'd tell her what had him so preoccupied. In the meantime, she hoped this visit with Aunt Jennie would cheer him up. "She seems happy enough, except for missing her little corgi." Diana led the way through the lobby. "Remember not to say any-thing about our project, though."

"Haven't forgotten."

They reached the door to apartment 18C. Diana tapped lightly, then peeked in. "It's me, Aunt Jennie. I brought your favorite cream-filled chocolate dough-nuts. And I brought a friend."

"Come in, come in!" Face aglow, her great-aunt sat forward in the blue recliner. "I've been on pins and nee-dles waiting for you, honey. Introduce me to your—" Aunt Jennie's brow furrowed, and then her face lit up in a smile. "Oh, my, Tripp Willoughby, as I live and breathe!"

"Hi, Mrs. Stewart. It's great to see you again. Wasn't sure you'd remember me." Tripp strode forward to give Aunt Jennie a kiss on the cheek.

"Of course I remember you!" Clutching Tripp's hand, Aunt Jennie clucked her tongue. "And what's this 'Mrs. Stewart' business? I've always considered you family." Her pointed glance at Diana said she'd like her great-niece to make it a reality.

Behind Tripp's back, Diana cast Aunt Jennie a raised-brow stare: *Don't you dare make a big deal out of this!*

Her great-aunt returned a smirk that only Diana would recognize as her get-over-yourself look. "Tripp, you and Diana sit here on this end of the sofa so I can hear you better."

"Yes, ma'am, thanks." Tripp motioned for Diana to seat herself nearest Aunt Jennie, then eased onto the cushion next to her.

"Closer, closer," Aunt Jennie urged, waving at Tripp to scoot toward Diana. "I don't want to miss a word of our visit."

When barely an inch separated them, Aunt Jennie sat back with a satisfied smile. Diana, on the other hand, could barely breathe. The doughnuts apparently forgotten, the sprightly little woman plied Tripp with questions about what brought him to Juniper Bluff, how he liked being a veterinarian and if he thought he might settle here permanently—*hint, hint*. Diana should have known Aunt Jennie would be all too anxious to play matchmaker.

Then the conversation turned to Tripp's family. With difficulty he described his mother's failing health, then revealed what his sister had told him on the phone last night.

Diana's heart constricted. "Oh, Tripp." She grasped his hand. "You said it was bad, but I had no idea. I'm so sorry."

"Just the mention of hospice makes it hit home with me." Grief darkened his eyes. He swallowed hard. "My mother is dying, and I've got to accept it."

"But your mother knows the Lord," Aunt Jennie said softly. "Find courage for the present and comfort for what is to come by remembering Jesus is already preparing a place for her in heaven."

Tripp nodded. "Thanks, that helps." Giving Diana's hand a squeeze, he stood. "I should get going. Enjoyed seeing you again, Mrs.—I mean, Aunt Jennie."

"Leaving so soon?" Aunt Jennie motioned him over. "You'll visit again, won't you?"

"Count on it." He bent to offer a goodbye hug.

Diana followed him into the corridor. She wanted so badly to share her own hug with him, to somehow ease his unbearable sorrow. "Tripp, my heart is breaking for you."

He lifted his hand to her face, his palm warm against her cheek. Just as quickly, he dropped his arm to his side. "Don't feel sorry for me. Please. I can stand anything but that."

His sharp gaze sliced through her before he turned and strode away.

"Tripp?" She started after him. "Tripp, don't leave—"

Without looking back, he waved halfheartedly. "I'll see you tomorrow at the obedience class."

Deflated and feeling utterly helpless, Diana returned to her great-aunt's apartment. She slipped inside and leaned weakly against the closed door.

"Your poor young man," Aunt Jennie said. "Should he be alone right now?"

"Maybe not, but he made it pretty clear he'd rather be." With a silent groan, Diana crossed to the sofa and sank down. Why did Tripp find it so hard to let someone share his struggles?

Aunt Jennie reached across to pat Diana's knee. "I still remember how inconsolable you were after he broke things off. Nothing anybody said seemed to help, and you finally told us all to leave you be."

"For all the good it did," Diana replied with a smirk. "You, Mom and Dad were all over me like fleas on a dog."

"Your daddy worried most. Scared him to death that you might do something foolish."

"No kidding. He came up to see me at school and spent nearly a week making sure I didn't decide to drop out." Diana rolled her eyes. "As if! The breakup only made me more determined to get my business degree and do something meaningful with my life."

Aunt Jennie sat back and folded her hands, a smug

look flattening her lips. "You've certainly made a success of Diana's Donuts."

Narrowing one eye, Diana frowned. "Okay, out with it. There's obviously more you mean to say."

"Only that there's more to life than running a successful business." Aunt Jennie motioned toward the little white bag Diana had set on the side table. "Speaking of doughnuts, though, I'm about ready for one. Care to join me?"

Diana could only laugh while thanking the Lord for her great-aunt's wisdom and humor.

When Diana didn't see Tripp at church Sunday morning, her concern increased. After leaving Aunt Jennie's yesterday, she'd been sorely tempted to call and check on him—or even drive out to Serenity Hills as she had the evening after the open house.

But perhaps giving him space was the best course of action for now, for both their sakes. Diana was still reconciling her softening feelings toward him, especially after Friday night and the unmistakable current of electricity thrumming between them. His arm around her shoulder as they sat on the sofa, the look of longing in his eyes as he'd said goodbye on her front porch— for a fleeting moment she'd had the feeling he wanted to kiss her.

It stunned her to realize she would have let him.

Following worship, Diana glanced around again, hoping she might have missed Tripp's arrival. Spotting Doc Ingram and his family, she casually asked if they'd heard from him.

Doc Ingram frowned. "Think he might be under the weather. He's got a standing invitation to Sunday dinner at our house, but he called earlier to say he couldn't make it."

Seth and Christina Austin, leaving the sanctuary with their two children, strode over. "Asking about Tripp?" Seth said. "I saw him this morning. Seemed okay, just kind of distracted."

Christina touched Diana's arm. "You look worried. Is there something we should know?"

"Tripp's mother is very ill." Diana hoped he wouldn't mind her mentioning it.

"I'm so sorry," Christina said. "He'd mentioned she wasn't in the best of health but didn't give us any details. Has she taken a turn for the worse?"

As briefly as possible, Diana related what Tripp had told her about Mrs. Willoughby's battle with kidney disease. "It looks like they're going to put her in hospice care. Tripp's taking it pretty hard."

By now, Diana's parents had joined the group. Her dad cast her a questioning glance, obviously wondering why Diana suddenly seemed to have the inside track on what was happening in Tripp's life. "You two must be seeing an awful lot of each other lately," he said.

Diana winced. Things had been happening a little too fast to keep her parents in the loop. "Um, yes, Tripp's been helping me with the therapy pets program."

"Has he, now?" Dad arched a brow.

"I was thrilled to hear about your program," Christina said. "If not for getting ready to have twins," she added with a loving smile for Seth, "I'd consider volunteering with Gracie."

"You and Gracie actually helped inspire me," Diana said. As time had passed since her accident, Christina didn't depend on the golden retriever quite as heavily as she once did, but Gracie remained a special part of the Austin family.

As everyone said their goodbyes, Diana's mother linked arms with her. "So you and Tripp are spending more time together? Hmm, I think you'd better come to lunch with us and fill us in."

Getting the third degree from her parents was the last thing Diana needed today, but she didn't see any chance of escape. Determined to get it over with as painlessly as possible, she agreed to meet them at Casa Luis. The after-church crowd typically packed the popular Mexican restaurant, which meant Diana could count on the noise level to keep Mom and Dad from getting too personal with their questions.

Because if they asked point-blank whether she was falling in love with Tripp Willoughby all over again, she wasn't sure how she'd respond.

Tripp pulled into the church parking lot at ten minutes before three. He drove around back, nearer to where the obedience class would be held, and glimpsed Diana talking with Sean, the trainer. Four or five dog owners chatted among themselves while their dogs got better acquainted.

Shutting off the engine, Tripp hauled in a steadying breath. He was doing a little better emotionally than he had been yesterday, when he'd left the assisted-living center so abruptly. Though he'd skipped church this morning, he'd spent a lot of time reading his Bible and trying to pray. Not easy while he still felt so at odds with God over the course his life had taken.

Well, except for one important aspect, and she'd just looked his way, her smile a beacon of welcome…and hope.

With a hesitant smile of his own, Tripp ambled over. He nodded at Diana, then offered his hand to the dog trainer. "Good to see you again, Sean. Thanks for doing this."

"Glad it worked out." Sean held the leash of a well-behaved boxer mix. "This is Brutus, my teaching assistant."

Two more dog owners arrived, including the Mussells with their friendly mutt, Darby. Diana introduced everyone to Sean, then turned the class over to him. She motioned Tripp to a nearby bench, where they could sit and observe.

"Looks like everyone showed up," Tripp commented.

"And they're all so enthusiastic." Diana's shoulders heaved with a grateful sigh. "Almost wish I had a dog so I could join the fun."

"Me, too. Maybe after I get a place of my own…"

She tilted her head, the sparkle in her big brown eyes warming him. "So Juniper Bluff is growing on you, huh?"

"Guess so."

"I'm glad." Diana braced her elbow on the bench back, head resting upon her fingertips as she gazed up at him. "Missed you at church this morning. I prayed for you…and your mom."

"Thanks. Sorry about yesterday. I was still in a really bad place."

"You don't have to apologize. I can't even imagine how hard this is for you."

In more ways than one, he didn't say. "Being with you, though—" His mouth went dry, and he couldn't finish the thought. He shifted to face her and cupped her elbow with his hand. "Diana, is this really happening? You, me…us?"

"I don't know." Her voice fell to a whisper. "Do you want it to?"

"Do you?"

"I never thought I'd say this, but…yes." Lifting her head, she slid her hand along his arm. When her fingers grazed his cheek, the gentleness of her touch made him shiver. "Can we get back what we had, Tripp? Is it even possible?"

"I'd like to find out." Angling his head, he leaned closer.

Suddenly a pair of giant-sized brown paws plopped on Tripp's lap, and he jerked aside. Instead of the kiss he'd almost shared with Diana, he suffered Darby's long, wet tongue lashing across his face.

Diana laughed out loud as Tripp grabbed the hairy beast's drooling muzzle with both hands. "Hey, big boy," he said through his own laughter, "enough is enough!"

"Sorry, Doc!" Vince Mussell jogged over and grabbed Darby's dangling leash. "Guess we have more work to do on the 'stay' command."

"Practice makes perfect." Tripp patted Darby's rump as Vince coaxed the dog toward the other class members.

Still snickering, Diana found a tissue in her purse and handed it to Tripp. "You might want to clean up a bit."

It would take more than a flimsy tissue to wipe away that much dog slobber. Until Tripp could wash his face with soap and water, he could kiss goodbye any further thoughts of kissing Diana.

Which was probably for the best. Number one, they

were sitting here in plain view of several townsfolk, some of whom might take great pleasure in spreading the word that Juniper Bluff's doughnut lady was making time with the new veterinarian.

Number two? It didn't matter that Tripp had once been on the verge of proposing marriage to the woman he loved. Their breakup had been a cruel one, thanks to his cowardice, and he had a lot to make up for. Even if Diana did seem willing to try again—which thrilled him beyond imagining—his personal life was currently in too big a mess. He had no idea when he might get that dreaded call from Brooke about their mother, and stressing over it wasn't doing his own health any good.

And he simply couldn't bring himself to lay all these concerns on Diana, not when things were going so well between them.

On Monday morning, Tripp discovered the Juniper Bluff rumor mill was alive and well. Doc Ingram had stopped by Diana's Donuts for coffee on his way to the clinic. He wore a mischievous grin as he set a to-go cup and a pastry bag on Tripp's desk. "Heard you and your sweetie were canoodling behind the church yesterday."

"That's a bit of a stretch." Heat rose along the sides of Tripp's neck. "We were just talking, that's all."

"*You* may have thought you were just talking, but half the town is already planning your wedding."

Groaning, Tripp set his elbows on the desk and palmed his eye sockets. "You got all this from picking up coffee and doughnuts?"

Robert plopped into the chair across from Tripp. He opened the bag, pulled out a paper-wrapped glazed doughnut and passed it to Tripp. "Here, drown your sorrows in sugar. Coffee's yours, too. I remembered the soy milk."

"Thanks, you're all heart." Stomach issues notwithstanding, Tripp was mortified enough that he couldn't stop himself from indulging in a little sugar-and-caffeine therapy.

"So," Robert began, taking a sip of his own coffee, "want to tell me what's really going on with you and Diana? The most I've gotten from you so far is that you knew each other in college, but something tells me there's a lot more to the story."

After two delicious but ill-advised bites, Tripp laid aside the doughnut. It was well past time to level with his partner, and maybe it could serve as the next logical step in moving toward full disclosure with Diana. "We were this close to getting engaged," he said, holding his thumb and forefinger millimeters apart. "But I was under a lot of stress at vet school, and the next thing I knew, I landed in the hospital."

Robert offered a grim nod. "The pressure can be rough—haven't forgotten. Was that what kept you from proposing?"

"I could have handled the pressure. What I *couldn't* handle was my diagnosis." Tripp lifted his coffee cup to his lips, then set it down without drinking. He met Robert's gaze. "I have Crohn's disease."

A noisy exhalation whooshed from Robert's lungs. "Wow. I'd never have guessed—although I have noticed you're pretty selective about what you eat." With a guilty glance toward the doughnut, he added, "Sorry if I contributed to the problem."

"It's okay." Tripp released a weak chuckle. "I've kept things pretty much under control for several years now."

"So your disease is what came between you and Diana?" Robert shook his head. "That's not the Diana Matthews I know."

"It wasn't her. I broke things off. Back then, I could barely deal with the diagnosis myself, let alone what it could mean for my future. I couldn't inflict all that on Diana."

Sitting forward, Robert pinned Tripp with a hard stare. "You never told her, did you?"

"I didn't know how." He closed his eyes briefly. "Still don't."

"Well, if things are getting serious again between you two…"

"I know. Believe me, I know."

A knock sounded on Tripp's door, and Yolanda peeked in. "Your first patient is here."

"Thanks, be right there." Tripp stood, as did Robert. "You'll keep this conversation between us?" he murmured to his partner.

"Just don't wait too long."

"Hey, Di," her not-so-favorite customer LeRoy hollered from across the shop. "Or should I be callin' you the future Mrs. Doc Willoughby?"

Diana tried not to cringe. It was turning into a busier Monday than usual, and this kind of banter had been going strong all morning. Not *quite* as vocally as LeRoy, thank goodness.

She carried the coffee carafe to his table and refilled his mug. "Now, LeRoy, you know I don't kiss and tell."

Not that there had actually been a kiss, but they'd come close. And now it seemed the entire town knew about it.

Seth Austin had just walked in the door. He ambled over, a mile-wide grin splitting his face. "What's this I hear about some kissing going on?"

Diana glared. "*Nobody's* kissing *anybody.*"

She set the carafe on LeRoy's table with a thud, then pulled out the chair opposite him. Carefully stepping onto the seat, she stood tall and shouted for attention. "Thank you all *so* much for your continued patronage. But the very next person who says one word about the kiss that *didn't* happen, or so much as hints about my marriage prospects, will be banned from this establishment for life."

Catcalls and applause broke out, a clear indication that no one took her seriously. Not that she expected them to—many of them, including Seth, had known her since childhood and probably felt they had as much of a stake in her future as her own family—but if she didn't at least try to establish some boundaries, she'd never hear the end of this.

The door chime sounded, announcing the arrival of another customer. All eyes turned toward the front, and the room immediately fell silent.

Tripp stood in the doorway, looking temporarily disoriented to find everyone's focus on him. He glanced around uneasily, his gaze finally settling on Diana, still high above the crowd on her makeshift pedestal. One eyebrow arching skyward, he cocked his head. "Did I miss something?"

Almost as one, Diana's customers returned to their previous conversations, acting as if nothing had happened. Diana climbed down from the chair, straightened her apron and held her head high as she marched to her station behind the counter. She would *not* give her patrons the satisfaction of seeing her pay Tripp any more attention than she would any other customer.

By the time she reached the cash register, Tripp stood across the counter from her. "What can I get for you?" she asked with a tense smile.

"How about a Greek yogurt and a bottle of spring water?" With a quick glance over his shoulder, Tripp murmured, "Any chance you could take a short break?"

She nodded. "I'll get Kimberly to cover for me. Wait for me at the gazebo."

After filling Tripp's order, she gave him a couple minutes' head start, then slipped into the kitchen to call Kimberly to the front.

Kimberly snickered. "Does this have anything to do with a certain veterinarian who just stopped in?"

Diana rolled her eyes as she hung up her apron. "I'll be back in fifteen minutes."

She briefly considered using the rear exit, but then she'd have to walk all the way down the alley and around the block. Might as well run the gauntlet since it wouldn't take her customers long to figure out her destination. Ignoring their stares, she headed out to the square.

As she joined Tripp on the bench inside the gazebo, he offered a shy grin. "Awkward, huh? Robert told me things were getting crazy over here. I had a little time between appointments and wanted to make sure you're okay."

She shrugged. "I'm used to the Juniper Bluff busy-bodies. Sorry you're getting initiated so soon."

"Guess it was inevitable." Tripp swallowed his last spoonful of yogurt, then tossed the container into a nearby trash receptacle. With a bemused laugh, he asked, "So what exactly were you doing up on that chair?"

"Threatening the busybodies with expulsion." Looking across the street, Diana glimpsed two tiers of peering faces lining her shop windows. She nudged Tripp's arm and nodded toward the onlookers. "Obviously, my words had no effect."

"Obviously." Chuckling, Tripp gave his head a brisk shake. Then, turning serious, he covered Diana's hand with his own. "How would you feel about *really* giving them something to talk about?"

Her heart thumped against her rib cage. "What did you have in mind?"

"I don't know…maybe the kiss we never quite got around to yesterday?"

"You mean right here? In the town square?"

"I promise, I've washed my face since Darby so rudely interrupted us." Tripp's eyes held hers. "Shaved extra close this morning, too."

"Why?" she said, barely able to breathe. "Were you already planning this moment?"

"Not consciously. But I haven't forgotten how you used to complain when my whiskers got scratchy."

"I never did care for the permanent five-o'clock-shadow look."

"Di…" His Adam's apple made a long, slow journey up and down his throat. "I really want to kiss you. Right now. In front of everybody."

She shivered. "Okay, then."

So he did.

Chapter Eight

I kissed Diana!

Even better, she'd kissed him back. Willingly, tenderly, as if the breakup and the intervening years had been wiped away in an instant. It didn't matter that half the town had looked on. It didn't matter that ten minutes later they had to say goodbye and return to their jobs.

All that mattered was not messing up this chance to win back the woman Tripp had once walked away from.

He practically floated back to the clinic. The pet owners he saw at his next appointments probably wondered why Doc Willoughby couldn't seem to stop grinning—even at the end of the day, when Sue Ellen Jamison returned with Cleopatra for another dose of worm medication.

"We may need to change Cleopatra's flea prevention," Tripp explained as he pressed a tissue to his bleeding left index finger. "Is she outside much?"

"Only in the backyard," Sue Ellen said, then sheepishly added, "although she does like to catch birds."

Thus ensued a lengthy conversation about the likely sources of Cleopatra's tapeworm infestation. At first shocked, then remorseful, Sue Ellen peppered Tripp with questions until he pointedly handed her an informative brochure, then ushered her and the ill-tempered cat out to the front and turned them over to Yolanda.

After hanging up his lab coat, scrubbing his hands and applying an adhesive bandage to his wounded finger, he collapsed in his office chair and phoned Diana. "How was the rest of your day? Any fallout from our rendezvous in the gazebo?"

"Nothing I couldn't handle. How about you?"

"Thought the day would never end so I could talk to you again." Hearing Yolanda shutting things down, Tripp lowered his voice. "I was hoping maybe I could take you to dinner."

"Sounds nice. But…maybe we could drive over to Fredericksburg?"

"Where there's a smaller chance of running into anyone we know?" Tripp chuckled. "Good plan. Can I pick you up at six?"

"I'll be ready."

Tripp had just enough time to rush out to the cabin and freshen up. Arriving at Diana's, he let out a low whistle when she answered the door. Her dark waves skimmed the shoulders of a gauzy aquamarine tunic top that complemented her coloring beautifully. Combined with skinny indigo jeans, strappy sandals and silver hoop earrings peeking from beneath her hair, the effect was entrancing.

Helping her into his SUV, Tripp waited till the last possible second before releasing her hand—and only after she cast him a dubious stare. On the drive over to Fredericksburg, she suggested a few of her favorite restaurants, and he chose one he thought most likely to accommodate his dietary restrictions. His insides were still talking back after the two bites of glazed doughnut he'd stupidly ingested that morning.

The restaurant offered a homey atmosphere, and the quiet corner booth where the hostess seated them made it easy to talk. And they talked plenty, long after the dishes were cleared away. Tripp had so many questions about Diana's family, what she'd done immediately after finishing college, where she'd gotten the idea for Diana's Donuts, how each of her pets had found its way into her life.

In turn, he answered her questions about his first years in veterinary practice and what his sister, Brooke, had done after getting her marketing degree, but he deliberately sidestepped any mention of his condition. Crohn's disease wasn't exactly pleasant dinnertime conversation, and he wouldn't put a damper on what essentially amounted to their first real date since college.

The date ended on Diana's front step with a goodnight kiss that Tripp had been waiting for all day. Memorizing the way Diana's brown eyes glistened beneath the porch light, he murmured, "Can we do this again soon?"

"Come over after work sometime and I'll fix dinner. How about Wednesday?" Her fingertips rested lightly against the hollow of his shoulder. "Afterward, we can watch a movie…or just talk."

"I'll be here."

On Wednesday, though, Tripp had to cancel when an emergency appointment kept him at the clinic until late in the evening. Someone had come upon a stray dog that had been hit by a car, but the injuries were too severe, and Tripp ultimately had to euthanize the poor animal. No matter how many times he'd been through that, it never got easier. He went home exhausted and with his stomach in knots.

Then he phoned Diana, and just hearing her voice soothed away the stress. After the call, he fell asleep imagining coming home to Diana every evening and sharing the day's highs and lows. "It is not good for the man to be alone," Scripture said, and Tripp was coming to believe it as he never had before.

He'd just told Diana good-night and was ready to crawl into bed when his phone rang with a call from Brooke. He squeezed his eyes shut briefly before answering. "Hey, sis."

Her tremulous exhalation sounded in his ear. "We had our first visit from the hospice nurse today."

His heart plummeted. Everything happening this week had helped to distract him from worries about his mother. "How'd it go?"

"She's very professional but also extremely kind and caring. We all liked her."

"And Mom? How's she taking it?"

"She's reached the point of acceptance." Brooke sniffled. "A lot faster than the rest of us, I'm afraid."

Tripp didn't doubt it. "I still wish I could help somehow."

"I know you do. But we're coping. The nurse will come every morning, and I've arranged my work schedule so I can get home earlier each day to help ease the strain on Dad."

"So...no more dialysis?"

Another shuddering breath. "No, Tripp. No more dialysis."

He didn't have to ask what that meant. "Dear God,"

he began, struggling for the strength to pray but unable to find the words. How did anyone pray in a situation like this? For a miracle of healing, for a few more weeks or months to say their goodbyes…or for death to come quickly and peacefully?

"Mom's doctor says she shouldn't be in any pain, so that's a comfort," Brooke said. "Mostly she'll just have less and less energy as things wind down."

Tripp pinched the bridge of his nose. "You'll let me know if it looks like I should come before Thanksgiving?"

"I promise. But Mom's already making plans for having all of us with her for the holiday, so you know she'll fight to hang on for all she's worth." A tear-filled laugh burbled from Brooke's throat. "She even had me pull out her recipe box the other day so I could start on the shopping list."

"That's our mom," Tripp said, shaking his head.

But the realization that this could be the last Thanksgiving he ever spent with his mother hit Tripp hard. After the call ended, he sat on the edge of his bed for several long minutes while his emotions ran rampant. If only he could hear Diana's voice again…

He dialed her number. Then, noticing it was nearly 11 p.m., he immediately disconnected. As early as Diana had to be at the shop in the morning, she was probably sound asleep already.

A second later his phone rang—Diana. "Tripp? Did you just call?"

"Sorry if I woke you. Didn't notice how late it was."

"Is everything okay?" Concern overshadowed the grogginess in her voice.

He told her about the call from Brooke. "I shouldn't

have bothered you, but after the day I had, and then this—" His voice broke.

"No, no, I'm glad you called." She paused. "I hate that you're alone out there. Do you want to come over? I can make us a late-night breakfast, and we can watch old reruns on TV to help get your mind off things."

Tempted as he was, he wouldn't disrupt Diana's rest any more than he already had. "I feel better just talking to you. These past few days…they've meant so much."

"For me, too, Tripp." Sincerity laced her tone. "And please, never, ever hesitate to call or come over anytime you need to talk. What your family's going through—I can't even imagine how hard it must be to watch someone you love deal with such a devastating illness."

Thanking her for listening, Tripp told her to get some sleep and said good-night. A twinge in his belly reminded him he'd forgotten to take his nightly medications, but as he stood at the bathroom sink with a pill bottle in one hand and a glass of water in the other, Diana's parting words penetrated.

When, if ever, could he bear to burden her with the possibility, no matter how remote, that his own disease could turn devastating? His doctors had prepared him for the various complications he could face, the worst of which involved extensive surgery and potentially traumatic lifestyle changes—adjustments Tripp couldn't imagine forcing on someone he loved.

And yet, a future without Diana scared him even more.

On Thursday, Diana phoned Tripp during the late-morning lull, catching him between appointments. "Any chance we could meet for lunch?"

"Sounds nice, but…another time, maybe? I've got to get some lab samples ready to send out." His tone suggested he was glad to hear from her, but he also seemed distant, distracted. Between work and family concerns, he had every right to be.

Still, Diana couldn't shake the feeling that he held something back, as if he regretted being so open with her on the phone last night. Was it only his natural reserve? Or had they tried too quickly to pick up the pieces of their relationship, and now he was having second thoughts? "Sure," she said, trying hard to sound upbeat. "Call me anytime."

She didn't hear from him again for two long days. In the meantime, she second-and third-and fourth-guessed exactly where this thing between them was headed.

On Saturday afternoon, as Diana and her crew wiped tables and straightened up before closing, Tripp walked in.

With a knowing smile, Kimberly relieved Diana of the broom and dustpan she'd been wielding. "Get going. I'll finish up and shut things down."

Hands perspiring for no obvious reason, Diana shrugged out of her apron as she strode over to greet Tripp. "Hey, stranger."

He looked as uneasy as she felt. "Sorry I haven't been in touch."

"I've been worried." *And not just about your mom.*

Tripp glanced around the shop, where Kimberly and two other workers bustled about. "Can we go somewhere?" he asked softly. His crooked smile turned wistful. "I've missed you."

Five minutes later, they sat in the gazebo, Diana's hand locked firmly in Tripp's and her heart hammering like that of a lovesick teenager. He hadn't said a word since they'd started across the street. Now, deep crevices etching the corners of his eyes, he stared at the scuffed floorboards.

"Tripp," Diana whispered, "what is it?"

"Just a lot on my mind, that's all."

She chewed her lip, a desperate ache squeezing her heart. "Maybe you should just pack up and go to California. Spend this time with your mom while you can. Doc Ingram would understand. Everybody would."

He gave his head a small shake. "No, I can't turn my back on my responsibilities here. Anyway, as Brooke keeps reminding me, Mom could—" A guttural sound choked off his words. He cleared his throat. "She could linger for weeks yet."

"But still—"

"Brooke will let me know if I need to fly out sooner than later. Until then, I just need to keep busy."

Diana nodded in understanding, all the while wishing she had any clue what to do to make things better. She suggested the first thing that came to mind. "Want to come over later? I could make us a light supper."

"Thanks, but I think I'll head home. I've got some veterinary journals I need to catch up on." Then, as if realizing how distant he sounded, he dipped his chin and sighed. "I'm sorry, Di. With everything I'm dealing with, I wouldn't be very good company."

"That doesn't matter to me. We don't have to talk at all if you don't want to. I just—" She released a sharp sigh and pressed his hand between hers. "I just want to help."

"I know," he said, barely meeting her gaze, "and I'm

not purposely shutting you out. I'm just trying to work through some stuff."

"I get that you're worried about your mom. But is it more than that?" Diana held her breath. "Is it…us?"

His grimace said it all.

Rising, she stood in front of him, arms locked at her waist. "It was all too easy, wasn't it? Falling back into the past and pretending like—"

Tripp shoved to his feet. His hands clamped hard around her shoulders. "There's no pretending here, Di. I'm still in love with you. I want us to be together as much as—no, even *more* than I did twelve years ago."

"Then why do you keep pulling away?" She searched his face but found no answers there, only those dusky blue eyes clouded with pain and uncertainty.

His gaze drifted toward the ceiling briefly before he drew her back to the bench. Leaving a few inches of space between them that felt like the Grand Canyon, he sat forward with his hands clasped between his knees. "You're right, it was way too easy slipping back into what we had, and now I'm scared to death of jumping into something neither of us is ready for."

Diana's fingertips curled around the edge of the bench. "I think I'm finally getting the picture. Basically you're telling me you're a commitment-phobe." Jaw clenched, she slowly shook her head. "All the signs were there. I should have figured this out years ago."

"Maybe you're right." Tripp straightened with a tired sigh. "But not for the reasons you think."

"Care to explain, then?" She couldn't mask the bitterness in her tone.

He glanced at her, his lips parted as if he was about to reply. Then his breath caught and he looked away.

"Okay, fine." Diana stood once more. "If you don't have the guts to be honest with me, I've got plenty of other ways to spend my Saturday afternoon."

Before she'd taken three steps, Tripp caught her and whirled her around, trapping her lips in a kiss that rocked her to her toes. When the kiss ended, they both stood breathless. Tripp drew her close and rested his head on hers. "I want to explain things, believe me. But I'm not thinking straight, and until I get through this thing with my mom, I can't trust myself not to hurt you...or mess things up even worse than before."

"You can't mess things up, not if you really love me." Diana moved toward him, arms outstretched. "Let me help you through this."

He accepted her embrace with a shuddering exhalation. "You already are, just by being here."

She tipped her head. "Then why doesn't it seem like enough?"

His gaze locked with hers for a searing moment before he lifted his head and took a purposeful step back. He dropped his arms to his sides. "I have to go, Di. Just please, don't give up on me."

"I won't," she murmured. But as he slipped past her down the steps, a tremor shook her insides, a certain, terrifying sense that she was on the verge of losing him again.

On Sunday afternoon, Diana sat alone on one of the benches on the church lawn to watch the obedience class. Tripp hadn't shown up yet, and though he hadn't exactly said he'd be there, she couldn't stop worrying. He'd seemed so conflicted and confused yesterday, and then had hardly spoken five words to her at church that morning, just hurried out to his car as soon as worship ended.

After checking her cell phone one more time to see if she'd missed a text or call, she made up her mind to drive out to the cabin as soon as the class ended. He might be holding her at arm's length, but his reticence was no match for her determination.

Forty minutes later, Sean ambled over with his boxer, Brutus. "Everyone's coming along real well."

"Wonderful." Rising, Diana forced a smile. "Do you think two more Sundays will have them ready?"

"Don't see why not. A couple of dogs still need to work on some skills, but if the owners keep up the practice between classes, they should be okay."

Encouraged, Diana chatted briefly with the owners. All seemed enthusiastic about earning their dogs' obedience certificates and passing Agnes Kraus's evaluation. Diana reminded them about the veterinary forms they'd need to provide before the group could be authorized as a Visiting Pet Pals chapter.

"No Doc Willoughby today?" Vince Mussell tugged on Darby's leash to stop him from sniffing a piece of trash.

"He's dealing with some serious family concerns. His mother isn't well." Diana glanced away briefly while composing her expression into something resembling a smile. "I know he would have been here if he could."

"Well, I hope everything turns out okay. Sure like that fella. Darby does, too." Vince scratched the dog behind the ears. "Yep, Doc Willoughby has a real nice way about him."

Diana couldn't agree more.

Then Tripp's warm baritone sounded behind her. "My ears were burning. Y'all talking about me?"

She swung around and came face-to-face with his hesitant half grin. "Tripp. I didn't think you were coming."

"Meant to. Went to my office this afternoon to catch up on a few things, then got on the phone with my mom and dad. We talked for so long that I lost track of time." He handed Diana a manila envelope. "Hoped I'd catch you before you left. I made copies of vaccination records and wrote up the health assessments you'll need for the evaluation."

Diana narrowed her eyes as she accepted the envelope. "You did all this today?"

"Just keeping busy." Tripp cast a polite nod at Vince and reached down to scratch Darby behind the ears. "This guy doing okay with his lessons?"

"Better than last week," Vince said with a snort, "but we still have some work to do. Good to see you, Doc. Heard about your mom. Janice and I will keep y'all in our prayers."

"Appreciate it."

Diana reached out to touch Tripp's arm. She'd rather hug him, but taking in Tripp's detached expression, she thought better of it. Plus, Vince was standing right there. Instead, she quietly asked, "How's your mother doing today?"

"About the same. Holding her own." With a brisk nod, Tripp returned his attention to Vince and his dog. "What exactly is Darby having trouble with? Any way I can help?"

Clearly, Tripp was heavily into avoidance mode. Crossing her arms, Diana stepped aside while Vince described Darby's training weaknesses.

"Biggest problem is he's a puller," Vince explained. "Can't get him to walk nicely beside me on the leash."

Frowning, Tripp scratched his chin, then knelt in front of the dog. He unsnapped the leash, flipped it around to the loop handle and wove it into a figure eight, which he fitted over Darby's neck and snout as a makeshift halter. "Try this," he said, handing the other end to Vince. "It'll give you more control in leading him."

Vince gave Darby the command to heel, then stepped out. The dog started to pull ahead, but the halter immediately drew his attention back to his master. He slowed his pace and trotted alongside Vince with new respect.

"Wow," Vince said, grinning over his shoulder as he led Darby in a broad circle. "You should be teaching this class, Doc. Any other quick tips?"

"The main thing is consistency. Just keep practicing every day. And lots of long walks. That'll burn off some of Darby's energy so he's more ready to focus on the training."

Burning off energy. Sure seemed Tripp was doing more of that himself. Diana wondered what it would take to reclaim his focus on their relationship.

Tripp had never felt so torn. He'd seen the look in Diana's eyes and sensed how much she wanted to reach out to him, to hold him and comfort him. Yet so much still stood between them, and he was way too close to blowing his second chance to have her back in his life permanently.

His brain kept replaying the phone conversation with his parents earlier. Dad had sounded so much older than the last time they'd talked, and when his dad had stepped away from the phone for a moment, Tripp had said as much to his mom.

Caring for an invalid will do that to you, Mom had said. *He's worn out, and so am I. Soon we'll both be able to rest.*

Those softly spoken words had nearly undone Tripp. All he could say was, *I'm sorry. I'm so, so sorry.*

And Mom had kept telling him he had nothing to be sorry about. Not one thing. *Let's talk about happy news*, she'd said. *Tell me more about your life in Juniper Bluff. Tell me more about Diana. I always did like that girl. She had spunk.*

Still does, and plenty of it, Tripp thought now as he and Diana walked out to the parking lot together...close but not touching.

He'd sidestepped any hints to his parents about the possibility of getting back together with Diana. Those first few weeks in Juniper Bluff, he hadn't held much hope. But now, painfully aware of what his mother's illness was doing to Dad—to all of them—he had even less.

"Gotta go," he said as they reached Diana's car. He opened her door for her. "Talk to you soon."

"I hope so." With one hand on the door frame, she clasped his hand. Before he could resist, she tugged him close for a goodbye kiss.

Her featherlight touch froze him to the spot. Jaw firm, he watched her drive away before climbing into his own car. But instead of heading home, he returned to the clinic. He sat down at his desk and dove into a stack of files and other paperwork that could easily have waited until Monday morning.

My grace is sufficient for thee...

The scripture he'd relied on so often whispered through his thoughts.

My grace...sufficient...

He closed the file he'd been reading, leaned back in his chair and took several long, slow breaths. And remembered what his dad had said on the phone this afternoon, *One day at a time, son. Only choice we have is to take this one day at a time.*

That's what Tripp had to do, too. He was smart enough to realize he was way too vulnerable these days—*not* the ideal frame of mind to make any radical decisions about his future. Especially where Diana was concerned. Like his dad, he needed to take each day as it came and make the best of it.

In the meantime, he'd pray that God would somehow show him—one way or the other—whether keeping Diana in his life was the right thing to do.

Chapter Nine

Diana didn't see much of Tripp the following week. He'd called on Tuesday but said he was between appointments and couldn't talk long. He hadn't sounded quite so distant, though, which eased Diana's mind. She could relate to his need to keep himself occupied—until he'd come back into her life a few weeks ago, she'd had plenty of practice herself.

But it didn't make being apart any easier.

On Wednesday, she invited him over for supper, and he surprised her by accepting. They spent a relaxed evening together, mostly talking about who had stopped in at the doughnut shop, Tripp's most interesting veterinary case of the day and—of course—the therapy pets program. When Diana asked Tripp about his mother, his simple reply was, "Not much change."

They spoke on the phone a few more times over the next couple of days, and on Saturday afternoon, Diana persuaded Tripp to go on a horseback ride with her. Rather than risk a replay of Mona's feistiness, she asked Seth if they could take out a couple of his calmer trail horses.

Out on the trail, it was as if Diana could see the tension melting from Tripp's shoulders. As they arrived in the clearing at the top of the hill, he reined his horse to a halt and looked up at the cloudless blue sky.

"I needed this," he said, then turned to her and smiled his special smile, the one that never failed to convey how much he loved her.

She grinned back, glad for the sunglasses to hide the wetness filling her eyes. "You know what they say. All work and no play..."

"Makes Doc Willoughby a very strung out, self-absorbed, inattentive boyfriend." His mouth twisted in an apologetic frown, but Diana took heart at the fact that he'd actually referred to himself as her boyfriend.

"No more doom and gloom, Doc Willoughby. Today's all about having fun." Diana nudged her horse closer, until the two horses were parallel. She scanned the far side of the meadow. Then, with a mischievous glance at Tripp, she pointed to a tall, skinny cedar. "Race ya to that tree. Loser buys dinner."

Before he could react, she kicked her horse into motion. Not that it did much good, since these trail horses rarely moved faster than a bone-crunching trot.

"No fair!" Tripp shouted behind her, but she heard the laughter in his voice. A couple of seconds later he caught up and even passed her.

She decided right then to let him win. He'd already won back her heart anyway—something she'd never have believed possible if anyone had asked her two months ago. Besides, seeing his face-splitting victory grin as he reined his horse around to wait for her was worth a zillion times more than the price of dinner.

"So where are you taking us?" he asked, breathing hard.

"Winner's choice." She feigned a look of chagrin. "But please have mercy on my poor, pitiful bank account."

Tripp opted for the restaurant in Fredericksburg where he'd taken her the last time they'd gone out for dinner. After they'd both had a chance to clean up from the ride, Tripp drove into town to pick her up.

His reserved side reemerged over dinner, though—a dinner he barely picked at, she couldn't help noticing. Losing her own appetite, she longed for the lightheartedness they'd shared out on the trail. She'd never admit it aloud, but the strain of trying to stay cheerful and positive for his sake was wearing on her.

He'd grown even more distant by the time he met her at the church the next afternoon to watch the obedience class. Diana finally coaxed out of him that Brooke had phoned early that morning to say his mother had had an especially bad night.

"You should have called me," Diana said, holding his hand as they sat on the park bench.

He glanced away, his mouth hardening. "You worry about me enough as it is."

She wanted to snap at him that two people who truly cared for each other would willingly share their concerns, but the retort froze on the tip of her tongue. Instead, she turned her attention to the class, just in time to see Darby army-crawling out of his "down, stay" position the moment Vince turned his back. In spite of herself, she couldn't hold back a snicker.

Tripp had noticed, too. He squeezed Diana's hand and smiled at her, the corners of his eyes crinkling in a silent plea for forgiveness. "I have a feeling Darby will turn out to be your star therapy pet. Who can resist such cuteness?"

Diana wiggled her brows. "Let's just hope Agnes Kraus agrees."

When the class ended, Diana and Tripp both nodded with satisfaction at the improvement they'd seen in each dog.

"One more class," Sean said as he checked off items on his roster. "So far, I'm expecting all the dogs will pass."

Diana drew air between her teeth. "Even Darby?"

Sean laughed. "Even Darby. He's a work in progress, but he'll get there."

After everyone had left, Diana walked with Tripp to the parking lot. "I promised Aunt Jennie a visit this afternoon. Want to come along?"

"Thanks, but no, not this time." Tripp pressed a hand to his side, and Diana caught a subtle grimace.

"Are you feeling okay? You're not catching something, are you?"

"It's nothing. Probably just too many long days and short nights." His smile seemed forced.

"Well, okay, if you're sure. Go home and get some rest." She stretched up for a quick kiss, then kept her hand on his cheek as she added, "Call me later if you aren't feeling better. I mean it."

His only response was a noncommittal nod.

Knees drawn up on Aunt Jennie's love seat half an hour later, Diana admitted her concerns about counting on a future with Tripp. "Too many times lately, it feels like he's pulling away. Am I being selfish for wanting reassurance?"

"No, sweetie, not at all." Aunt Jennie took a tiny sip

of the tea she'd brewed for them. "Just be mindful that with the terrible loss of his mother looming, he'll need time to grieve and heal."

"I'll give him all the time he needs." Diana set aside her empty cup. "The one thing I can't bear," she said with a shudder, "is losing him again."

Aunt Jennie scoffed. "Where's your faith, girl? If God went to all the trouble to send Tripp Willoughby back into your life, do you believe for a minute He won't see this thing through?"

"Of course not." Diana reached across to squeeze her great-aunt's wrinkled hand. "But what if God's plans for this reunion aren't the same as mine? What if He had an entirely different purpose for bringing Tripp to Juniper Bluff?"

"Well, then, it'll be up to the Lord to reveal it." With a wink, Aunt Jennie reached for the teapot.

Diana waved away the offered refill, while her thoughts skipped to a far less romantic reason for Tripp's reappearance in her life. Maybe he was only supposed to help her launch the therapy pets program— something she couldn't confide in Aunt Jennie without spoiling the surprise.

But if that were the case, surely there were a dozen other experienced veterinarians God could have sent Diana's way. Why did it have to be the one man she'd never been able to get out of her heart?

When Tripp's bedside alarm sounded Monday morning, he'd already been up for two hours dealing with a Crohn's flare-up. He limped over to the nightstand and silenced the insistent clamor.

This wasn't looking like a good day to handle

squirming puppies and temperamental cats. Reluctantly, Tripp reached for his cell phone.

"Robert, it's Tripp," he began, his whole body tensing as another cramp rolled through him. "Not doing so good this morning. Can you cover my appointments, or should I have Yolanda reschedule?"

His partner agreed to see the morning patients and said he'd take care of rescheduling the afternoon appointments so he could make his farm calls. "You just take it easy and get better, okay?"

Tripp thanked him, then took another dose of his meds and crawled into bed.

Shortly before noon, a call from his sister woke him. Seeing her name on the display, he sat up with a start, ever fearful she'd be calling with bad news. His voice cracked as he answered. "Brooke?"

"Hey, big bro. Sounds like I woke you."

"I, uh… I had to call in sick today. Been napping."

"Oh, no. With all this stress, I bet you haven't been eating right, have you? Remembering your meds?"

"Usually." One hand pressed against the throbbing pain in his abdomen, he was glad his sister couldn't see him just now. "And I'm the big brother, remember? So you can quit bossing me around."

"The big brother who still needs looking after, apparently." Brooke scoffed. "You've let Diana know what you can and can't eat, haven't you?"

Her question only reinforced the doubts he'd been wrestling with. Between his sister giving him the third degree and the cramp twisting through his gut, he was on his last nerve. "I don't need you lecturing me about how I'm handling my stomach issues—or my love life."

"Tripp, I didn't mean—"

"Forget it." Tripp drew a tight breath. "Just tell me how Mom's doing."

"Still declining." Brooke hesitated, her tone growing shaky as she continued. "But her spirits are good. She's amazing, Tripp, shaming us all with her strong faith and how at peace she is about waiting for Jesus to—" Her voice broke.

For a moment, Tripp couldn't find his voice, either. He forced down a painful swallow. "Are we still looking okay for my Thanksgiving trip?"

"For now. The doctors still won't commit to anything definite, and you know Mom's a fighter. Having you here for the holiday is about all she talks about."

Brooke's tentative assurance that their mother could last another month relieved a small measure of Tripp's anxiety. "I've already bought my plane ticket. But if anything changes—"

"I'll call right away."

After saying goodbye, Tripp decided he'd slept long enough and went to the kitchenette to look for something safe to eat. He opened a snack-sized container of applesauce, grabbed a spoon and shuffled out to the porch.

He'd barely sat down when the distant ring of his cell phone sounded from inside the cabin. He almost let it go to voice mail but couldn't take the chance that it wasn't Brooke calling back.

In the bedroom again, he snatched up the phone without checking the display. "Hello?"

"Tripp, are you okay?" Diana. "Doc Ingram just stopped in at the shop and mentioned you called in sick this morning."

"I'll be fine. Probably a…stomach bug…or something." He grimaced at the evasion.

"I'm on my way out there. Could you handle some chicken soup from the deli?"

"Diana, no." Tripp clawed the back of his head. "I'm okay, really."

He could hear each breath she took. "No to the soup," she said slowly, "or no, you don't want me there at all?"

Either answer would get him in deeper trouble than he was already in, so he went with another deflection. "Don't you need to be at the doughnut shop?"

"Kimberly can handle things for the afternoon. Please, Tripp, let me take care of you."

Having Diana "take care of him" through one of these episodes, or something even worse, was the absolute last thing he'd ever wanted. But he sensed turning down her offer now would only raise more questions he wasn't ready to answer. "Okay," he said with a sigh. "Chicken soup might just do the trick."

"Great. I'll be there within the hour."

By the time Diana arrived, Tripp had finished his applesauce and swallowed more cramp meds. The pain had finally subsided. He waited on the porch as she stepped from her car with a white paper sack from the supermarket deli.

She darted up the steps. Standing toe-to-toe with him, she searched his face, then felt his forehead. "You don't feel feverish. How's your stomach?"

"Better." Offering a reassuring smile, he pointed to the bag. "I hope you brought enough for two."

He showed her inside to the kitchenette, where he brought bowls and spoons to the table. While Diana dished out the soup, Tripp filled two glasses with ice water.

As they sat down together, Diana cast him one more look of concern before bowing her head to bless the meal. "And, Lord," she finished, "please knock some sense into this hardheaded man so he doesn't feel like he has to power through troubles on his own."

The first spoonful of soup nearly choked him, but he kept his cool and managed to polish off the entire bowl. It settled well, and Diana's company actually felt nice. Still worn out from the flare-up, though, he soon dozed off in one of the easy chairs. He was vaguely aware of Diana rustling around in the kitchenette, interesting aromas of something on the stove drifting through the cabin.

Sometime later, she jostled his shoulder. "I have to go home and see to my pets, but I found a few things in your fridge—ground turkey, veggies and stuff—and mixed up a casserole. It's warming in the oven whenever you get hungry."

"Thanks," he said, sitting up with a yawn. "Sorry I slept so much."

"You obviously needed the rest." Diana bent down to kiss his forehead, then shook her finger at him. "If you feel worse later, you'd better call."

He only nodded, unwilling to promise. "I'll be fine. Don't worry about me."

"As if." She rolled her eyes and marched to the door.

As it closed behind her, Tripp fought the sudden impulse to go after her and ask her to stay.

Not worry? Tripp had to be kidding. Seemed all she did these days was worry—about being ready for the therapy pets evaluation, about Tripp's mom, and—most of all—whether this romantic revival meant they really could have a future together. Because lately Tripp was giving off all kinds of mixed signals—pulling her in, pushing her away—and Diana was having a terrible time keeping her balance.

Twice after she got home that evening, she almost called Tripp to ask if he was feeling better, then abruptly changed her mind. He'd seemed grateful for her help but also uncomfortable, as if allowing someone else— her?—to take care of him strained some macho part of his psyche.

At least she hoped that's all it was.

By the next morning, she couldn't keep herself from calling. His cell phone went to voice mail, which she took as a sign he was feeling better and made it to work. He returned her call over the noon hour.

"Got your message," he said. "Sorry I couldn't call sooner. We had a full appointment schedule this morning."

Diana pushed aside the salad she'd been eating at her desk. "Are you sure you shouldn't have taken another day to make sure you're over this?"

"I told you, I'm fine." A note of impatience tinged his tone.

"Well, you looked pretty sick yesterday. I was—"

"How many times do I have to tell you, Diana? I *don't* need you worrying about me."

His sharp tone made her flinch. "All right, fine. I have plenty of other things I can be worrying about that don't require dealing with your attitude."

She jammed her thumb on the disconnect button and slammed the phone facedown on her desk, then dropped her head into her hands.

She'd scarcely moved ten minutes later when Kimberly leaned in the doorway. "Don't tell me—lovers' quarrel?"

Massaging her temple, Diana released an exasperated sigh. "Can we rewind the calendar to last summer? Life sure seemed a lot simpler then."

"Simpler. But a lot less interesting."

"I can do boring. Boring is nice. Boring is—"

Diana's part-time counter girl, Nora, tapped on the door frame. "Hey, Diana, somebody's asking for you out front."

"A customer?"

Nora smirked. "Your boyfriend."

"Tripp?" Diana's stomach plummeted. "Tripp's *here*?"

Kimberly cast her an enigmatic smile. "Guess you'd better go see what he wants."

Nora and Kimberly both slipped out, while Diana squeezed her eyes shut and prayed for calm. Then, head held high, she marched from the office.

Tripp paced on the other side of the counter. Seeing her, he halted, his eyes pleading. "Di. Please don't be mad."

"Don't I have a right to be?" Sniffing back a surge of emotion, she scanned the shop. Good, no other customers at the moment. She pressed her fingertips into the countertop. "Tripp, what's going on with us? You have me so confused I can hardly think straight."

"Not my intention. I'm just…" He pulled a hand down his face, his gaze sweeping up, down and sideways as if searching for words.

Too tired to argue, Diana decided to make it simpler for him. "Just slowing things down for a while. I get it."

He winced. "It's not the same, not like before."

"That's what I'm counting on." She took his hand and squeezed hard. "If you need slow, we'll go slow. I'm not going anywhere."

Diana didn't hear from Tripp for the rest of the week, and it took every bit of willpower not to call or stop by the clinic. She began to wonder if he'd even put in an appearance at the final obedience class on Sunday. But if he needed space, what choice did she have but to give it to him?

When her parents invited her to go to lunch with them after church, she begged off. Instead, she spent the first part of the afternoon reviewing her therapy pet notes and making sure she was still on track with the paperwork.

As she'd feared, Tripp didn't make it to the class. And neither did one of the students. A few minutes after Sean got started, Diana's cell phone rang.

"Sorry for not letting you know sooner," the woman said, "but my daughter's work schedule got changed unexpectedly and I need to watch my grandson. Afraid I can't make it to the class."

"That's okay," Diana said. "I'll ask Sean if he can offer a makeup session."

"No, don't bother. It looks like I'll be keeping my grandson fairly regularly from now on, so you'd better not count on me as a volunteer."

"Oh, I see." Covering her disappointment, Diana expressed her understanding and invited the woman to get in touch if her situation changed.

Great. Agnes Kraus's final evaluation and therapy pet volunteer training was only a week away. If Diana lost one more volunteer, she'd be below the minimum necessary to get her therapy pets chapter approved.

Back home again, she pored over the original list of possible volunteers and zeroed in on those whose dogs already had obedience training. Could any who'd initially declined be convinced to reconsider? Maybe Tripp would help—

Diana bit her lip. No, she was on her own for now.

At the rate things were going, she might *always* be on her own.

It sure felt like it when she and Tripp hardly spoke at all over the next week. They shared brief phone calls, but their conversations mainly touched on how his mother was doing and if Diana was ready for Agnes Kraus's visit on Saturday.

"I'd really like you to be there," Diana said when Tripp called her Friday evening.

"I'll try," was all he said. "But either way, you'll do great."

At the doughnut shop on Saturday, Diana spilled more coffee in a single morning than she usually did in an entire year. She shouldn't be so nervous—she still had a full contingent of volunteers, all eight with obedience certification and the required veterinary forms. But Agnes Kraus would be judging by her own set of criteria. Whether Diana's loyal band of dog owners could pass the strict criteria to form a Visiting Pet Pals chapter, she wouldn't venture a guess.

As she mopped up yet another spill on the service counter, Kimberly came in from the kitchen with a tray of muffins. "For pity's sake, Diana, go do some book-keeping or something. Let Ethan take over the register."

"He's busy busing tables. Anyway, I'd rather spill

coffee than risk transposing numbers in the accounts."
Pushing out her lower lip to blow a strand of hair from
her eyes, Diana gave her attention to the next customer.

Over her lunch break, she reviewed her checklist
one more time to make sure she hadn't overlooked anything. Shortly after three, Kimberly shooed her out the
door with strict instructions to call later and tell her
how it went.

She'd arranged for the volunteers to gather once
again on the lawn behind the church. By 3:25, seven
of the eight dog owners had shown up. A few minutes
later, a dark blue SUV pulled into the parking lot, and
a tall, red-haired woman in a tailored blouse and dressy
slacks stepped out. With the added effect of the woman's
dignified bun and square-shaped tortoiseshell glasses,
Diana felt like she was back in high school and about
to be disciplined by the principal for too many tardies.

Wiping sweaty palms on her jeans, and suddenly
feeling completely underdressed, Diana strode over and
introduced herself. "So nice to finally meet you in person, Mrs. Kraus. Did you have any trouble finding us?"

"Not at all." Head tilted, the woman surveyed the
group now walking their dogs around the lawn and
chatting with each other. "Only seven?"

"The last one should be here any minute." *I hope!*
The only person missing was Kelly Nesbit with her ter-
rier mix, Freckles. Kelly rarely arrived late for anything,
and Diana was growing concerned. "Do you want to
wait, or should we get started? I have the signed agreement from the assisted-living center, along with all the
dogs' health records and temperament assessments, if
you want to look at those first."

When Mrs. Kraus agreed, Diana led her over to the

bench where she'd left her tote. While the woman perused the paperwork, Diana kept an eye on the parking lot. Shortly, her cell phone buzzed with a text from Kelly: Emergency at the walk-in clinic. Can't get away. So sorry!

Drawing a bolstering breath, Diana informed Mrs. Kraus. "But I know Kelly really wants to participate, and her dog went through obedience training last year." She riffled through the file folder. "See? Here's the copy of his certificate, plus all the veterinary forms."

"I'm sorry, but I can't approve a dog and handler without personally observing them." Rising, the woman returned the forms she'd just been reviewing. "Unfortunately, without eight qualified volunteers and dogs, your group doesn't meet the qualifications for a Visiting Pet Pals chapter."

Diana rose and stood in front of Mrs. Kraus. "But you've come all this way. Surely you won't turn us down because we're short one person?"

"We have strict guidelines. If I were to make an exception for you—"

"But you just said they were guidelines. People make exceptions to guidelines all the time."

"I can't, not without approval from our board of directors." With an apologetic smile, Mrs. Kraus withdrew her key fob from her handbag. "Contact me again after the first of the year. I'll be happy to reschedule."

So much for Aunt Jennie's birthday surprise. Diana had already arranged with the director at the center to hold their first pet visit a week from next Monday. She'd reserved the community room and had been working on plans all week to make it a fun celebration for Aunt Jennie and all the residents.

"No," Diana said, hoping she sounded more authoritative than whiny. "No, it *has* to be today. You can't—"

Someone's firm but gentle grip settled on her shoulder, and the next voice she heard was Tripp's.

"Hello, Mrs. Kraus. I'm Dr. Willoughby, and these dogs are my patients." He stepped up beside Diana. "Surely we can work something out. Diana's invested too much time, energy and heart in this project to have it fall through on such a minor technicality."

The pressure of Tripp's hand brought the welcome reassurance Diana needed. Now she could only hold her breath and hope their combined pleas would change Mrs. Kraus's mind.

"As I was telling Ms. Matthews," the woman said, "I don't have authorization to make such a decision."

Tripp glanced at Diana. "Who are we missing?"

"Kelly and Freckles," she murmured. "Kelly got caught at the clinic."

With a thoughtful nod, Tripp addressed Mrs. Kraus. "Then how about this? Go ahead and evaluate these dogs and owners now. If the last volunteer doesn't make it before you're ready to begin the volunteer training session, I will personally arrange to get her and her dog to your location sometime within the next few days."

Indecision played across the woman's face. "Well, I suppose that's an option. Nothing says the evaluation and training can't be done elsewhere, or that all dogs have to be seen on the same day."

"So," Diana said, confidence returning, "once all the dogs and owners are approved, you can certify our group as a chapter, right? And we can start our visitations."

"Correct." Mrs. Kraus retrieved a clipboard from her satchel. "Very well, then. Shall we get started?"

As the woman strode over to where the owners mingled with their dogs, Diana released her pent-up breath. She swiveled to face Tripp. "Thank you. I didn't think you were coming."

"Nothing could keep me from being here today. I—" He wavered, his gaze shifting toward the bench. "Can we continue this discussion sitting down?"

Noticing his pallor, Diana tugged him over to the bench. "Are you okay?"

His gaze slid sideways as he mumbled, "Still having some stomach problems. It's nothing."

"It's the stress of everything, isn't it? Have you been to see a doctor?"

"It's under control." Tripp reached for Diana's hand. "Can we talk about something else?"

He was closing himself off again. Diana yanked her hand away and folded her arms. "So you're feeling sick and yet still found the strength to swoop in here like Superman to save my therapy pets program. And now you won't talk about it? What does that say about our relationship?"

Tripp's gaze locked with hers. "It says I care."

He had her there. Lips pursed, she glanced away. As much as she'd like to pursue this discussion, today wasn't the ideal time, not with so much riding on today. She released a huff and pushed up from the bench. "This isn't over, Tripp. One of these days, maybe you'll finally be ready to share all of yourself, not just the parts you think I can handle."

She lifted her hands in an exasperated gesture, then with a brisk shake of her head she marched across the lawn.

Chapter Ten

Once all the dogs had passed Agnes Kraus's evaluation, Tripp decided not to stick around to watch the training session. He wasn't feeling that great anyway—and he hadn't been lying when he went along with Diana's suggestion that it was stress. Between agonizing over the thought of losing his mother and doing his best not to permanently wreck things with Diana, his life couldn't get much more stressful.

He skipped church Sunday morning in an attempt to nip his latest flare-up in the bud so he wouldn't have to take any more time off from work. On Monday he followed through on his promise to Diana and contacted Kelly Nesbit to see if she'd be willing to take Freckles to San Antonio to meet with Agnes Kraus. Kelly had a day off on Thursday and said she'd be happy to make the drive, so Tripp phoned Mrs. Kraus to set up the appointment.

On Thursday evening, Diana called. "I thought you'd want to know, Kelly and Freckles passed with flying colors and my chapter's been approved."

"Never had any doubts. Congratulations."

"We're holding a practice session on Saturday to get ready for our first visit to the assisted-living center. Any chance you can come?"

The hopeful lilt in her tone tugged at Tripp's heart. He pushed aside his half-eaten plate of scrambled eggs. "I'll see how things go this weekend." Hoping to distract her from any health-related questions, he changed the subject. "Found a home for another kitten today. Just one left now, plus mama cat."

"Really? I'm so glad. I'm still working on Pastor Terry's wife. She's hinted a few times she'd love to have a kitten." Diana sighed. "I don't know what to do about the mama. Nobody seems interested in a full-grown cat. They just don't have the cute factor kittens do."

Tripp shifted and stretched out one leg. "I had an idea about mama cat. She's made herself right at home at the clinic. What if we adopted her as the clinic cat?"

"You could do that? Oh, Tripp, I love the idea!"

He smiled to himself, glad he could bring a little more happiness into Diana's life. "We'll probably change her name, though. Yolanda's been calling her 'Sandy.'"

"A perfect name."

A brief but pleasant silence settled between them. Then Tripp asked, "How are the party plans coming?"

"Everything's set for Monday evening at the assisted-living center. I can't wait."

"Hope I can come by, at least for a bit."

"Me, too. I know your California flight leaves pretty early the next morning." A pause. "Tripp? Take care of yourself, will you?"

"Yeah. Thanks." He pressed his lips together. "I'll

do my best to be there for your practice session this weekend."

On Saturday, though, Tripp got drafted by Robert to assist with emergency surgery on a horse with an impacted tooth that had become infected. They wrapped things up too late for Tripp to make it to the practice session, and by then he barely had enough reserves left to clean up and fall into bed.

By Monday morning, a November cold front had blown in, bringing gusty winds and intermittent rain showers. The miserable weather seemed apt for Tripp's gloomy state of mind, a perfect day to bury himself in work.

As he entered the clinic through the back door, he caught Yolanda's voice as she spoke with a client.

"I'm sorry, Vince, but Doc Willoughby seems to be running a little late this morning," she said. "He's been fighting a stomach bug off and on for the past couple of weeks."

"But I've got to get Darby fixed up quick." Vince's tone sounded urgent. "We're doing our first Visiting Pet Pals event tonight."

"Let me try to reach Doc Willoughby. Can you—"

Tripp stepped into the area behind the reception counter. "What's going on with Darby?"

Yolanda whirled around. "I thought you might be under the weather again."

"I'm okay." Giving Yolanda's shoulder a pat, he peered over the counter for a look at Vince's mutt. "What happened, fella?"

Seated on his haunches, Darby whined softly and held up his left forepaw.

"I let him out to take care of business after breakfast, and he decided to chase a squirrel," Vince explained. "The grass was slippery from the rain, and he tripped on a tree root. Been limping ever since."

"Let's take a look. Bring him on back."

In the exam room, Tripp pulled a rolling stool over and sat down to perform his examination. He palpated Darby's leg from shoulder to paw, then gently flexed the joints to determine which movements caused discomfort.

"Nothing appears to be broken," he said, straightening. "Most likely a simple sprain. The best thing for Darby is rest and an ice pack."

Stroking the big dog's head, Vince heaved a sigh. "Then we shouldn't join the rest of the group at the center this evening?"

Tripp gnawed the inside of his lip. He hated disappointing Vince, but even more, he knew how much a full contingent of volunteers tonight would mean to Diana. "See how he's doing later this afternoon. If the swelling has gone down and he isn't favoring the leg so much, it would probably be safe to take him over for at least part of the evening."

"Well, you'll be there, right, in case we have any problems?"

"Uh, not sure I can make it."

Vince's mouth fell open. "What? After all you did to help Diana make this happen? Come on, Doc, you gotta be there."

Tripp sat forward, elbows on his knees. "The thing is, I'm leaving in the morning to spend Thanksgiving with my family, and—" He clamped his teeth together against the heartbreaking ache in his chest. "It could be the last time I see my mom."

"Aw, Doc, I'm real sorry. We all understand you've got a lot on your mind."

"Which is why I'm not sure my being there tonight is a good idea. I'd just put a damper on everyone's enjoyment—especially Diana's."

"That's just plumb crazy. You mean the world to her. Should have heard how she talked about you last weekend at our volunteer meeting."

Tripp swallowed. "What exactly did she say?"

"Mostly what a hard time you were having with your mom being sick and how we might still be waiting on approval if you hadn't stepped in with Mrs. Kraus." Vince quirked his mouth in a dubious frown. "So you better not let her down, Doc. Or the rest of us, either, because we're all counting on you."

Warmth spread through Tripp's insides. "I'll think about it," he promised. "Maybe I'll see you at the party, after all."

Prickles of excitement darted up and down Diana's spine as she tapped on Aunt Jennie's door. When her great-aunt invited her in, she swept the little woman into a hug. "Happy birthday!"

Aunt Jennie released a hearty chuckle. "Got plenty to be happy about. Making it to ninety-three is nothing to sneeze at!"

"Mom and Dad are meeting us in the dining room. Ready to go over?"

"Just let me get my sweater. It's always so chilly in there." Snatching a baby blue cardigan off a chair, Aunt Jennie took Diana's arm. "So glad you and your folks could come over and have dinner with me. Makes my birthday extra special."

Diana could hardly wait to make her great-aunt's day even more special.

In the dining room, her parents met them at a festively decorated table for four. As Diana's dad seated her, Aunt Jennie gasped with delight. Her smile stretched even wider when the server brought out plates heaping with some of her favorite foods: sugar-cured ham, marshmallow-topped sweet potatoes, baked apples, creamed peas and yeasty dinner rolls.

"Don't forget to save room for ice cream and cake," Diana said with a wink.

Laughing, Aunt Jennie squeezed Diana's hand. "Oh, my, you're spoiling me."

Taking a quick peek at her watch, Diana replied with a tight-lipped smile. Her volunteers should be checking in at the front desk anytime now. They'd be ready to make their entrance shortly after Aunt Jennie and the other residents finished dinner and gathered in the community room.

Halfway through dinner, Aunt Jennie remarked, "How is your sweet young man doing, honey? You haven't brought him to see me in a while."

Releasing a tremulous breath, Diana clutched the napkin in her lap. "He's been busy. And still very worried about his mother."

"Oh, yes. Please let him know I'm keeping him in my prayers—" Aunt Jennie's eyes narrowed as she looked toward the opposite door. "Could be mistaken, but I think I just saw him peek in."

Heart hammering, Diana twisted to look but caught only a glimpse of a plaid shirtsleeve before whoever it was disappeared around the corner. She'd hoped Tripp would try to be there, but she hadn't dared to count on it.

Excusing herself, she rose on shaky legs. She found him in the community room mingling with the therapy pet volunteers. Tripp glanced up from his conversation with Kelly Nesbit, his gaze locking with Diana's. He said something to Kelly, then ambled over. His mouth twitched in a nervous smile. "Looks like everything's going according to plan."

"So far. Aunt Jennie's going to be so surprised." Diana studied him. "How are you feeling?"

"Better." He shoved his hands into the pockets of slim black jeans. "Couldn't bear to miss your great-aunt's expression when she's greeted by all these furry friends."

"I can't wait, either." Diana glanced up with a sincere smile. "You helped make this happen, and I haven't begun to thank you enough."

"No need. I've enjoyed every minute of it." He looked past Diana, a flicker of uncertainty in his expression. "Mr. Matthews. Nice to see you again."

"Hello, Tripp." Diana's father rested a protective arm around her shoulder. "Sweetie, they're ready to bring out Aunt Jennie's birthday cake."

"Be right there, Dad." She waited for her father to step away, then murmured, "I should make sure my volunteers are all set."

"Right. If there's anything I can do, just ask."

She replied with a quick nod, then shared some last-minute instructions for the volunteers before rejoining her family in the dining room. Her mother signaled the server to bring the cake to the table, and Aunt Jennie's eyes sparkled brighter than the twinkling candles atop

the German chocolate cake. As they began the birthday song, the other residents took notice and chimed in.

As the applause died down, Diana took the opportunity to make her announcement. "Don't forget, the
party continues in the community room right after dinner. Please join us!"

"There's *more*?" Aunt Jennie asked.

"Oh, yes." Diana grinned. "The fun is just beginning."

Finding a chair in an out-of-the-way corner of the
community room, Tripp settled in to watch as residents
began to gather after dinner. Those first glimpses of
eight mannerly pooches of all shapes, colors and sizes
brought varied reactions—everything from bewilder-
ment, to curious smiles, to full-out grins and laughter.

Tripp couldn't help smiling, himself. This was even
better than when he'd worked with a therapy pets group
while doing his veterinary internship. Not that tonight's
experience was so different, but because he was getting
to share it with Diana.

He looked toward the entrance to see her escorting
her great-aunt into the room. The tiny, white-haired
woman's eyes grew big as saucers. She threw a hand
to her mouth to cover a gasp.

"Oh, my, look at all the puppies!" Laughing, Jennie clutched Diana's wrist. "How delightful! Can we
pet them?"

"That's why they're here." Beaming, Diana showed
her great-aunt to a chair near the center of the room.
"This is your birthday surprise, Aunt Jennie."

One by one, Diana had the volunteers come over
and introduce their dogs. Jennie oohed and aahed over
each of them, caressing their heads and tickling them

under their chins. After she'd had a few minutes to enjoy the dogs, the volunteers began taking their pets around to meet other residents. Some responded shyly, others eagerly, but Tripp could see in each face the pure joy of giving and receiving this singular gift of affection.

While he watched from his corner, Vince and Janice Mussell wandered over with Darby. "You're awful quiet over here," Vince remarked.

"Just taking it all in." Tripp gave Darby a pat while unobtrusively checking the dog's leg. "Looks like this fella's doing better this evening."

"Followed your orders with the cold packs and kept him off his feet most of the afternoon. He was rarin' to go by suppertime."

"Isn't this the most fun ever?" Janice's gaze swept the room. "And so rewarding. Diana says we're going to try scheduling visits twice a month."

A stooped gentleman hobbled over, leaning on his cane. "Can I pet this boy again? Reminds me an awful lot of Duke, my boyhood dog. Never stopped missing that sweet old guy."

Vince and Janice sat down with the elderly man, and while he showered Darby with attention and reminisced about Duke, Tripp decided it was time to slip out.

He made it as far as the foyer when Diana caught up with him. "You're not leaving already, are you?"

"I've got that flight to catch in the morning, remember?"

"Oh, Tripp, I wish I could go with you."

"You have your shop to run. Besides, you should be with your own family for the holiday."

Diana dropped her forehead against his chest. He was right, she couldn't exactly skip out on her mother's

Thanksgiving feast. They'd have Aunt Jennie with them this year, too. "You'll keep in touch, though?"

"I promise."

She sniffed loudly and raked her hand across her cheeks. "If your mom—I mean, when the time comes—"

"I'll let you know." He pulled her close, his throat closing over the words he had to say before he left. "Don't ever forget how much I love you, Di. Always have, always will."

"Tripp—"

"Walk me to my car. I need to get on the road to San Antonio."

Her steps faltered as he guided her toward the exit. "Now?"

"My flight leaves at six a.m. I booked a room for tonight at a hotel near the airport."

He was back to all business again. And not fooling her for a moment. They stopped beside his SUV. "Tripp?"

"Yeah?" He climbed in behind the wheel.

"I'm still in love with you, too."

Chapter Eleven

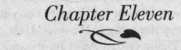

Watching Tripp drive away, Diana felt her heart ripping in two. She'd have given anything to be with him during what could turn out to be the most difficult Thanksgiving anyone could face. Instead, all she could do was pray for him.

For the present, though, she took comfort in knowing she'd made her beloved great-aunt's birthday special. When Diana telephoned Aunt Jennie the next day during a break at the shop, the sweet woman spent almost the entire conversation raving about the party and the time spent with all the adorable, well-behaved dogs. According to Aunt Jennie, everyone else at the center had fallen in love with the dogs, too, and couldn't wait for their return.

"I'm scheduling another visit in a couple of weeks," Diana assured her. "In the meantime, I've gotten the okay to bring Alice, my rabbit, for an afternoon visit next Sunday. She's not as playful as the dogs, but she's great for cuddling."

Changing topics, Diana reminded Aunt Jennie

she'd be picking her up on Thursday morning to spend Thanksgiving with Diana's parents.

"I can't wait. Much as I've enjoyed the meals they serve us here, I'm ready for your dad's famous smoked turkey and your mother's delicious corn bread dressing."

On Thanksgiving morning, Aunt Jennie already had her coat on and was waiting for Diana in the lobby. The day held just enough nip in the air that Diana hoped her parents had a cozy fire going in the wood-burning stove. They did, and Diana settled Aunt Jennie in a padded rocker close by, then brought her a steaming cup of tea with honey and lemon.

"Dad's out back keeping an eye on the smoker." Diana tuned the TV to a holiday parade broadcast for her great-aunt to watch. "Need anything else before I help Mom in the kitchen?"

"I'll be just fine, sweetie." Aunt Jennie patted Diana's hand and looked up with a concerned smile. "Any word from your young man today?"

Glancing out the broad picture window at the barren pastures, Diana sucked in a tiny breath. "No, not yet."

"You should call him, let him know you're thinking about him."

"Maybe later. I don't want to intrude on his family time." Diana gave her great-aunt a quick kiss on the forehead, then excused herself to help her mother with dinner preparations.

It didn't take Mom long to notice Diana's preoccupation, especially after she accidentally dropped one of her mother's crystal water glasses on the tile floor.

"It's okay, honey," Mom said, swooping in with a broom and dustpan. "It's just a glass."

"I know, but—" Making a growling noise in her

throat, Diana tore off a handful of paper towels and wet them at the sink, then knelt to help her mother clean up the remaining glass fragments.

When they finished, Mom pulled Diana close for a hug. "This is all about Tripp, isn't it?"

"I hate being so conflicted." Diana pressed her temple against her mother's. "Right before he drove away Monday night, I finally told him I'm still in love with him."

Chuckling, Mom shifted to face Diana. "And that has you conflicted?"

"Actually, more like terrified. Because I can't shake the sense that something's going to happen to keep us apart."

I'm still in love with you, too.

Every time Diana's words whispered through Tripp's mind, he thought his heart would burst right out of his chest. The memory had carried him all the way to San Antonio, comforted him through a restless night at the airport hotel and buoyed his flagging hopes during the long flight to Los Angeles.

The next two days and nights spent at his mother's bedside, though, blurred such hopes into oblivion. Mom had grown so weak and pale, she was a shadow of the woman he remembered from the last time he'd visited. She seemed to sleep most of the time, and whether she heard the conversations going on around her, Tripp couldn't tell. He could only thank God he'd made it in time to spend this last Thanksgiving with her.

As he sat holding his mother's hand on Thursday morning, Brooke asked him for some help in the kitchen. Reluctant to leave his mother's side, he rose and brushed the papery-thin skin of her forehead with a kiss. His dad immediately took his place beside Mom's bed, and the tragically endearing expression on Dad's face as he gazed at his sleeping wife just about did Tripp in.

Halting outside the kitchen door, he squeezed his eyes shut as a vision of Diana someday wearing that same expression at his bedside smacked him hard.

I'm still in love with you, too.

His belly cramped. He didn't realize his groan was audible until Brooke called his name.

She jabbed her finger toward a chair at the dinette. "Get in here and sit down. And don't pretend with me that you're not hurting. It's written all over your face."

One hand pressed against the pain in his abdomen, he glared at his sister. "Drop it, will you? I don't need—"

Their father's anguished cry rang out from the other room, and they both rushed to Mom's bedside. The hospice nurse stood on the opposite side, her stethoscope pressed to Mom's chest. Moments later, she silently shook her head.

That quickly, it was over. Within the hour, two gentlemen in dark suits arrived from the mortuary and took Tripp's mother away.

Sick with grief, worsened by his unrelenting remorse over not being able to save Mom with one of his own kidneys, Tripp collapsed on his bed and stayed there for the rest of the day.

Dusk was falling when Brooke peeked in on him. "Hey, brother mine. Come eat something. We've still got all this Thanksgiving food in the oven." She sighed. "And we all need to keep our strength up for what happens next."

With a barely suppressed moan, Tripp eased his legs off the side of the bed and sat up. "Not hungry, but I'll try."

"Good." Brooke tucked an arm around his shoulder. "Oh, and I left messages for Diana about the funeral. I know you don't feel like talking yet, but you should call her. She'll be anxious to hear from you."

Nodding, Tripp made a vague promise to call Diana soon. The problem was, he had no idea what he'd say to her. The last thing he wanted was to break her heart again, but these last few days had reaffirmed his convictions that he had to spare her even the remotest possibility of suffering through what his dad had just endured. But if he suddenly told her there was no chance of a future together, she'd beg for explanations and, once again, he'd hold back, because Diana was just stubborn enough to stay with him no matter what.

And the thought of seeing her again at Mom's funeral? He hated himself for thinking this, but a part of him hoped Diana would be too busy to come.

Diana had barely walked in the door at home after dropping off Aunt Jennie at her apartment when her cell phone rang. The display showed an out-of-area phone number but no name, so it couldn't be Tripp. Probably another of those annoying robocalls. With her suddenly starving cats yowling at her feet, she let the call go to voice mail.

Later, after all the pets were taken care of and she'd warmed some leftovers for her own supper, she listened to the message. When she heard Brooke Willoughby's voice, her heart plummeted to her toes.

"Hello, Diana. It's been a long, long time, huh?" Brooke sounded as if she'd been crying. "I'm calling for Tripp because he's…well, he's taking this pretty hard. But he said you'd want to know when Mom passed away—the funeral arrangements and such."

With a sniffle, Brooke reported that their mother had slipped away peacefully in her sleep around eleven that morning. A quick time-difference calculation told Diana she would have been helping her mother sweep up the broken crystal around that time.

"We're taking Mom home to Austin for the burial," Brooke's message continued shakily. "Services will be next Monday. Soon as I hang up, I'll text you the details." A pause. "I'm sure you're worried about Tripp. He's just…he's going to need some time. And I really hope you can come to the funeral, because we'd all love to see you again."

The voice mail ended, and Diana switched over to view the text. Tears rolled down her cheeks as she read the name and address of the church she used to attend with the Willoughby family whenever she visited Tripp back in college. Those had been such happy times, sharing smiles while they sang the worship songs, holding hands as they bowed their heads for prayer. And Peggy Willoughby always planned the most fun Sunday afternoons. She'd have the whole family pitching in to put homemade pizzas together for lunch, or the girls would chat as they chopped salad veggies while the guys went out to the patio to grill steaks. Afterward, sometimes they'd walk to a nearby park and play disc golf, or if it was cold or rainy, they'd gather round the dining room table and play board games until Diana, Brooke and Tripp had to pack up for the drive back to campus.

The memories kept coming, until Diana had soaked several tissues and decided it was time to get practical.

First, she called Kimberly and asked her to cover the shop for a couple of days. "I'll drive over to Austin on Sunday afternoon and probably return sometime Tuesday. Will that work for you?"

"Absolutely. No worries, hon. Got someone lined up to take care of your animals?"

"My teenage neighbor knows the routine. I'm calling her next." Diana thanked Kimberly and said she'd see her in the morning. A few minutes later, she'd made arrangements for the pets and also reserved a room at the hotel Brooke had mentioned in her text.

Now all she had to do was survive the next few days until she could see Tripp again.

After the Sunday worship service and a quick bite of lunch with her parents, Diana climbed in her car and headed for Austin. The drive took just over two hours, and by four o'clock, she had checked in to her hotel room and hung her dark navy dress in the closet so the travel wrinkles would hang out.

Sitting on the bed, she stared at her cell phone and pondered giving Tripp a call to let him know she was in town. He'd texted yesterday afternoon, a curt message informing her they were in Austin and staying with church friends.

She'd texted back, Glad you made it safely. See you soon. Praying.

No reply.

She had to assume they were all exhausted beyond imagining, and with burial arrangements still to be finalized, Tripp had plenty on his mind without engaging in chitchat. Tomorrow would come soon enough, and Diana could finally surround him with the love she'd been storing up since he left after Aunt Jennie's party last Monday night.

For the past twelve years, if she were honest. The bitterness she'd clung to in the beginning, then the couldn't-care-less pretense that came later, had only masked her true feelings. No matter how staunchly she'd claimed to be over Tripp Willoughby, having him back in her life these past several weeks had proved her wrong. Utterly and completely wrong.

The next morning, after a few bites of the hotel's complimentary breakfast along with three cups of strong coffee to counteract a virtually sleepless night, Diana dressed for the funeral. She left shortly after nine thirty for the ten o'clock service. The route was so familiar, but there had been a few changes since the last time she'd traveled these streets—a new strip shopping mall, more fast-food restaurants, a business plaza. Across the road from the church, a modern, up-scale apartment complex filled what used to be a vacant lot. The church itself had grown, too, a breezeway now connecting the sanctuary to a two-story educational building and gymnasium.

Time hadn't stopped. Not for the community, not for this church, not for Diana and Tripp. Their feelings for each other had grown and changed, as well. The budding romance of their college years, though unexpectedly cut short, now held the promise of growing into something much deeper and more mature. More lasting, too, Diana prayed. It made her heart flutter to imagine what came next.

Stepping from her car, she strode across the rapidly filling parking lot and joined other mourners on their way into the sanctuary. An usher handed her a memorial bulletin and invited her to sign the guest book. She waited her turn at the stand by the inner doors, then found a seat about halfway to the front.

Sorrow billowed in her chest at the sight of the closed coffin and floral arrangements in front of the altar. Peggy Willoughby's portrait sat on an easel nearby—soft, brown curls sprinkled with gray framing smiling eyes so much like Tripp's, it made Diana's heart clench.

A few minutes before ten, a side door opened to the left of the chancel. The pastor emerged—someone new since Diana had been here last—followed by Brooke and Tripp, their father supported between them. The poor man, thinner and more stooped than Diana recalled, had a dazed look about him. Brooke had changed little. Even her red-rimmed eyes didn't betray her innate self-assurance, evident in the set of her chin and purposeful steps.

But Tripp—oh, Tripp! Taking in his haggard appearance, Diana nearly started from the pew. Hollow cheeks, dark circles under his eyes and the grim set to his mouth testified to the agony of grief he'd endured these past several days. She wished he'd look her way so that she could silently convey her love and support, but he barely glanced up before taking the front pew with his father and sister.

The service began, and Diana could hardly tear her gaze from the back of Tripp's head. Though his father wept openly and Brooke dried her eyes several times, Tripp sat stoically, even when Brooke strode to the lectern to say a few words about their mother.

Following the concluding prayers, the pastor invited family and friends to proceed to the cemetery for the graveside service, after which the Willoughbys would receive guests at a luncheon in the fellowship hall. Diana filed out to her car with the others. The cemetery was only a few blocks away, and soon she stood weeping silently on the periphery as the pastor read the Twenty-third Psalm and commended Peggy to her heavenly Father.

Still, Tripp didn't seem aware of her presence, and before she could approach him, the funeral director whisked him and his father and sister into a limousine for the return to the church. There, at least, Diana hoped to finally have a few minutes to hold and comfort him.

Arriving back at the church parking lot, she followed the other mourners to a large, first-floor room in the new building addition. Tripp and his family stood inside the main doors to receive greetings and accept condolences, and with each step that brought her nearer, Diana's pulse notched up.

At last, she stood in front of Brooke. Her former roommate gasped in happy surprise and wrapped her in a warm hug. "Diana! I'm so glad you came."

"Me, too." Diana's voice cracked. "I'm so, so sorry about your mom."

Breaking away, Brooke looped her arm through her father's. "Dad, here's Diana."

Mr. Willoughby's smile broadened. "How are you, honey? Gracious, you look just the same. I wish—" Tearing up again, he pulled her close for a kiss on the cheek, then whispered, "It made Peggy so happy to know you and Tripp found each other again."

Unable to speak, Diana merely nodded as Mr. Willoughby handed her off to Tripp. Holding both his hands, she felt suddenly shy as she looked up at him. His lips trembled in the beginnings of a smile that quickly faded. She moved closer to draw him into a comforting embrace but sensed him stiffen before he edged away.

"I, uh...we can talk later," he murmured, nodding toward the line behind her. "Sorry."

"Of course." Diana stepped away. She had no right to feel snubbed, but she couldn't help it. It felt as if Tripp had just slammed a door in her face.

Brooke reached past her father and Tripp to catch Diana's arm. "We have a reserved table at the far end. Sit with us, okay?"

"Are you sure?" Diana glanced at Tripp, hoping for his agreement, but he'd turned away to speak with someone else.

"Absolutely," Brooke said, then added with a meaningful smile, "You're practically family."

Brooke's reassurance restored a measure of Diana's confidence. Tripp's detachment had to be grief related. It must have been torture knowing nothing could be done to help his mother, then to witness her rapid decline, to be with her as she breathed her last... Diana couldn't imagine losing one of her own parents, or even Aunt Jennie, to a lengthy and devastating illness.

With a sobering breath, she crossed to the buffet table. As she filled a plate, a few of the Willoughbys' old friends recognized her from years gone by and welcomed her back. Their kind words warmed her, especially when they spoke to her as if she, too, had suffered a loss. She truly felt as if she had, because if things did work out between her and Tripp, she'd never get to experience knowing Peggy not just as her boyfriend's mother but as her cherished mother-in-law.

By the time the receiving line had dwindled and the Willoughbys could get some lunch, Diana had almost finished. Arriving at the table, Tripp faltered as if surprised to see Diana there. With a hesitant smile, he took the chair at her left, and she noticed his plate held little more than a slice of ham and a small serving of green beans. Before she could comment, though, Brooke and her father sat down on Diana's other side.

"I'm worn out." Brooke released a muted groan and took a sip of iced tea.

Diana touched Brooke's arm. "Thanks again for inviting me to sit with you. It's an honor I wasn't expecting."

"Wouldn't have it any other way." With a wink, Brooke added, "And don't tell anyone, but I'm kicking my shoes off under the table."

"My lips are sealed."

Tripp and his father both ate in silence—or rather, mostly picked at their food—while Brooke asked Diana all kinds of questions about what she'd been doing since college. Diana couldn't tell whether her old friend's chatter was genuine interest or just her way of dealing with grief. Recalling what she knew of Brooke from their college days, probably both.

A sudden motion to her left made her glance at Tripp. A grimace marred his features. Short, moaning breaths slipped between his dry lips as he leaned forward and clutched his abdomen.

Diana swiveled to face him. "Tripp, what is it?"

Eyes squeezed shut, he shook his head. His face had gone deathly pale, and the moans had become one long, keening cry.

Panicking, Diana whirled around to get Brooke's

attention, but she'd already shoved her chair back and was hurrying around to Tripp's side.

"Hospital," Tripp gasped. "Now."

Chapter Twelve

Before Diana realized what was happening, several people had rushed to help. She scooted out of the way as someone Brooke addressed as Dr. Halvorson stepped in. By then, Tripp was doubled over in obvious pain and verging on unconsciousness.

After a brief debate about whether to call for an ambulance, the doctor recommended driving Tripp directly to the emergency room. Two other men came over and, looping Tripp's arms over their shoulders, walked him out to Brooke's rental car, parked just outside.

Terrified, Diana hurried after them. She caught Brooke as she climbed in behind the steering wheel. "Where are you taking him? I want to come."

Brooke named the hospital. "It's not far. Meet us there."

By the time Diana got to her own car and brought up the hospital location on her map app, the Willoughbys were a good five minutes ahead. Then she had to deal with traffic and got stuck in the right lane when she needed to make a left turn. When she finally found her way to the parking area outside the emergency room, she was ready to claw through the windshield.

She raced through the double doors and surveyed the busy waiting area. No sign of Brooke, her father or Tripp—and she knew this was the right hospital because she recognized Brooke's car parked at the drop-off curb.

Her worries skyrocketed. Nobody got seen this quickly in the ER unless it was a life-or-death situation. *Dear Lord, please. I can't lose him now!*

Fighting down panic, she approached the check-in desk. "Can you tell me anything about Tripp Willoughby? He would have just been brought in."

A nurse in aqua scrubs consulted her computer, then raised an eyebrow in Diana's direction. "Are you family?"

She couldn't lie. "No. But I'm a close friend. Please, anything—"

"I'm sorry. You'll have to wait until someone from his immediate family can answer your questions."

With a reluctant nod, Diana turned away and scanned the room for an empty seat. She found one facing the doors to the treatment rooms and plopped down, hugging her handbag to her chest. How long would it take before someone brought news? Would Brooke even remember Diana was there?

Before she'd finished the thought, the doors opened and Brooke appeared. Diana scrambled to her feet and rushed over. "How is he? What's happening?"

"They're prepping him for emergency surgery." Brooke grasped Diana's hand. "Come with me to the surgical floor waiting room. Dad's already gone up."

"Surgery?" As Brooke hurried them to the elevator, Diana tried to process everything. The only thing that made sense was a ruptured appendix. What else could cause such sudden, excruciating pain?

Brooke jabbed the button for the third floor. "If he wasn't already hurting so badly, I'd strangle him. I warned him several times this could happen if he didn't eat right and take better care of himself."

Recalling Tripp's recent stomach bug, Diana wondered now if it had actually been the early warning signs. "It's his appendix, right?"

"Appendix?" Brooke's mouth dropped open in an incredulous stare. Then, shoulders collapsing, she expelled a noisy breath. "He never told you, did he?"

"What? What didn't he tell me?"

The elevator doors opened at the third floor. Brooke draped her arm around Diana and marched her through the opening. "Girl, we need to sit down somewhere and have a long, long talk."

Had Tripp fallen into an echo chamber? Over the constant ringing in his ears, other sounds seemed amplified by a factor of ten. His eyelids felt like twenty-pound cement blocks. He tried to swallow, but his throat hurt like the worst case of strep ever.

"Tripp? You in there?" His sister's voice.

Little by little, he pried his eyes open, only to be blinded by a fluorescent light overhead. "Where—" It was all he could push past his raspy vocal chords.

"The hospital. You just had surgery for a blockage." Elbows braced on the side of the bed, Brooke hovered over him. "You could have died, you know. I'm half-tempted to kill you myself, you big, brainless—"

"Brooke." Their dad appeared at the bedside. "Enough."

Tripp couldn't think clearly enough to grasp why he was in so much trouble with his sister, so he decided this was a good time to drift back to sleep.

The next time he opened his eyes, the room lay in darkness. His whole body felt stiff and sore, but when he tried to shift his position, a twinge in his abdomen made him suck in a breath.

Oh, yeah. Surgery…blockage… It was coming back to him now, the recurring belly cramps over the past few weeks, the stabbing pain that grew steadily worse the day of Mom's funeral.

Mom's funeral. He sank into his pillow with a moan. The whole day had been one long, painful blur, both physically and emotionally.

And Diana. He remembered sitting next to her in the fellowship hall, right before he collapsed.

Great, just great. By now, Brooke would have told her everything. Tripp's best intentions of finally being honest with Diana about their breakup, of allowing her the chance to love him for who he was today—forever taken away from him by his own stubborn stupidity.

A brown-skinned man in scrubs pushed a rolling computer terminal into the room and switched on a muted light over the bed. His name tag read James Fessler, RN. "Doing okay, Mr. Willoughby? Any pain?"

Not the kind medicine could relieve. "Just a few twinges."

James checked Tripp's vitals, then changed out his IV bag. He handed Tripp a cord with a button on the end. "This will release pain meds. Don't worry, there's no chance of overdose. You want to stay on top of the pain so you can rest and heal."

"I know. I'm a veterinarian."

"Ah, so it's *Doctor* Willoughby. Where do you practice? I just got my kids a puppy."

"Not around here. In Juniper Bluff." For how much longer, Tripp wouldn't hazard a guess. The thought of facing Diana again terrified him.

"Over near Fredericksburg, right? Well, you get some rest, Doc. I'll check in on you later, but don't hesitate to buzz the desk if you need anything."

As soon as the nurse left, Tripp gave himself another dose of pain meds in hopes it would make him drowsy. Lying there in the dark with only his troubling thoughts to keep him company, sleep seemed his only escape.

A couple more doses got him through the night. About the time his breakfast tray was delivered, Brooke and Dad arrived.

"Wow. You look a hundred times better than when we left here last night." Brooke peeked beneath the metal lid on his tray. "Oh, joy. Broth and lime gelatin. No worries about me snitching a bite."

Dad circled to the opposite side of the bed. "How are you, son? You scared us silly."

"I'm okay. More worried about you." Tripp gripped his father's hand.

"Hangin' in there, best we can." Dad shared a glance with Brooke, who gave a quick nod, obviously some kind of private communication Tripp wasn't supposed to interpret. "I'm just gonna step out to the nurses' station and see if they have some coffee."

As the door closed behind his father, Tripp pinned his sister with a hard stare. "All right, what's going on?"

Arms crossed, Brooke plopped down on a chair. "Eat your breakfast and I'll tell you."

The beefy aroma of the broth was slightly nauseating, but if Tripp wanted to get stronger, he'd better try to get it down. He took a few careful sips. While his stomach settled, he glanced over at Brooke. "So...?"

"So... I'm pretty mad at you right now." She sat forward. "Do you have any idea what it was like for *me* to have to explain to Diana about the Crohn's? Tripp, why didn't you tell her?"

The broth churned through his insides. "I was waiting for the right time. And then—" He swallowed and looked toward the window. "What Dad went through with Mom, the thought of putting Diana through that— I just couldn't do it."

"You big baby." Lips pursed, Brooke shook her head. "She's in love with you, Tripp. Don't be an idiot. Don't let her go again."

"You don't understand—"

"No, *you're* the one who's totally clueless." Rising, Brooke approached the bed. "Just talk to her, Tripp. Apologize and make things right, before it's too late. She's in the waiting room right now. Let me go get her—"

"No." Tripp's chest muscles clenched. He fought for breath. "Not like this. Not while I'm lying in a hospital bed with tubes in my arm."

Brooke glanced toward the door. When she faced Tripp again, the frustration in her eyes had turned to worry. "She's hurt and angry, Tripp, and she has every right to be. If you don't reach her now, you may never get another chance."

Long moments of indecision passed. Tripp's thoughts sped through the uncertain future, and when he contemplated facing it without Diana, his heart twisted.

The door whispered open, and Tripp jerked his head

toward the sound, both hoping and fearing he'd see Diana.

It was his father. Exhaling tiredly, Dad caught Brooke's eye and murmured, "I tried, but she wouldn't stay."

Only then did Tripp realize how ready he was to stuff all his fears about the future into a deep, dark hole and do whatever it took to convince Diana of his love. Ignoring the pang shooting through his surgical incision, he pushed himself upright in the bed. "What— she left already?"

"Sorry, son, but she was real upset." Hands stuffed in his pockets, Dad shuffled closer. "Said she only stopped by to make sure you were all right and had to get back to Juniper Bluff."

Brooke cast him a sad smile. "I'm sorry, Tripp. I tried to tell you."

"Not your fault." He looked away. "I brought this on myself."

Diana used almost an entire box of tissues during the drive home. Between the flood of her own tears and the spitting rain smearing the windshield, the road ahead was a misty blur, and she could only be thankful there hadn't been much traffic on a Tuesday.

Pulling into her garage, she shut off the engine and hammered the steering wheel with her fist. "How could you, Tripp?"

All those wasted years, simply because he was both too proud and too insecure to be truthful with her about his health condition. Did he have so little respect for her, so little trust in her love?

Now, how could she ever trust him again? Even if she

could forgive him—and she wanted to, desperately—every time she replayed Brooke's description of Tripp's battle with Crohn's, along with the potential complications she'd read about later on the internet, her thoughts raced with the terrifying possibility that any future they might hope for could be cruelly and painfully cut short.

It didn't matter how many sources quoted statistics indicating Crohn's was rarely fatal. What if Tripp proved the exception? What if another episode like this one—and Brooke had said it wasn't the first—turned into something much worse?

She had to stop thinking about it before she drove herself crazy. Hauling her travel bag from the trunk, she entered through the kitchen door, only to be loudly greeted by three howling cats and a squawking parakeet. Alice the rabbit was quiet, at least, hunkering near her crate door and wiggling her nose.

"I missed you, too, guys. All right, all right, don't trip me." Stepping gingerly around the cats, Diana made her way to the bedroom and started unpacking. It was still early. She could grab a bite of lunch and then relieve Kimberly at the doughnut shop.

Just keep busy. If she could focus on work and her therapy pets group, maybe she'd get past the anger and find a way to deal with the revelations of the last couple of days.

When Diana walked in the back door of the doughnut shop an hour later, Kimberly looked up from her mixing bowl with a start. "Didn't expect you back so soon."

"Nothing to keep me in Austin." Barely looking at her assistant, Diana took an apron from a hook. "Who's up front?"

"Nora. And don't have a conniption, okay? She, um,

had a little accident with the cappuccino machine this morning."

Good, a problem to deal with. Today, problems were Diana's friend. She started for the front before Kimberly could bombard her with questions about the trip. Or Tripp. She didn't want to talk about either one.

Avoidance worked fine for the rest of the day. And the day after that. And on into the weekend, at least until Sunday morning, when Doc Ingram caught her on her way into church.

"Awful thing about Tripp," he said. "First his mom dying, then him getting sick like that."

"Yes, awful." Diana offered a pinched smile. Out of politeness she asked, "How are things at the clinic? Are you managing okay?"

"Hasn't been easy. Good to know Tripp's on the mend. Can't wait to have him back." With a nod to his wife, waiting at the sanctuary doors, Doc Ingram excused himself. "You take care of that boy, you hear?"

"But I—" No use explaining. The vet was out of earshot anyway.

Then Marie Peterson arrived with her great-grand-children, Seth Austin's kids, and bustled over to say hello. From Marie, Diana learned Brooke and Mr. Willoughby had driven Tripp home and were staying in one of the guest cabins.

Diana blinked. "He's back already?"

"You didn't know?" Marie's eyebrows bunched. "I just figured—I mean, I heard you two—"

The opening praise music began, saving Diana from an uncomfortable explanation. "We'd better go in to church."

She sidestepped into the pew alongside her parents

and grudgingly accepted her father's sympathetic one-arm hug. Dad's "Spidey sense" where Diana's boyfriend issues were concerned had kicked in big-time after she returned from Austin, and she hadn't been able to escape confiding the truth about Tripp and all that had happened.

"Heard he's back in town," Dad spoke close to her ear. "Planning on seeing him?"

Keeping her eyes on the song lyrics scrolling across the projection screen, Diana shook her head. "Still processing. Not to mention I've been busy getting organized for another therapy pets visit this afternoon."

"Sounds like an excuse to me."

Diana bit her tongue. "I—I just need more time."

And a whole lot more prayer.

From a cushioned chair in the cabin's sitting area, Tripp watched his sister puttering around in the kitchenette. "You really don't have to stay," he told her for the tenth time since they'd brought him home. "I can take care of myself."

"Uh-huh, like you've totally been doing lately." Crossing to his chair, Brooke handed him a plate of baked chicken breast and steamed green beans. Bland, but at least it wasn't hospital food.

"So I had a minor setback."

"Minor?" Hands on her hips, Brooke glared. "Have you forgotten you just had *major* surgery?"

"I've learned my lesson this time, I promise." Shifting to ease the strain on his healing incision, Tripp glanced over at his dad as he settled onto the sofa with his own plate of food. "How have you put up with this bossy kid for so long?"

"She's a handy little thing to have around." Dad cast his daughter a loving, misty-eyed smile. "Don't know what we'd have done without her this past year."

Tripp's first bite of chicken stuck in his throat. He forced it down with a gulp of iced tea. Dad was right, of course. Brooke was the glue keeping them all from falling apart.

Well, except for Tripp. He'd fallen apart mightily these past few weeks. But the pieces were coming together again, praise the Lord. Long talks with his father during his hospital stay and in the days since had helped him regain some perspective—about his mother's courageous battle with kidney disease, about the ups and downs of his own condition and especially about not letting fear of an unpredictable future rob him of happiness in the here and now.

But would Diana see it the same way? Would she give him another chance, first to explain and apologize, and then to try again to build a life together?

None of it would matter, though, if he didn't take his health more seriously. The obstruction was his own fault for ignoring the warning signs of an impending crisis. Now that he was thinking more clearly, he could see how his negligence had been a form of self-punishment for his "crime" of not being able to give his mother a kidney and save her life. As Brooke and his parents had been telling him for years, he needed to stop blaming himself for something that was never his fault.

When they'd finished supper and Brooke had washed the dishes, Tripp insisted she quit fussing over every little thing and sit down with him and Dad. "I'm serious," he said. "Brooke, you've got a job to get back to, so there's no point in y'all sticking around. I'll manage fine on my own. Besides, the Austins and Petersons are right next door, and Marie's already offered to bring meals over for the next few days."

"That's all well and good," Brooke said with a scowl. "What I really want to know is when and how you're going to start repairing the damage you've done with Diana."

Tripp matched her stare. "I fully intend to—or at least I plan to try. But not with my daddy and baby sister nagging me at every turn."

"Nagging? *That's* what you call making sure you don't ruin the rest of your life—or kill yourself in the process?"

The chinks in Brooke's armor were showing, and it saddened Tripp to realize he'd only added to her stress and strain. "I won't let that happen, sis. You have my word."

She sniffled and turned away, but not before Tripp caught her wiping away a tear.

"Brooke, my sweet girl," Dad said with a weary sigh, "it's time you took a rest from the caregiving. Let's do what Tripp says and get on home. Time we all got started on finding our way through this—" his voice wavered "—and on to whatever comes next." He pushed up from the sofa and patted Tripp on the shoulder. "Get a good night's sleep, son. We'll come say goodbye in the morning before we leave for the airport."

It was early yet, but as soon as his dad and sister returned to their guest cabin, Tripp crawled into bed. He'd been cleared for limited activity but had been up and around more today than he should have been. It just felt so good to be out of the hospital and back in his own place.

His own place—a rental cabin more suitable for a short-term stay than a permanent residence? He'd have to remedy that soon because he'd had plenty of time to think it over recently, and he felt more certain than ever that he wanted to settle down right here in Juniper Bluff.

And not just settle down but, Lord willing, make a home with the woman he loved.

Chapter Thirteen

Another week went by while Diana pretended everything was okay. Which wasn't easy when she jumped every time her cell phone rang, hoping and yet dreading she'd see Tripp's name and number on the display. He'd called three times already, but she hadn't been ready to talk. She hadn't even found the nerve to listen to his voice mails and had systematically deleted them. He probably figured she'd given up on him completely. If so, it served him right. Served them both right for believing in something they could never have.

On Saturday morning, as she mechanically filled customers' orders, Seth Austin walked in. Glad for the distraction of a good friend, she managed a weary smile. "Seth, hi. Haven't seen you in here on a Saturday in a long time."

"No Camp Serenity kids this weekend, and our only two guests are honeymooners." Seth's mouth quirked. "More interested in quiet walks around the lake than guided horseback rides."

"Ah." Diana glanced past Seth. "No Christina?"

"She'll be along. She's over at the drugstore refilling her prenatal vitamins."

"Won't be long now, huh?" An unexpected twinge of regret stabbed Diana's heart. The likelihood of her ever knowing the joy of having a family of her own had all but disappeared because she couldn't imagine it happening with anyone but Tripp. With a brisk inhalation, she shoved aside such futile thoughts. "So. What can I get you?"

"Regular coffee for me, extra strong. Christina asked for raspberry tea." Seth nodded toward the bakery case. "And a carrot muffin and cheese Danish."

"You two are so predictable." Smirking, Diana turned to fill Seth's order.

"Haven't seen you out at the ranch lately," Seth said as she set two mugs on the counter. One eyebrow slanted in an accusing frown. "This isn't like you, Diana. At least it didn't used to be."

Diana clamped her teeth together. "You know what it feels like to have your heart broken by someone you loved and trusted, so don't judge me."

"No judgment intended. Just an old friend who'd really like to see you happy with the man you love." Leaning closer, Seth braced his elbows on the counter and lowered his voice. "Look, with Tripp recuperating at his cabin, he and I have had plenty of time to get better acquainted, so I know all about the Crohn's and how it's the reason you two aren't together. I also know it's not like you to run from something just because it's a little scary."

"Isn't that exactly what Tripp did when he broke up with me in college?"

"For which he's paid dearly, sounds like to me. He's

crazy in love with you, Di, and the only reason he hasn't pushed harder to get in touch since he came home is because he understands you need time to come to terms with everything."

"Come to terms with the fact that he kept the truth from me all these years? That's going to take a while." Conscious of being in full view of her other customers, Diana swiveled sideways to swipe away an escaping tear. "Here comes Christina. I'll get those pastries for you."

She served Seth and Christina and was grateful neither said anything more on the subject of Tripp Willoughby.

She wasn't so fortunate when she stopped in to see Aunt Jennie later that afternoon. Her parents happened to be there, too, and their presence made it even harder to calmly justify why she'd avoided all contact with Tripp since he'd returned home.

"You need to settle this once and for all," her father said. "Either go patch things up or make a clean break. You owe that much to yourself and to Tripp."

Squashed between her parents on Aunt Jennie's love seat, Diana sat with her arms folded tightly against her chest. "I have no idea what I'd even say to him."

Aunt Jennie scoffed. "Words are highly overrated. Just go be with him, honey. God will take care of the rest."

While Diana shook her head and sniffed back a tear, her mother tugged her hand free and gave it a squeeze. "I have an idea," she said. "Let me call Tripp. I'll invite him over for Sunday dinner tomorrow—a gesture of kindness as he recuperates."

"I don't know, Mom…"

"Give this a chance, sweetie." Her mother kissed her cheek. "Your dad's right. This has to be settled, and you need to do it face-to-face."

An anguished sigh ripped through Diana's throat. "All right, but I should be the one to call him. And if Tripp agrees to come, no pressure, okay? Whatever happens, happens."

Her mother nodded. "Whatever happens, happens."

Steeling herself, Diana carried her phone out to the corridor. As she found Tripp's number in her contacts, a huge part of her hoped he wouldn't answer.

He did.

"Tripp, I, um…" She swallowed the nervous lump in her throat. "I wanted to find out how you're doing."

"Better, thanks." A kind of calm strength undergirded his reply. "Actually, I've been a lot more concerned about how *you're* doing."

She had no way to answer that without sounding cruel. "I'm coping," was all she said. "I know we need to deal with…everything. But you've just had major surgery, and I don't want to do anything to hinder your recovery."

"Diana, don't worry about that. I'm getting along fine."

"I'm sure you are. But—well, let me just get to the point. My mom would like you to come over for Sunday dinner tomorrow."

Tripp hesitated. "I hope this isn't strictly a pity invitation."

"No. Absolutely not." Diana marched to the end of the corridor. "Actually, I'm insulted that this is even an issue. That you would think so little of my family. Of *me*—"

"I don't." A sigh rasped through the phone. "That's a mistake I will never make again. Can we just chalk it up to pea-brained male pride?"

She scoffed. "Now *that* is a condition I definitely consider pitiable."

Another moment of silence elapsed. "Can we back up to the part where I said yes to your mom's invitation and let me add a simple thank-you?"

"That would be best. I'll text you directions to my parents' place."

"No need." His voice dropped to a nostalgic murmur. "I remember like it was yesterday."

Diana's throat clenched as she recalled the last time she'd brought Tripp home to spend a weekend at the ranch. She'd been so certain he was on the verge of proposing, and then he'd taken ill with what they'd all assumed was either a stomach bug or food poisoning. Tripp must not even have known about the Crohn's at that point. Then, only a few weeks later, she'd received the fateful phone call ending it all.

She cleared her throat. "So Mom usually serves dinner around one thirty. Come on over whenever you're ready."

"I'm looking forward to it…more than you know."

Diana wished she could say the same, but the mere thought of facing Tripp tied her insides in knots. "Okay, then. See you tomorrow."

"See you tomorrow."

When Tripp arrived at the Matthews ranch shortly after 1 p.m. on Sunday, Diana met him at the front door. The look on her face was anything but welcoming. In fact, she looked ready to bolt.

Mrs. Matthews rescued them both. She waved from the kitchen, a slotted spoon in her hand. "Come on in, Tripp. You can help Diana set the table while I dish up the veggies."

"Glad to, ma'am." Following Diana to the kitchen, Tripp cast a poignant glance toward the family's freshly cut Christmas tree, a sad reminder he'd never have another Christmas with his mom. "Thanks for having me over. It's really good to be here again."

With a kind smile that suggested she'd read his thoughts, Mrs. Matthews handed him a stack of plates. "You're welcome anytime, Tripp."

Diana barely looked at him as she gathered up napkins and flatware. "Dining room's this way."

"I remember."

The simple act of arranging place settings on the dining room table seemed to help Diana relax. When she reached past Tripp with a knife and spoon, she stood close enough that he caught the subtle fragrance of lavender.

To break the awkward silence, he asked, "How's it going with the therapy pets?"

"Pretty good. We visited the assisted-living center again last weekend."

Tripp released a gentle laugh. "I'll never forget the look on your great-aunt's face when she saw all those dogs for the first time. The therapy pets are going to be real blessings to all the residents."

"I hope so." Diana inhaled a shaky breath. "I should ask what else Mom needs help with. Dad's roasting chickens on the grill. Why don't you go ask when the meat will be ready?"

"Uh, okay. Sure." Tripp disguised a nervous gulp,

knowing if he really wanted to make up for lost time, convincing Diana's father of his honorable intentions was as good a place as any to begin.

Stepping onto the patio, he tried hard to keep his tone friendly and light. "Hey, Mr. Matthews, how's it going?"

"Thought I heard you drive up earlier." Diana's father opened the grill, releasing a burst of flavorful aromas that made Tripp's stomach growl in anticipation. "Chickens look done. Pass me that platter."

So Mr. Matthews wasn't in the mood for conversation, and Tripp couldn't help being relieved. The business of getting the meat to the table had saved them both from an uncomfortable father-to-hopefully-future-son-in-law interrogation. Tripp could wait for the next one until he'd actually slipped the engagement ring on Diana's finger—a day he prayed would be soon in coming. But first, he had to find a way to assure her he was in this for the long haul and would never let her down again.

The dinner was every bit as good as Tripp remembered from when he'd dated Diana in college. He appreciated Mrs. Matthews's frankness in questioning him about his dietary restrictions. Apparently, Diana had prepared her, because he could eat just about everything on the menu without hesitation, and he savored every bite.

Afterward, he offered to help with kitchen cleanup. Once all the leftovers had been put away, Mr. and Mrs. Matthews excused themselves to the family room, leaving Tripp and Diana with the dishes. The intimacy of working alongside her like this—Tripp rinsing plates and handing them to Diana to set in the dishwasher—brought back all kinds of pleasant memories from their college dating days, along with dreams of many similar days to come.

"This is nice," he murmured, his hand brushing hers.

"Mmm-hmm," she replied without looking up.

He handed her another plate but didn't let go. "Di," he said, waiting for her to meet his gaze. When she did, tension lines radiated from the corners of her eyes. With a tender smile, he reclaimed the plate and set it on the counter, then took both her hands in his. "This is the best day I've had in a long time. Please tell me there can be more."

Pulling away, Diana backed up a step and folded her arms. "What do you want me to say, Tripp? That all is forgiven and I'm fine with spending the rest of my life worrying about whether you'll end up in the hospital again? Or—or maybe even—"

The intensity of her response caught him off guard. Stunned, he reached out to enfold her against his chest, holding her close until she stopped resisting. "Yes, Crohn's can be a miserably annoying condition, and there are bound to be setbacks. But it's not a death sentence. I know what I need to do to keep it under control."

"I'm overreacting, I know." Slowly, hesitantly, her arms tightened around his torso. "I just can't lose you again."

The desperately sweet sound of those words wrapped around his heart and squeezed. "I'm not going anywhere." Cupping her cheek, he tilted her head and lowered his lips to hers in a kiss he hoped would convey the depth of his love and his enduring commitment to making a life with her. Ending the kiss, he smiled down at her. "Do you believe me now?"

Tears filled her eyes. "I want to, more than any-thing."

"Then take a leap of faith with me. Let's spend the rest of our lives making up for what we've been miss-ing out on since I got stupid and scared and let you go."

"You make it sound so easy."

Tripp thumbed a droplet from her cheek. "It could be…if you'd let it."

She pulled out of his arms and turned away. "I don't know if I'm ready. I… I'm still sorting things out."

"I'll wait as long as it takes." Knowing there was nothing more he could say, Tripp slipped out. After offering Diana's parents his sincere thanks for dinner, he said goodbye.

As he drove down the lane toward the main road, an idea began to form. He just might know a way to con-vince Diana once and for all that he was here to stay.

Over the following week, Diana heard nothing from Tripp. Had she been too adamant about needing more time? If so, he'd taken her at her word, and she wasn't sure how she felt about that. Because the bald truth was she missed him. Missed him terribly.

Besides, after those moments of closeness they'd shared at her parents' last Sunday, she thought for sure he'd stop in or at least call. If they really did have hopes of restoring their relationship, a little more communi-cation might be in order.

Where was he?

When he didn't show up for church Sunday morn-ing, Diana's doubts increased. Catching Marie Peter-son after worship, she nonchalantly asked about Tripp.

"Oh, far as I know, he's just fine." Marie glanced

around distractedly. "I know he's been busy catching up on work at the clinic. Also mentioned he had some business to attend to this weekend."

"Business? Like, out of town?"

"Could be." Waving at her husband, Bryan, across the foyer, Marie excused herself. "Got a roast in the oven, sweetie. Don't want to burn the house down."

"Of course. Don't let me keep you." Watching the plump woman hurry away, Diana had the distinct impression she'd just been given the brush-off.

Was Tripp keeping more secrets from her—and enlisting the aid of his landlady to cover for him? Diana did a slow boil as she marched out to her car. Apparently, the man had learned nothing about the cost of not being honest.

It wasn't until late Sunday afternoon that Tripp finally called.

"Where have you been all week?" Diana's effort to keep the peevishness out of her tone had failed.

"Busy with patients, mostly. And I'm still supposed to be taking it easy, so lots of naps and early bedtimes."

Slightly mollified, she drew her lower lip between her teeth. "Well, it's good to know you're taking care of yourself."

"I really want to see you, though. Any chance you're free for dinner tonight?"

Tiger crawled into Diana's lap, circled three times, then plopped down and began purring. "Well, I don't know," she grumbled, stroking the big cat's head. "I might have had a better offer by now."

"Rain check, then?" The flippant tone of his voice infuriated her. "Give me a buzz when you're free."

"Tripp Willoughby! I'm sitting here on my sofa in

ratty sweats, and you should know perfectly well I have no better plans than microwaving leftovers and dining with three cats, a rabbit and a parakeet."

"So can I pick you up in an hour?"

If not for yearning so badly to see him, she'd give him an earful about his presumptuous attitude and then hang up. "Okay, fine. But only because it'll be a lot more satisfying to chew you out in person for ignoring me for an entire week."

He chuckled softly. "If you still feel like that two hours from now, I will humbly oblige."

Two hours from now? What could he possibly have up his sleeve? With a gruff goodbye, Diana nudged the cat off her lap and went to change into clean jeans and a sweater. After freshening her makeup, she tried three different hairstyles before settling on wearing it loose. She spent another ten minutes deciding whether to wear her new brown boots with the legs of her jeans tucked inside or pulled down over the top. Tucked inside won out. She decided it made her look more assertive—and where Tripp was concerned, she needed every ounce of fortitude she could muster.

She'd just given the pets their supper when the doorbell rang. Drawing several long, slow breaths, she took her time in answering. Tripp had made her wait for an entire week. He could stand to cool his heels on her front porch for a couple of minutes.

When she opened the door to his apologetic grin as he clutched a bouquet of fragrant flowers in bright, Christmasy colors, her resolve crumbled. "For me?" she asked, and then wanted to kick herself for sounding like a simpering female.

"No," he replied with a completely straight face, "I

brought them for Alice. Thought she'd like munching on them."

Diana's mouth fell open. "Tripp—"

"I'm serious." He pointed at the various flowers in the bouquet. "Daisies, roses, pansies—rabbits love these. And I checked with the florist. No harmful chemicals."

"Um, okay…" Brows in a twist, Diana reached for the bouquet.

He didn't let go. His grin returned, while his eyes softened into a look that weakened her knees. "I'm kidding. These are totally for you."

"Ever the practical joker, aren't you?" With a quick shake of her head, Diana seized the flowers and spun on her boot heel before Tripp could notice the effect he was having on her. "Come on in. I need to find a vase."

Once she'd placed the flowers in water and set the vase on the kitchen table, she retrieved her purse and jacket. "So. Where are we having dinner?"

"We'll get to that." Tripp paused on the front step while she locked her door. "There's one stop I want to make on the way."

Diana didn't have much choice except to go along with whatever Tripp had planned. She sat stiffly in the passenger seat of his SUV and tried not to be obvious as she noted the route he took. After reaching Main Street, instead of heading downtown or toward the highway to Fredericksburg, he wound through another residential area.

Finally, her curiosity got the best of her. "I don't know of any restaurants around here. Care to clue me in?"

At that moment, Tripp pulled up in front of a ranch-style brick house with a white porch rail. The house looked empty, and a For Sale sign stood near the curb-side mailbox. Tripp shut off the engine and pushed open his door. He cast Diana an enticing smile. "I've got the key. Want to go inside and look around?"

She glanced from Tripp to the sign and back again. "You're buying a house?"

"The owners accepted my offer on Friday."

"You're *buying* a house."

"I think you just said that." Rolling his eyes, Tripp stepped from the car. He strode around to Diana's side and helped her to the curb. "The place is structurally sound, but the interior needs updating. I was hoping you could help me with some ideas."

Still in disbelief, Diana stumbled along beside him as he strode up the front walk. "*This* is what you've been doing all week between patients and naps—house hunting? But Marie Peterson gave me the impression you had business out of town."

Glancing her way, he wiggled his brows. "Oh, so you cared enough to ask about me?"

"Has anyone ever told you how infuriating you can be?"

"You. Several times."

"Well, it's no compliment. Seriously." As they reached the porch, she set her hand on his arm. "Why the sudden rush to buy a house?"

He pulled a key from his pocket, then turned to her with another of those beguiling smiles, this one fraught with meaning. "Because Juniper Bluff is my home now, and I decided it was time for more permanent living arrangements. This town has everything—absolutely *everything*—I've ever wanted in life."

Diana's breath grew shallow. "Tripp, I—I can't—"

"Just come in and tell me what you think." He unlocked the door and pushed it open. "Our dinner reservations are at six, so we don't have much time."

Speechless, Diana followed him through the empty, echoing rooms as he flipped light switches and pointed out various features. It was a nicely arranged house, with small formal areas, a den with a stone fireplace, an eat-in kitchen and three spacious bedrooms. Diana had to agree, though—updates were in order, especially in the straight-from-the-'70s kitchen.

"By the way, I *was* out of town this weekend," Tripp confessed. "The owners have agreed to let me move in now and rent until closing, so I drove over to Austin to arrange to get my apartment furnishings out of storage."

"Oh. That's nice." Between the swiftness of Tripp's decision and the reasons he'd given her, Diana felt like she was still playing catch-up.

The den faced the rear of the house. Tugging on a cord, Tripp drew open the dingy, olive-green drapes covering a sliding patio door. "Nice backyard, don't you think?"

Diana fanned away a cloud of dust emanating from the drapes before peering through the glass. "Wow, it's big. A privacy fence, too."

"Yeah, I thought it would be great for a dog or two… and maybe kids someday."

The implications of this show-and-tell grew clearer by the moment. "Last time I checked, you didn't have a dog. As for kids, I didn't think… I mean, after what Brooke told me while you were in surgery…"

Tripp fingered a lock of hair falling across Diana's shoulder. "What exactly did she say?"

She couldn't look at him. "That you were scared of

having children because they might inherit the propensity for developing Crohn's."

"It's true, I let the possibility worry me for a long time." Breathing out softly, he rested his arms across her shoulders and dipped his head until their foreheads touched. "But I had some long talks with my mom during her last days, and then with Dad after my surgery, and it finally sank in that spending my life with the woman I love outweighs every problem we could ever face."

Emotion tightened Diana's throat. "When you got sick at the funeral—when I thought I might lose you—" Her eyes pressed shut, she shook her head. "If that happened to one of our children—"

"*If*, Diana, not when. Genetic predisposition is just a percentage number, not an absolute. And remember, we've got God on our side. He's carried us this far, hasn't He?" Tilting her chin, he kissed the tip of her nose. "I want a family, Di. I want it more than I ever dreamed possible. And I want it with you."

Pulse thundering, Diana wrapped her arms around him and held on tight. "I never, ever stopped loving you."

"Then you have to believe as I've come to accept, that God brought us back together because we were never meant to be apart." Easing from her embrace, Tripp drew something sparkly from his breast pocket, then took her left hand in his.

She gasped. "Is that…a *ring*?"

"I've been holding on to this for twelve long years."

"You mean—"

"I bought it just a few days before my first serious hospital stay, before I learned I had Crohn's." Tripp's eyes darkened. His voice grew thick. "When I called you to break up, I was clutching this ring against my heart. I'd convinced myself I had to let you go, but I was never able to part with this one tiny symbol of hope."

"Oh, Tripp." Scarcely feeling the tears slipping down her face, she cupped his cheek. "If only you'd trusted me. If only you'd trusted our love."

"It's a mistake I'll never make again. I can't undo the past, but if you'll have me, we can start right now working on the future we always dreamed of." Still holding her hand, he sank to one knee. "Marry me, Diana. Let's not waste another minute."

Sinking down next to him, she threw her arms around his neck. "Yes, Tripp Willoughby, I will marry you—and the sooner, the better!"

Epilogue

One month later

Making a rush trip to the ER was *not* the way Tripp envisioned spending his wedding day. At least this time it was for a much happier occasion than dealing with his personal health issues. Seemed Diana's matron of honor, Christina Austin, insisted on going into labor three weeks early—and two hours before Tripp and Diana were supposed to say their "I do's."

"Honey, sit down." Diana looped her arm around his waist. "Wearing a groove in the waiting room carpet isn't helping Christina and Seth in the delivery room."

"Maybe not, but it makes me feel like I'm doing *something*." Tripp snuggled Diana under his chin. His stomach was in knots, and it had nothing to do with the Crohn's. He couldn't help imagining both the terror and the elation of someday being with Diana for the birth of their own child.

Except there needed to be a wedding first, and the whole day had just been turned upside down.

A sudden commotion drew his attention to the door.

The widest grin Tripp had ever seen split Seth's face. Wearing a blue paper gown over the dress pants and shirt he would have worn to the wedding, he strode into the waiting room. "Jacob and Elisabeth Austin have officially arrived!"

A collective whoop of joy filled the room. Bryan and Marie Peterson rushed over with Seth's older kids, Joseph and Eva. All four of them smothered Seth with laughter and hugs, while Diana squeezed Tripp until he almost couldn't breathe. Eyes filling, he hugged her back. He'd calmly delivered any number of puppies and kittens during his years as a vet, but this was an entirely different kind of thrill—and it wasn't even his baby.

Diana tugged on his arm. "Let's congratulate the new dad."

Joining Seth and his family, Tripp and Diana listened as Seth recited the statistics. "Jacob weighs five pounds, nine ounces, and Elisabeth is five pounds, two and a half ounces. And they both have healthy sets of lungs!"

"How's Christina?" Diana asked.

"Tired, but so, so happy." Seth still hadn't stopped grinning.

Tripp pumped Seth's hand. "You look like you could use some rest, yourself, *Daddy*."

Eyes widening, Seth palmed his forehead. "Aw, man—your wedding!"

"Hey, no worries. We'll just reschedule." Although delaying making Diana his wife was the very *last* thing Tripp wanted to do.

Diana stretched up to give Seth a kiss on the cheek. "We should go. Give Christina our love, and tell her we'll see her soon."

"I will. And thanks for being here." Seth winked.

"Once y'all tie the knot, I'll be happy to return the favor someday."

After a round of goodbyes to Seth and his family, Tripp escorted Diana down to the parking lot. The January day had grown blustery as the sun sank toward the western hills, and Diana minced along in spiky heels, a short jacket and the shimmery waltz-length white dress Tripp wasn't supposed to see until she started down the aisle at Shepherd of the Hills Community Church.

She did look amazingly beautiful, though, and Tripp told her so for probably the twentieth time that day as he helped her into his SUV.

"At least my dress is bought and paid for," she said. "Your rental tux is due back tomorrow."

With a tight-lipped nod, Tripp closed her door, then dashed around to climb in behind the wheel. He sat there for a minute while his thoughts raced. "What if… what if we go over to the church right now and have Pastor Terry marry us in a private ceremony?"

Diana stared at him, her brows forming a V. "Are you serious?"

"Never more so." He shifted to face her. "Unless you'd be too disappointed not to have your big church wedding?"

She lifted her hand to his cheek and lightly kissed his lips. "The wedding isn't nearly as important to me as spending the rest of my life as Mrs. Dr. Tripp Willoughby."

"Then…"

Facing forward, Diana snapped on her seat belt. "Let's do it."

When they arrived back at the church, Diana spotted her parents' car outside the fellowship hall and figured they had stayed to pack up the reception food and decorations.

"That looks like Brooke's rental car, too," Tripp said.

"Great, they're all here. I'll go tell them the plan while you track down Pastor Terry." With a quick kiss, Diana shoved open her door.

Hurrying into the fellowship hall, she shouted, "Mom, Dad, everybody! The wedding's still on."

"What?" Brooke whirled around and nearly toppled a floral arrangement. "I thought you'd decided to postpone."

Diana's mother rushed out of the kitchen. "Everyone's already gone home, honey. And the food's all packed for freezing."

"None of that matters." Diana took Brooke's hand on one side and her mother's on the other, then smiled toward her father and future father-in-law as the men strode over. "Our families are here, and Tripp's rounding up Pastor Terry. We'll save the food and hold a reception in a week or two, after we get back from the honeymoon."

"I'm so glad," Brooke said, beaming. "I didn't know how I'd get time off work again so I could make the trip to be your bridesmaid."

The door flew open and Tripp marched in, the pastor in tow. He swooped Diana into a hug. "Let's get married!"

"Wait," Diana burst out. "There's still one person missing. Aunt Jennie will be so disappointed if she misses my wedding."

Mom shook her head. "We took her back to her apartment hours ago. I'm not sure she's up for another outing so soon."

"Then let's take the wedding to her." Diana looked to Pastor Terry for ~onfirmation.

He nodded in agreement. "I'll call the administrator right now and explain what's happening."

Tripp pulled Diana aside. "With this last-minute change of plans, I've got something else I need to take care of. I'll meet you at the center in a few minutes, okay?"

Arching a brow, Diana straightened the boutonnière pinned to his lapel. "Might this have anything to do with a surprise wedding gift?"

"It might." He winked. "You'll have to wait and see."

Already feeling as if her heart would float right out of her chest, Diana did her best to contain her curiosity.

By the time everyone arrived at the assisted-living center, an aide had brought Aunt Jennie to the community room. A few other residents had also gathered, which was fine with Diana since she'd gotten to know them during the regular therapy pet visits. They seemed almost as excited as Aunt Jennie to be able to attend Diana's wedding.

Even some of the staff looked on as Diana and Tripp recited their vows. Following the brief ceremony, the family joined Aunt Jennie in the dining room for the evening meal. Diana's mother had brought the wedding cake, and everyone applauded as Diana and Tripp fed each other the first few bites from the upper tier, specially made with Crohn's-friendly ingredients. Afterward, the staff served generous slices to the residents.

As they sat around the table finishing their cake and sipping decaf, Tripp leaned close to kiss Diana's cheek. "Be right back, okay? By the way, this would be a good time to invite everybody back to the community room."

"Tripp...what are you up to?"

His only reply was a mischievous grin.

A few minutes later, with Aunt Jennie settled in a comfortable chair and other residents filtering in from the dining room, Diana glanced toward the foyer to see Kelly Nesbit, Vince and Janice Mussell, and a few other therapy pet volunteers with their dogs. Before Diana could gather her wits to ask what was going on, the grinning volunteers paraded into the community room. One by one, they peeled off to stop and say hello to the elderly residents, who were delighted by the unexpected visit.

Then Tripp entered, a perky tan-and-white corgi prancing alongside him. He and the dog headed straight for Aunt Jennie. Yipping with excitement, Ginger danced on her hind legs as she stretched up to shower Aunt Jennie with doggie kisses.

"Oh, my Ginger! My sweet little Ginger-dog!" Tears streamed down Aunt Jennie's face as she cuddled the companion she'd missed so much.

Dumbfounded, and loving this man more than ever, Diana captured Tripp's hand. "When did you do this?"

"I made a quick trip to see Mrs. Doudtman in San Antonio few days ago. Kelly's been keeping Ginger for me until I could spring the surprise." He slid his arm around Diana and tilted her chin for a kiss. "We can always use another therapy pet, right? Besides, I told you when I bought the house that it had a great yard for dogs."

"Yes, I do seem to remember that. I just hope Ginger will make up quickly with my menagerie."

"Mrs. Doudtman said she adapted very well to both

her shelties and a cat she adopted recently. Her grand-kids, too, so I'm not anticipating any problems."

"Good." Diana squeezed in closer. "Because I also remember you said something about having kids of our own someday."

"Speaking of which..." Passing the leash to Diana's father, Tripp nudged her toward the exit. "What do you say we get started on our honeymoon, Mrs. Willoughby?"

"Why, Dr. Willoughby, I thought you'd never ask!"

* * * * *